THE
STRING
DIARIES

STEPHEN LLOYD JONES

D1363248

headline

First published in 2013 by
HEADLINE PUBLISHING GROUP

First published in paperback in 2014 by
HEADLINE PUBLISHING GROUP

1

Cataloguing in Publication Data is available from the British Library

ISBN 978 1 4722 0468 4

Typeset in Bembo by Avon DataSet Ltd, Bidford-on-Avon, Warwickshire

Printed and bound in Great Britain by Clays Ltd, St Ives plc

Headline's policy is to use papers that are natural, renewable and recyclable
products and made from wood grown in sustainable forests. The logging and
manufacturing processes are expected to conform to the environmental
regulations of the country of origin.

HEADLINE PUBLISHING GROUP
An Hachette UK Company
338 Euston Road
London NW1 3BH

www.headline.co.uk
www.hachette.co.uk

STEPHEN LLOYD JONES grew up in Chandlers Ford, Hampshire. He now lives in Surrey with his wife, three sons and far too many books. *The String Diaries* is his first novel.

'*The String Diaries* is a page turner, and will keep you awake late into the night' *SFX*

'I just couldn't put the book down. A definite must read' www.jonturner1974.wordpress.com

'This is very much a superior supernatural story, intelligently plotted and well written' www.curiousbookfans.co.uk

'Impossible to leave alone for too long' www.bcfreviews.wordpress.com

'Will keep you reading long into the night . . . a totally unique reading experience . . . an author to watch' www.falcatatimes.blogspot.co.uk

'Intensely readable' www.drying-ink.blogspot.co.uk

'[An] enjoyable read . . . an entertaining thriller which moves at a good pace' The British Fantasy Society

t-turn-on-
cancel-all-
bag.co.uk

'It's a story that will hold you in its grip,
not only while you are reading but for
some time afterwards as well'
www.jerasjamboree.com

'Jones hit all the right notes in this clever
and exciting novel, which delivers both action
and mystery with a dash of the supernatural'
www.afantasticallibrarian.com

'This is a splendid debut'
www.theeloquentpage.co.uk

'A brilliant first novel and a truly
gripping read' www.welovethisbook.com

'Lloyd Jones is a master of the cliff-hanger.
Every chapter is consuming and page-
turning . . . this book grabs you by the
throat and refuses to let go from page
one!' www.wordandpiece.wordpress.com

'I was completely hooked by *The String Diaries* . . .
The premise is refreshingly original. The ending
to the book is perfect . . . a terrific read'
www.summerreadingproject.blogspot.co.uk

'An exciting novel, an original bad guy'
www.thelittlereaderlibrary.blogspot.co.uk

For Julie

and for three boys
who have already changed the world

CHAPTER 1

Snowdonia

Now

It was only when Hannah Wilde reached the farmhouse shortly after midnight that she discovered how much blood her husband had lost.

They had spoken little during the drive to Llyn Gwyr. Hannah concentrated on the road ahead, her vision blurred through rain and tears. Beside her, Nate slumped in the Discovery's passenger seat, a crooked shadow. She tried to glance over at him as the distance to what they'd left behind increased, but it was impossible to comprehend the full horror of his injuries while they were on the road. Each time she suggested they pull over Nate shook his head and urged her on.

Get to the farmhouse, Hannah. I'll be OK. I promise.

Close to midnight, after four hours behind the wheel, she watched the English place names flashing past the Discovery's headlights surrender to their Welsh cousins: Cyfronydd; Llangadfan; Tal-y-llyn.

No other vehicles shared this night with them. And although Hannah could see little more than what lay directly ahead, she could feel the country growing wilder, opening up around her.

The road bucked and twisted, tried to throw them loose. For a time they chased a rushing mountain stream, the fractured diamonds of moonlight on its surface the only clue to its presence. When the road looped, climbing higher, the reflections winked out, lost to the night.

Half a mile from Llyn Gwyr, near the crest of a hill, Hannah slowed the 4x4 to a crawl and turned off its headlights. She inched the vehicle up the final few yards of the slope, to where a clump of ash trees grew. For a moment she watched the silhouette movement of their naked branches.

Hannah switched off the ignition. The sound of the engine had masked the voice of the wind until now. Here, at the summit of the hill, it sang around them, buffeting the car on its springs.

By God, what were you thinking? Did you really believe this place would be safe?

In the passenger seat, Nate roused himself, lifting his head. He squinted out of the window. 'What do you see?'

Beyond the trees, the land dropped away below them, receding towards the shore of an almond-shaped lake. Although the moon had draped itself in rainclouds creeping in from the west, a phosphorescence lingered on the water's surface. The black line of a river, snaking down from the mountains, fed the lake at its westernmost point.

Llyn Gwyr's farmhouse stood on the lake's far shore. A steep gravel track, crossing the river at a stone bridge, linked it to the main road.

'I can hardly see a thing from this far away,' she told him. 'Not in the dark, anyway.'

'There should be some binoculars in the door well. Check the bridge first. See if it's clear.'

Hannah found the glasses, raised them to her eyes. Trained them in the direction of the river. She needed a moment to orient herself, and then she found the bridge. Its crumbling stone arch looked barely robust enough to support the weight of their Land Rover.

No debris on the bridge itself, that she could see. Nothing lurking beneath it. No signs of a potential ambush.

'It's clear.'

'OK, now check the house.'

She heard him shift his weight in the seat and try to conceal a gasp of pain. Immediately she wrenched the binoculars from her face. 'Nate? What is it? What can I do?'

'Nothing, Han. I'm fine.' His voice was husky with exhaustion. 'Go on. Check the house.'

She raised the glasses back to her eyes, trained them on the farmhouse this time. Its whitewashed stone walls glowed with the reflection of a nebulous moon. She found the outline of what she knew from photographs was a sagging slate roof. 'What am I looking for?'

'Check the windows first. Are they intact?'

A pause while she checked all four. 'Yes. The ones that I can see.'

'That's good. What about the door? Is it open? Does it look like it's been forced?'

'It's difficult to tell but—' She frowned. 'No, I think it's secure.'

'That's good, Han. That's great. OK, look. I don't think anyone is here. I don't think anyone *can* be. But we're going to be cautious all the same. We're going to keep the lights out until we're off the main road, and we're going to drive slowly. The entrance is just up ahead. From what I remember of this place, it's rough going until we get down to that bridge. Then it flattens out. We'll park around the far side of the house so that nobody can see our car from the road.' He paused, hissing through his teeth as he shifted his weight again. 'Are you ready?'

Hannah blew air from her cheeks, nodded. 'Take the binoculars for me.'

She held them out to him. Felt his hand brush against hers. His fingers were wet, sticky. She felt her throat constricting. 'Nate, are you still bleeding?'

'Doesn't matter. Come on. We're nearly safe now.'

She suddenly had to know. Despite his calming words, his encouragement, she was still reeling from the shock of tonight's events. Before they went any further she needed to know exactly what she faced. On impulse, her hand went to the overhead light. She snapped it on.

Some of the hope Hannah had been clinging to died then, as she saw the true state of him. She clenched her teeth and forced her jaw to still itself, determined not to reveal how acutely his appearance affected her.

Blood drenched him.

His woollen jacket was saturated with it. The fabric of his shirt glistened and dripped. Blood pooled between his legs. It collected in the folds of the seat. It soaked his jeans.

When Hannah raised her eyes to his face her emotions betrayed her and she sobbed. He was dying. She could have no doubt. Scarcely any life could remain inside him. His lips had lost all of their colour. His cheeks, where he had not wiped blood over them, were as pale as milk. Despite the cool air inside the 4x4, sweat stood out in beads upon his skin.

Nate tried to smile, but when his lips drew back from his teeth she saw a corpse leering at her. 'I think the bleeding is starting to slow down.'

Her voice trembled, on the verge of a scream. 'We need to get you to a hospital, Nate. *Right* now.'

He shook his head. 'No. We can't. I'll be all right. I promise you.'

'Nate, we—'

'*No*. Hannah, listen to me.' Nate paused, and she saw he was gulping for air. 'We can't take any risks with this. You know that, I know you do. What happens to me is irrelevant. We have to protect Leah.'

The scream pressed at the back of Hannah's throat, taunting her. At the mention of Leah's name, she turned to look at their daughter, asleep on the back seat. The sight of her smooth face, so fragile and so serene, terrified her and rallied her in equal measure.

He was right; they had no choice. But how did she meet

Nate's eyes and accept his words without protest? How could she become an accessory to sacrifice like that? It tore something within her. Only two people in the world she loved like this. Putting one before the other was unthinkable. As was the alternative.

Nate eased his hand out of his jacket, stared at his bloodied fingers. 'This is survivable, Han. Believe me. I've lost a lot of blood, I know that. I realise how bad it looks, but I've seen injuries like this before and I can make it, I swear. As long as we can get inside soon.'

Hannah batted tears from her eyes. She didn't believe him. He was a ghost. But she found herself swallowing the scream and twisting the keys in the ignition. 'Hold tight, then. We'll be there in a few minutes. Are you comfortable?'

'Are you serious?'

She forced herself to laugh. It sounded like she was choking.

Easing off the handbrake, she nudged the 4x4 into motion. They coasted over the brow of the hill and followed the road down the other side, descending through forest that reached for them with arms of spruce and Douglas fir. She saw the turning on the left and took it.

Once they were off the main road, boxed by tall conifers, she risked using dipped beams. The track below them was little more than a rocky slope. She had to keep their speed under walking pace to navigate around the larger boulders and avoid jolting Nate as much as possible. Even so, every couple of yards he groaned as the wheels alternately skidded and gripped on the stones. She flinched at his every sound.

Damn the odds, keeping fighting until you have nothing left.

Wasn't that her father's favourite phrase? This sense of help-lessness, this fear, served no one. She forced herself to consider what she knew about blood loss. If Nate were to stand any chance of survival, she had to prevent him going into shock. His laboured breathing and sweating were symptoms of serious hypovolemia.

She had to stop the bleeding. She had to keep him warm. And she had to get liquids into him.

They drove past a wooden sign, black lettering on a rotting whitewashed plank. LLYN GWYR. One of her father's prepared bolt-holes.

At the bottom of the incline, the track's surface improved. She followed its curves, easing the Discovery over the arched bridge and swinging it towards the farmhouse. Its headlights swept the front of the building, illuminating all but Llyn Gwyr's windows. Those black countenances remained stubbornly impenetrable.

The driveway looped around the far side of the house. They passed stone-built stables and an empty cowshed. Gravel crunched under the Discovery's tyres as she pulled up behind the house.

Hannah switched off the engine, then the lights. She pulled the keys from the ignition. 'I'm going to unlock the house. I'll be back in a minute to help you inside.'

'Take the torch.'

She nodded, reaching behind her seat and grabbing their powerful four-cell Maglite. Leaning forward, she kissed him. His lips were clammy, cold.

'Don't go wandering off anywhere,' she said.

'Forgot my hiking boots anyway.'

Good that he could still joke. But she could barely hear his voice.

Hannah put her hand on the door handle, hesitating. Now that they had arrived, she was reluctant to get out of the Discovery; it had been their haven for the last five hours. As if seeking to dissuade her further, the wind railed with greater force.

Every minute mattered now. She could delay no longer. Hannah opened the car door and jumped down on to the driveway.

Immediately the wind slammed into her, rocking her back on her feet. It gusted and eddied, an angry wraith, pasting her hair to her face and squeezing fresh tears from her eyes. Swinging the car door shut, tucking her head down, she zippered her fleece and stepped away from the Discovery.

Although her vision had not fully adjusted to the darkness, she could discern the outline of the farmhouse against the sky, the deeper black of its windows, the back door, the conservatory. A vague impression of outbuildings off to her left.

Quickly, Hannah closed the distance between the car and the main residence, wondering what she would find. She knew the place had stood unoccupied for years. Her father paid someone to check on it every now and then, but she had no idea how often. She noticed that one of the ground-floor windows – of what might be a living room – had been smashed. Not good. But there was no time left for caution. She had to get Nate inside.

Hannah reached the back door and peered through the kitchen window. Nothing but darkness within. She found the key and was sliding it into the lock when she heard movement behind her.

She froze, right hand on the doorknob, left hand holding the key fob. The sound vanished as abruptly as it had arrived. And then she heard it again: a skittering of loose gravel on the drive behind her.

Once more it disappeared, overtaken by wind and rain.

She had tucked the Maglite under her left arm. Although she had nothing else with which to defend herself, the torch was solid: machined aluminium. The sound behind her couldn't have been Nate. She would have heard him opening the car door.

Hannah transferred the flashlight to her right hand, gripping it towards the bulb like a club. Her index finger hovered over the control switch. In her ears she felt the pulse of blood in her arteries.

They're depending on you. Nate and Leah. You're all they've got.

Slowly, ever so slowly, she turned on the spot.

Beyond the gravel driveway stood a neglected kitchen garden. At the end of the garden, on the far side of a post-and-rail fence, lay the fields attached to the farm. She could see the moon-dusted heads of vegetation bending in the wind. In the distance, silhouetted mountain peaks.

Between her and the garden, just a few yards away, something loomed on the driveway. She was unable to see it clearly in the darkness, but it was large. Bigger than her.

Hannah heard a bass grunt. A snort of breath.

Whatever it was, it was nearer to her than the car. Tensing, she thumbed the flashlight.

Caught in the brilliance of the Maglite's beam, washed in light, stood the largest stag Hannah had ever seen. Its coat was a reddish brown, darkening around the throat. Antlers, each displaying a cluster of individual tines, swept upwards and forwards from its head. Two liquid eyes regarded her. She found herself locked in their gaze.

The torch had clearly startled it. She could see muscles twitching and contracting in its flank. But for some reason it did not bolt. The stag sidestepped, gravel dragging under its hooves, and raised its nose high to sniff the air. It stood motionless for a few seconds, then tilted its head.

Hannah noticed that she was holding her breath. If it chose, the animal was powerful enough – and its antlers sharp enough – to run her through.

She saw its muscles bunch again, felt herself tense in response. Now it moved its head to the right, appraising her with a single glossy eye.

So abruptly that she nearly cried out in shock, the stag twisted about in an explosion of gravel chippings, and with three leaps was gone.

Hannah stared into the dark, transfixed by what she had just seen. It had been a red deer. But she had never heard of a population in Snowdonia before.

Dismissing it, needing to focus on Nate, Hannah turned back to the farmhouse. She opened the door and stepped into the kitchen. A cursory sweep with the torch revealed a large room with an uneven flagstone floor. An inglenook fireplace. A sofa and two chairs. Glass-fronted kitchen cabinets above dusty countertops. Two Welsh dressers: one displaying crockery, the other spilling over with paperback books, fishing reels, candles, seed packets, matches, a first-aid kit. A round table by the window. A doorway leading to an unlit hall.

Spotting a light switch on the nearest wall, Hannah toggled it. Dead. She remembered Nate telling her the place was too remote to be on the grid. There must be a generator in one of the outbuildings. It, and the electric lights, would have to wait.

Grabbing a box of matches, resting the Maglite on the floor beside her, she knelt by the fireplace. Someone had left logs and kindling stacked in the grate. In under a minute she had a fire going. She took two candles from the dresser and lit them, placing one on the table and another on the counter. She would light more later. Right now she had to get her husband inside.

Outside, the wind's intensity had increased. Frozen air sluicing down from the mountains brought an aching chill. Ducking her head, Hannah hurried to the passenger side of the Discovery. She wrenched the door open.

Nate slumped inside, unconscious, skin as white as linen.

'Hey!' Slapping his face, she managed to rouse him. He lurched up in his seat, and she could see he was trying to focus, but his eyes were rolling in his head. 'I've got you, Nate, OK? Don't try to speak. It's only a short walk. I've got a fire going. You'll have to help me just for this next bit. I'm afraid it's going to hurt a little.'

Hannah braced herself as somehow he managed to lean forward and topple out of the car into her arms. It took all her strength to stop him from falling to the ground, and all her resilience to ignore his scream. 'Good. Good, Nate. That's the hard part. Just a few steps more.' She cast a look back at her sleeping daughter.

Nine years old. How can this be happening to us?

'Leah, sweetheart, I'll come back for you.' Hannah kicked

the passenger door closed, shutting the girl inside, away from the storm.

Side by side, Nate's arm around her shoulders, they managed to hobble to the kitchen, where the fire was already warming the room.

'Sofa,' he slurred.

'That's where we're heading.' She eased him down on to it. Pushed a cushion under his head. Raised his legs. 'I need to see under your shirt.'

Nate's hands fell away from his sides. She opened his jacket and ripped his shirt open, scattering buttons. His torso glistened with blood.

Immediately, she saw the two puncture wounds, each an inch in length. One was just above his lowest rib. She couldn't tell if his lung had been pierced, couldn't remember from biology how far down the ribcage the lung extended. The second wound sat even lower, in his abdomen.

Hannah fetched the first-aid kit – a green plastic briefcase – from the dresser. Popping the catch, she threw open the lid, rummaging through its contents. She found wipes and quickly cleaned his wounds. Within a couple of seconds blood began to seep from them. At least it wasn't flowing freely. Then again, he had lost so much already. Finding a bag of wound closure strips, she tried as best she could to tape him up. She placed dressing pads over the strips and bound them to his body with bandages, wrapping them tightly by passing the rolls underneath his spine.

It wouldn't save him, she knew. Only professional medical care could do that now.

With a blanket from one of the armchairs, she covered him up. 'Nate, stay awake, OK? We need to get some fluids into you.'

He nodded, whispered, 'I love you.'

Saying goodbye.

Hannah turned away from him, wiping her eyes, unable to reply. At the sink, she found a glass and filled it with water. In one of the cupboards she found a packet of sugar and poured some into the glass, stirring it with a spoon. 'Drink.' She held it to his lips, lifting his head as he slurped it down.

He drank two more glassfuls before he indicated he'd had enough. Then he took a shallow breath. 'Han . . . in the hall. Cupboard.' His voice was so low she could barely hear him. 'Gear . . . for the lake.'

'What gear, Nate? What do you mean?'

'Scuba.'

Hannah frowned, then his meaning hit her. She stepped into the dark hallway. Using the Maglite, she found the cupboard under the stairs. Inside, among coats, overalls and hats, stood a diving tank and regulator. She directed her beam at the chipped white cylinder. On its side in printed black letters: *Enriched Air NITROX*. In handwriting on a peeling sticker above this: *MOD 28M. 36% O2*. She rapped on the tank with her knuckles, tilted it. Full.

The enriched air would help him to breathe, allowing more oxygen to enter his system. It might just win them some time. Buoyed by her discovery, she dragged the tank into the kitchen, attached the regulator and pressed it into Nate's mouth. 'OK, you're not going to win any fashion prizes, trust me. But keep breathing. Nice and slow.'

He was too weak to reply, but he held eye contact with her. Hannah felt a thousand things pass between them in that look. She took his hand. Squeezed it.

Inside the room, the crackle of the logs in the grate and the mechanical sucking of the regulator made the only sounds. Outside, the wind hurled fistfuls of raindrops against the windows.

Hannah got to her feet, took a deep breath and was just about to go outside to Leah when something heavy crashed against the front door of the farmhouse.

CHAPTER 2

Balliol College, Oxford

1979

Charles Meredith asked himself two questions that July morning, as he made the drive from his Woodstock home to the Balliol College library. First, would the girl be there for a fourth morning in a row? Second, how much did it matter to him?

While he wouldn't be able to answer his first question until he arrived on campus, the fact that he found himself navigating summer tourist traffic on a Saturday morning to find out suggested it mattered to him quite a bit.

The girl was both pig-headed and short-tempered – traits, Charles conceded, that he shared. Inevitably, it had led them to an entanglement. Yet as well as being pig-headed and short-tempered, the girl was also an enigma, a puzzle demanding his attention.

Her sudden appearance, crashing into his life like thunder in a restless sky, could hardly have come at a worse time. In less than six weeks he was due in Princeton, New Jersey, where he was to deliver a lecture to academia's finest – and fiercest – scholars of early medieval history. Not only was that work incomplete, he had just discovered a weakness in the architecture of his central tenet so severe it threatened to bring the entire edifice crashing down.

Wednesday morning, he had arrived on the campus with his six-week deadline bearing down on him like Theseus's Minotaur. Carrying a satchel of research papers, scribbled thoughts and books, he walked through Balliol's library to his table near the wooden statue of St Catherine. It was the table Charles used every time he visited. From here, surrounded by printed works, he could look through the arched windows to the front quad, and could also see the portrait of George Abbot, former Canterbury Archbishop, and one of the forty-seven translators responsible for the King James Version.

Lately, Charles had discovered that the table was not the only one he *liked* to use; it had become the only one he *could* use. If he tried to place himself anywhere else in the building, at any other desk, he found his concentration ebbing, his temper fraying. At first he told himself he simply drew comfort from having St Catherine and old Abbot gazing down on him while he worked. It had – he now accepted – been a lie.

Like the precisely ordered shirts hanging in his wardrobe, the carefully stacked cutlery in his kitchen drawer, the tins of food meticulously arranged in his larder, the collection of flattened foil milk-bottle tops on his sill, the table represented another symptom, another warning sign, another encroachment of the compulsions beginning to haunt him. Charles had been embarrassed to discover that both colleagues and students had sensed his fixation and were content to indulge him, with the result that whenever he visited the library, at whatever time of day, he found the table empty and waiting for him. That was until Wednesday morning, when he discovered his squatter.

She was young. At least ten years his junior. When he arrived she had reference books scattered before her like the picked-over leavings of a carrion feast. It would, he thought, take her an age to pack up all her materials and move to another desk. Since he had left his house, a dozen new ideas and worries had occurred to him. He needed to commit them to paper before they evaporated. Charles felt a tic pulling at his right eye.

He made a show of opening his satchel and noisily removing documents and pens. The girl looked up at him, blinked, and returned to her book. This left him standing in the middle of the library, awkwardly clutching a sheaf of papers and a swinging satchel. He glanced around. Few other scholars were using the library at this hour. Certainly no other women. Balliol had only accepted its first female Fellow a few years earlier. The first intake of female undergraduates was not due to arrive until the Michaelmas term. That meant she was a visitor, rather than a member of the college.

He could see Pendlehurst working his way down the stacks, paper in hand, mouth moving wordlessly. The librarian spotted Charles, saw the girl occupying his table and elected to drift out of sight.

Charles felt his jaw clenching. He cleared his throat. Stared.

The girl had a long face, almost equine. Chocolate-brown eyes. Auburn hair tied back in a ponytail. Again, she looked up at him. Holding his gaze a moment longer this time, she raised a challenging eyebrow. When he didn't respond – it was difficult to as his own eyebrows were already raised – she returned to her work, picking up a pencil and writing something down on her notepad. Charles glanced at the cover of her nearest book.

Gesta Hungarorum.

'Miss?'

She looked up. 'Yes?'

'I'm sorry, you're sitting in my seat. Can you move?'

She leaned back in the chair, considering him with a puzzled expression. When she spoke, her accent was French. 'You are sorry?'

'No, I'm not sorry.' Charles hesitated, frowned. 'I'm not sorry. I meant . . . Look, that's my chair.'

'This is your chair?'

'Yes, at my table'

'Your table.'

He felt his fingers tightening around his papers. Tried to

calm himself. 'Look, it's not a problem.' He gestured around the library. 'There are plenty of free tables.'

She followed his gaze. 'Yes. The library is quite empty.'

He waited for her to say something else, or to begin packing her belongings. Then, appalled, he realised that she intended to do neither. Her eyes continued to examine him.

He smiled. Rather, he widened his mouth, exposing teeth. 'I come in here every day. And I always sit at this table.'

'It is a nice table.'

'Yes.'

'If I came here every day, I would want to sit here too.'

'If you came here every day, you'd quickly discover that I am always to be found in that seat.'

Now she returned his smile. 'Except today.'

Charles sucked in a breath, held it. Exhaled. He tried to ignore the muscle twitching in his cheek. 'Indeed. Well, I don't want to hold you up any longer, and I'd also like to get started please, so can you . . .' He left the sentence hanging.

'Can I what?'

He flapped his hand in the direction of the other chairs. 'Just . . .'

'Just what?'

'Look. I gather you're not a student of this college. So perhaps you don't know who you're talking to, but—'

'I've a feeling I'm going to find out.'

'I'm *Professor* Charles Meredith, and—'

'And I am Nicole Dubois.'

'Well . . . that's wonderful.' Charles paused, shook his head. 'For God's sake. Will you just get *out* of my seat?'

'I think . . .' She paused, tapping her pencil against her teeth. 'No.'

The library opened at nine o'clock on weekdays during the summer. The next morning Charles intended to be there the minute the doors were unlocked. After leaving the campus the day before he had been so angry – so fixated on the fact that she had not yielded to him in what, after all, was a perfectly simple request – that he had been unable to concentrate all afternoon. As a result he was yet another day behind schedule.

Traffic delayed his arrival, meaning he did not reach the library until ten minutes after it had opened. Already vexed, he pushed through the door, marched past Pendlehurst and came across the girl, sitting in his seat, with her books spread out all over his desk in such a disorderly heap that they virtually screamed at him to be dusted, alphabetically sorted, straightened and stacked.

'You!'

She glanced up and smiled, but the trace of ice in her expression was not lost on him. Her hair, he noticed, was in bunches today. 'Good morning.'

'What are you doing here?' he snapped.

The girl – Nicole, he thought, her name was Nicole – indicated the spew of books with the palm of her hand. 'The same as yesterday, you see? Reading. Writing.'

'I have a lot of work to do today.'

'Then I wish you well.'

Instantly, he felt his cheeks growing hot. She possessed an instinctive grasp of the exact turn of phrase, the most casually mocking manner, guaranteed to incense him. 'You're interfering with my work, jeopardising a critical deadline. I don't know what it is you're researching, but why don't you take it some-where else?'

She opened her mouth, considered his expression, hesitated. Then: 'Go on. Say it.'

'What?'

'Please say it.'

'Say what?'

'Ask me if I know who I'm talking to.'

'Look, I've had about—'

'Go on. Ask me.' She rummaged through her notes. 'I wrote it down somewhere here.'

'This is preposterous!'

'Preposterous! Good word, Charles. Pre–pos–ter–ous.' Nicole rolled it slowly off her tongue, savouring each syllable. 'What a lovely sound it makes.' She indicated the rest of the room. 'The library is almost empty. But you must sit here. And you call me preposterous. It's ironic, no?'

'Will you let me have my seat?'

'OK, I'll ask for you.' She contorted her face into a grimace. 'Nicole, do you know who you're talking to?' Now her expression relaxed. 'Yes, a strange man whose Ph.D leads him to believe he owns Balliol College library.'

'No it doesn't.'

'The arrogant and obsessional Professor Charles Meredith.'

'How dare you!'

She raised her eyebrows. Charles stared at her, speechless. Then, with a sudden feeling of impotence so crippling that he could no longer hold her gaze, he turned to the nearest table and threw down his papers. He sat down. Searched for one of his documents. Spread it out before him. Found a pen and uncapped it. Hunched forward, feeling his ears burning, his hands shaking. Tried to concentrate. Found his eyes flickering over sentences and phrases, retaining nothing.

From the next table he heard a snort and glared up at the girl. She was shaking her head at him, openly displaying her amusement. Feeling the arteries in his neck beginning to throb, Charles stood, gathered up his belongings and marched down the aisle.

'*À bientôt*,' she called after him.

Outside the building, pacing back and forth, he urged himself to calm down. The Princeton lecture was thirty-seven days away. Theseus's Minotaur was growing tusks and horns. He could not afford to lose another day of work.

After a minute of clenching and unclenching his fists, and casting baleful looks at the undergraduates hurrying past, Charles went back inside the building. He found Pendlehurst at a desk.

Beckoning him over, he laid an arm around the man's shoulders. 'I'm going to need a key to get in early tomorrow, Pendlehurst,' he said. 'Lots on.'

Charles let himself into the library at eight o'clock the following morning, before the other scholars had arrived. He found his table blissfully unoccupied. Glancing up at the placid wooden face of St Catherine, giving old Abbot a silent nod, he sat down and opened his satchel. Removing its contents, he carefully stacked his books in a pile, largest at the bottom, smallest at the top, each volume precisely centred upon the one beneath it, making the beginnings of a pyramid. He selected a notebook and placed it in front of him, one handspan from the nearest desk edge and equidistant from each of its sides. From his case he removed three pens and a single pencil. He lined them up in a row above his notebook, the lettering of each instrument at a forty-five degree angle towards him.

Content with the arrangement of his tools, Charles let his eyes drift across the library, deciding where to begin. It proved difficult. However hard he tried to focus on the Princeton lecture, he found himself returning to the exact choice of words he would use when the girl arrived at opening time to claim the territory.

Nothing petulant. He would not demean himself. He required something subtle. Elegant. Something that underlined his ascendancy while demonstrating graciousness in victory.

The exact content of that sentence changed several times over the next hour, as he polished it, refined it, added and subtracted hidden subtexts.

By ten o'clock she still hadn't appeared. By eleven, he persuaded himself that she was not coming. By quarter past eleven, he noted with dismay that he had produced no work all morning and had spent nearly three hours devising a pointlessly smug sentence to reel off to a girl he had met only twice. By midday he had wound himself into such a maelstrom of fury that he leaped up from the desk and scraped his papers back into his satchel. Deciding to abandon the campus altogether, he strode out of the library and crossed the street to where his car was parked.

The Jaguar – a silver E-Type Series 3 indulgence – was where he had left it in front of a brick wall. Now he discovered that a dark green Hillman Hunter had parked horizontally behind it. His vehicle was trapped against the wall.

Frowning, Charles approached. He bent to the driver's side of the Hillman and peered through the window. No one sat inside. Nothing lay on the black vinyl seats that provided any clue to its owner. He rested his hand on the bonnet. It was warm, but it was also in the full glare of the midday sun. The car could just as easily have been here a minute as an hour. Searching around him he saw an elm tree, set back from the road and shading a patch of grass. Nicole Dubois was reclining against its trunk.

Sighing, Charles walked over. 'Let me guess. That car,' he said, pointing at the Hillman, 'belongs to you.'

Nicole looked up at him, squinting in the sunlight. Her face remained impassive, her tone neutral. 'Charles. What you did this morning was disappointing.'

'What?'

'It was ungracious, unbecoming, ungentlemanly. Rather than playing by the rules, you used the advantage of your position to get what you wanted. I am not impressed.'

He opened his mouth to protest and discovered with dismay that despite his morning rehearsing for their next clash, he was utterly unable to think of a retort. When she forced him, unexpectedly, to defend his behaviour of the last few days, he found he could not. Now that he was outside the sombre environment of the library, with the sun on his face, he was chagrined at just how irrational – how *ungracious* – he had been. And all over a table.

She was waiting still for his answer. Casting about, he noticed the book she had been reading, a thumbed translation of *Gesta Hunnorum et Hungarorum*, by Simon of Kezá. 'You realise that's a work largely of fiction,' he said.

'Of course. And you will also realise that it's one of the earliest texts available.'

'What are you trying to find out? I might be able to help.'

'If I need to locate a table, Charles, I'll let you know.'

He nodded. 'OK, I deserved that.'

'Yes. You did.'

'Look, perhaps I could buy you a cup of tea. To say sorry.' He blinked, aghast. Where on earth had that come from? 'I meant, if you wanted to discuss a particular aspect of Hungarian history.'

Nicole closed the book. When she jumped to her feet he was surprised to see that they were almost the same height. 'No, Charles. I don't want to talk about it.'

He held up his hands. 'That's fine.'

Rummaging in her bag, Nicole produced a set of keys. 'I must go.'

'Yes. Of course.' He stood back, allowing her to pass him, the awkwardness between them now painful.

She unlocked the Hillman and threw her bag on to the passenger seat. Starting the car, she reversed into the street. Nicole wound down the window. 'You need not worry, Charles. Tomorrow is the last you'll see of me.' Putting the Hillman into gear, she drove away up the street.

Which brought him to Saturday morning, negotiating summer traffic on the way to the campus and asking himself whether she would indeed make a final visit. Apart from her name, he still knew nothing of her, or quite why it seemed so important that she left Oxford with a better impression of him. He did know that getting to the library before her and taking a seat at the wretched table would be disastrous, which was why he refused to allow himself near the building until just past ten o'clock.

The library was quiet, with only a few readers occupying

desks. He ventured into the stacks and found St Catherine and old Abbot gazing down at him.

His table was vacant.

Charles stood for a long moment, quite unprepared for the disappointment he felt. He pulled out the chair and sat down, thinking.

He knew the girl's name. And the fact that she was French. It was little more than nothing, really. He sat in the seat for a further half an hour, his mood gradually darkening, before accepting that she was not going to appear. He stood up to leave and as he passed the front desk, Pendlehurst called out to him, 'That French girl left something for you.'

Immediately, he felt his spirits lift. 'She's been in?'

'She was here first thing this morning. Sat at your table for a bit, passed me a note for you and left.'

Cursing, he realised he had missed her by just thirty minutes. Pendlehurst handed him a folded sheet of paper torn from a notepad. Quickly he opened it.

Ki korán kel, aranyat lel

It was Hungarian. But he could not translate it.

'Did she say anything?'

'Just that she couldn't wait any longer and that she had to leave.'

'Did she say where she was going?'

'I didn't ask.'

'Damn it.'

'Is everything all right?' asked Pendlehurst.

'Do you know any Hungarian speakers?'

'I think Beckett is your best bet.'

'Can I use the telephone?'

It took Charles ten minutes to locate Beckett, and only a further minute to get the translation.

He who wakes early, finds gold

A Hungarian variation of an English proverb: *the early bird catches the worm*. Charles found himself smiling for the first time that morning, and then an idea struck him. He tracked down Pendlehurst. 'She must have contacted us in advance to access the library.'

'Of course.'

'So you should have a record of her.'

'I believe so. Professor, are you sure there isn't something wrong?'

'It's imperative that I get back in contact with her before she leaves Oxford. Can you hunt out her details for me please?'

Giving Charles a strange look, the librarian beckoned him behind the desk. He opened a box of filing cards and began walking his fingers through them. 'Here we are. Dr Amélie Préfontaine.'

Charles shook his head. 'No, her name is Nicole.'

'The tall girl? French accent?'

'Yes.'

'Carried a big canvas bag.'

'That's her, yes.'

'It says here Dr Préfontaine.'

Charles realised that he was frowning, and that Pendlehurst was beginning to look uneasy.

'If something odd is going on,' said the librarian, 'I think you should tell me. She was looking at some very rare manuscripts while she was here.'

'No, it's fine. I must have misheard her. Thank you, Pendlehurst.'

The card details revealed an Oxford address and a local number. Charles walked across the street to a telephone box. It was sweltering inside the booth. He loosened his tie. Picking up the receiver, he pushed ten pence into the slot and dialled the number. It rang fifteen times before someone answered. He heard static on the line.

'*Oui?*' A female voice. But not the girl's. This woman sounded much older.

'Hello?' He listened to the crackle and pop of the connection, framed by the woman's breathing.

The voice came back in heavily accented French. 'Who is this please?'

'My name is Charles Meredith. Professor Charles Meredith. I lecture at Balliol. I'd like to speak to Dr Amélie Préfontaine.'

A pause. Then, '*Je suis desolée.* There is no Amélie here.'

'Wait. What about . . . Nicole Dubois?'

This time he heard an intake of breath, followed by rapid French in the background, too faint to make out. The woman on the other end of the telephone covered the mouthpiece. The muffled sounds of conversation continued. He could hear the alarm in both voices but not the words. The clarity of the line was suddenly restored.

'Jakab.' She spat the name at him.

'No, this is Charles—'

'*Démon. Allez au diable!*' The line went dead.

Charles recoiled from the handset, shocked at the vitriol in the woman's voice. He stared at the receiver for several seconds before replacing it in the cradle. Despite the heat inside the phone box, goose bumps had risen on the flesh of his forearms. He opened the door of the booth and stepped out into the fresh air outside. Then, without understanding why, unaware of how his next actions would echo though every single day of his remaining years, Charles Meredith broke into a sprint towards his car.

Phoenix Avenue, the address on the library card, was only five minutes through the centre of the city. Perhaps longer in Saturday traffic. But not if he was aggressive. A conviction filled him that if he did not act now, immediately, his chance to see her again would be lost.

His car was parked near the same tree as the day before. Today, a Triumph Stag. After his shaming yesterday, he had left the Jaguar at home, uncomfortable at the degree of opulence it suggested. Right now he could have found good use for it. No matter. The Stag was still a powerful car.

Charles slid in behind the steering wheel and slammed the door. After reversing into the street he accelerated along St Giles and past the Ashmolean on Beaumont Street.

You're insane, he told himself, as he sped through the city. *You've met this girl three times. The one thing you thought you knew about her turned out to be a lie, and that telephone conversation was not just unusual, it was downright chilling.*

Arriving at a crossroads, he braked hard behind an Austin Cambridge held up by a red light. Phoenix Avenue lay to his left, a long tree-lined row of Victorian redbrick townhouses. As he waited for the lights to change he spotted a green Hillman Hunter at the kerb, a hundred yards along the avenue. It sat outside a decrepit-looking three-storey townhouse, the front garden overgrown to weeds. Nicole Dubois was hurrying down the front steps. She was guiding an older woman with a white shawl draped across her shoulders. Both of their faces looked drawn with fear. Nicole shepherded the woman into the passenger seat and closed the door.

At the junction, the lights still glowed red, vehicles crossing from both directions. Nicole went to the back of the car. She threw two large bags into the boot, ran to the driver's side and jumped in.

Through the Austin's rear-view mirror, Charles made eye contact with its driver, willing him to move. But there was nowhere for him to go.

A belch of blue smoke erupted from the Hillman. Nicole pulled away from the kerb and headed away up the avenue.

In frustration, Charles rammed his fist down on the horn. The driver of the Austin frowned.

'Come on, come *on*.'

The Hillman followed the curve of Phoenix Avenue and disappeared around the corner. In front, the stream of traffic ceased. The lights changed to amber, then green. When the Austin remained stationary, he hammered the horn again as the driver continued to frown at him.

Charles ran out of patience. He hauled the wheel clockwise and stamped on the accelerator. Overtaking the car in front, he spun the wheel to the left and cut across it, foot flat to the floor, tyres protesting.

Accelerating up the avenue, he followed it for two hundred yards before reaching a tail of traffic at a T-junction. The Hillman was nowhere in sight. The two cars in front of him pulled away, one to the right and one to the left.

Sitting at the top of the junction, Charles slapped his hands on the steering wheel. Which direction? To go left would take him north, skirting anticlockwise around the city. Turning right would take him to the London Road and the motorway. He had no time to debate his options further. The latter seemed a sensible choice so he swung the Stag to the right and felt its three-litre V8 press his seat into his spine as he moved up through the gears.

Within minutes, houses on both sides gave way to fields. He overtook a lumbering Talbot Sunbeam and found clear wide road in front of him. Charles watched the needle on the speedometer creep past eighty. He marvelled at his new-found recklessness. But Nicole – or Amélie, or whatever she was really called – was fleeing, and the only way he was going to catch her was by taking a risk.

He saw the green glint of a car in the distance.

Spurred on, Charles pushed the Stag harder. He quickly closed the distance between himself and the Hillman and had to brake violently as he came up behind her. He knew she would not be able to hear his horn at this speed so he flashed his lights instead. The distance between them was too great to see her clearly in her rear-view mirror. He jinked the car left and right, flashing his lights again to attract her attention.

In front, the older woman strained around in the passenger

seat. Then, instead of slowing, the Hillman began to gain speed. Both cars were rapidly approaching the rear of a large articulated lorry. The Hillman swerved out into the oncoming lane. It overtook the lorry and canted back in front of it just in time to avoid a collision with a car heading towards them.

'Jesus Christ!'

What was she doing?

The artic swerved, rocking back and forth on its suspension. Its air-horn blasted.

Hugging close to the back of the lorry, Charles was forced to wait for another three cars to pass in the opposite lane before he could overtake. It took him a further minute to close the distance to her Hillman again.

She was not going to stop for his flashing lights, but his Stag was a far more powerful car. Checking the road ahead was clear, he pulled out to the right and accelerated. She anticipated the move, also moving right, and he braked just in time to avoid clipping the Hillman's rear.

Charles pulled back in behind her, swearing and shaken.

Perhaps thinking that he was going to try the same move on her left, she swerved to block him. This time she reacted too aggressively and as the car rocked over, its left-side wheels drifted on to the grass of the siding. Brake lights flared red, and suddenly the back end of her car was weaving wildly. Charles went right to avoid the fish-tailing Hillman, which bobbed, slid, and veered off the road towards the field on its left. It tore through brambles, hit a bank. The front end reared up and the car lifted into the air, sailing clear of a hedgerow. It seemed to hang in the air for an age. Then the front end nosed downwards and smashed into the field's sun-baked earth.

The first impact tore off its front wheels. Glass shattered. Metal body panels sheared and spun away. The Hillman bounced, steaming and smoking. When it landed a second time, it slewed around to the right.

With shocking and violent energy, the vehicle flipped.

CHAPTER 3

Snowdonia

Now

Hannah Wilde was still gripping Nate's hand in the kitchen of Llyn Gwyr when something hammered against the front door of the farmhouse. Her stomach muscles clenched and she felt herself doubling over, as if reacting to a physical blow. Panic swelled in her, a tangible pressure in her chest. For a long moment she felt too frightened to think or move. Her eyes darted to the darkened hallway. They returned to her husband's face.

A single unvoiced question: who?

For the space of three breaths, silence dominated. Then the hammering resumed. Four heavy resounding bangs that made her flinch as each one landed.

Leah.

Her daughter was still asleep in the back of the Discovery.

Alone. Unguarded.

Hannah felt her scalp shrinking, her skin prickling.

How could anyone have found them so soon? Even her father didn't know their whereabouts. Hours earlier he had made Hannah promise not to tell him which of the safe-houses she was heading for. It meant he was less able to betray her, less likely to endanger them.

Surely no one could have followed them here? She would

have spotted their headlights. It would have been suicidal to attempt the winding mountain roads without them. Unless, of course, they had other means to follow.

She needed to think. Act.

It was pointless trying to pretend that nobody was home. Anyone standing outside the porch would see the glow of candle-light spilling into the hall. And she knew that whoever this intruder was, he – it would be a *he*, she was certain of that – would not be diverted simply because she refused to answer the door.

While it felt monstrous, she thought Leah was probably safer in the car for now, wrapped in the darkness behind the house. If only she had locked the Discovery's doors.

Hannah disengaged her hand from Nate's. She moved to the doorway of the unlit hall. Stepped through it. Kept close to the wall, balancing on the balls of her feet. All the while her fear maintained a physical presence in her chest, forcing her to take quick shallow breaths.

Enveloped in shadow, she crept across bare wooden floor-boards. Past a staircase leading to the first floor. Towards the end of the hall.

The air here was frigid after the warmth of the kitchen. Beneath her feet, the boards flexed, threatened to creak. Ahead stood the front door. Solid oak, except for a bulbous glass pane. On each side, leaded half-windows allowed a trickle of moonlight to pool on the floor.

Hannah eased closer until she had a view through the nearest window out to the porch.

No one stood outside.

She craned her head further. Held her breath. Kept the rest of her body concealed. She now had a clear view of the entire front drive. Still no sign of their intruder. But something else. Something just as frightening.

An ancient Land Rover Defender now stood on the gravel a few yards from the door. This close, she could hear the tick of its engine as it cooled.

Claws of panic punctured her skin, clenched her intestines. Twisted. Whoever the driver of the Defender was, if he wasn't outside the front of Llyn Gwyr, he was probably moving around the side of the farmhouse.

Back towards the Discovery.

And Leah.

A moan escaped her. Breaking cover, all sense of stealth forgotten, she sprinted down the hall to the kitchen.

'*Han!*'

On the sofa, Nate had removed the oxygen regulator. His face was translucent. A death mask. As she passed him he reached out and his fingers closed on her wrist, his strength as delicate as cobwebs. When he pulled her to him, his voice was little more than breath against her cheek. 'Pantry . . . left shelf.' His eyes rolled with the effort of talking. 'Shotgun. Loaded last time I checked.'

'Leah's outside.' Hannah heard herself sob. A wretched sound. She was losing her husband. Perhaps her daughter too.

'Go.'

She stepped towards the pantry door. Sensing movement, she glanced around at the kitchen windows and saw something butt its face up against the glass.

The candlelight had transformed the windows into flaming mirrors, reflecting everything except what lay directly behind them. In the window beside the door, a large dog stared in at her, front paws resting on the sill. Hannah halted halfway across the kitchen, locked into the gaze of its rust-coloured eyes. Although the transforming effect of the candlelight disguised its true colouring, she saw a muscular chest covered by a short, thick coat.

Hannah remained motionless until another face appeared behind the glass. This time she gasped and took a step backwards as she saw not another dog, but a man.

He was ancient. At least eighty. Tall in defiance of his age. Deep lines and creases ran in patterns across his face. Little fat or flesh clung to his bones. A fuzz of white hair, cropped close, covered his head and a mist of stubble sprouted on hollow cheeks. His eyes startled her the most. They shone bright, green, and wicked, sparkling with the flicker of reflected flames. The instant he noticed her he froze, and they stared at each other, both of them still.

The dog skittered a paw across the glass and tilted its head. It barked once and began to whine, the thin sound discordant over the wind's voice. Without taking his eyes off Hannah, the stranger raised a hand and caressed the animal's ears. Immediately it fell silent.

Hannah retreated a step towards Nate, grateful that the high back of the sofa concealed his presence. As if sensing her thoughts, the dog glanced over at where he lay.

The old man lifted up his hands. 'Didn't mean to startle you,' he shouted. His voice was strong, as dry as straw, and his accent was strange: an influence of Welsh laid over something less identifiable.

Could this really be him?

She could think of nothing that would have allowed him to find them so quickly. Had he simply made a fatefully lucky guess?

'What do you want?' Hannah surprised herself with the steel in her voice. She forced herself to avoid looking down at Nate. There was nothing he could do; she was in this alone.

'Saw your lights approaching from my place. Just seeing if everything's all right, is all.' The old man moved towards the door. As he passed the window she risked a glance down. Nate had lapsed back into unconsciousness. The oxygen regulator lay useless on his chest.

Her eyes snapped back up. 'Why wouldn't it be?'

'Not been people at Llyn Gwyr for a long while. Sometimes when a place lies empty around here, you get trouble turning up. Making itself at home when it's got no business doing so. Damn fool time of night to be making a visit, if you ask me.'

'I wasn't.'

He continued to stare at her, his intentions unreadable in the furrows of his face. 'There's a young girl sleeping in your car. She yours?'

Hannah felt a scream building. At least it would relieve some of the pressure. Nate was waning, his life trickling away every moment she delayed. Leah was stranded in the Discovery, cut off from Hannah by this outlandish stranger and his creature. Her throat throbbed with clenched emotion. 'My daughter.'

'Are you trouble?' he asked. If truly this was Jakab, the odd exchange of words was like nothing she had previously contemplated.

'No. We're not trouble.'

He nodded. 'Maybe you are, maybe you aren't. Maybe you are, and just don't know it. For a moment I thought you might be robbers, or at least people up to no good. But now I've seen you. Well, there never was much of value here to start with, I suppose.'

Hannah sorted through her options. She had no weapon to hand. Nate had told her of the shotgun, but the kitchen door was unlocked, and in the time it took her to get into the pantry, he would be inside the house. If she needed more than a second to locate the weapon, or if Nate's recollection was wrong, then it would all be over. Yet what if the old man was genuine?

He turned his eyes up to the skies, as if losing interest. 'This storm's going to roll in any moment. Just figured if you were alone, you might need help getting the power on.'

Hannah forced herself to make a decision. She could not trust this stranger's identity or his intentions. But if he was really from a neighbouring farm out on a mission of charity, she could not risk rousing his suspicions. More than anything, she needed help.

You have to take a chance. Please God let this be the right one.

Senses screaming, she walked to the kitchen door, and before she could change her mind she opened it. Wind eddied into the room, baring teeth of ice. 'I'm sorry,' she said. 'You just startled me. Let's start again. It's good of you to check up.'

Fanned by the air rushing into the room, the flames in the hearth set emeralds dancing in the old man's eyes. 'Don't need an apology. Sometimes when you live out here alone, you forget how to treat with people.' He held out a hand, the skin around his eyes crinkling. 'They call me Sebastien.'

Hannah hesitated. She focused on steadying the shakes that tried to betray her. Reached out her hand.

If he grabs me, I'll scream. But it won't matter. It'll be too late. I will have failed them.

She felt the old man's fingers close on her hand. His skin felt like soft denim, dry and warm. He gripped her hand. Tight.

And then he let go.

Sebastien indicated the dog. 'This here's Moses. It's been a time, but there used to be a diesel generator in your outhouse. If the motor hasn't seized, I could try getting it started for you. Won't give you any hot water but at least you'll have light. Why don't you get your little sprite inside while Moses and I go and take a look?'

'You're very kind. Thank you.'

She didn't know nearly enough about who he was and why he was here, and something about him unsettled her. But that would have to wait. Hannah watched as he whistled to his dog, pulled up the collar of his Barbour and turned away. He walked out of the candlelight towards the stone buildings.

Whatever happens, don't leave him alone with Nate.

If she allowed that, she faced losing the one thing to which she could cling: the knowledge, the utter conviction, that the man lying on the sofa was the father of her child, the man she loved, her confidant, her friend. Hannah opened the kitchen door, ducked outside and ran towards the 4x4.

The wind battered her, furious, and tried to push her back inside the house. Gusts flung squalls of stinging rain. She lifted an arm across her face, screwed up her eyes. Peering through the darkness at the car, she wondered what she would do if her daughter wasn't inside. The thought nearly made her retch.

Don't think about it. Not yet.

Moving to the Discovery's rear door, she wrenched it open and found Leah illuminated in the milky glow of the overhead light.

Relief. Joy. Anguish.

What would you have done if she'd gone? What would you have done, Hannah?

Trying not to wake the girl, she unfastened the seat belt, gathered her daughter into her arms and carried her across the driveway to the house. In one of the outbuildings, she saw torchlight and heard the clacking of a hand crank.

Back inside Llyn Gwyr's kitchen, she lowered Leah into an armchair. The girl opened her eyes, blinked. Hannah hushed her, pressing a cushion into her arms. She smoothed her daughter's hair until Leah closed her eyes again and curled up.

She turned to Nate. Lifted back his blanket. Spots of blood had begun to stain the bandages that bound his dressings.

The kitchen door banged open and before she could cry out to stop him, Sebastien walked inside, wiping his feet on the mat. He flicked the light switch. When the overhead bulb winked on, he nodded to himself. 'Reckon you've got enough diesel to get you through two or three nights. Tomorrow you need to check your LP tank. You might have warmth now, but there's not much wood in your store and with the roof blown in, what you've got is soaked. If there's any left, the gas should give you hot water. If there isn't, you need to order some. Not wise to be unprepared up in these mountains. Especially when there's little folk around.' He turned towards the door. 'Moses, come. Let's get this door shut.'

Hannah rose to her feet as the dog trotted inside. When the old man closed the door, she felt her muscles tense. He opened his mouth to say something further, and then he seemed to notice her alarm. This time her eyes betrayed her. She glanced down at her husband.

Sebastien leaned over the sofa. He stared down at Nate. At the blood dried to his milk-white face. At the oxygen tank. The regulator.

Without a word, he reached out and laid two fingers against the pulse point on her husband's neck.

He looked up at Hannah. 'Thought you weren't trouble.'

'We're not.'

'Maybe. Maybe not. Either way, I reckon you need more help than I thought.' He licked his lips. 'You want to be straight with me. Pretty quick. This boy's as good as dead.'

She sobbed. 'Don't say that.'

'Doesn't mean he *is* dead.' Sebastien rounded the sofa and knelt down at Nate's side, knees cracking. He lifted back the blanket and surveyed the dressings. 'You want my help?'

'Yes.'

He raised his head and his eyes pierced her. 'You're willing to do as I say and tell me exactly what I ask?'

'Anything.'

'What happened?'

'He was stabbed. Twice.' Tears streamed down her face. 'I don't know if his lung is punctured. I can't tell.'

'When did it happen?'

'Five hours ago.'

'And you didn't take him to a hospital? You're a bloody fool.'

'I know. I *know*.'

'As good as killing him.'

'Don't. Please.'

'Who stabbed him?'

'I . . .' She hesitated. How could she explain that?

'I said be straight with me,' he snapped. 'Never mind. You can tell me later. For now, stay here. Moses? *Légy résen.*'

The dog moved around the sofa and sat down on its haunches, close to Nate.

'Where are you going?'

'Outside. I have a medical kit in the car.'

'There's one here.' She indicated the plastic briefcase.

'No good. I'll use my own.'

He was gone for less than a minute. When he returned he was carrying a bulky canvas roll and a black holdall. The canvas looked ancient, military, but when he unrolled it she saw it contained medical supplies that were modern and clean.

'Let's have a look at you, boy.' Sebastien rolled back Nate's blanket, selected a pair of scissors from his roll and snipped away the bandages. He nodded at the regulator. 'What's that?'

'Oxygen.'

'Wake him up. We need him conscious. And get that back into his mouth. It's no good if he's not breathing it.'

Hannah complied, sliding past Sebastien to rouse her husband. She pressed the regulator back into place. Nate moaned.

The old man peeled away the dressings, swearing at what he saw beneath. Gaping wounds, pooling with blood. 'Did you clean these?'

'Yes.'

'Not properly, you didn't.' Shaking his head, muttering more curses, Sebastien withdrew a pair of surgical gloves from a canvas fold and snapped them on. He spent a long time swabbing Nate's wounds with alcohol. Probing the edges of the first, he scowled as fresh blood welled. 'Deep. Very deep. But the lung isn't punctured. It's too low for that, and you'd probably see air bubbling up.'

He moved on to the second wound, air whistling in his nose as he concentrated. 'It's this one that concerns me. It's in the right place to have sliced through his intestine. I can't tell yet.' He selected a shiny metal instrument and teased apart the sides. Dark blood overflowed and ran down Nate's torso. 'I need to stitch this. And quickly. We're going to have to do it a layer at a time.'

'What do you want me to do?'

'You know how to rig up an IV?'

'Yes.'

'Get a catheter into him. You'll find one in there.' He nodded towards the canvas roll. 'Saline bags in the holdall. And a line.'

They worked together for nearly an hour, their only words his instruction and her compliance. Hannah inserted a cannula into a vein on the underside of Nate's arm. She taped it in place and set up a gravity-fed drip, wondering how an ancient hermit could have access to medical saline bags. She guessed that he couldn't. Realised that her family weren't out of danger; worried that they might be in even more danger.

Hannah watched as Sebastien sutured Nate's wounds layer by layer, hands working with delicate haste. His green eyes glittered as he concentrated on his task, and his breathing grew more nasal. Without looking up, he asked her to pass him a swab and when she placed it into his upturned hand she saw a mark, or tattoo, on his wrist: faded, blue and indistinct, but plainly the silhouette of a bird of prey.

Moses sat by the fire, tail sweeping the flagstones, eyes fixed on the windows. Abruptly Sebastien sat back and pulled off his gloves. He passed a hand across the top of his skull. Massaged his scalp. 'It's done.'

Hannah studied the neatly sewn wounds on her husband's torso, his shockingly pale skin, the dark, sunken patches around his eyes. His blue lips. 'Nate?'

Her husband stared at the ceiling, eyes unfocused and dull. Corpselike. After a moment, he moved his head and looked at her. When he opened his mouth to speak she shushed him, telling him that it was OK, that he was going to be OK.

Hannah turned to the old man. 'What now?'

Using an arm of the sofa for support, Sebastien pushed himself to his feet. He flexed his shoulders. 'Now he rests. I'd prefer it if we could get him into bed, but it's best that he lies here for now. We don't want to risk those opening up again.'

'Can we let him sleep?'

'Let's get some more liquids into him first.'

Hannah got to her feet and mixed another glass of sugar water. She held it to Nate's lips. He gulped it down. Closed his eyes. Within seconds he was asleep. Hannah found Sebastien's gaze upon her.

'I think,' he said, 'it's time for some answers.'

'Will he live?'

'That's a question.'

'It's the only question right now.'

He frowned. 'You agreed to be straight with me.'

'He's my husband.' Hannah gestured to the armchair where Leah slept. 'You're looking at our daughter. They're the two most important people in the world to me. They're all I have. And I need to know if he's going to live.'

'If your husband survives the night, he's got a good chance.'

'And his chances of surviving the night?'

'Do you believe in God?'

The question ambushed her, choked her. She couldn't speak.

Seeing her distress, Sebastien's face softened. 'If you do, pray. Because that's all either of us can do.' He sat down on a wooden chair at the table by the window. Moses padded across the room, arranging himself at the old man's feet.

Sebastien caressed the dog's head. 'OK,' he said. 'I've helped you as much as I can. If you're bringing trouble to the valley, I want to know about it. Question one: who stabbed him?'

Hannah remained still a moment, weighing up everything that had transpired. She felt her heart begin to thud in her chest. Moving to the cooker, she twisted the dial for one of the hobs and heard the hiss of gas. She found a box of matches and lit the range. Then she filled a kettle with water and placed it over the flame. 'You're right. You deserve answers,' she admitted. 'I'll tell you. But before we do anything else, let me make some tea.'

Sebastien's face relaxed. 'That would be most welcome.'

'I think there's powdered milk from the last century somewhere around.'

She knew she couldn't leave him with Nate for more than a moment. She had seen how quick and agile he could be. Opening the pantry door, heart a staccato drumming, she ducked inside. Found what she needed.

Back in the kitchen, Sebastien had not strayed from his chair by the window. He glanced up at her as she aimed the shotgun at his chest and thumbed the safety switch.

'I've seen that tattoo before, old man,' she said. 'You'd better start talking.'

CHAPTER 4

Oxford

1979

Charles had only a moment to witness Nicole's car flip over before a line of trees blurred past on the left, blocking his view.

Hands tight on the steering wheel, teeth clenched in shock, he glanced once into his rear-view mirror before jamming his foot on the brakes. The Stag's bonnet dived and its tyres shrieked. Charles's seat belt snapped taut against his chest. He spun the wheel and turned around on the empty road.

What was she thinking?

Then another thought overtook him. Far darker than the first.

What have you done?

Driving back to the place where the Hillman had left the road, Charles turned through another U and nudged the Stag up on to the bank, out of the path of following traffic. He switched off the engine and rubbed his face. Examined his trembling fingers.

Was he responsible for the accident? Certainly, he had wanted to help her. But he could not pretend that his motivation had been entirely altruistic. He had been driven, just as much, by an urge to satisfy his curiosity. And a desire to see her again.

He opened his car door and jumped out. Bracing himself for

what he might be about to see, he scrambled up the raised grass verge. A bramble-choked drainage ditch separated him from the field. Beyond the ditch stretched a brittle carpet of close-shorn wheat stalks, except where Nicole's car had gouged a dark scar.

The Hillman was a buckled and twisted box, caked in earth and dust. It must have flipped full circle at least once, because it had come to a rest on its broken axles. Smoke fluttered out of the engine block, dispersing on the breeze. Behind the car lay a litter of metal and broken glass, evidence of its destructive progress through the field.

Charles slid down the far side of the verge and into the drainage ditch, his shoes slipping on weeds and stones. Grimacing, he pressed through a tangle of gorse, blackberry and ragwort. Thorns tore through his shirtsleeves. Barbs pricked his arms. He felt blood running long before he fought his way clear.

Dragging himself up the far side of the ditch and out of the last clutches of undergrowth, Charles fell into the field. His arms burned where brambles had raked him and nettles had brushed his skin. His scalp itched from the burrs he had collected. Something buzzed near his ear. He waved it away and studied the Hillman. Close up, he saw it was even more damaged than he had first thought: a contortion of jagged metal.

And then, with a lurch of adrenalin and fear and excitement, he spotted Nicole's passenger. She was moving gingerly, picking her way around the far side of the vehicle as if feeling her way through mist. Blood seeped from a cut on her forehead, and her cheek was swollen and red. But she was alive.

Jubilant, Charles shouted out to her. On hearing his voice, the woman looked up, hesitated. She glanced back at the wreckage. Then she raised a hand and stumbled towards him.

The sun had baked the earth to a hard crust. Beneath the bristling mat of stalks, the ground was fissured with cracks. It made fast progress difficult, and by the time he reached her, he was panting with effort.

She had once, Charles saw, been a handsome woman. Age lines – he could not have called them *laughter* lines – criss-crossed her face, but they had not concealed the defined features beneath. When her eyes flashed over him, he thought they looked almost black. Her hair was the same rich auburn as Nicole's, but it had lost its lustre long ago. He wondered if the scowl that tightened her lips into a thin line was caused by pain.

As he closed the last few feet, she bent at the waist and moaned. Concussion, he wondered? Broken ribs? He stared down at the top of her skull, at the speckled white skin of her crown that peeked through a frizz of unstyled hair. It reminded him of chickens' feet. 'Are you all right?'

She ignored him. Or perhaps she did not understand him. Or was in too much discomfort to answer. From this angle, he couldn't tell whether her eyes were open, whether they were haemorrhaged, whether she was suffering.

Charles reached out to her and as he did she straightened. He saw what she clutched in her hands just before she swung it up at him.

The blunt edge of the rock crunched into his nose, snapping back his head. Pain rushed screaming into his face. The world tilted, unbalancing him, and he found himself on his back, the air knocked out of him, blinking up at the sky. He lifted his hands and cupped them around his nose. Their touch triggered an electric spasm of agony. He felt the gushing warmth of blood on his fingers.

Points of light skittered and danced. Bright fireflies of pain. He squinted through eyes blurred from tears and sun, seeking the old woman. Her expression terrified him. She stepped across his chest and raised the rock above her head.

'No!'

The shout came from inside the Hillman. Charles's eyes slid over to it. Dizziness was beginning to overcome him, but he had enough sense left to raise his arms against what was coming.

A crash and groan of metal. A car door being kicked off its hinges.

'*Mama*. No!'

His attacker turned, rock still raised high. Nicole struggled free of the vehicle. She fell on to her hands and knees. Gasped. Climbing to her feet, she raised a flat palm and shook her head. *Stop*.

The woman stared at Charles. Her black eyes seemed devoid of emotion, but he saw that tears had traced clean lines through the grime on her cheeks. She pitched her rock off to the side and stepped away from him. When Nicole appeared beside her, the older woman began to gabble in French, jabbing her finger at him. The pair engaged in rapid-fire conversation. Charles was too dizzy to follow it.

Nicole broke off and scowled at him, eyes blazing. 'What are you doing? Why are you here? You could have killed us.'

He rolled over on to his side and spat blood into the soil. 'That's rich. She just tried to stave my bloody head in.'

Nicole lunged for the discarded rock. 'I'll finish the job unless you tell me what you're doing here.'

He forced himself up on to his hands and knees and shook his head to clear it, dislodging a flurry of sparks. 'I don't *know* what the bloody hell I'm doing here. I wish I wasn't, I can tell you that much. You were the one who left me a note in the library. What the hell was that about?'

'Were you the one who telephoned the house?'

'Yes.'

'Why did you ask for Préfontaine?'

'Because that's the name you registered at the library. Why are you using a false name?'

'*I'm* asking the questions, Charles. Why are you in a different car?'

He realised, too late, that without the distinctive Jag, she would not have understood who pursued her. 'I have two cars.'

'Why?'

'I like cars. Jesus.'

'You're a university professor.'

'I can't like cars?'

'Not on a lecturer's salary.'

'I'm not just a university professor.'

'What do you mean?'

'Just that.'

She brandished the rock.

'Look, for Christ's sake, there's nothing sinister! There was some inheritance, that's all. Land, mostly. Some of it I developed. It worked out quite well.'

'Why did you follow me?'

'I told you; I don't know. I was . . . I wanted to see you again. And after the bizarre conversation I had with your delightful mother here, I wanted to make sure you were all right.'

Nicole's mother snatched at her daughter's arm. She pointed past Charles's shoulder. '*Dépêche-toi.*'

He turned to see the lorry they had overtaken pulling to the side of the road. Air brakes hissed. He felt the tension between the two women intensify.

Nicole switched her focus back to him. 'You just wanted to see me again.'

'Yes.'

'Why?'

'I don't know, really. I just—'

'You just felt compelled.'

Charles gambled that she was not going to strike him with the rock unless he did something particularly reckless, and climbed to his feet. She moved backwards, granting him space.

'Idiotically compelled,' he said.

'Instinct.' She was searching his eyes.

'Something like that.'

'And what does your instinct tell you now?'

He fished a handkerchief from his pocket and dabbed at the

blood pooling on his upper lip. 'That you're a couple of lunatics.'

'Charles. Look at me. I am deadly serious.' She stole a glance at the lorry. 'What does your instinct tell you now? About me?'

'I don't know you.'

'That doesn't matter. Forget for one moment what just happened. If you can. When you first met me, and this very moment as we stand here – do you think you can trust me?'

She was speaking faster, looking more anxious.

'I don't know.' He paused, shrugged. 'Perhaps.'

'Then listen to what I have to say, Charles. We have to get away from here right now.'

'Why?'

'I don't have time to explain. I need you to make a leap of faith. I'm asking for help. It doesn't happen often and I'll only ask once. If you want to help us you need to get us away from here.'

This was crazy.

'OK. Just . . .' He nodded. 'OK. I will. I'll help. But what about your car? We can't just walk away.'

'Charles—'

He blew out a breath. And accepted a step into the unknown. 'Fine. Come on. Let's get out of here.'

Nicole turned to the woman. She spoke rapidly, pointing first at Charles and then at the road. The woman protested, but she seemed to have lost the argument.

'Passports.' Nicole ran to the rear of the Hillman, twisted the boot lock and cursed when it would not move. She banged on the crumpled lid, jiggling the lock in frustration.

'What's wrong?'

'It's jammed. Our bags are inside.'

'Let me try it.'

'There's no time. It's stuck fast.' She went to the driver's side, reached through a broken window and pulled out a large bundle tied up with string. It looked like a collection of old leather-bound books. 'Come on. We need to go.'

'You can't leave your passports here.'

'Let's *go*.'

Nicole crossed the field, slipped down the slope of the ditch and pushed her way through the brambles, pulling the woman behind her. Charles found himself following.

The lorry, an old Bedford with a red bonnet and black wheel arches, had pulled up twenty yards behind the Stag. A man appeared from the far side. Pot-bellied, green vest, lank hair. He cupped a cigarette in his hand. ''S'why we have speed limits, son. Everyone still got their arms and legs?'

Charles ignored him. He followed the two women to his Stag, opened the passenger door and loaded them in. Jumping behind the wheel, he started the car and accelerated away from the verge.

In his rear-view mirror, he watched the receding figure by the lorry. The man stared after them. After a moment he flicked his cigarette into the bushes and turned away.

They swept through Oxfordshire countryside. Charles rolled down the windows, grateful for the purifying rush of air. The fields they passed were mostly empty, the harvesters having stripped them of their grain. The heat of the sun had scorched the earth that remained. It had been a hot month, although nothing like the summer of '76 three years earlier, when the government had introduced the Drought Act.

Where they passed dairy farms, cows grazed on pasture right up to the fences bordering the road. The animals raised solemn faces as the Stag sped past. Nicole turned often in her seat to scan the road behind them. Charles wondered if she was searching for something in particular, or if her habit was so ingrained she found it impossible to stop.

Either way, he resolved to say nothing for a while. He needed to give himself a chance to think about what had happened. His nose ached like hell, and a headache was pinching and pricking behind his eyes. Again, he asked himself what he was doing, why he had felt such a compulsion to get involved, to follow this girl.

He cast glances at her as she fidgeted in her seat. On her lap lay the bundle of books tied with string. Some of them were so old they were falling apart, the leather of their bindings cracked and dusty, the pages clumped and brown. Nicole rested her hands on top of the pile, her fingers fiddling with the knotted string. Her face remained impassive as she studied the road ahead, eyes narrowed against the wind and the glare. She looked strong, determined, yet at the crash site he had seen a fear in her as fleeting as it was unsettling. He knew she had been telling the truth when she told him she seldom asked for help. It was clear in her every interaction with him – in her speech, even in the way she held herself – that she was used to standing alone. He wondered what events, what life blows or choices, had chiselled her that way. He wondered if he would find out.

The London Road out of Oxford led to the motorway, and rather than following it south he chose the northern branch. He took the exit near Wendlebury and circled Bicester before taking country roads back west towards Woodstock. It was a circuitous route, but he sensed that Nicole needed time to gather her thoughts. By the time he was on the homeward stretch, she had ceased checking the road behind them and had fallen into a daze.

Charles examined himself in the rear-view mirror. His nose, never a graceful appendage, was swollen and purple. Blood caked the rims of his nostrils and flecked his chin. His clothes were scuffed with mud and torn from brambles. His forearms were scratched white and streaked with crimson where thorns had punctured his skin.

Strange, but despite the pain of his throbbing face, the pressure building behind his eyes, he felt *exhilarated*. He knew some of that was due to the adrenalin racing through his system.

But there was more to the feeling than adrenalin alone. It felt as if a hidden part of him had been unlocked, and as the daylight flooded in it was beginning to rejoice.

Thinking of the woman who had so efficiently clobbered him, he angled the mirror to get another look. Nicole's mother caught his reflection and returned his stare. No warmth resided in that look, no trust. He supposed that had he not chased them down so impetuously they would never have crashed off the road. She owed him little gratitude. Yet her behaviour when he had gone to help her defied understanding. She had been ready to kill him, genuinely intent on cracking open his skull and letting his brains leach into the earth. Charles recalled his conversation with her as he stood in the telephone box outside Balliol College. She had called him *démon* and *Jakab*. Clearly she believed he was someone intent on doing them harm. If it wasn't for the memory of her black eyes as she stood over him and clutched the rock above her head, he could even feel pity. But it was far too soon for that.

He angled away the mirror.

They crested a hill. An avenue of oaks flanked the road below them. Thick trunks thrust into the sky, their crowns forming an arch of foliage. As the Stag barrelled into a tunnel of green they were plunged into shadow, the sunlight flickering and dappling as it fought through the leaves.

In damp mulch at the side of the road, bloated and ripe, lay the carcass of a deer. Something – presumably another vehicle – had shattered its jaw and twisted its head around its neck. Blood had flooded from its mouth and ears and nose, and flies crawled and danced in its fluids. Charles winced as they drove past.

'Where are you going?' The sight of the dead animal had shaken Nicole out of her reverie. She sat up in her seat, instantly alert. 'Charles, where are we?'

He heard the suspicion in her voice, and it depressed him. He knew he needed to tread carefully, needed to avoid his natural inclination to lead. It was not ground that they could occupy in harmony. 'We're north of the city,' he told her. 'We just passed through Bunker's Hill. I have a house in Woodstock, a few more miles from here. If you want I can take you there. If not, I can drive you anywhere you want to go.' He closed his mouth, resolving to say nothing more. He could feel her considering her options.

Nicole twisted round in her seat, looked at the woman behind. 'Can we all go there? To your house?'

'You can even bring Joan of Arc, if she behaves herself.'

'Charles, watch your tongue,' Nicole snapped. 'That's my mother.'

'Yes,' he told her. 'I've noticed a charming similarity.'

Charles felt her glaring at him. He concentrated on the road ahead but when he sensed, a few moments later, that she was still examining him, he met her gaze and found that she was grinning. It transformed her face so spectacularly that he found himself grinning in return.

'What's funny?' he asked.

She laughed, quick and guilty. 'Your nose, Charles. It's like a strawberry.'

'Nice of you to mention it.'

'Does it hurt very much?'

'Yes, it bloody hurts.'

Nicole laughed again. 'I'm sorry.'

He nodded. 'How about you? Are you OK? When I saw the state of your car, I didn't think anyone could have survived.'

'I'll live. I'm sure I'll feel a lot worse tomorrow.'

'What are you going to do about the Hillman?'

'We can't go back to it now. It's rented. There'll be a—' She stopped, and he knew she had caught herself, dismayed at what she had been about to reveal.

'It's OK,' he said. 'You don't have to talk about it.'

'No, it's fine, Charles.' She seemed ready to say more, but he could feel her tensing again. She stared at the road and swept her hair away from her face. Quietly she added, 'Our passports are gone.'

They drove through the open gate to his cottage shortly afterwards. Nicole peered out of the window as he parked next to the Jaguar, under the shade of a silver birch. 'It's beautiful, Charles.'

Cotswold stone framed tiny sash windows gleaming with pale green paint. Wisteria vines twisted about the stone, bunches of purple flowers hanging thick and heavy with pollen. Above it all a tiled roof sagged with age.

Charles climbed out of the car as Nicole helped her mother from the back seat. He led them inside the cottage and along the hallway to the kitchen. As they assembled inside the low-ceilinged room, he felt a sudden flush of awkwardness. 'I'm sorry, I've forgotten my manners. You'll have to forgive me. I don't often have guests. Please.' He indicated a rectory table in the corner and ushered them to chairs. While her mother took a seat, Nicole placed the bundle of books on the table and went to the window. She looked out at the garden.

Impeccably manicured lawn stretched to a rear border of blackcurrant and raspberry bushes, with wild meadow beyond. Beds spilled over with dahlias, foxgloves, chrysanthemums, geraniums: a barrage of pink, purple, and red swaying on dark stems. Wild flowers clustered around the trunks of apple trees, cherry and Japanese maple. Bees hovered and buzzed, bodies sticky with nectar. On one side stood a shed in front of a tilled vegetable patch. A metal water butt collected rainwater from its guttering.

Charles felt another pang of self-consciousness, uncomfortably aware of how feminine his garden looked. He moved to the sink and filled a kettle with water.

'You surprise me,' she said. 'I never would have pictured this.'

'You've caught it at the best time of the year, of course.'

She looked past him at the blossoms, smiling.

Charles made tea in a china pot and carried it to the table on a tray loaded with cups. He waited until the leaves had steeped and then he poured. 'Look,' he said. 'I don't know what you're involved with, what situation you've found yourself in. But it's clear you're worried about telling me much about it. I'm not going to pry, I promise you, but I do want to help, and it's going to be difficult to do that very well without knowing at least something about you and what you're facing. It's pretty obvious that you're running from someone. You've been concealing your identity too. At this point I don't even know if I should call you Nicole or Amélie.'

'It was probably a stupid thing to do, but I told you the truth when we met. Like you, I just felt compelled. One of those things. I can't explain it. My name is Nicole Dubois. This is my mother, Alice. The doctor bit is also true. I earned my Ph.D at Paris-Sorbonne. My field is early medieval history, the same as you. I lecture at the university in Lille.'

Charles extended his hand in mock formality. 'Well, *Doctor* Nicole Dubois. It's good to meet a fellow academic.' When Nicole placed her hand in his he nearly jumped at the sensation of her fingers on his skin.

She treated him to a tired smile. 'I don't know where we go from here.'

'Catch-22.'

'What do you mean?'

'You don't feel able to confide in me, and I can't help you until you do.'

She sipped tea. 'We need to get to Paris. We'll be safe there, both of us. We have identities we can use in France. Préfontaine, others.'

He frowned. 'OK.'

'We're not professional criminals, Charles, if that's what you're thinking. Yes, we have other identities, documentation, but none that would stand up to the scrutiny of an international border. When we travel it's under the names on our passports. Coming here was a risk. We planned to visit only briefly. With the car crash, insurance report, investigation, there will be an easy trail. And without passports to leave England . . .' She left the sentence hanging.

'What were you looking for at Balliol?'

'Charles, I can't tell you that. It's not that I don't want to. It's for your own sake. I'm not in any personal danger. Not really. But it's not the same for anyone close to me. It is better you do not know. Believe me.'

'You can't expect me to—'

Her temper flared. 'Charles, have you listened to anything I've said? I will tell you what I can, but not that. I don't even know you.'

'My exact words earlier when you asked me if I trusted you.'

'That was different.' She glanced around the kitchen, at the copper pots hanging from the ceiling rack, at the vase of lilies on the windowsill. When she looked back at him, her face had changed. Hardened. 'How do I even know you're who you say you are?'

He sat back in his seat. 'That's an odd thing to say. You met me at the university. You're in my house.'

Alice Dubois leaned forward and laid a hand on her daughter's arm. She spoke for the first time, in accented English. 'Nicole, you can find out. Validate him. If that's the only way you can trust him, then do it.'

Nicole looked at her mother, then back at Charles. 'How long have you lived here?'

'Four years. Since I—'

'Tell me something about this room. Something only you would know.'

'Like what?'

Anything. Just something I can verify.'

He cast about. A line of cookery books stood on the work surface, squeezed between two mason jars.

'There's a small notebook bound in brown paper in that stack. My mother's old recipe book. Sellotaped towards the back is a folded recipe for pavlova taken from a magazine. There's a cross mark in pencil on it,' he told her. 'The pavlova was a disaster.'

Nicole rose from the table, found the book and riffled through the pages. She found the scrap of paper tucked at the back, and the cross in the location he had described. She came back to the table and laid it down for her mother to see. 'Thank you. I'm sorry that I had to—'

'Don't apologise. Look; stay here, tonight. The spare room is already made up. We can talk more later if you want. And if you don't, fine. I'm afraid I don't have much in the way of supplies. So let me pop out. I have a few errands to run first, but I can pick up some food and make us dinner. Perhaps all this will become clearer after that.' He stood, hoping that by demonstrating his full trust in her she would begin to lower her defences. 'Treat the place as your own. Use anything you need. I'll be gone for a couple of hours at most.'

Nicole stared into the tea leaves at the bottom of her cup.

Charles returned at seven o'clock that evening with three paper sacks filled with groceries. For supper he cooked them linguine with mussels and tarragon in a cream and white wine sauce. He opened a Chablis to accompany their meal, and he soon found himself fetching a second bottle from the fridge.

While they ate, Charles talked of his work at the university. Remembering the texts he had seen her reading – early histories of the Hungarian people – he steered the conversation towards his knowledge of Eastern Europe. Nicole contributed little, but she did ask questions of him and listened intently to his replies.

He told them of his other projects. How the BBC had commissioned him to write and present a five-part radio series on medieval Europe. The first two episodes had aired in the past few weeks. He had received only a modest fee, but ratings had been promising so far and his producer was talking about a larger follow-up project.

Afterwards, they cleared the table and Nicole helped him wash the dishes. She brewed a pot of coffee and they took it into the living room. Nicole and her mother sat on the small sofa, across from his armchair.

'I've thought of a way to get you back to France,' he told them. 'It's going to take me a few more days to arrange things, but you're welcome to stay here with me until then.'

'Get us back to France?' Nicole asked. 'How?'

Charles could not resist a grin.

CHAPTER 5

Snowdonia

Now

Hannah kept the stock of the shotgun tight into her shoulder, sighting down the barrels and aiming at the centre of the old man's chest. She was only a few yards away from him but she had seen how quickly he could move. She would not give him a chance to react.

His eyes flared as he saw the weapon, and Hannah felt cowed by the power they conveyed. As he raised his hands, his expression remained inscrutable.

'Don't,' she snarled. 'Put them back down. Into your lap. *Now.* Don't misread me and think I won't pull this trigger. Give me the slightest reason to shoot you and you're dead, I promise you that. If you move out of that chair, you're dead. If I ask you a question and I don't like your answer, you're dead. If your goddamned dog does something weird, this ends very quickly for you. Understand?'

He glanced briefly at Moses sitting by the fire, then carefully measured out his words. 'If you are who you say you are, you have nothing to fear from me.'

'I'm the one holding the gun, old man. I have nothing to fear from you at all.'

He continued as if she had never spoken. 'If you're not Hannah Wilde, if you're the other one, then I know your secrets. Do what you will. I'm too old to be scared by guns. I've made my peace and I'm ready to face whatever comes next. You can send me on in the knowledge that we're closing in on you and that this may well be the last murderous act you commit.'

She could see from the quick rise and fall of his chest that he was not as calm as his demeanour suggested. It had taken a feat of will to keep his voice steady as he uttered those words. 'That was quite a speech.'

He inclined his head. 'Perhaps a touch dramatic, but heartfelt nonetheless.'

'How do you know who I am?'

'I don't. Not for certain. Let me ask you a question.'

'I don't think so.'

'Then pull the trigger.' He waited, never taking his emerald eyes off hers. When she didn't respond, he said, 'When you were fifteen years old your father bought a farm in south Oxfordshire and inherited a herd of cattle. Which breed?'

She stared, stomach roiling. Not only did this stranger know who she was, but he was trying to verify her identity just like her father had taught *her*. She wondered what advantage she might give him by answering truthfully, and could not see one. If he was trying to win her trust, it was a laughable ploy. He could have forced the answers out of her father.

When he saw that she was hesitating, he added, 'This is not to help you verify my identity, Hannah. It's to help me verify yours.'

'They were Ayrshires.'

'Shortly after you arrived, there was an accident. What happened?'

'I tried to milk one of them by hand,' she said. 'I must have pinched, because it kicked out and broke my wrist.'

'What happened to the cow?'

'Nothing. We named her Footloose.'

The old man closed his eyes. When he opened them, they

sparkled with intensity. 'Hellfire, for a minute there I thought I was talking to *him*. That was a bit of excitement, eh? I was all ready to gut you.' He chuckled, then he cast a look at Nate and the laughter faded on his lips. 'Hannah, I'm so glad you're all still alive.'

'Thanks, I'm touched. But the rules haven't changed. You move off that—'

'Yes, yes, I know,' he snapped. 'I move, I die. Very poetic.' Now that he seemed satisfied with her identity, his brashness had resurfaced. 'I'm not moving, am I? I'm sitting on this damned uncomfortable chair with an aching back, after bending over your husband for the last hour trying to save his life. Even if I wanted to move I think it'd take me a week to straighten myself out. I thought you were making some tea.'

'How do you know my name?'

'Because we've met before. A number of times. Not for a good few years, I'll grant you, and I can see your manners haven't improved in the meantime. Last time I saw you was out in Hungary when your father brought you. And still with that look on your face sour enough to curdle milk.'

'You know my father?' she asked, frowning.

'Of course I know him. Was with him when he picked out this place. You made a lucky choice, by the way, coming here.'

'Your turn.'

'My turn to what?'

'Validate. Before you say anything else, I want some proof.'

'OK, fine.' He started to worm his right hand into the pocket of his Barbour.

'Whoa, there. Easy with the hands. Nice and slow.'

With exaggerated care, he eased his finger and thumb into the pocket. He withdrew a wicked-looking hunting knife, its metal dull but sharp, its wooden handle smooth with age.

'Careful,' she warned, keeping both barrels high.

He nodded, then dropped the knife back into his pocket. 'I will be, now I know who you are. 'Course, I don't know what would have happened if you *had* been him. I reckon maybe he'd be a bit quicker than me. Who knows? I'm getting on a bit these days. But then again, so is he. The gun's empty, Hannah. If you'd pulled that trigger I would have buried this knife in your throat. Lucky for you, and for my conscience, you didn't.'

'What are you talking about?'

'When I last checked in on this place, I found a loaded shotgun in that pantry. Second shelf up on the left-hand side, wasn't it? Just where you must have found it. Knowing the types we sometimes get in empty properties like this, I didn't want to leave a loaded weapon there. So I removed both rounds. I know you didn't have time to check when you hopped back there to fetch it. If it makes you feel better, you'll find the cartridges back in their box in the drawer of that Welsh dresser behind you. The one with all the crockery on it. Now, please – point that thing away from my face. It's very rude.'

Hannah stepped backwards, widening the gap between them. When she was nearly at the door to the hallway, she broke the shotgun and checked the chambers.

Empty.

'Tell me something else,' she demanded.

'The day your father met your mother they fought over a table. I can't remember where exactly, but one of the Oxford colleges, where he lectured.'

She knew how unlikely it was for anyone to know that story unless Charles had told them personally. Coupled with his knowledge of the shotgun, she decided he had to be telling the truth.

Hannah felt exhaustion wash over her. Somehow, she had managed to get Nate and Leah away from her father's place alive. For the moment it seemed as if they had not been followed. Nate's condition was dire. The possibility that he might not survive the night, however shattering, was something she had to consider. But they had found a safe-house. A temporary respite from what hunted them. They still had a chance.

'Hannah?' he asked.

She blinked away weariness. 'I'm sorry, Sebastien. When I saw the tattoo, I panicked. Knew I'd seen it, just not where.'

'Don't be sorry. If you ever need to validate again, for whatever reason, you don't hesitate. Better to be safe. If I don't answer quickly enough, or I seem insulted, puzzled, you shoot me. Aim for my head next time, not my chest. Charles made those rules very simple for a reason. They work, and they're the only way you have of keeping your family safe. Later I'll tell you a few things you can use to validate me when you need to.

'Now, I'm not a patient man by nature, I'll admit that. So I hope for both our sakes you're going to keep to your word and make that tea.'

She forced a smile at his words, even though she didn't feel like smiling. He was trying to lighten the atmosphere, and he deserved something for that; he had already done so much more. 'I think that's the least you've earned. Thank you. Thank you for being here. For helping Nate.'

Sebastien waved away her gratitude.

She went to the dresser, found the box of cartridges and loaded two of them into the gun. Returning the weapon to the pantry, she emerged with tea bags, powdered milk and sugar. 'These don't look too ancient,' she said, indicating the supplies.

'They're not. I make sure everything's up to date, just in case something happens.' He paused, then added, 'I'm sorry something has.'

This time it was Hannah's turn to brush aside a well-meant comment. A childish part of her still hoped that by refusing to dwell on what had happened tonight, it might still magically right itself. Nate, lying pale and motionless on the sofa, was testament to the foolishness of that thought.

The kettle on the stove began to boil. She switched off the gas, added tea bags to two mugs and poured water. While the tea brewed, Sebastien lowered himself into an armchair by the fire. Once he had settled, Moses padded over for some attention.

'You already knew something was wrong when you got here, didn't you?' Hannah asked him. 'Even before you saw Nate.'

He nodded. 'I spoke to Charles this evening.'

She felt jolted by the admission, felt her emotions churning. 'You spoke to him? When?'

'Shortly before he talked to you, I suspect.'

'What did he say? Have you heard from him since? Is he all right?'

Sebastien held up a hand and signalled Hannah to lower her voice. 'I spoke to him once, that's all, quite a few hours before you turned up. I haven't talked to him since you managed to get away, and he hasn't tried to call back. I doubt he would. He told me you'd been compromised.'

She nodded. 'Did he tell you how?'

'He said someone from his solicitor's office called him. They were worried they might have let something slip. He didn't give me the details. It was a very quick conversation. Can I ask what happened? How Nate got injured?'

'I don't even know that myself. Dad called us in to see him. Told us we needed to leave right away and not to tell him where we were going. Nate and I split up. He went to pack a few things, I went to get Leah. I was out in the field when I heard the shots.'

'Shots?'

'It sounded like a pistol. I think Nate shot him. When I heard it I didn't know what to do. I called Nate on my phone and he told me to reverse the Discovery up to the side of the house. We pulled up and Nate climbed into the car. I didn't even know how badly he was hurt until we got here.'

Sebastien frowned, and glanced across at her husband. 'Did you see your father before you left?'

'No. No I didn't.'

'Has he tried to contact you since?'

She shook her head, not wanting to voice it aloud and admit to herself what that probably meant.

'I'm sorry, Hannah. It's an evil thing, this. It has to end. I'll do everything I can to help you.'

She fought back tears. Hooking tea bags out of the brews, she stirred in powdered milk and handed Sebastien a mug.

Cupping his hands around it, he watched Leah. She was curled in the opposite armchair. 'Can I make a suggestion?'

'Please.'

'We put your little one to bed upstairs. There's a child's room with a bed already made up. The next few days are going to be tough on her, and she's going to have to adjust fast.'

Hannah looked over at the girl, resisting the urge to gather her into her arms. Before Leah's birth, she had believed the emotions Nate stirred in her the pinnacle of what a human being could feel: love and terror, in equal quantities; love so powerful that it overwhelmed – but never conquered – her fear of exposing him to the shadows stalking her; terror that she could lose someone who made her *feel* like this. Yet when Leah arrived in their lives, she was startled once more by the power and complexity of her feelings: love and terror again, hopelessly intertwined, now on a colossal scale; love that did not compete with what she felt for Nate but reached out and gathered all three of them in its arms; terror multiplied, magnified now by the awful possibilities of losing them both, losing one and seeing that loss in the face of the other, or – this last thought one that whispered only in her darkest moments – having to choose between them, sacrificing one so the other might live.

From that first day, she had promised herself she would not allow the events that destroyed her own childhood to spill over into her daughter's. But already history seemed to be repeating, with Hannah a helpless witness. That it had to end was an easy thing for Sebastien to say. She had always told herself that when the time came, she would fight rather than flee. But flee was what she had been forced to do.

It was, she vowed, a temporary flight. She could still fight. She still had Leah, and Nate still clung to life. If he lost that battle – she felt her throat constrict at the very possibility – then while a fundamental part of her life would be over, the responsibility to keep Leah safe would fall even more heavily upon her. And while she wasn't ready to contemplate a world without Nate, she would readily trade her life to secure her daughter's future.

Yet what if the worst did happen? What if Nate lost his battle and Hannah traded her life for her daughter's? Leah would be left utterly alone. After tonight's appalling events, Hannah had to presume that her father was dead. That left no one. No one on Nate's side. All her own family gone. For Leah's sake, one of them *had* to survive this. Which led her back to the same dilemma. Fight or flee. She was starting to understand just what impossible choices those who had gone before her had been forced to make.

Hannah made herself list the positives. The farmhouse could still function as her father had intended: a safe-house, a reprieve from the hunt. She had won them some time now – time to make plans, time for Nate to recuperate, time for her to explain things to Leah as best she could.

She looked at Sebastien sitting in the armchair before her. She knew his eyes measured her, assessing the levels of her strength, her resolve. What part did he play in this? After his initial abruptness, the gentleness of his words had betrayed the warmth in him. She felt she had an ally here. But she also suspected there were things he had not told her. Knowledge had always been the most important weapon in all of this. It was still the one thing she lacked the most.

She needed to earn Sebastien's trust. And quickly. Everything he could tell her – about Jakab, and about her father – had the potential to be useful, had the potential to swing the needle of probability in their favour.

Fight or flee.

'You're right, she needs to sleep in a proper bed.' Hannah finished her tea and placed the mug on the counter. 'But I don't want her waking up alone. Not after all this. Can you show me around upstairs? There must be a master bedroom.'

'Front of the house.'

'Then she can sleep in there with me.'

Sebastien nodded, wincing as he pulled himself out of the armchair. He clanked his mug down on the counter next to hers.

Hannah went to the sofa and knelt at Nate's side. He was still asleep, his pallor as awful and as frightening as when she had first turned on the Discovery's overhead light. He breathed in shallow spasms. She wanted to check under the pads to see if the bleeding had stopped, but Sebastien had warned her not to disturb the bindings. She kissed the top of his head and smoothed his hair.

The Maglite was by the fireplace where she had left it. Hannah picked it up. Even though Sebastien had managed to start the generator and they had electricity to power the lights, she found the solid heft of its aluminium casing reassuring. 'Let's go and check out upstairs,' she said.

Sebastien turned to the dog and gestured in Nate's direction. 'Stay here. Keep watch.' Moses pricked up an ear. His tongue lolled out of his mouth and he panted agreement.

In the hallway, Sebastien flipped the light switch. A frosted bulb lit up a chandelier hung with dust-coated crystal. The light cast an eerie patina of shapes on to wallpaper lifting at its seams and brown with age. A door opposite the kitchen led to a dark living room. She could see the outlines of old furniture. Chill air leached from the doorway. Further down the hall a second door, this one closed, concealed what she presumed was a dining room.

She followed Sebastien to the front door. He turned and led her up the stairs, wooden treads creaking beneath his feet. The passageway grew murkier as they ascended, the light from the downstairs hall unable to banish the shadows from the upper level of the house.

They came to a landing and a tall chest of drawers. A display case stood upon it, the front smeared with grime. Inside, the glass eyes of a stuffed peregrine falcon watched her. The specimen was pitiful with age, its feathers brittle, some of them missing. A stain of brown had spread across the front of its chest. She vowed to get rid of it first thing in the morning.

Off to their right, the stairs rose again. Sebastien went first and they arrived at a long passageway. He flicked on a light switch. The ceiling bulb, enclosed in a fabric shade, remained dark. He toggled the switch back and forth and shrugged. 'Must have blown. Come on, this way.'

At the end of the hallway he opened a door and turned on another light. She stepped into a large bathroom. In one corner stood a cold and uninviting roll-top, a verdigris stain around the plughole. A rusted metal shower hose snaked up from the mixer unit, its head hanging limp from a bracket, as if its neck had been broken. The shower curtain was spotted with black mould. On the basin next to the toilet, a plastic tub contained a dried brown sliver of soap.

'Probably could do with a once-over,' Sebastien muttered.

'You don't say.'

'We can spruce it up a bit tomorrow. Come on, I'll show you the master bedroom.'

'I can't wait.'

He indicated a door and she poked her head inside. The room was huge, two tall sash windows overlooking the driveway below. The wind was fiercer up here, howling as it battered itself against the walls. Sebastien reached for the bedroom light switch but she knocked his hand away. 'Don't. We're more exposed on this side of the house. Let me close those curtains first.'

'As you wish.'

'I know it's unlikely, but I'd feel better if I knew no one could see inside.'

'Can't blame you for that.'

Hannah went to the heavy drapes and pulled them across the windows, flinching at the feel of the mildewed cloth. The house needed a good blast of heat to chase out the damp.

Once she had shut away the sounds of the storm, Sebastien turned on the light. An ancient four-poster bed rested against the wall opposite the windows. A crimson bedspread covered it. Two mahogany wardrobes, with carved crests and ornate corbels, stood against the far wall. A dressing table and chair, in the same Renaissance style, completed the room's furniture.

Between the two wardrobes, a stone fireplace surrounded a grate with logs, kindling and a box of matches. A further supply of wood had been stacked in a basket on the hearth. 'Did you do that?' she asked.

He nodded. 'I'll get it started for you.'

'No, I can manage.' She moved to the grate, struck a match and quickly had a fire going. 'You can turn the light off now.' Sebastien obliged. Lit only by the glow of the flames dancing around the logs, the room felt a fraction more welcoming.

Hannah sat on the corner of the bed. 'How did you meet my father?'

Fetching the chair from the dressing table, Sebastien lowered himself down on to it. He rubbed the small tattoo on his wrist. 'Charles tracked down a Council contact in Geneva. The Council selected me to go and meet him. We thought your father might be one of *them* at first. I was sent to discover the truth.'

'The Eleni Council?'

'The same.'

'You're Eleni?'

'Was. No longer.'

'What happened?'

He opened his hands. Studied the veins criss-crossing the backs of them. 'I got old. Needed to find some peace. And I didn't like the way things were going. The direction the Council was taking, I mean. There was a new generation and the whole thing was getting a lot more militant. Losing its way, I thought. Then again, I can't deny that I've grown a lot less tolerant than I once was. So maybe it was just me that changed.'

'What brought you here?'

Sebastien lifted his head and met her gaze. Emerald fireworks glittered in his eyes, and she thought she detected great sadness in them, a loneliness so stark that it frightened her. 'What I told you was true. I live here now. When your father was scoping out locations for his hideaways years ago, I came here with him. This was his first, you know. It just seemed a beautiful area, what with the mountains, the solitude. When he bought Llyn Gwyr, I found another place up for sale a few miles west. I've been here ever since.'

'Alone?'

'There's Moses.'

'A dog.'

'Better company than some humans I've known.'

'Which breed is he?'

'Vizsla. An old Hungarian hunting breed.'

'Hungarian?' she asked, eyebrows arching.

Sebastien smiled. 'They're not just great at tracking game, either.' He shrugged. 'Perhaps that's what they were bred for, back in those days. Nobody knows for sure. You'll find most Eleni keep them.'

'Tell me about the tattoo.'

His fingers moved back to the blue symbol on his wrist and he smoothed away the wrinkles. 'The Imperial Eagle. It used to be the heraldic animal of the Austro-Hungarian Empire. And yet these days they're all but extinct. All Council members have the bird's head marked on them. Higher ranks receive more of it.'

'You have the whole silhouette.'

'Yes. I was *signeur* when I left.'

She frowned. 'You're kidding.'

'You know what that means?'

'I know about the Eleni from what my mother told me, and from the snippets my father shared when he was in the mood. And I know that the *signeur* is one of the three chairs. And traditionally the holding seat for the *Presidente*.'

He nodded. 'Whereas you look at me and see an old hermit with bad manners and creaking joints.'

'No, I—' She paused, then shrugged. 'Fair enough. Yes, I do.'

He cackled. 'We'll get along fine, you and me.'

'We'd better. I'm pretty short on friends right now.'

Sebastien put a hand on her shoulder and squeezed. Hannah found herself absurdly grateful for his touch. 'I'm not the only one,' he told her. 'But you can rely on me to do what I can to protect you.'

'He's not really after me. He's after one of those two downstairs.'

'I know. And . . .' He hesitated. Appeared to consider something. 'We'll work together to stop that happening.'

She nodded, warmed by his reassurances and quiet humanity. 'You're a good man, Sebastien.'

He withdrew his hand and stood up, crossing the room to the door. Stepping out on to the landing, he peered over the rail to the stairs below. Satisfied, he walked back into the room and closed the door behind him. He returned to the bed and sat down opposite her, his voice barely a whisper. 'Tell me again exactly what happened when you left Charles tonight.'

The seriousness of his expression, and the care he had taken to ensure their privacy, sent fear crawling like a rash across her skin. She felt her heart accelerate in her chest. 'I already did.'

'Just do it.'

After the gentleness he had displayed moments earlier, his sudden bluntness jarred.

'Dad called me into his study. He was distressed, really paranoid. He said Jakab was already at the house. That he'd supplanted one of the staff. He told me and Nate to take Leah and leave.'

'Keep your voice down. Then what happened?'

'Leah was playing outside. Nate went to pack a bag and I grabbed her from the garden. I heard shots. I dialled Nate on the phone.'

'Why?'

'Because I was right around the other side of the house. It's a big estate. Stables, the works. I didn't want to bring Leah out to the front unless I knew what was happening.'

'And Nate answered.'

'He told me to get Leah into the car, to reverse it up to the side of the house. I've never been so scared. I didn't know what was happening. I even considered driving away with Leah there and then. Hated myself for that. But I reversed up and Nate limped out.'

'Did he say what happened?'

'Just that there had been a fight, and that he'd been stabbed. I think he was trying to protect me, trying to stop me from panicking too much.'

'And you think Nate shot Jakab.'

'Yes.'

'Did you see anyone else?'

'No.'

'No one else at all?'

'No. I—'

'Hannah, listen to me very carefully.' Sebastien took both her hands into his. 'Have you validated Nate since he got into the car with you?'

'No, I—'

She stopped. Suddenly knew why he had gone to the landing. Why he had closed the door. Why he was whispering.

Horror embraced her, thrusting its talons deep. 'Oh my God, no,' she said.

CHAPTER 6

Gödöllö, Hungary

1873

Lukács was sitting in the toolshed playing with the mole rat when he heard his father calling his name.

He knew why József wanted him. He also knew, without any doubt, that he had no chance of escape. Tomorrow's journey loomed with a dark inevitability; Lukács could no more halt the events lined up before him than he could halt the clocks in his father's workshop with a hopeful breath.

It did not make the thought any easier.

His first *végzet* night. One of four over the coming months that would symbolise his entry into adulthood. A night of celebration, of discovery, of girls flush-faced with the excitement of reaching womanhood.

If, he reflected, he had been born whole like his brothers, instead of bringing them disgrace. Lukács suspected his own passage through *végzet* would be greeted with little enthusiasm by his peers.

On the sawdust floor of the toolshed, the mole rat lurched from left to right, dragging its shattered hind legs behind it. It had no eyes to speak of, testing the air with a wrinkled pink nose, the folds of which, his older brother assured him, resembled a woman's vulva. He watched it quiver and twitch as the creature searched for an escape route. The comparison disgusted him. Typical of Jani.

Sensing open space behind it, the mole rat turned and used its front paws to pull the rest of its body through the dust.

Lukács blocked its progress with a stick.

'Here he is!'

Two figures had appeared in the doorway, one tall and broad, the other a child. Summer sun silhouetted them but he knew their shape, recognised the voice that had spoken. The taller one ducked inside the shed, walked over and stared down at Lukács, hands on hips. 'Well, well. What's the saying? A bad penny always turns up.'

'Go away, Jani.'

'Can't you hear father calling you?' Jani looked round to little Izsák, who was still peering around the door jamb. 'So he's deaf now as well. Our brother is truly blessed.'

'I'm not deaf.'

Jani hunched down and stared into Lukács's face. 'Then why do you linger here like a disobedient pup?'

'He'll find me soon enough.'

'Yes, he will. When he does, he's going to be angry with you for ignoring him. Perhaps you'll get a whipping. Although probably not today. He needs his runt as pliable as possible if he's any chance of getting rid of him at the *végzet*. Pity there isn't a runt's *végzet*, eh, pup?'

Lukács said nothing in reply. To answer Jani too readily would incite violence. Not that he particularly cared.

His brother looked down at the struggling mole rat. They both watched as it raised its vulva-like snout and sniffed the air. As if finding something distasteful in Jani's presence, the rodent turned away.

'Appropriate pet for you,' Jani sneered. 'Listen to me, runt. Tomorrow night, at your *végzet*, if any one of them asks, you don't tell them about your brothers. You don't *have* any brothers. Understand?'

Lukács scowled.

'You know no one called Balázs Jani. I'm not having my name associated with a cripple.'

'He's not a cripple, Jani.' Izsák stepped into the toolshed. The boy only reached Jani's chest in height; he kept a careful distance.

'You shut up, 'Sák,' Jani spat. He turned back to Lukács. 'You don't mention any brothers. You especially don't talk to any girls from the Zsinka family. If you're as deaf as you seem, you won't have a problem acting mute, will you? Understand?'

He shrugged.

Jani snatched a handful of his hair and yanked his head back. 'I said do you understand?'

'Leave him alone!' Izsák took another step towards them.

Lukács refused to struggle in his brother's grip. 'Fine, Jani. No mention of brothers. And I won't talk to any Zsinka whores, I promise.'

He heard Izsák snigger. Before he even saw it coming, he felt Jani's fist slam into his cheek. The blow knocked him sprawling. Pain bloomed in his face but he controlled it, pressing his lips together and raising his head, daring Jani to strike him again.

'Remember what I said, runt.' His brother cracked his knuckles and turned for the door. 'I'm fetching Father.'

Once Jani had gone, Izsák scampered over. 'Does it hurt very much?' he asked.

Lukács laughed. The pain of his lacerated cheek was nothing compared to the sting of his older brother's words. The truth of them drew blood from wounds that had festered in him as long as he could remember, a litany of individual scars: an older brother so ashamed of him that he would deny his existence; a father who cared only for the old traditions and who paid scarce attention to him now that their mother had gone; a younger brother too immature to understand the deeper currents that ran within their family, and whose scorn would arrive as surely as the next harvest the instant he was old enough to understand.

'I'm fine, Izsák.'

'He's in love with the older Zsinka girl. But she's not as keen. That's why he's so cross.'

'She sounds like a wise girl.'

Izsák sniggered. 'I hear she's a dirty *kurvá*.'

'Hey! Where did you hear words like that?'

'It's what I heard father calling her. He says all the Zsinkas are sluts.'

Lukács grinned at that, until a new silhouette appeared in the doorway. He flinched when he heard his father's cough, deep and low.

'Izsák, leave us. I want to talk to your brother.'

'Yes, Papa.' Flashing Lukács a sympathetic glance, the boy skipped outside.

His father stood in the doorway for a time before he stepped over the threshold. Pulling a wooden stool from underneath a workbench, he dusted it down and sat his frame upon it. He smelled of old tobacco and mint oil.

Rifling through the pocket of his leather waistcoat, Balázs József pulled out a clay pipe and pushed it into his mouth. The spark of a match illuminated an oiled mustache and thoughtful, heavyset eyes. 'Dark in here.'

'Yes.'

'Is that why you like it?'

'Don't know. Maybe.'

Velvet threads of smoke drifted across the shed, carrying scents of dried apple and scorched paper. 'Heard what your brother said.'

'It's what you all think. At least he's honest.'

'He'll get my belt later.'

In between them, the mole rat hesitated in its explorations, its nose trembling as it tested the air, hunting for options.

Lukács glanced up from the rodent and into his father's face. József's features had not lost any of their strength as he had aged. His face rarely betrayed emotion, yet now Lukács detected a softening. Was that pity? He wanted none of that. Certainly not from his father. It was partly his seed, after all, that was responsible for Lukács's condition.

József leaned forward. 'Your cheek is cut. We cannot have that. You need to stop the bleeding.'

'It hurts to make it stop.'

'Do as I say. I will not have you looking like that tomorrow.'

Reluctantly, Lukács focused on the throbbing in his face. As he had been instructed many times before, he tried to empty his mind of the distractions of his environment, tried to ignore the pressure of his father's gaze. Instead, he concentrated on the sensation of the swelling, the bright lance of pain where Jani's knuckles had split his skin. Gritting his teeth, he forced the muscles of his cheek to press together, bracing himself as the swelling dissipated through the right side of his face.

'Relax, boy. You're too tense.'

He realised he was holding his breath. Tears brimmed in his eyes as the line of the cut flared with white-hot heat and then, as with the swelling, began to subside.

'Now wipe off the blood.'

Lukács complied, looking at the smudge of crimson on the back of his hand.

József inhaled smoke, sighed. 'None of this comes naturally to you, does it?'

He shook his head.

'I swear, Lukács, if I knew how to help you in this . . .' His father reached out a hand and tilted his son's face up to meet his own. 'Show me your eyes. Look into mine.'

Unwillingly, Lukács obeyed. His father's eyes seemed, at first, as they always did: a flat and unremarkable grey. But as he watched, Lukács began to notice changes. Striations of green appeared, flecks of indigo. The streaks of colour began to evolve and diversify, like diamonds rising and sinking in a twilight lake, a prismatic display of pigments that mesmerised Lukács with their range and beauty. Engulfed, he felt the confines of the shed fade as his father's eyes became his universe. He swam in an effervescent sea glittering with pinpricks of turquoise and jade, copper and gold, on a rising wave where sequins and rubies and emeralds tumbled and danced in the surf.

At the centre of all this, József's pupils gaped like forsaken voids into which Lukács would flounder if he did not pull himself away: yawning maws, reaching for him with serrated grins the colour of charcoal. Beauty and horror; at first seductive and then threatening. Did he fear what lurked inside the darkness of his father's eyes? Or did he fear the *absence* of what resided there?

Lukács blinked, breaking the spell. He knew his own eyes were dull, lifeless – the colour of river mud in comparison. And for a fleeting moment he was glad.

Suddenly he found his voice. 'Maybe another year, maybe if we waited. We could go to the *végzet* next summer. Maybe I will have learned by then.' He saw his father begin to shake his head, but he pressed on. 'Or maybe we could just forget about the *végzet* altogether. I could stay here with you, helping you in the workshop. You know I've become more accurate with the instruments. I've done all the bevelling over the last month and—'

'*Enough*, Lukács! I have heard *enough*! You will *not* disgrace me. Nor your mother's memory.' His father breathed deep, swallowed his anger. 'You will go to the *végzet*. You will do your best. We will see what happens. There are qualities in you that any sensible girl should find attractive. I will not allow you – a Balázs – to carry the shame of a *kirekesztett*. Now, I want you inside the house within the hour. We have preparations to make. At noon tomorrow we leave.'

Standing, his father exhaled a plume of pipe smoke. At the doorway, he paused. 'You know, Lukács, your brother Jani might seem cruel, but we all have an interest in your success. Think on that. You may not believe it, but the life of a *kirekesztett* is a curse, one that would weigh on you many score years from now. Trust me, son; it is not a path you wish to walk.'

With his father's departure, the silence returned. Lukács watched the mole rat squirm and twist about in the dirt as it tried to manoeuvre its broken body.

We all have an interest in your success.

That was really all they cared about. József professed a concern for his son's life as an outsider, but it was empty sentiment. None of them cared a damn for *his* feelings – his fear, his absolute certainty – that tomorrow night would bring the first humiliations of many before the reality of that life presented itself anyway.

He saw no reason why he could not stay here, living a simple life in his father's mansion, learning the skills of a horologist and moving about in the world free of the social burdens imposed on the *hosszú életek*. His father's pride alone condemned him to this path.

Reaching for the mole rat, Lukács picked it up in his fist and studied it. The rodent struggled between his fingers, and he could feel its tiny bones moving under the thin grey fur of its coat. It was a repulsive creature, virtually blind from the skin that grew over its eyes to protect it as it burrowed through the earth. In many ways it reminded him of himself. He knew what it was like to have a sense partially formed.

His frustration blistered into anger. He tightened his grip around the animal. The mole rat thrashed, mewling a thin sound of distress. Lukács increased the pressure, watching it intently until a glutinous scarlet thread spurted from its mouth on to his fingers. Disgusted, furious, he squeezed harder, feeling the rodent's bones cracking and collapsing under his hand. He flung its body across the shed where it hit the wooden boards with a wet slap.

Wiping his fingers clean of the mole rat's fluids, Lukács realised just how long he had been sitting here. The sun had crept across the sky and now a single beam of light shone through the gap in the doorway. He held up his hand and looked at the shadow his fingers cast on the wall.

He rearranged them and the shadow became a mole rat, one twitching knuckle a perfect reproduction of the creature's nose. Lukács made the shadow rat cavort and play for a moment, before he switched the arrangement of his fingers and the shadow rat morphed into the profile of a wolf. The wolf yawned and dissolved into a horse that bucked its head twice, and transformed into the silhouette of an eagle. The bird moved its head from side to side.

Lukács watched the eagle for a while, then shook out his fingers and made a deer, the top of its head smooth and antler-free. Taking a breath, he braced himself for the pain he knew would follow, and focused on the shadow animal. The deer twitched. Gradually, twin bumps appeared on its head. Lukács felt his teeth grind together as he concentrated. The knuckles of his hand felt like they were trapped in a vice. With an effort that made him cry out, the bumps on the deer's head suddenly elongated and branched. Before his eyes, antlers grew up and out, developing individual tines. The pain was now unbearable, glass daggers slicing him from the tips of his fingers to his elbow.

On the wall, as if checking for potential predators, the deer raised its head and looked from left to right. Lukács gasped with exhaustion and the animal's image collapsed. As he regained his breath, he contemplated the silhouette of his limp fingers, fingers that burned now as if touched by fire.

Tears streaked his face. He wiped them away with his free hand and studied the one that pained him. Blood welled from under the nails of each finger and dripped onto the toolshed floor, where it mingled with that of the mole rat in the dust.

They left for Budapest at noon the next day. Lukács climbed on to the cart next to his father as the two horses flicked out their manes, impatient to be on the move.

His brothers had gathered in the courtyard to watch them

leave for the city. Jani's face betrayed his scorn, but he raised an arm and waved Lukács off, as if sensing his father's displeasure and calculating the cost of defiance too high. Little Izsák, his face filled with excitement at the prospect of a night alone, skipped and bobbed on the gravel. József whistled to the horses. The cart lurched forwards and Lukács felt his stomach lurch in tandem as they drove out through the gates.

The horses led them through the town and soon they were passing the white walls and red tile roof of the huge Gödöllö palace. The building's magnificence captivated Lukács every time he saw it. The knowledge that the Royal Palace in Budapest dwarfed it both awed and perturbed him.

'Will I see Franz Joseph at the palace?' he asked, after they had been riding for an hour. Once they had left the outskirts of Gödöllö the road had narrowed, and they journeyed now past fields and forest.

'There's no chance of that,' his father replied. 'For a start, the king is in Austria. That's the only reason we've been granted permission to hold the *végzet* at the palace this year.'

'He doesn't know what goes on in his own palace?'

'Of course he does. But there are appearances to maintain. The Crown doesn't officially recognise us as subjects.'

They ate lunch on the road: cured sausage spiced with paprika, a hard cheese and hunks of bread. His father washed it down with mouthfuls of red Villány wine, then handed the bottle to his son. It was the first time Lukács had tasted wine. He enjoyed the feeling of warmth that spread through his belly.

'Will all the great families be arriving at the palace on a horse and cart?'

'Don't be insolent, boy. You won't be arriving on this. I've hired a carriage for tonight. It meets us at Szilárd's house. The manner of your arrival is the least of our worries.'

They reached the Pest district by late afternoon. The city was hot and dusty, and the sounds of the crowded streets filled Lukács's ears. When they finally arrived at the waterfront, he gazed out at the vast expanse of the Danube for the first time in his life. Jani had told him to expect a sight, but this was the largest body of water he had ever seen. Its sheer size confused him at first, and he found it difficult to believe what his eyes were showing him. How could such a wonder of nature exist?

The river, his father explained, originated in the Black Forest of Germany, winding its way through Europe for nearly two thousand miles before emptying into the Black Sea. The afternoon sun, low in the sky, winked on its brown waters.

József halted the cart outside a three-storey townhouse with tall leaded windows. A boy came out to lead away their cart and horses while another servant conveyed them inside. After brief introductions with Szilárd, Lukács was shepherded into a dressing room where clothing had been laid out for him.

The polished shoes he recognised; the rest of the outfit he had never seen before. While it resembled the formal evening wear worn by the nobility in and around Gödöllö, the cloth and the tailoring before him was of an even finer standard.

Wearily, he peeled off his travel clothes. He washed himself using water from a jug a servant had left him, then pulled on dark trousers and a stiff white shirt. The winged tips scratched at his neck. He tied a white silk bow tie at his throat, shrugged into the waistcoat and finally the wide-lapelled frock coat. Its fabric was heavy, smooth, luxurious.

On a separate side table, the last item waiting for him was a polished pewter mask. He picked it up and turned it over in his hands. The artistry was stunning. He remembered the lengthy sitting he had endured six months earlier; the pewter face bore an unsettling resemblance to his own, although the artist had clearly used licence in its construction. The mask's expression conveyed strength, confidence, compassion – qualities he sus-pected his father had requested, rather than anything the visiting journeyman had witnessed for himself.

At nine o'clock that evening, obediently following József, Lukács climbed into an enclosed black carriage. The sun was setting as their driver turned on to the Széchenyi chain bridge that linked Pest in the east to Buda on the west bank. The bridge sat upon two enormous stone river piers, the roadbed suspended by chains of iron, each link several yards long. It was the only bridge in Hungary to have mastered the Danube.

'See the stone lions?' his father asked, pointing at the guardians on each abutment. 'I knew the sculptor, Marschalkó. A fine man. They say the famous bronze lions of Trafalgar Square are based on them. Such mastery.'

As they crossed the bridge, Lukács studied the vast edifice of Buda Palace on the opposite bank. The building overwhelmed the hill on which it stood, its tall walls of stone, washed golden in the setting sun, rising up proud of the surrounding trees. Verdigris roofs, turrets and domes blazed with colour.

'The finest building in Europe,' József told him. 'Graced tonight with the finest of its residents. You're privileged indeed, my son. I've never visited the ballroom. They say its opulence is not to be matched.'

Their carriage clattered up the hill, rolling to a stop in front of the palace entrance. József laid a hand on Lukács's shoulder and reached into a pocket. 'Before you go,' he said, 'I have something for you. Tonight you become a man. It's fitting that as my son, you wear my finest work.' From his pocket he withdrew a gold watch on a heavy chain. 'This is yours. I've kept it from you until tonight. I've been working on it this last year. You won't find a more accurate, finely balanced piece, even if I say so myself. Here, take it.'

Stunned, Lukács took the watch from his father, immediately feeling its weight. He opened the hunter case and gazed at its face, marvelling at the craftsmanship, and the work that must have gone into it. Turning it over, he saw an inscription on the back plate.

Balázs Lukács
Végzet 1873

'I don't know what to say, Father.'

'Then say nothing. Go. Don't lose it. Put on your mask before you open the carriage door. And take this purse. You shan't need it but you should have money. Make me proud, son. I wish you well. Whatever happens tonight . . .' His father paused. Then he nodded towards the door. 'Go on. It's time.'

Lukács followed two footmen through the palace grounds as the sun dipped below the hill. Candlelight shone out of a plethora of palace windows. Once through the grand entrance, he ascended wide stairs and followed an endless corridor hung with life-sized paintings of Hungarian royalty. The identities of most of the monarchs were lost on him, but he noted several images of Franz Joseph.

Two huge gilt doors stood at the end of the corridor. Music and conversation drifted from beyond. As the footmen moved to the doors and opened them for him, Lukács lifted a hand to the pewter mask on his face. The metal was cold beneath his touch. Taking a breath, he stepped into the palace ballroom, utterly unprepared for the splendour that greeted him.

Hanging from brackets at least sixty feet above the floor, three enormous chandeliers dominated the room, each fes-tooned with scores of burning candles. So intricate and delicate was the white-golden stucco that adorned the ceiling that Lukács found it difficult to believe anyone capable of producing such beauty. Along the east wing of the room, several arched recesses housed windows that stretched forty feet in height, with views down to the mighty Danube and to Pest on the far bank. Frescos adorned the long wall opposite the windows, and all along its length stood gilt chairs upholstered in red velvet.

A string ensemble played on a stage at the far end of the ballroom. Across the main floor, young men – perhaps a hundred of them – stood together in groups. All of them wore the same formal attire as Lukács, and all of their faces were hidden behind individually crafted pewter masks. They conversed loudly, holding thin-stemmed champagne flutes and long cigars.

While the young *hosszú élet* men were an impressive sight, the ladies stole the main focus of Lukács's attention. Like so many tropical birds, their finery bewitched him. Their dresses were a kaleidoscope of colours and fabrics. Bustles were *de rigueur,* as were plunging necklines and short off-the-shoulder sleeves that would have scandalised his father. There was uniformity too in the style of their hair: scooped up from each side of the face, into either a high knot or a cluster of ringlets. Instead of masks, they wore lace veils that covered their faces just below the eyes. Mirroring their male counterparts, they chattered in small clusters. Lukács saw several in the nearest group break off from their conversation to examine him, and he felt a pleasurable prickling of his skin as their eyes flashed over him.

Intercepting a waiter bearing a tray of champagne flutes, he helped himself to a glass, selected the nearest group of young men and walked into their midst. Immediately they widened the circle to accommodate him. One by one they came forward to shake his hand. He received no named introductions, but he had been advised to expect that.

As each young man spoke to him, he watched the eyes behind their mask. He was used to seeing the striations of green and indigo in his father's eyes, but now he saw a multitude of variations: flecks of silver, swirls of purple, vivid tiger stripes of orange. Grimly, he noted their looks of confusion as they studied him. Did they wonder if an impostor lurked in their midst? Or simply a weakling? The constraints of protocol prevented anyone from challenging him, but he saw several of them exchange questioning glances.

As the champagne flowed, the conversation flowed with it, moving from the exploits of the king to the latest on the unification of Buda and Pest into a single metropolis. Lukács found it difficult to contribute at first, but as glasses were refilled and everyone began to relax, the talk turned to the night's proceedings and, more pointedly, to the other half of the room's occupants. Lukács noticed that some of his group had already started to drift away to initiate conversations, and it was not long before he found himself standing alone in the arch of one of the huge windows. Turning his back on the reception, he gazed down at the Danube below. Darkness had fallen. The great river was a wide strip of black, flickering with the reflected lights of Pest. Beyond the city, somewhere out there, lay Gödöllö, his home, his bed. He wondered what Jani and Izsák were doing. He wondered if they thought of him.

'Beautiful, isn't it?'

Startled, Lukács spun around. Close to his elbow, a girl almost his height studied him with a critical eye. He noticed a smirk on her lips beneath the translucent lace of her veil. Instinctively, he backed into the recess, away from the lights of the chandeliers.

'Ah, a shy one.' The smirk widened. 'Don't worry. I shan't bite. I saw you come in. I thought you might have introduced yourself by now but you've been standing there with that dull group of boys all evening. And now you're all alone. You haven't even talked to any of us.'

'I hadn't realised I was being observed.' He winced; it had been a clumsy thing to say. Quickly, he added, 'You're right, of course. It is a magnificent view.'

She glanced out of the window and Lukács used the opportunity to examine her. He could not say that she was pretty – or even charming – but there was something in her brash confidence, in her obvious ripeness, that interested him.

'Is this your first time at the palace?' she asked.

'Yes. And you?'

'Gods, no. My father's an ambassador.' She laughed. 'Am I allowed to say that? Perhaps not. Indeed, certainly not. But now I have and there is little to be done. All this secrecy, it's just a bit of theatre, wouldn't you say? I mean we're all *hosszú életek*.

'I've accompanied my father here many times. Official engagements. Impossibly stuffy, to tell you the truth. Nothing at all like this.' With a gloved hand she touched his arm. 'Come over into the light. I can hardly see you, standing in the shadows like that.'

He felt his heart lurch. This was it. A first approach. The moment for which his father had coached him, and his older brother had taunted him, for so long. He knew the etiquette, knew he was being flattered, knew that outside of the *végzet* this girl doubtless moved in far higher social circles. Yet that was the point of the *végzet*, was it not? A levelling ground that allowed all *hosszú életek* to mingle. A tradition, as she had indicated, and one that stretched back hundreds of years. He did not find her attractive but that was not the point. Tonight was for first introductions. It would only be at the next gathering that the more intricate sexual fencing would begin.

'Would you not wish to admire the view a while longer?' he asked.

'Oh, nonsense with the view. The Danube will be there in the morning. It'll be there a thousand years from now.' She lifted a pointed chin and challenged him. 'Come out with me.'

Inclining his head, heart accelerating, he followed her out of the alcove and into the light. As they passed along the wall, the girl paused underneath a gilt wall ornament that held a branch of candles. She turned to him, reached a finger up to his face and tilted his head towards her.

Breathless, Lukács looked into her eyes. Around the black of her pupils, her irises were a startling cornflower blue. As he watched, he noticed other colours begin to emerge. Whorls of magenta, shooting lines of gold. He felt blood begin to fizz through his arteries. His chest swelled with anticipation.

But even as he drank her in, the display faded. Still transfixed by what he had seen, Lukács did not notice the disdain on her face until she asked, 'What's wrong with you? Your eyes. They're . . . *lifeless*.'

He felt his face reddening. 'It's a . . . a birth defect. The rest of me—'

'You're not even *hosszú élet*!'

'Yes, I am. Of course I am. It's just that my eyes . . . my eyes never took. No one knows why. But the rest . . .' He floundered.

'I heard a rumour we had a freak in our midst,' she hissed. 'I never imagined I'd be tasteless enough to pick him.' The girl turned away, searching for friendly faces in the crowd.

Lukács's temper flared. He grabbed her by the arm and twisted her to face him. 'How tasteless of *me* to attract the only filthy *kurvá* in the palace.'

The girl curled back her lip, revealing a row of white teeth. 'Manners to match your deformity, I see. Let go of my arm.'

Wanting to punish her, he tightened his grip. Beneath his fingers he felt the muscles of her arm contract and harden, fighting his pressure.

Lukács gritted his teeth and squeezed, wanting to hurt her now, willing his fingers to force themselves into her flesh. He snarled when he saw pain register on her face. 'Filthy *kurvák* should keep their opinions to themselves,' he whispered, guiding her back towards the recess.

An ugly blotch of red had appeared at her throat. She took an unwilling step with him into the arch. 'I'll scream.'

'Make it a good one.' He knew she would not cry out, knew she would do almost anything to avoid drawing attention to their sordid little confrontation, even if that meant clenching her teeth and tolerating the pain he was inflicting. He increased the pressure on her arm. She gasped, sucking the lace veil taut against her lips, and then a hand appeared on Lukács's shoulder.

Sharp fingers sank into him. The pain was immediate and brutal.

'Enough of this. Let go of her this *instant*.'

Lukács twisted around. Three men, ancient and lean, had gathered behind him. Each wore a styled grey wig and navy frock coat. None of them wore masks.

The oldest of the three clutched his shoulder. Lines of age mapped the man's face, a network of creases spreading out from his mouth as his lips pressed together. The skin of his throat sagged like a ruined net, but his eyes were clear, strong, furious. His fingers clenched and Lukács suppressed a curse.

The elder's voice was a dangerous whisper. 'Remove your *hand* from the lady's arm.'

Holding on to her a moment longer, a futile gesture of defiance, Lukács relinquished his grip and the girl shrank away from him. Her eyes had lost their scornful expression. She watched him now with fear. Free, she took a few uncertain steps backwards and lost herself in the crowd.

'I can imagine the gist of your encounter,' the elder continued, removing his hand from Lukács's shoulder.' That's no excuse for your behaviour. There is *never* any excuse for that kind of behaviour. You bring shame on your family with your actions. I know who you are. I know that you face some challenges. Your father is a good man, an excellent man. He is the only reason I do not ask these gentlemen to march you down to the river and hurl you in. We'll overlook this. *Once.* Do you understand me?'

Lukács's temper still burned. He glared, but when the old man glared back, Lukács glimpsed something in those eyes that terrified him. His palms grew slick, and he felt his heart gallop in his chest. He adopted a look of contrition. 'Yes. Completely.'

'I suggest you take some air. It is not too late to redeem yourself tonight. Thankfully there was little audience to witness your performance. We shall talk to the girl. Now go. Outside. The fresh air will bring you back to your senses.'

'Thank you, sir. I will.'

Striding across the floor of the ballroom, Lukács wanted to tear the mask from his face and mop away the sweat. He fought the impulse. Between the gilt doors he walked, along the corridor of kings, down the grand staircase and out into the night air beyond.

The girl's reaction had hurt, but he had expected it. Jani, with his sarcasm, had at least prepared him. What puzzled him, what *interested* him, was the arousal he had felt as he dug his fingers into her flesh.

How many hours had passed? How much had he drunk? Lukács squinted at the tankard on the scarred wooden table before him. The watch his father had given him nestled inside his waistcoat pocket, but even as inebriated as he was, he knew better than to take out a valuable object like that in a place such as this. The tavern was filled with punters: their noise and their stink and their smoke.

Across the table sat his two drinking partners. Márkus, that was the first one's name. Brash, opinionated, the young man's debauched humour had been making Lukács laugh for over an hour. Márkus's lady friend Krisztina perched next to him. She was pretty, he thought. In fact, a better word was *sexual*. She had an easy, suggestive manner, the cut of her dress accentuating the slimness of her hips and the fullness of her breasts. Her rich blond hair was tucked under a white cap.

After leaving the palace for his prescribed fresh air he had, on a whim, continued down to the river. He discovered Márkus and Krisztina larking about on the bank. They had both been drinking and, after running out of money at the tavern, had decided to take a stroll. Lukács was drunk for the first time in his life and wanted to carry on drinking. He also had a purse of money. Márkus and Krisztina needed little encouragement to help him spend it. While they initially showed surprise that someone so obviously high-born would choose to share their company, their determination to get drunk outweighed any reservations.

Lukács did not have to manoeuvre through any political debate with these two. The conversation was degenerate but amusing, naive but fun. He knew they made a bizarre three-some. Yet that was the spirit of *végzet* night, he told himself drily: social interaction free of the constraints of class. His new friends might scratch around in the dirt by day, but Lukács was having the best evening he could remember.

Márkus swigged from his ale and gesticulated. 'You never told us. What was that thing going on up at the palace? That's where you came from, isn't it? You had one of them masks, just like all them others we saw.'

'A masked ball,' Krisztina said, her eyes flashing. 'Very grand.'

'And very dull.' Lukács drained his tankard and slammed it down on the table. 'More drink!'

'That's the spirit!' Márkus shouted. 'But I've got an even better idea. Kris, are you game?'

She met Márkus's eyes, smirked, and then looked at Lukács. Her eyes held a challenge. 'I am if he is.'

'What are you talking about?'

Márkus slapped a hand onto his shoulder. 'Lukács, old friend. Have you ever tried opium?'

A minute later, they were ushering him through a side door and up a flight of stairs. Down a filthy corridor and through a stained curtain, they emerged into a long room. A few candles offered a low copper light, and the air held an astringency he could not identify. Mattresses lined each wall, some of them occupied by groups of men, some by couples, a few by individuals. Márkus found an empty spot and they collapsed down on to a mattress. Slowly Lukács's eyes adjusted to the gloom. On the floor in front of them he saw an oil lamp on a tray.

A man came, standing over them. 'How many?'

'Three pipes,' Márkus told him. Then: 'Well, *pay* the man, Lukács!'

He handed over coins from his purse and the man brought the pipes. A small brown smear lay in each bowl. Lukács watched as Márkus lit the oil lamp and warmed his pipe in its flame. He raised the stem to his lips and inhaled the vapours, holding the smoke inside him before gently exhaling and resting back on his elbow.

'Your turn.'

Lukács copied his friend's actions, drawing in the vapour and trapping it in his lungs. It was a harsh sensation at first, bitter against the back of his throat. He breathed out and watched Krisztina light her pipe, giggling at something Márkus said to her.

They continued to chat, their conversation just as irreverent as before, and the man brought more pipes. After a while, Lukács felt a strange peace settling over him. A numbing sensation had spread throughout his limbs, and he felt as if his vision had softened. He found himself studying Márkus and Krisztina, thinking how fortunate he had been to bump into them. Warming his pipe, he sucked long and hard on opium smoke.

'Lukács. *Lukács!*' Márkus's grinning face leered at him. 'Look at him, Krisztina, look at his eyes! You enjoying yourself, Lukács?'

Laughing, he nodded. His lips felt like jelly. 'Want another pipe.'

'Where's that purse of yours?'

Lukács threw it at him. He realised he was leaning into Krisztina's torso, his arm brushing her breast. He could not remember how they had become so close, but he was reluctant to move in case she pulled away. From his vantage point, he could see the slopes of her breasts, and could follow her cleavage into the shadows of her bodice. Krisztina's sexuality, her very immediacy, was beginning to intoxicate him as powerfully as the opium. He blinked, looked up and discovered that she was watching him. Aghast, he glanced over at Márkus, but his new friend was too busy with the lamp to notice.

They smoked more pipes. The conversation waned. A feeling of utter calm and *rightness* washed over him. It occurred to him that Márkus did not mind how close Lukács sat to Krisztina, or whether she flirted with him, because the man was confident of his worth, and equally trusting of Lukács's honour. Both of those insights delighted him. 'You know, Márkus,' he said, after a moment's contemplation. 'You've chanced upon the most beautiful woman. I salute you for your impeccable taste.'

Márkus chuckled, raised his pipe. 'I salute your salute.'

Lukács felt Krisztina staring at him. When Márkus occupied himself once more with the pipe, he dared to meet her eyes. They exchanged a lot with that look. Ironic, he thought, that his *végzet* could go so badly while here he seemed expert in communicating with his eyes alone.

Taking a risk as Márkus hunched over the oil lamp, Lukács reached up, brushed a blond curl from her face and traced his finger down her cheek.

Krisztina's mouth dropped open. She shot a glance at Márkus to see if he had noticed. When her eyes returned to Lukács, he saw a flush rising on her cheeks. They exchanged no words, and she did not pull away.

They remained on the mattress, virtually comatose, for another hour, until he remembered the carriage. Pulling the watch from his pocket, he swore. The driver would not wait for him all night, and he could not remember the route back to Szilárd's district. Rousing his two friends, he told them that he needed to leave. They pulled themselves up, blinking, thanking him in slurred voices.

'I want to do it again,' he said. 'I'm back in Buda in a week. Where can I reach you?'

Márkus found a scrap of paper and scrawled a crude map on to it. 'Meet us at the place I've drawn.' He grinned, slapping Lukács on the shoulder. 'And bring that purse!'

Lukács pulled himself to his feet. His legs felt like someone else controlled them. He shook hands with Márkus, and made theatre of kissing Krisztina's hand when she proffered it.

'I look forward to seeing you again, Lukács,' she said.

Her eyes told him everything he needed to know.

CHAPTER 7

Oxford

1979

When Charles walked into his kitchen the morning after bringing Nicole and her mother to his cottage, two things struck him as odd. First, the back door hung open. He knew he had left it closed and locked. Second, the pile of books Nicole had liberated from the Hillman Hunter stood on the kitchen counter. The string that usually bound them lay in a loose heap.

Frowning, Charles looked through the window to the garden outside. In front of the raspberry bushes that marked his property's border, Alice Dubois stood motionless, her back towards the cottage. Arms folded against the early morning chill, she gazed into the meadow beyond, where low sun kissed the grass with a buttery light.

Charles watched her with a prickle of unease. Again, he asked himself what had scarred this woman and her daughter so deeply, what it was they feared, and from whom they fled. He also wondered at his compulsion to find out more about Nicole. How many times had he met her? Twice at the library, a third time outside the college campus, and yesterday's near-fatal meeting on the road out of Oxford. Four encounters in the space of a week, that had started to consume him as nothing had before.

His eyes travelled to the pile of books. Curious how they appeared chronological in age. The bottom-most volumes were cracked and blistered, their leather bindings crumbling, their pages stained and yellow. One ragged specimen had almost been destroyed by fire, edges blackened where flames had taken a bite. None bore titles on their spines. The books towards the middle of the stack were more recent, their leather worn but still supple. Some of those nearer the top showed a year printed in gold numerals, and the one uppermost was the volume Nicole had been writing in when he met her at Balliol's library.

This collection of texts, Charles knew, held the answers to many of his questions about her predicament. She was still deeply distrusting of him. So far, even though he had taken the leap of faith Nicole had demanded, had ferried them away despite her mother nearly braining him — had even taken them into his home — she had revealed virtually nothing. Surely, if he was willing to do all that, he deserved to at least know something of what she faced? He knew his mind, his intentions. He wanted nothing more than to help her tackle whatever problem she faced. OK, perhaps he did want a little more than that. But the less she told him about her predicament, the more difficult it was to offer his help.

Nicole's mother still stood at the bottom of the garden, watching the meadow. With an impulsiveness that surprised him — justifying his actions even as he reproached himself — Charles picked up the uppermost book and opened it.

Nicole's handwriting was neat, compact. Much of it was in French, but here and there he noticed phrases in Hungarian. It made him think of the texts she had been studying in the library: *Gesta Hungarorum* on the first occasion, and *Gesta Hunnorum et Hungarorum* by Simon of Kezá on the second.

He spotted passages she had written in German, and phrases in a language he could not place. On some pages he found sketches of locations, of buildings and costumes. Slipped between two leaves he discovered a faded black-and-white photograph. It depicted a silver mask, the date on the back indicating it had been taken in 1946. He flicked forwards, finding various attempts at a family tree. Nicole's name appeared at the bottom of each. The names immediately above hers were French, but higher up they were of German origin. Above that they seemed to move into Eastern Europe.

In all the notes one phrase stood out.

Hosszú életek.

Charles had never before heard or read the term, and could not begin to guess either its meaning or significance. It clearly obsessed Nicole. She had written it many times, sometimes underlining it, sometimes scratching it on to the page so forcibly that her pen had torn through the paper. Another word he saw repeated was a name.

Jakab.

The name her mother had called him on the telephone. Again, it was circled, crossed out, gouged out.

'*What* do you think you're doing?'

Charles spun around. Nicole stood in the doorway, eyes blazing. She lunged forward and snatched the book from his fingers.

Dismayed, he lifted up his hands. This was, he knew, the worst possible transgression of the small amount of trust she had placed in him so far. 'Nicole, I'm sorry. I'm a bloody idiot. I came down here and they were just lying there, open. I couldn't help myself. I thought there might be something in there that—'

'Damn *right* you're a bloody idiot. You thought there might be something in there that . . . what? Helped you find out everything you wanted to know about us? After everything I warned you about last night? Did you understand or believe a word I said?'

'You've hardly *said* a word except to tell me you won't tell me anything,' he protested.

'And that gives you the right to snoop through my papers, does it?'

'Hardly snooping. They were left out on the counter.'

'Where they spontaneously untied themselves.'

'They were loose like that when I walked in.'

'Liar! I can't believe I was foolish enough to think I could trust you.'

'*Nicole!*' Alice Dubois had appeared by the back door. Her face was pale as she stepped into the room. 'Why are you shouting? What has happened?'

'*He's* happened. He untied the diaries. I caught him rifling through them like a sneak thief.'

Her mother frowned. 'He didn't untie them, Nicole. That was me. I brought them downstairs this morning. I went into the garden to watch the sunrise and left them here.'

'You left them out, where anyone could look at them?' Nicole asked, her eyebrows raised incredulously.

'I thought you were all still asleep,' Alice snapped. 'Just calm down. And as for you,' she added, jabbing a finger at Charles. 'Do you think you can help yourself to our belongings just because they're under your roof?'

'Help myself?' he asked. 'I hardly—'

Nicole interrupted him. 'You've betrayed our trust.'

Charles felt his temper fraying. His swollen nose began to throb. Reading her notebook had been stupid, but he resented accusations like that. 'I've done nothing but try to help you ever since we met.'

'Thanks Charles, we really appreciate it,' she retorted. 'Yesterday we nearly died because of your help. And now we're stuck here without our passports. If it wasn't for you we'd be back in Paris by now.' She barged past him to the counter, snatching up the books. 'I've had about as much of your help as I can stomach.'

He folded his arms. 'Fine, then. Go.'

She stopped, tilted her head at him.

'Do you have any friends here?' he asked. 'Any contacts? Money? No? Face it, Nicole. You need my help. You both do.'

'We've got this far without you.'

'I'm sure you have. But that was then, and now you're here. And actually you do need my help, and despite the fact that you're a volatile lunatic with an equally volatile mother, it's still on offer.'

Nicole stared at him, trembling with anger. He could tell that his words had caused her to pause, even if they had outraged her. Charles opened his mouth to continue, but something told him that he had said enough, that he had pushed his luck – and his argument – as far as it would go.

He sensed that the three of them balanced on an apex.

'He's right, Nicole.'

Charles turned. He had not been expecting support from her mother.

'We don't have any choice,' Alice said. 'Let this go. Take a breath. I don't like the situation any more than you. But I believe him. We can forgive one error of judgement after what he's done. Let him make his plans and see if he can get us home. For the moment we have to accept that he is our best hope.'

Nicole's shoulders slumped. She dropped the books down on the counter, took up the string and began to secure them. Chagrined, she met Charles's eyes. She started to say something, changed her mind, and shook her head. Chewing her lip, she picked up the books and strode out of the room.

Charles watched her go. He felt Alice's gaze upon him.

'This volatile mother can forgive one error of judgement,' she said, eyes flat. 'But two would be dangerous. Don't think I'm not watching your every move.'

'Does the term *hosszú életek* mean anything to you?' Charles asked.

Ensconced in the Rabbit room of the Eagle and Child public

house, he traced a bead of foam down his pint glass and looked across at his colleague, Patrick Beckett.

'Charles, I'm astonished!' The professor of comparative philology was a tall man, with quick birdlike mannerisms and teeth too enormous for his mouth. He leaned forwards on his stool and snapped out a hand to retrieve his ale, slurping down a mouthful. 'I never thought this night would come.'

'What night is that?'

'The night you came to ask my advice on something. You honour me greatly, my friend. I must have risen up the ranks of academia to deserve such an accolade. I'd better drink this quickly before you change your mind, hadn't I? I knew there was a reason behind you buying the beer. Do you think this might be the first time you've dipped into your wallet this year?'

'Don't be daft, Patrick.' Feeling foolish in spite of himself, Charles glanced out of their wood-panelled hideaway by the fireplace before adding, '*Életek*. I've been looking for a reference everywhere, but I'm damned if I can find anything.'

'Well, I'm glad you've seen the light, that's all I'll say. You'll learn just as much about a society studying its myths as its history.'

'I don't follow you.'

'It's not a historian you need, Charles, it's a folklorist.' Triumphant, Beckett indicated himself. 'Enter Beckett stage right.'

'I was under the impression that linguistics was your bag.'

'Of course. And to understand any language fully, one has to understand the society in which that language developed. What better way to do that than by familiarising oneself with its folklore? Now I'll admit that I've spent far more time reading the old tales than most, but it's fascinating stuff. Much better than any of the guff produced this side of the twentieth century.' He held up a quick hand. 'Ah, aha, I forget our surroundings, of course. That was crass of me, and entirely untrue. But you understand my general sentiment.' He rapped on the table with his knuckles, for no reason that Charles could fathom. Beckett was full of these odd little quirks, tics and contradictions. It made conversation with him exhausting.

'So what can you tell me about *életek*?'

'Probably very little.' Beckett raised a finger in caution, taking a break to sip from his beer. 'Although saying that, more than most, I'm sure. On the other hand, who knows what I know or whether what I know is even true? When I say true, of course, I mean correct, or at least what I mean to say is, *authentic*. You see? We're already getting into difficulties.'

'In that case,' Charles said, 'putting aside the potential *inaccuracies* of what you've heard for a moment, could you at least enlighten me with what you *have* heard before they call last orders?'

Beckett clapped twice, delighted. 'Beautifully phrased. Of course I will. I'd have to go back and check my sources, as this is straight off the top of my head. I can't remember if it's from the German *Märchen*, the Slavic folktales, or somewhere else entirely. It doesn't matter, I suppose. In fact, I think there may be tales about them in a number of different sources, which is entirely normal. They're not always referred to that way either. In fact, *életek* – or to be more accurate, *hosszú életek* – is a Hungarian phrase.'

'They?'

'A people. *Hosszú életek* translates from the Hungarian into Long Lives. Or perhaps it's Long-lived.' He paused again, clicked his fingers. 'I'm not entirely sure if it's a direct translation, anyway. It could be a slight corruption.'

'OK, let's not dwell on the etymology.'

'Perish the thought.' Beckett drained his beer. 'Is it your round again?'

Shaking his head, Charles picked up his wallet. A few minutes later, settled with fresh pints of ale, he waited for Beckett to resume.

'I've been thinking about it while you've been at the bar. I told you I knew more than I thought, didn't I? It's all coming back now. I must have come across them several times over the years, and clearly from different sources, because the tales diverge. Amazing, the brain. Anyway, the Long Life part is only half the story. The real meat of the legend is the fact that the *hosszú életek* could change their shape.'

'Shape-shifting?'

'It's a common theme in mythology, isn't it? Sometimes punitive, sometimes defensive. Often predatory. You even have your more contemporary psychological shifting. Jekyll and Hyde, as an example.'

'And the *életek*?'

'Well that's where the stories diverge. Many of them talk about *hosszú életek* just as we would talk about a different society or culture. You wouldn't classify the French as essentially evil or predatory, would you? Or all the Japanese as crooked? The *életek* are simply another aspect of our heritage. Rare, but present all the same. Moving through the world, largely invisible, known only to the nobility in whichever country they reside. Many of them actually *are* nobility. You would assume that longevity and disguise would give one a certain advantage in political circles, after all.' Beckett laughed. 'Well, any sort of circles, let's face it.'

'But not all the folklore agrees on that point.'

'No. And that's where it gets interesting. There does seem to be a clear split. You'd obviously expect a few renditions of a tale like this to have a more sinister edge. Stories told to young children to keep them in line, for instance. And there are plenty of those as well. But what I remember finding fascinating is the fact that those stories come much later. In fact, you can't find many of them at all if you go back more than a couple of hundred years or so. It's as if something happened back then to turn opinion against the *életek*.'

'You speak of them as if they exist.'

'No, I speak of them as if society believed them to exist. And there's lots of evidence for that. When you piece the folklore together, throw in a few assumptions and stir it all up with a bit of imagination, a tale emerges of a race that lived in secret in Eastern Europe until about five hundred years ago. It's not surprising that the shape-shifting aspect of their nature comes to the fore. Think about the context. In the ninth century you have Árpád the Magyar leader, with his Covenant of Blood, taking and unifying the whole of the Carpathian Basin, of which Hungary was a part. His descendants rule quite happily – well, perhaps *happily* is not the right word at all, but let's not allow it to delay us – until the thirteenth century, and then . . . *bang*!' Beckett thumped the table with his fist, spilling beer. 'Disaster! The Mongols invade. Millions slaughtered. Women and babies. Cats and dogs. Massacre after massacre. Nobody safe. The Mongols raid and raid. They burn, plunder, rape. It's not difficult to understand how a myth centred around shifting develops in that environment.'

'Defensive shifting.'

'Exactly. And that is perhaps the birth right there of the *életek*. Their root, as it were. And if it's a defence mechanism we're talking of, then you'd expect them to be secretive. Who knows? Maybe after the threat of the Mongols had dwindled by the end of the century, the *életek* were able to step forwards. And live quite happily side by side until, for whatever reason, they were driven underground again, or interest in the myth began to wane.' Beckett drummed his fingers on the table, evidently pleased with his oratory. He sipped his beer.

'It's an interesting tale.'

The academic nodded sagely. 'You know, Charles, I have to say I've enjoyed this conversation immensely. You've completely reinvigorated my enthusiasm for the Carpathians. There's something I feel I ought to ask you.'

'Go on.'

Beckett's expression became serious for the first time that evening. 'Would you be at all interested,' he asked, 'in joining our battle re-enactment society?'

★ ★ ★

Nicole and Alice stayed with him a further week. It took him longer than he had expected to arrange their passage back across the Channel. His boat-owner friend had agreed to the crossing readily enough, but the avoidance of French Customs had been a negotiation point that resulted in him parting with several cherished bottles of Château Latour.

But even with that complication resolved, Charles admitted to himself that he had played for time. The longer he spent in Nicole's company, the more he realised it was not just curiosity that led to his procrastination but an obvious attraction. They had argued less as the days passed – although on a few occasions their differences of opinion had forced Alice to intervene and separate them. They ate together, walked together, talked, laughed. Nicole asked to listen to a tape of his radio documentary, and then mocked him ruthlessly while she listened. He saw a different side to her during those evenings. When her defences were down, they bantered affectionately. He was often left feeling intoxicated from the experience.

The night before the two women sailed, he managed to persuade Nicole to leave the cottage and accompany him to a French restaurant in the heart of Oxford. Whomever she was running from, he reasoned, the chances of meeting him in a particular restaurant in a particular city on a particular evening were remote.

Sitting in the tiny bistro, Nicole delighted him by ordering *escargots*, and Charles delighted her by tasting one. He watched her across the table, trying to memorise her face as best he could. Her hair was down tonight, auburn locks falling over her shoulders. Summer sun had browned her face, revealing a dusting of freckles.

Nicole glanced up at him, raising an eyebrow. 'You have that look again.'

'Which look?'

'I don't know. *That* look. I never know what you're thinking when I see it.'

'I'm thinking that this is certainly the last I'm going to see of you for a while. I'm hoping it's not going to be the very last.'

Nicole took a sip of wine, replaced her glass. She looked down at her food and then into his eyes. 'Oh, Charles. This has been difficult for you, hasn't it?'

'Don't say it like that.'

'Like what?'

'It sounds like you're brushing me off.'

'I'm not. But it *has* been difficult. Is difficult. This, I mean. Us.'

'It doesn't have to be.'

She shook her head. 'Please. Don't start that.'

'I want to see you again.'

'You will.'

'Will I?' he asked. 'You haven't told me where you're going. You haven't given me an address. Or even a telephone number. You won't tell me your plans.'

'I know.' Nicole dropped her fork and reached out to take his hand, squeezing it before retreating. 'It's daunting, isn't it?'

'What?'

'Trust.'

He nodded slowly. 'You're asking me to trust you.'

'Haven't I always?'

'You'll come back?'

'I can't promise that. But we'll see each other again, I think. Just maybe not here.'

'And without sounding desperate, can I ask when?'

She laughed. 'You do sound desperate. It's completely out of character. And completely touching. The answer is I don't know. But I think I'll be going crazy in Paris if I haven't had another argument with you at some point in the next few months.'

He smiled, and then he thought about what he needed to

say, and his face grew serious. 'We keep coming back to trust. I think I've done enough to earn yours by now. But I've made a few mistakes along the way. I should never have read your diaries without asking.'

'Duly noted.'

'And equally I'd be betraying your trust if I didn't confess to you what I read when I dipped into them. Or where that trail led me.'

Across the table, Nicole laid down her knife and laced her fingers together. 'I'm listening.'

He paused, alert for her reaction. Glancing around the restaurant, more for her benefit than the chance of anyone overhearing them, he said, '*Hosszú életek.*'

She flinched in her seat. Ever so slightly. As if she had been stung.

But she didn't throw her wine in his face, didn't storm out of the restaurant, didn't do any of the things he had been half expecting. Her breathing accelerated, but aside from that she simply watched him.

Charles waited until another diner had passed their table, and then asked, 'Well?'

Raising her eyebrows, she opened her fingers, indicating that he should continue.

He cleared his throat. Then, he began to relay everything he had learned from Beckett, and everything he had managed to read since. He omitted nothing, talking about the conflicting mythologies, about Beckett's own speculations. And when he had finished she was still sitting there, still watching him, still silent.

'You haven't said a word,' he said, picking up his wine glass and draining it.

'What do you want me to say?'

'I don't know. React? Tell me I shouldn't have done it? Tell me the significance of all this?'

'Charles . . .' She floundered, looking away from him, and

he saw tears in her eyes. 'How do we even have this conversation? How do we? I value your friendship. I respect you. But you could never understand this. That's why it's best that—'

'I understand enough, Nicole. I understand that, for whatever reason, this isn't a mythology to you. I understand that you and your mother are running from someone. Something happened, I don't know what. And for whatever reason, you think someone is hunting you, and you believe them to be *hosszú élet*. Is that true?'

She choked a sob, and it took all his restraint not to leave his seat and comfort her.

'Nicole, you've been asking me to make a leap of faith all this time. I don't know anything about this, other than what I learned from Beckett. I think I'm in love with you.' He shook his head. 'Damn, I've said it. But I can't make that leap of faith unless you confide in me.'

Nicole was silent for moment, contemplating his words. 'What was your view on what you heard?'

'Of *életek*?'

'Yes.'

'I don't have a view. It's an interesting myth. What else can I say?'

'Could you have a relationship with someone you thought was deluded?'

'No.'

'You see our dilemma.'

He gambled, played one last hand. 'His name is Jakab, isn't it?'

This time she reacted more violently. She rocked back in her seat, spine arched away from him, eyes scanning the restaurant – the same furtive expression he had seen the day she crashed her car. A bird trapped in a cage with a predator. It chilled him.

Nicole breathed quickly, hands gripping the table, knuckles white. Slowly, incredibly, he watched her recover herself. They sat in silence for a few minutes, and he waited as she looked from his eyes, to the table, and back to him.

'Charles, we need to get out of here,' she said. 'Somewhere darker. Somewhere with stronger drink.'

They found a suitable watering hole two streets away. Dimly lit, noisy, anonymous. Wooden booths lined the wall opposite the bar. Nicole slid into one while he ordered two large cognacs and brought them over. A sputtering candle sat in a dish upon the table. She blew it out as he sat down, an indication of just how much he had managed to shatter her demeanour in the last half an hour.

Charles watched her take a swallow of her drink. She hunched over in her seat, fingers laced around her glass. He sipped his brandy, wanting to hear her story but careful not to pressure her. He was still astounded that he had told her he loved her, and dismayed both by his atrocious timing and her lack of reaction.

'Jakab.' She shuddered. 'God, how I hate to say that name. When I was a little girl, my mother told me the tales of our family, told me why we had to be careful, keep our heads low. My grandmother, Anna, was Hungarian by birth, but she fled with her husband to Germany before the start of the Second World War. His name was Albert. Something happened in Hungary to make them flee. It was all very quick, in the middle of the night. They said goodbye to their families and that was it – never saw them again.

'They settled well enough in Germany. My grandmother gave birth to my mother, Hilde, shortly after they arrived. When war broke out, Albert was conscripted by the Nazis. He survived for about a week until a sniper got him at Stalingrad.'

'Hilde? I thought—'

'Her real name. When the war ended and the Allies occupied, Anna was itching to move again. I don't know if she had a near miss with Jakab or she was just concerned about the borders opening up again. Either way, she decided to move further west, this time to France. She took Hilde with her.'

'Not a good time to be in France, if your husband was a dead Nazi.'

'Conscript. But yes, you're right. They were outcasts. Moved around a lot. My mother changed her name to Alice and then she met my father, Eric Dubois. By this time, Anna had passed away. I never met her.

'My mother always warned me to be on the lookout for anything strange, to watch the behaviour of the people close to us, in case it changed. She told me there had been a man in Hungary – Jakab – who grew obsessed with her grandmother. There was a chance he was still out there. With Anna dead, there was a chance he would come for us.'

Nicole glanced up at him, measuring his expression. 'Of course, she thought he was a *hosszú élet*. And by this time, I had read the diaries. When you read that kind of thing . . .' She took another drink. 'This is the bit I don't expect you to understand. Or believe. But let me put it like this. Imagine you are *hosszú élet*. Imagine the myth you heard was true, that you have that ability. And imagine that the woman you're obsessed with is married to another. And hates you. And imagine that, even knowing how she feels, you don't care, you want only to possess her.'

He shook his head, opening his hands.

'Charles, you *become* the man that she loves. You *supplant* him. My mother had been guarding against that all her life. But at the time, with no real experience of what was coming, it still seemed like a superstition, an eccentric set of hand-me-down diaries and warnings from a family too carried away by its own fireside tales. That was until we started noticing the changes.

'My father, Eric, was a quiet, lovely man. A carpenter by trade. When he wasn't in his workshop making furniture, he was churning out toys for me and my friends in the village. We were living in a tiny place just outside Carcassonne. A newcomer came to town. Petre, we called him. He and my father became very close. Petre came to dinner with us, was at the house all the time. He began apprenticing to my father, even though they were almost the same age. Work was scarce. People took what they could get.

'But as time went on, Petre began seeking out my mother. He would visit the house when he knew my father was out. He started buying presents for her. My father must have seen what was coming. I think he was reluctant to act because he cared so much for his friend. It came to a head one afternoon when Petre made a pass at her. Father was a passive man, but it pushed him over the edge. He went berserk. He found his apprentice and beat him. We never saw Petre again. Everyone in the village knew what had happened. The man had nowhere to stay, nowhere to drink, nowhere to work. Everyone loved Eric and no one was going to forgive someone who betrayed him like that.

'Shortly afterwards, we began to notice changes in my father. He stopped making toys, for a start. That was the first thing I noticed, anyway. My mother – she would never tell me – but I think their relationship . . .' Nicole swallowed, choking on her words. 'Let's just say their physical relationship went from healthy and loving to violent and perverse. The arguments started. My father would forget huge chunks of our previous life together. I would make up stories about things we had done and he would nod in agreement, or laugh alongside me. Even though none of it was true.

'Then one day, outside the village, they found the body. It had been buried for a while, and the face was gone. Sliced off. The gendarme failed to identify it. But my mother knew.'

Charles nodded, transfixed by her words, filled with concern for Nicole's state as she talked. 'What happened?'

'One evening, my mother packed me off to friends. She plied my father with drink until he was virtually comatose, put him to bed and locked the door. Then she went downstairs, boarded up the house and torched it.'

'My God.'

'She collected me in the middle of the night and we headed north. We never went back.'

Nicole leaned back in her seat. She smiled at him, brushing tears from her eyes. 'And that's it. What do you think? Still interested in me?' Her tone verged on hysterical.

'Want me to play devil's advocate?'

'Sure.'

'It's difficult to say this without the risk of hurting you, but your father could have been ill.'

'A degenerative disease that would explain his behaviour. Alzheimer's.'

'Perhaps. Or something similar.'

'And my mother burned an innocent man.'

'That's the bit that's difficult to say.'

Nicole nodded.

Then he asked, 'So if Jakab burned in the house, why are you still running?'

'Because my mother had one friend in the village she confided in. She called her a few years later to find out what happened. By the time the fire reached the upper floor, it had drawn the villagers out of their beds. They saw a man screaming at one of the windows. Some said later he appeared to be writhing. *Rippling*. He broke the window and threw himself out, from a height that would have killed or crippled most men. And then he got up and ran away.'

'And he's still after you.'

She picked up her cognac, gulped it. 'And that's why I'm in England. In Oxford. I've been researching all this time. There are texts here: original sources, documents I can't access anywhere else. *Hosszú élet* means Long Life but it doesn't mean immortal. I want to find out how much longer this can last.'

Charles breathed deeply. He found it difficult to respond to the enormity of what she had just told him. It was impossible to believe any of the more sensational aspects of the story. But clearly something tragic had happened to the Dubois family. Whether Beckett's tales had any relevance suddenly didn't matter to him. Eccentric or not, he would take another leap of faith if she asked him to, would put the mythology to one side until he had worked out what to do.

Reaching across the table, he took her hand. 'Will you let me help you?'

She laughed, tears falling this time, and put her own hand over his. 'Of course, Charles. Thank you.'

'Will you let me read the diaries?'

'If that's what you want.'

'Will you leave them with me for a while? Maybe one or two of them?' She hesitated, then squeezed his hand and nodded. Charles glanced at his watch. 'We'd better get back to the cottage. You sail for France in the morning.'

'There's one more thing, Charles.' She still held his hand, and now she really did smile. 'It sounds better in French.'

'What is it?'

'Je crois que je vous aime aussi.'

It was the most beautiful phrase he had heard.

CHAPTER 8

Snowdonia

Now

A wave of nausea threatened to overwhelm Hannah as the full impact of Sebastien's words seized her.

Have you validated Nate since he got into the car with you?

She took a gasping breath. Another. Felt a buzzing in her ears, a dryness in her mouth.

Could she even conceive that the man downstairs was someone other than her husband? The possibility that Nate had not been the one to travel with them to the farmhouse brought consequences so dire she could hardly even consider them.

She searched her memory frantically for any proof that it was Nate – *her* Nate – that lay injured on the sofa in the kitchen. She reran their flight from her father's place, the words they had exchanged in the car. What words, though? He had hardly spoken. Had hardly even told her what happened.

But he was dying!

And unless we've managed to stop the bleeding in time he may STILL be dying!

Unbidden, a memory rushed at her: the day she married Nate. No guests. No fuss. Her husband, her father and a single minister in a church on the shores of Lake Annecy. Charles booked them into the bridal suite of a hotel overlooking the lake, but Hannah bundled Nate into their car and drove him into the mountains instead. That night she made love to him on a blanket and they fell asleep watching a cold moon dust the lake with wedding diamonds. The next morning they drove back to the hotel in time for a breakfast served by staff who did their best not to notice the dirt on their clothes and the flush on their faces.

Tears blurred her vision. She clenched her fists, forced herself to lock away the memory. Focused instead on hatred. On rage.

She would not yet believe that her husband was gone, but she would go downstairs and find out. If it was Jakab she found – if he had supplanted Nate – then God pity him because the only thing left for her would be vengeance and hers would be terrible. She would destroy him. Utterly. Pulverise his flesh. Shatter every one of his bones. Stamp him into the earth. Gut him. Burn him. Obliterate him.

Hannah realised that she was shaking. Eyes gritty, she jumped up from the bed.

Sebastien climbed to his feet. 'What are you thinking?'

'I need to know.'

He nodded. 'I'm coming with you.'

No need to be stealthy now, she reasoned. Either her husband lay on the couch downstairs or a monstrous counterfeit.

You left Leah with him.

The grotesque reality of that thought swamped her, a capsizing black wave that closed over her head and pushed into her lungs.

You left Leah.

Hannah gagged, stumbled. Would he harm their daughter? Everything she had read in the diaries described a creature whose mind was so broken, so incapable of empathy or love in the way she understood those concepts, that any attempt to predict its behaviour was an exercise in insanity.

The possibilities she had discounted moments ago were now so real they seemed like probabilities. As Hannah crossed the room she realised with horror that she had already started to grieve.

She had been raised to survive: to flee, to fight, to grieve, accept, protect. She had been taught by three decades of fear, of loss, of snatching moments of joy in a world of instability. She could not remember a time, even during her happiest moments – *especially* during her happiest moments – when she had not caught herself wondering when it would end, how it would end, and how the entries in her own diaries might read if they survived long enough to be passed down.

Act.

Stop thinking. Don't hesitate. *Act.* The mantra had served her tolerably so far. Looking into the future would immobilise her if she allowed it.

Earlier, after verifying Sebastien's identity, she had put the shotgun back on the pantry shelf. The old man's arrival had reassured her, and she had been more worried about leaving a loaded weapon within Leah's reach than their immediate discovery. How costly might that mistake turn out to be?

Hannah stepped out of the bedroom, began to move down the stairs. As she passed the landing, the eyes of the stuffed falcon followed her with a dead stare.

She had little need for stealth. But she found herself creeping down to the ground-floor hall nevertheless. Little need for stealth, but little need either to alert him to her approach. She kept tight to the wall, minimising the creak of the treads beneath her feet. Sebastien followed, close behind.

At the bottom of the stairs Hannah paused, listening.

Wind. The knocking of window-panes. Rain bouncing like rice grains off the glass. Inside, the house breathed silence.

She padded along the floorboards to the kitchen. Winced at the hard shadows cast into corners by the dull light of the chandelier. Sought them anyway, rejecting her fear.

The first door on her right was closed. Dining room. Further down, the living-room door gaped open. The darkness within emitted a chill breeze. She remembered the smashed window she had seen. Remembered that she had not investigated it. Another mistake.

The hallway twisted a dog-leg before arriving at the kitchen. She would have to turn her back on the living-room doorway, on that black void.

And that's when he would grab her. She'd feel his fingers slide around her throat, hear him whisper her name, and she would scream and kick and bite and claw and gouge but when she turned and saw the ghoul wearing her dead husband's face, she would know she had lost everything.

Hannah stopped in the hall, and when Sebastien butted up against her she nearly cried out.

You left Leah with him.

She turned away from the toothless mouth of the living-room doorway. Balled her fists. When nothing leaped out at her, she stepped into the kitchen.

Hannah had left candles burning and a fire crackling in the grate. As she entered the room the light was soft and warm. The sofa where she had laid Nate and they had treated his wounds was empty. The hose of the drip she had set up lay on the floor, discarded.

In the armchair where Leah had slept, a solitary cushion remained.

Hannah felt something wrench inside her. She opened her mouth. Wanted to scream. A million dark thoughts flooded her. Thirty years of nightmares condensed into a single moment.

Yet this was real. This was happening.

Don't think about what it means. Don't. Just think of Leah.

Sebastien walked into the kitchen behind her. He hissed when he saw the empty sofa. His eyes flicked to hers.

Gun, she mouthed, and he nodded in response.

The pantry door was ajar. Hannah slipped inside. She felt around for the shelf where she had left the weapon. Even as she wondered what she would do if the shotgun was missing, her hands touched the shelf and slid along the wood. Empty.

Hannah wasted a few more seconds, feeling blindly, knowing the truth but needing to convince herself that the weapon had really gone.

She backed out of the cupboard.

Sebastien still stood in the doorway, but he had turned to face the hall. She heard him take a slow, measured breath. 'It's OK,' he said, the timbre of his voice startling after the silence of the last few minutes.

Something odd in his tone. Something terrifying.

She couldn't make her legs work. 'What is it?'

'It's OK,' he repeated. 'Everything's OK. I've found Nate.'

Sebastien took a step backwards, then another. As he reversed into the kitchen, Hannah saw that the shotgun's twin barrels were pressed against his chin. Sebastien backed further into the room. The shotgun followed. Holding it was a nightmarish, corpse-like version of her husband.

'What you . . .' he said to Sebastien, voice cracked and rasping. He licked his lips. Tried again. 'What . . . you doing here?'

Hannah's feet remained fastened to the floor. 'Nate, where's Leah?'

He advanced into the room, using the barrels as a prod to keep Sebastien at a distance, never taking his eyes off the old man. 'Back up. Couch . . . Sit.'

'Where's *Leah*, Nate?'

'Safe. When . . . he sh'up?' A breath. 'Show up.'

The knife block on the kitchen counter held six blades. It was two yards from her. 'Just after we arrived. It's OK. He's a friend.'

Sebastien sat down on the sofa and rested his hands in his lap.

'You d'know any . . . anything 'bout him, Han.'

'Nate, he checks out. Please. Give me the gun.' Nate swayed on his feet, rested a shoulder against the door frame. The barrels of the weapon swung towards her. She tensed. Wondered what a chest full of buckshot would feel like. Wondered if it would kill her instantly. 'Nate, you're going to pass out and you're holding a loaded gun. Give it to me. I've got a better chance of shooting him than you have.'

Nate took his eyes off Sebastien for half a second as he glanced at her. Removing the hand that clutched the barrels, he wiped sweat from his face. A wrack of pain seemed to lash him. He bent, grimaced. If this was an act, it was the best she had ever seen. He looked like he could collapse at any moment.

Of course it'll look good. It WILL be the best you've ever seen.

Then, when she was least expecting it, he handed her the shotgun.

Before she had even grasped what was happening, Hannah found herself holding the weapon. Quickly, she stepped away from him.

The safety lever was off. She thumbed it back on – could not risk shooting her husband. *If* that was who this corpse-creature turned out to be. She lifted the barrels and aimed. 'I'm sorry, darling, I love you. I love you so much and I have to do this. I need you to tell me the name of the hotel where we stayed, the night of our wedding.'

Nate stared at the shotgun pointing at his head and then he looked at his wife. 'I hope you don't think I'm dishonouring you,' he said, gasping for breath. 'But you've never been the sort of girl to . . .' He swallowed, winced. Reaching out a hand to steady himself, he closed his eyes as another tide of pain coursed through him. When he opened them again they were filled with love. '. . . to settle for a hotel bed when you had the chance of a tumble under the stars.'

Hannah sobbed then, feeling her life's axis tilting, her world seesawing back into alignment. That they had lost their home, their livelihood, their peace, no longer mattered. Only her family mattered. What was left of it.

Leah. Nate.

He slumped further against the door jamb and she ran to him, holding the shotgun in one hand and cradling him with the other.

He pointed a finger towards Sebastien. 'We haven't finished here.'

'Nate, he saved your life.'

'Then he won't mind a few questions.'

From the sofa, Sebastien said, 'Hannah, remember what I said. Let him ask. It's important.'

Nate nodded. 'We've met before. Where?'

The old man smiled. 'A number of times. But only ever with Charles. I remember a particular occasion when we had lunch in Budapest and you ordered a steak so rare you virtually had to drink it.'

Nate stared at Sebastien. His mouth twisted first into a grin, and then a grimace of pain. 'You old dog. What . . . brought you here?'

'We have a lot to talk about. But it can wait. First we need to get you well.'

Clenching his teeth, Nate sagged in Hannah's embrace. 'Leah's in the next room. Asleep still. You need . . . put her to bed. I need . . . lie down.'

Sebastien helped her guide him to the sofa. 'Can I ask what you've done with Moses?' he asked, as he reattached the drip to Nate's arm.

'Great guard dog,' Nate muttered. 'Threw a chocolate outside and he . . . out like a shot.'

It took Hannah a few minutes to carry her daughter upstairs and tuck her under the covers of the four-poster bed. Leah woke once, asking where they were, but Hannah managed to soothe the girl back to sleep.

Downstairs, seeing that Nate had also drifted off, she led Sebastien into the living room. She spotted the smashed window, resolved to fix it in the morning. With so many potential entry points, the security risk of a single broken pane was minimal. It did, however, make the temperature of the room uncomfortable. She closed the curtains and switched on the dim electric bulb that hung from the ceiling.

Settling into a chair, Sebastien said, 'I can only try to imagine how traumatic that must have been for you.'

Hannah rubbed her face. She filled her cheeks with air and allowed them to deflate. 'If I'd lost Nate . . .' Finishing the sentence would bring tears and lower her defences. She left it hanging, watching as Moses nosed his way into the room. The dog collapsed at Sebastien's feet.

'Do you have a plan?' he asked.

'We can't stay here indefinitely. But Nate's in bad shape.'

'He's remarkably resilient. I have to admit, when he came at me with that shotgun, I didn't think there was any chance it was really him.'

'He's a fighter, all right.'

'I can't pretend to know him well, but our paths have crossed a few times over the years, via your father. And it's always been clear that everything he does, he does with you and your daughter in mind.'

'It's a largely thankless task.'

'After what I just overheard in the kitchen,' Sebastien replied archly, 'I'm sure it has its rewards.'

She glanced over at him and noticed with surprise the wolfish grin on his face. 'I'm not sure how I feel about someone as ancient as you are making dirty remarks like that.'

'Ancient.' He cackled. 'You're your father's daughter, aren't you?' His expression darkened the instant the words left his lips. He clamped his mouth shut.

'Do you think there's any chance . . .'

'Let's not dwell on that tonight. We don't know enough to speculate.'

'We haven't heard from him.'

'No.'

'So it doesn't look good.'

Sebastien sat in silence. Then he said, 'Tell me about your plan.'

'It really depends on Nate. I don't want to move him until I have to.'

'He's going to be very weak for some time. And he's going to be even worse tomorrow. Once the adrenalin wears off and the stiffness sets in, he'll be virtually immobile.'

'I think we'll be safe here for up to a week. Even if Jakab discovers the whereabouts of all the places we could have gone, he'll have to be incredibly lucky to pick this one straight away. We've left plenty of red herrings that will seem like more attractive options. They should tie him up for a while.'

'You've planned this well.'

'Not me. All of us. It's become second nature. A way of life.'

'Where will you go?'

She looked at her hands. 'I'm sorry, Sebastien. I think it's better if I don't say.'

He nodded, and she could see the empathy in his eyes.

'What you've done,' she said. 'I owe you so much.'

'You don't need to thank me. Or apologise for not telling me where you'll go. You've kept Nate alive because of your actions so far. You've given Leah prospects for a future. I'll bet you don't hear this enough, Hannah – you're incredibly brave, incredibly strong. I can't say I've met another who would have achieved what you have.'

She shook her head. What had she done that was so praiseworthy? Run? Flee? It was all she ever did. How many years had she thought about taking the fight to Jakab? How many nights had she fantasised about killing him? Time and again she had told herself that as long as Nate lived, as long as someone remained to care for Leah, she would do whatever was needed to end this nightmare and offer her daughter the chance of a life she had been denied.

But that's all it is, isn't it? A fantasy. When the opportunity came knocking, what did you really do?

To Sebastien, she asked, 'Do you think we're doing the right thing? Running, I mean? Do you think we should make a stand? Set up some kind of trap for him? Try to end this once and for all?'

'I debated that with your father many times.'

'It's difficult to defeat an enemy when you don't know his face.'

'And it's not as if it hasn't been tried before. I've read those diaries too.'

'How long have the Eleni been operating?'

'Over a century, if you add it all up. Around seventy years, in its current incarnation.'

'And how many *hosszú életek* have you encountered in all that time?'

'You know the answer to that, Hannah. It's like searching for raindrops in the ocean. At the moment, Jakab remains our best hope.'

'So you think we should react. Stop running.'

'Only you can answer that. I won't play God with your lives.'

She stood up. 'I'm going to get some rest. What will you do?'

'I'll go home.' He climbed to his feet. 'I'll be back tomorrow. You need groceries, fuel for the fire, diesel for the generator. It's safer if we leave the gas supply for now. You don't need any more eyes around here if we can help it. If you're willing, I'll leave Moses with you too. Despite what Nate said, he's a good dog. He won't let any harm come to you.'

'Thanks Sebastien.' At the front door, she planted a kiss on the whiskers of his cheek.

Up in the bedroom, watched by the dog, Hannah stirred the dying embers of the fire and moved to the window. Pulling open one of the curtains, she looked out at the night. The moon had reappeared through gaps in the cloud, and its light glittered on the surface of the lake. She watched Sebastien's Land Rover cross the bridge, crawl up the track to the main road and disappear over the ridge.

Hannah still thought there was more to his story than he was sharing. But that would have to wait. She had done all she could tonight – had managed to get Nate and Leah to the farmhouse alive. She hadn't managed to save her father.

Sebastien's words echoed in her mind. *We don't know enough to speculate.*

But she knew.

Climbing into bed next to Leah, she kissed her daughter's hair and lay down in the darkness. She thought she would not sleep. But she did.

Hannah woke once during the night. Moses was at the window, his paws on the sill, nose to the glass. Casting off the remnants of her dream, she slipped from the bed and moved to the dog's side.

A red deer stag stood at the edge of a copse on the far shore of the lake. It gazed across the water towards the farmhouse, the felt of its antlers glowing in the moonlight. For the briefest of moments, the stag locked eyes with her. Then it stepped back into the undergrowth, and was gone.

The ashes were cold in the grate and the windows stubbled with frost when Hannah woke a few hours later. Dawn had broken, muting the colours in the room to a flat blue. She rolled over in the bed and saw Leah lying on her back, staring up at the filigree of cracks that ran across the ceiling.

Noticing that her mother was awake, the girl turned to face her and asked, 'Did the Bad Man come?'

Reaching out and pulling her daughter into her arms, Hannah forced a smile. She had long feared this moment. While she had resolved to shield Leah from fear as much as she could, she had also vowed never to lie to her. If she had learned one thing more clearly than any other from reading her ancestors' diaries, it had been not to shy from the truth or avoid the difficult questions.

'Yes, darling, he did. But we got away from him and we're safe.'

'Did he see me?'

'No, he never saw you.'

Leah twisted out of her mother's embrace and sat up in the bed, rubbing her arms. 'It's cold in here. Where are we?'

'We're in the mountains. We drove through the night to get here. Do you remember being in the car? You were fast asleep when we arrived, and you didn't even wake up when I carried you upstairs.'

'I remember leaving Grandpa's.'

Hannah climbed out of bed. She had slept in her clothes, unable to relax enough to strip off. Stepping into her boots, she laced them up.

'Mummy, there's a dog in our room.'

'That's Moses. Do you want to say hello?'

'Funny name for a dog.'

Moses came to the bed and licked Leah's hand. The girl laughed, pulling it away.

'Is Daddy here?'

'Yes, he's downstairs.' Hannah went to the other side of the bed and perched next to Leah, brushing a tangle of hair out of her daughter's eyes. 'But he had an accident yesterday. He's hurt himself and we're going to have to look after him.'

'Will he be all right?'

'I hope so, honey. I really do.'

'Can we go and see him?'

She slapped Leah on the leg. 'Come on, then.'

In the kitchen, they found Nate still asleep. Dark circles shadowed his eyes. His complexion was pale, but his breathing was regular. Hannah could have asked for no more. She watched Leah's reaction carefully as the girl went to her father's side.

'Did he hurt his tummy?'

'Yes. That's why it's all wrapped up. To make him better.'

'What happened to his arm?'

'We put a little hole in it so we could pour in the medicine.'

Leah glanced round at her mother, her expression betraying her scepticism. 'I never heard of *that* before.'

Hannah tossed the remaining logs onto the fire, and managed to coax a flame into life. At the sink, she filled the kettle with water, put it on to the stove and lit the gas.

As the logs began to burn and the kettle boiled, Nate stirred and opened his eyes. He blinked, looking around the room to orient himself, then winked at Leah. 'Hello scamp,' he said. 'Come over here and give me a kiss.'

'We've got a dog called Moses, like God did,' she told him solemnly.

Nate laughed, choked, and launched into a fit of coughing. 'Is that so?' He looked up at Hannah. 'How are you doing?'

She took a glass from the cupboard and filled it with water, bringing it over to him. 'I'm fine. We're all fine. Worried about you but fine all the same. Here. I'm making tea, but sip this first. How are you feeling?'

'Like I've been run over by a train,' he replied. 'I don't think I can move.'

'You're not meant to. You should never have got up last night. That's a battlefield repair Sebastien's given you. I'm not doubting our friend's handiwork but if I see you off that couch again I'll have to knock you on the head with a frying pan.'

Leah giggled at that.

'Where's Seb?' he asked.

'He went back to his place. Said he'd drop in later with supplies.'

Nate nodded, drinking his water. When the kettle boiled,

Hannah made tea for them both. She found a dusty can of Coke in the pantry and gave it to Leah, whose face lit up.

'What are you going to do this morning?' he asked.

She rolled her eyes towards the back of Leah's head. 'I need to have a talk. Explain a few things. I thought we'd go for a stroll. Get some fresh air.'

Nate nodded his agreement, then indicated the dog. 'Do you want to take Mutley here?'

'I'd feel better if he was here with you,' she said.

Hannah retrieved Leah's coat from the car and waited while the girl shrugged into it before taking her outside. The wind had blown itself out overnight, but low grey clouds promised fresh rain. Water dripped from guttering. Moisture clung to the stems of plants and the gravel of the driveway. The chill air sliding down from the mountains brought a bite that made her eyes water but invigorated her nonetheless.

Leah ran over to the cowshed and popped her head inside, disappointed to find it empty. Together they investigated the stone-built storehouse. Its roof had partially collapsed, just as Sebastien had indicated; the stacked logs of wood were soaked and useless. In the second outbuilding they found the generator clacking away. Nate had taught her how to maintain one, and she agreed with the old man's assessment of its diesel reserves. Back outside, they walked past the abandoned stables and crossed the garden to the fence that delineated the farmland beyond. The fields attached to Llyn Gwyr had not been grazed in a long time. High grasses and wild flowers stretched before them, surrendering to scree, boulders and the rocky ascent up the mountain.

Hannah crouched down beside Leah and pointed to the horizon. 'You see that peak? That's Cadair Idris, one of the highest mountains in Wales. It means Giant's Seat.'

'Does it have glaciers?'

'Not any more. But once it did. Do you know what they

say? If you spend a night at the top, the next morning you'll either wake up a poet, or mad as a hatter.'

Leah laughed. 'That's silly.' She bent down and pointed. 'Look at these.'

Hannah followed the line of her daughter's finger to the mud around the bottom of the fence.

Animal prints. Lots of them.

Odd to see so many in one place. Hannah spotted the hoofprints of deer, what could have been wild goat, fox, and others too tiny to identify. She pointed out all the tracks she recognised, as well as a harvest mouse nest clinging to a thistle.

Leah noted it all with interest, and then said, 'Is the Bad Man coming here?'

Hannah stood up. She took the girl's hand. 'Come on, let's go and look at the lake. We can talk as we walk.'

She found it surprisingly easy to explain what had happened, and was encouraged to see how well Leah seemed to handle it. She knew the girl was worried by what she heard, despite Hannah's attempt to remain upbeat – or at least neutral – in the language she chose. Over the last two years she had begun to use the diaries to tell Leah stories. While she had not bluntly divulged their content, she had used them to spin cautionary tales, fables she hoped would allow her daughter to grasp the broader implication of their situation without exposing her to the horrific detail.

'Is Grandpa going to meet us here?' Leah asked, as they traipsed past the outbuildings towards the lake.

The question brought an agony of grief. 'I don't think so,' Hannah replied. She'd left her father with Jakab; the chances of her seeing him again were remote.

They had forged a tempestuous relationship during her adult years. Although she had not inherited Charles's quick temper, he had passed on his stubbornness, and that had led them to some spectacular clashes. He had not been a perfect father, and she had not been a perfect daughter, but they had loved each other fiercely, even if they did not always get along.

Hannah wrapped an arm around her daughter's shoulders. They skirted a patch of boggy ground and found a path of slate and stones. Looking about her, she realised just how well her father had chosen this bolt-hole. The valley in which the farmhouse nestled made them invisible to anyone travelling the main road. If it had not been for the farm buildings behind her, there would be no evidence of human activity within sight.

They rounded a rise and came upon the lake. The overcast sky had turned it to the colour of steel, a breeze dimpling it like a sieve. A flock of Canada geese flew in formation above their heads.

'Mummy, a boat!'

Hannah stared out across the lake, her skin prickling. Sure enough, a white wooden rowing boat bobbed on the water a few hundred yards from the shore. Two fishing rods jutted from its side. In the middle of the boat sat a man bundled up in a jumper and hat.

She felt her heart beginning to race. The man was watching them.

'Who is it, Mummy?'

'I don't know, darling. I've no idea.'

She felt Leah wrap an arm around her waist. 'Is it the Bad Man?'

What could she say to that?

The man lifted an arm and waved to them. Hannah stared back. Now he stood up. He pointed at himself, pointed to their side of the shore, and mimed the actions for rowing. This last act seemed to unbalance him, because the boat rocked violently beneath his feet. He leaned forwards and backwards in quick succession, trying to stabilise himself. Finally he lost his balance and tumbled into the bottom of the boat.

'He nearly fell in the water!' Leah screeched, laughing.

The fisherman's ineptitude had blunted the sting of fear in Hannah, too. She watched as he recovered himself and threaded his oars. Putting his back to them, he began to row the boat towards the shore.

Think, Hannah. What do you do?

She had no option but to stand her ground. It was obvious where they had come from; Llyn Gwyr stood directly behind them. If they abandoned the shore before the stranger reached them, they would have no clue who he was, and would be trapped inside the house with questions they could not answer. Worse, they would doubtless leave him curious and puzzled by their behaviour.

Don't take your eyes off him.

The boat was closer now. Hannah could hear the creaking of the oars in their rowlocks and their splash as they parted the water. She could only see the fisherman's back. He wore a rope-knit jumper of cream wool, ragged at the sleeves and collar. A blue hat was pulled down over his head, and from beneath poked a shock of jet-black curls. He was about Nate's build. Perhaps not quite as broad.

'Stay close to me, Leah. Do as I say. Don't say anything about Daddy. Or the Bad Man. Do you understand?'

The girl slid behind Hannah, mumbling her agreement.

As the boat glided to the shore and nudged up on to the shingle, the man pulled in his oars. He turned, looked both of them up and down, and broke into a wide grin. The whiteness of his teeth was a shocking contrast to the pallor of the day.

'Well, hello there, ladies!' he said. His voice was rich with a musical Irish brogue. Blue eyes, a vivid cobalt shade, twinkled with merriment. When they failed to respond he hesitated, tilting his head to one side. 'Ah, will you look at that. Caused offence already, I have, and before I've even known your names.' He flashed them another sharp smile.

'We weren't expecting any company,' Hannah replied, folding her arms. 'I understood this lake belonged to the farm.'

'Ah, but surely it's God's lake, is it not?'

Leah burst out from behind her mother's back. 'We've got God's dog!'

The man threw his head back and laughed. 'Have you now? Well, there's a thing. God's dog. And what do you call the fine animal?'

'Moses.'

He laughed again, looked up at Hannah and winked. 'A fine name for a dog, that. Listen, I was only pulling your leg. It might be God's lake but it also, by rights, belongs to your farm. Which makes me, for want of a better word, a poacher. But!' He held up his fishing rods. 'An unsuccessful poacher. So I'm sorry. For being on your lake. And not nicking your fish.'

Hannah nodded. 'And what's a born-and-bred Irishman like you doing in the heart of Snowdonia?' Despite all the alarms chiming in her head, she found herself unaccountably charmed by him, and knocked slightly off balance by his openness. The more sober part of her mind screamed one word.

Danger.

'Running away from Ireland, of course,' he replied, laughing.

'Were you running *from* something?'

'Aren't we all running from something?' His eyes shone, and she did not miss the challenge they held. 'Oh, but I haven't introduced myself. Allow me. Name's Gabriel. You can call me Gabe, if you like.'

'Nice to meet you, Gabriel.'

'And I'm sorry for invading your privacy. I had no idea there was anyone staying at the farm. Renting it, are you?'

'A holiday.'

'Grand. Me, I've a place over the hill.' He pointed. 'Just myself, a smallholding, and the horses.' He turned his attention to Leah and the flashing smile returned. 'Do you like horses, little miss?'

'Yes!'

Gabriel nodded, then cast his eyes appreciatively over

Hannah's body. 'And what about your ma now? Can she ride?'

His lascivious double meaning was not lost on her; every sentence he uttered seemed to contain a private joke. She scowled.

'Mummy's the best. She used to compete.'

Hannah laid a hand on her daughter's shoulder, determined to curb the girl's excitement before she let something slip. 'Come on, that's enough. It was nice to meet you, Gabriel. I'm sorry you haven't managed to catch anything, but I gather there are plenty of lakes around here. Perhaps you'll have better luck elsewhere.'

Chastised, Gabriel flicked his eyes to Leah, then nodded his agreement to Hannah. He replaced his oars in the rowlocks. 'Well,' he announced brightly. 'I won't hold you up any longer. It won't take me long to row back. I'll be out of your hair before you know it. It was a delight to meet you both. Little miss. Tall miss.' He pulled off his hat and raised it theatrically. Dark curls spilled out to frame his face. 'Now, I wonder. Is there any chance of you ladies giving me a shove-off?'

Hannah planted her boot on the boat's prow and shunted it out into the lake. Gabriel lurched backwards. He gripped the gunwales and just about managed to keep his balance. Leah laughed.

On the way back to the farmhouse, holding her daughter's hand, Hannah glanced back at the rowing boat as it moved across the lake. Gabriel lifted an arm and waved.

Turning away from him, she heard the same word echoing in her head.

Danger.

CHAPTER 9

Gödöllö, Hungary

1873

The week leading up to the second *végzet* passed unbearably slowly for Lukács. His father, as was the custom, asked him nothing of his evening at the palace. Even Jani seemed content to leave him alone. Izsák had hounded him to share his story, but Lukács brushed off his little brother's enquiries with an abruptness that sent the boy crying from the room.

He could hardly work out how he had occupied his time prior to his journey to Budapest. Krisztina consumed his thoughts, consumed his blood. When he closed his eyes he could feel the soft weight of her breast pressing against his arm, the warmth of her skin as he traced his finger down her cheek, the suggestion in her eyes as she said goodbye to him.

I look forward to seeing you again, Lukács.

He needed to see her. It took him days of debate, but Lukács decided he would not attend the second *végzet*. Nor would he attend the others. The ambassador's *kurvá* bitch daughter and her coven of privileged and pampered butterflies were welcome to their masked harlequins. Lukács refused to settle for the life prescribed for him. He would no longer allow others to dictate what he wore, what he thought, how he behaved. He would not observe the ridiculous social dance a millennia of conceited *hosszú életek* had designed for their offspring. Before his evening with Márkus and Krisztina, he had felt suppressed by fear: fear of rejection, fear of solitude. But the humiliation he had experienced at the *végzet* had been immediately counterbalanced by the acceptance he had received from the young couple. For the first time, he had mingled with low-born, and had found that he preferred their company by far to any sour-faced *hosszú élet*.

Lukács was confident he would not be missed until the third *végzet*, perhaps even the last. At that point, of course, his absence would be obvious. The consequences for his position in the community would be catastrophic; his relationship with his father, his brothers, would be destroyed. But although József had tried to scare him with his talk of life as a *kirekesztett*, Lukács had now tasted a piece of that life. Far from fearing it, he *coveted* it. Yes, he would lose privileges, the easy passage through life his identity afforded him. For the first time, he would need an income, somewhere to live. But he would be free.

He had made preparations. Already, a few valuable time-pieces had disappeared from his father's workshop. While he had not yet dared to remove any of the gold bullion from its hiding place beneath the drawing-room floorboards, he had calculated the value of the extraordinary quantity his father stored there, and discovered that it would fund him a luxurious life several times over. Although he would not leave his family destitute, he would feel no shame in taking what he needed when the day arrived.

On the evening of the second *végzet*, his father drove him to Pest as before, and they visited Szilárd's house, where Lukács changed into starched shirt, waistcoat and frock coat. This time a different mask awaited him on the dressing-room table. It was much lighter than the first, wrought from a delicate leaf of copper and polished to a high shine. Unlike the pewter mask that preceded it, this one covered less of his face – just a narrow strip above his cheekbones.

He would not wear it for long.

Looking at himself in the mirror and liking what he saw, he slipped his pocket watch into his waistcoat and walked outside. The journey from Szilárd's house was farcically short. They did not cross the Danube this time, but pulled up instead outside a sprawling mansion in Pest that overlooked the water.

'Make me proud,' József said, as a porter opened the door of the carriage.

Smiling, Lukács patted his father's arm and stepped down into the courtyard. He marched up the steps of the property and waited until József's carriage had turned the corner. Then he pulled off the mask and walked back out of the gates.

It was a warm evening, so he decided to cross the Széchenyi bridge by foot. He enjoyed the exhilaration of being so far above the water. The sun was setting, a glowing disc that painted the stone lions of the bridge with fire. Halfway across, he stopped and turned full circle, surveying the unified cities separated by the great river. Leaning out over the water, he fished the mask from his pocket. Whatever it meant to the *hosszú életek* hierarchy, to him it symbolised a shackle. On a whim, he launched the mask into the air, watching it spiral down, a glinting flicker of copper, towards the water below. He saw it touch the surface of the Danube, and kept sight of it a moment longer before it slid beneath the ripples. Lukács drew a breath, exhaled, and walked the rest of the way across the bridge.

Márkus's directions led him to a tavern as raucous and grubby as the first. Even though he had removed his coat and had rubbed grime into the front of his shirt before he entered, his finery still jarred. He felt hostile eyes upon him as he fought his way through the crowd.

He found Márkus at a bench, nursing an empty tankard. Krisztina sat beside him. When they spied him, their eyes widened in surprise. Márkus jumped to his feet with a laugh and embraced Lukács, slapping him hard on the back. Krisztina welcomed him with a smile that made his heart pound and his stomach flip.

It was strange seeing her without a fog of alcohol clouding his judgement. She aroused him still, but she was not as pretty as he remembered, nor as clean. His tongue left him and he mumbled a greeting at her, noting as he did that she wore the same dress as before. It was grubby and stained, but accentuated her curves no less as a result.

He suggested drinks and Márkus congratulated him heartily. Soon Lukács was swigging back mouthfuls of beer and laughing as his friend related the week's events, the highlight of which seemed to have been a riverside collision between a merchant and two sailors lugging a barrel of spoiled fish.

They talked, joked, drank. As the beer flowed, and Márkus became more animated and less observant, Lukács traded glances with Krisztina, and her flirtation became more daring. Once, beneath the table, her leg bumped against his and he almost leaped off his stool with surprise. He cursed himself for blushing.

Finally Márkus, red-faced, pulled himself to his feet. 'A piss!' he announced, staggering into the noise of the crowd.

Heart racing, Lukács met Krisztina's eyes. 'I would ask an imposition of you, if you would allow it.'

The corners of her mouth twitched. She leaned forward and planted her elbows on the table, cradling her chin on her fingers. 'I would allow it.'

He cleared his throat, stared at the table. 'There's something I would like to discuss with you. Alone.'

'I see.'

Lukács glanced back up at her. Her expression was flat, one eyebrow raised in a challenge. He decided to test his luck. 'Your answer?'

Her smile returned. 'I'm intrigued to hear what it is.'

'Good. I confess, though, I don't know how to engineer an opportunity for me to tell you without . . .'

'Márkus.'

'You see my dilemma.'

She chewed her bottom lip. 'Do you know the new statue of the king, on the riverbank?'

He nodded. Krisztina opened her mouth to continue just as Márkus arrived back at the table. She clamped her lips shut.

Frustrated, Lukács ordered more drinks. They bantered for another hour. By the time Krisztina stood up, he was drunk.

She placed a hand on her chest and turned to Márkus. 'You know, I think I'm going to leave you two rogues to it. I've an early start, and last week my head hurt all day after you both led me astray like that.'

Laughing, Márkus waved her off. Lukács continued to drink for another ten minutes, then picked up his coat.

Márkus frowned. 'You're going too? Already?'

'Things to do, I'm afraid,' he said. 'But I enjoyed it.' He rolled some coins towards his friend. 'That should see you through.'

Márkus snatched up the money. 'You, sir, are a gentleman among gentlemen. Will I see you again?'

'Oh, I'll definitely see you again.'

Shrugging on his frock coat as he left the tavern, Lukács hurried down to the river. Night had fallen, and the moon was hidden behind a bank of cloud. It was far darker along the riverbank than he had been expecting.

He found Krisztina leaning up against the statue of Franz Joseph. She pushed herself away from it as he approached, and fell in step with him.

'Let's keep walking,' she said.

Lukács nodded. He stole glances at her as they strolled along the bank, and she met his eyes once, her expression unreadable. The expectation that hung between them was palpable. The air crackled with it. He told himself to savour the moment, and he tried to absorb every detail of her: the swish of her dress as it rubbed against her legs, the sway of her hips, the taunting shadow of her cleavage.

'For someone who wanted to talk,' she said, 'you're remarkably quiet.'

Lukács went to the railing overlooking the water. He leaned against it. Krisztina came to a stop beside him, so close that he thought he could feel the heat radiating from her.

For the first time he noticed her smell. Not the delicate perfume of the coiffured *hosszú élet* ladies. This was an earthy smell, a musk of sweat and woman and sex that filled his nose, overpowered his airways and inflamed him. It made him feel nervous and joyous and invincible all at once.

'You know exactly what you do, don't you?' he said.

She turned towards him and looked up, her face inches from his own. 'Do I?'

Lukács reached out and pulled her to him, pressing his mouth to hers. She responded instantly, parting her lips and pushing her tongue into his mouth. He nearly cried out, outraged at the filthiness of the act yet fired with lust as their saliva mingled and he tasted her.

Her hands reached up to caress his shoulders. They moved around to the front of his chest and lingered there as the kiss deepened, and then with unexpected force she shoved him away.

Krisztina panted, grinning, eyes greedy for him but shaking her head. 'That's all you get, Lukács. I'd love to, but no more.'

'What's wrong?' He moved towards her but she held him at bay with a single finger.

'You. Me. This. It's wrong, and we both know it. Márkus might be Márkus, but what I've got with him has a future, at least. This doesn't.'

Lukács frowned. 'Why not?' He lunged at her but she pushed him off easily, laughing.

'Why not? Are you joking? Look at you – your fine clothes, your gold watch. I've never seen such wealth so naively displayed. I live in a house with two rooms and share it with my parents and six siblings. My father works the river and I wash linen for a pittance. You'll ride home tonight in a carriage, no doubt. I know what you want. And I'm a silly girl for being tempted. But it's not yours to take.'

His lust, frustrated, became annoyance. 'Why isn't it?'

Krisztina's eyebrows creased and her eyes flashed with anger. 'You think your purse can buy a night with me, is that it?'

'It's bought two nights with you.'

She slapped him.

He slapped her back. Hard.

Krisztina cried out, more in indignation than pain. She touched her hand to her cheek. Eyes narrowed, she backed away from him. 'Don't *ever* come near me again, Lukács,' she spat. Gathering up her skirts, she marched off.

Lukács's fingers stung where he had slapped her cheek. He was breathing hard: from excitement, from anger, from arousal. The smell of her lingered in his nostrils, her taste on his lips. He watched her stride along the bank of the Danube until the night wrapped her up in its arms.

Lukács's scowl of anger became a smirk.

The third *végzet* was conducted without masks. It represented the symbolic entry of the *hosszú életek* youth into adulthood, and allowed the participants to interact free of the constrictions of childhood. It was also the first time the celebrants could make known any interest they bore. Potential partnerships would be weighed and judged by the *tanács* at the final *végzet*. Appropriate matches would be approved, and courtship could begin.

Although he did not consider it a blessing, Lukács knew that to have two siblings was a rarity. *Hosszú életek* did not produce offspring easily, and even then for only a short period in their lives. The low birth count, along with the extreme nature of their longevity, meant that the entire community had an interest in the successful courtships of its youth.

Lukács had been making alternative preparations.

His riverside encounter with Krisztina had incensed him at

first. He could understand – just about – the scorn of the ambassador's bitch, but rejection by a Buda tavern slut was a different matter. He would not let it stand. He had felt the changes within him accelerating during the last few weeks. Despite the pair of rejections – perhaps, ironically, because of them – he was feeling comfortable with himself for the first time in his life, and could see a future where he made his own decisions free of the constraints imposed by the *tanács*.

He could not, obviously, attend the third *végzet*. Although the consequences of his continued absence loomed closer now, he viewed the coming confrontation with József as the fulcrum on which his new life would turn.

When he told his father he wanted to revisit the city, József lent him a horse, gave him money and ushered him out of the house, professing his delight at the changes he was witnessing in his son. Lukács used the opportunity to go drinking with Márkus and Krisztina.

The atmosphere at the table that night amused him greatly. He knew Krisztina could not divulge what had happened between them. She had too much to lose. Lukács sat there laughing with Márkus, ignoring her until she made flush-faced excuses and left them. Together, the two young men drank late into the night, swapping stories and details of each other's lives.

Lukács mined Márkus for information on how the low-born citizens of the city lived. He needed to learn a great deal, and quickly. He asked questions about his friend's work, his home life, where he ate, his courtship of Krisztina and the places he had visited up and down the Danube. As long as the beer flowed, Márkus was happy to answer any question he asked.

This afternoon, crossing the chain bridge to Buda on the third *végzet* of the summer, Lukács travelled in his carriage alone. This time he did not even bother with a subterfuge. He paid the driver a large tip and asked him to convey him directly to Márkus's workplace.

At the Ujvári boatyard, amid the stench of boiling pitch and the clattering of hammers, he found his friend planing the raised hull of a de-masted river schooner. When Lukács's carriage pulled up and he stepped out of it, Márkus straightened and whistled, long and low. 'Hell's teeth, Lukács, you travel like a king, don't you? I reckoned you was a proper gentleman, but just look at the brass on that thing.' He watched the carriage speed away, wiping sweat from his forehead. 'What are you doing here?'

Lukács clapped the young man on the back. 'I know you meet Krisztina on Tuesdays, but I was in the area. I thought I'd see if my hard-working friend needed a beer to quench his thirst before he met his sweetheart.'

'Do I ever!' Márkus shook his head. 'I keep asking myself what I did to deserve bumping into a fellow like you.'

They spent two hours throwing back tankards of beer in an alehouse around the corner. Lukács laughed heartily at his friend's jokes, and was gratified to see that he could make the boatwright smile at the anecdotes he invented of his life at home. 'Márkus,' he said. 'There's something I would ask you.'

'Ask away.'

'It's a trifle . . . delicate.'

'Do I look like I offend easily? Go on – out with it.'

'I've decided to leave Hungary,' Lukács said, bizarrely pleased by the disappointment he saw in the young man's eyes. 'My father isn't going to like my decision. In fact, no one is going to like it. I've been making plans, but I need your help to look after a few things once I've left.'

'Then you've got it.'

Lukács nodded. 'I'm grateful. Just a few ends that need tying. Perhaps you'd accompany me back to my lodgings and I can show you what I need. I've rented a suite at the Albrecht.'

Márkus raised his eyebrows. 'They probably won't even let me inside.'

'Yes, they will. You'll be with me.'

The Albrecht was a grand hotel, five minutes' walk from the Ujvári yard. A porter outside its imposing frontage opened the door for them, greeting Lukács while examining Márkus with disdain. In the lobby, Lukács approached the desk and waited for the concierge to spot him.

'Ah, Mr György, sir. How wonderful to see you. Your room has been prepared, I am pleased to say.'

'Thank you. I don't wish to be disturbed.' He pushed a coin across the counter and the concierge bowed, handing him his key.

Leading Márkus up to the third floor, Lukács unlocked the door to his suite and went inside. At a drinks cabinet, he selected two crystal tumblers and poured whisky into them. He handed one to his friend.

Márkus slugged it back in a single gulp and wiped his mouth. 'I'll do another one of those.'

'Gladly.'

'Look at this place, Lukács. Four-poster, lace on the cabinet.' He went to the bed, reaching out his hand. 'Just feel these sheets. Smell them.'

Lukács laughed at the wonder in the young man's voice. 'Have you seen the view?'

Márkus knocked back a second whisky, put down his empty tumbler and walked to the window, looking out at the street below. He shook his head, marvelling at what he saw. 'I could live like this. I really could.'

'Could you? You might think so, but don't be so sure. I can't. And I won't. You don't know the restrictions that go with this kind of life, Márkus. It has its advantages, admittedly. Its comforts. But it brings with it complications that stop you taking any enjoyment.' Lukács found that articulating those feelings made him feel morose. He changed the subject. 'Where are you meeting Krisztina tonight?'

'Near the church of Saint Anne on Batthyány tér.'

'No, you're not.' Lukács clubbed the young man around the

head with the whisky bottle. Lips curled back from his teeth in
a snarl of excitement, he was grateful when his makeshift
weapon did not fracture or explode. Márkus spun as he fell,
tangling in the floor-length curtains before pitching forwards on
to the floor, where he lay still.

Lukács returned the bottle to the cabinet and began to strip
off Márkus's clothes. It was an unpleasant task. Boat-building
was energetic work, and as he removed his friend's underclothes
he winced at the stench rising from his body.

Halfway through, Lukács realised that he had not checked to
see if Márkus was still alive. Admonishing himself, he lifted an
eyelid, and when that exploration revealed nothing, he lowered
his ear to the young man's mouth. The moist air rising from his
lips confirmed he was still breathing. Lukács was gratified by
that. He had not known how hard he would need to hit Márkus
to knock him out, and so he had put all his force into the blow.
While he only wished to incapacitate his friend, he'd accepted
that the blow might kill him. He examined Márkus's head and
felt the large swelling that had risen there. But there was no
softness to the skull. He hadn't shattered bone.

Once Marcus was completely naked, Lukács reached under
the bed for the lengths of rope he had stowed there. He tied
his friend's hands together, his feet, and lashed him to the legs
of the heavy four-poster. He made a gag from a flannel and a
piece of twine. Testing all his knots, satisfied that his friend
could neither escape nor broadcast his whereabouts, Lukács
stripped off his own waistcoat and shirt and draped them on the
bed.

Squatting on the floor, he ripped a chunk of auburn hair
from Márkus's head and walked to the cabinet, depositing the
heap on the polished wood. Lukács studied its colour, then
looked up at his face in the mirror.

He had been practising this for weeks. No longer did he cast
mere shadow animals on to the wall of his father's toolshed.
József had been right; it did not come easily to him. But he was

proud of how far he *had* come, and of the agonies he had endured to get there.

Gritting his teeth, Lukács gripped the sides of the cabinet with both hands. He closed his eyes, took three long, deliberate breaths, and *pushed*.

A million needles pricked his skull, tattooing his scalp with fire. He concentrated, willing himself not to scream, and pushed again, harder this time. Hitting the barrier where the pain was simply too great, he battered himself against it once, twice, three times, until suddenly it collapsed and he forced his way through.

Lukács panted for breath. He opened his eyes and saw sweat standing on his brow. His face was a blotch of red and white. Lifting a hand to his head, he tugged at a clump of hair. It pulled loose from his scalp. Lukács examined the skin beneath and saw a coarse stubble of auburn. The colour matched exactly the heap of hair on the cabinet.

Closing his eyes, he endured another minute of suffering, of searing heat in his scalp. A dreadful thirst came upon him. He gulped water from a jug while he recovered his strength.

Going to Márkus's body, he began a meticulous examination. He got down on his knees and peered at the man's face from all angles, so close that he could see the individual pores of his nose, the smattering of hair in his nostrils, the wax in his ears, the food crusted at the corners of his mouth. His picked up Márkus's right hand and felt its texture, examining the calluses of his fingers, the ripped fingernails and scuffed knuckles. He searched all over for blemishes, birthmarks, bruises or cuts. He inspected the hairs on the man's chest, his nipples, his genitals.

Leaning even closer, he sniffed the breath rising from Márkus's mouth, the stink from his armpits. He lowered his face to the mound of pubic hair and inhaled. Recoiling, he moved back up the body, pressing his fingers into muscle, testing the firmness of bicep and tricep, deltoid and pectoral.

Finally satisfied, Lukács removed the last of his clothes and lay down on the floor next to his friend. Canting his head to one side so that he could still see Márkus's body if required, he exhaled fully and closed his eyes.

He would not cry out.

As the agony began, as the fire whipped through him, as his skin stretched and his muscles ripped, as his back arched and the soles of his feet beat upon the floor, Lukács thought his teeth would crack and his eyes would haemorrhage in his skull. His fingers dug into the wood of the floor, fingernails scraping, knuckles cracking. His heart beat crazily in his chest, so laboured he thought it might burst.

When it was over, he lay there in stupefied paralysis. Tides of pain washed over him. He rode them silently, forcing himself to breathe, to endure, until they gradually began to ebb away.

Shivers of sensation fluttered over his altered shape. He felt the hairs on his body register the tiny movements of air in the room. The ambient sounds of the hotel had a different quality now. He could feel the rush of breath into his lungs more noticeably than before. He brought together the fingers and thumb of one hand, feeling the calluses on the pads.

Opening his eyes, he pulled himself to his knees and crawled on to the bed. Hunger burned in his belly but he had prepared for that. Tearing open a parcel of food, he gorged on spiced meat, hard cheese, sweet cakes. Saliva dripped from his chin. He felt his stomach attacking the food, breaking it down into fuel the moment he swallowed it.

When he had sated his craving, he dressed, went to the cabinet and gulped down the water that remained in the jug. Then, finally ready to see, he lifted his chin and looked into the mirror.

The reflection that stared back at him was a statue, silent and still. After a minute, it bent forwards and examined teeth, nose, lips. It brushed a hand through its hair. Opened its mouth to speak. 'Do I look like I offend easily?' it asked. The reflection turned its head from side to side, touching its cheek, feeling the roughness of its jaw. It took a long breath. And then a smile twisted on its mouth. 'I could live like this,' it said. 'I really could.'

Márkus Thúry strode out of the hotel suite.

He walked the streets of Buda until sunset. Excitement boiled in him as he wandered through the crowds. The city's sounds seemed louder, its colours more vivid, its stench more cloying.

On Batthyány tér he spotted Krisztina on a bench beneath a stone statue. She wore the same stained dress as always, with its tight waist and voluminous skirts. Leaning back on her hands, she seemed lost in daydreams, staring up at the sky. Márkus Thúry watched her for a while before he approached. He wanted to set this image of Krisztina in his mind, wanted to capture the scene as accurately as he could. He would enjoy reliving it later.

The sun had slid below the hill and the sky was darkening, patched here and there with purple cloud. At the windows of apartments, candles were being lit. Children were being called in from the street.

In the day's dying heat, Krisztina's forehead shone with a light sweat. He wondered how long she had worked before coming here. Her tanned cheeks were streaked with grime, but her hands and forearms were clean and raw where the oxalic acid she used to bleach the laundry had scoured them.

Krisztina spotted him as he crossed the square. She stood, tilting her head to one side. Márkus drew up in front of her, blood pumping. He was about to kiss her when he noticed she had not greeted his arrival with a smile.

'You're late,' she said, scowling. 'I've been waiting here nearly an hour.'

'There was a problem at the yard. It took a while to sort out.'

Krisztina leaned forward and sniffed his breath. 'That's a lie.

You've been drinking. Where did you get the money for that? I thought you were saving.'

He opened his mouth to protest, and thought better of it. 'OK, I admit it. Lukács came to see me at the boatyard. Told me he needed a favour and took me to a tavern nearby. Said he wanted to get out of Budapest for good, that we wouldn't see him again. I organised passage for him on a steamer. He sailed north an hour ago.'

'Good.'

She started walking, and Márkus raced to catch up. 'Good?'

'Yes, good. You've been spending far too much time with him. It's not normal.'

'I thought you liked him.'

She stopped in the street, a frown creasing her forehead. 'When have I ever said I liked him? When has *either* of us ever said that?'

'What do you mean?'

Krisztina put her hand on her hips, angrily thrusting out her chin. 'What do I mean? You've suddenly changed your tune. "Let the dim-witted *hülye* spend his coin if he wants to, Krisztina,"' she sneered. '"A few of his dull tales are worth a night of good drink." You think you're being so clever, Márkus. I'll admit I was taken in by him at the start. But that man's been using you just as much as you've been using him. You just don't see it.' She twisted away from him and strode up the street.

He followed. 'How can he be using me?'

'I don't want to talk about him. I'm glad he's gone and that's that. Where are we going anyway? What are we doing? I'd like a drink too but we can't afford that.'

He grinned at her. 'Oh, yes we can. Look.' From his pocket he withdrew Lukács's purse.

'Where did you get that?'

'He gave it to me.'

'He *gave* it to you?'

'I swear, Kris. I don't know how his mind works, do I?

When we said goodbye at the dock, he looked me in the eye, shook my hand and gave me this. He asked me to tell you he was sorry he couldn't say goodbye. Said he wished you a good life, and that he hoped the purse would give us what we needed to achieve it.'

Her mouth fell open. 'He said that?'

'What a *hülye*, eh?'

Krisztina stared at him for a long moment. Then she shook her head. 'Márkus, what *will* I do with you?'

He grinned. 'Walk with me. Up to the woods.'

'The woods? At this time of day? Why on earth—'

He put a finger to her lips, jingling the purse of coins in his hand. 'There's something I want to ask you, Krisztina.'

Now her mouth opened even wider, eyes flickering over him, trying to read his face. He saw her chest swell in expectation. Arms linked together, they walked up the hill.

As the light of the day faded, shadows began to gather under the trees. Birds sang evening songs, calling to each other in the branches above. Márkus found a comfortable spot beneath an oak. Taking Krisztina's hand, he eased her down on to a patch of soft moss. He reclined next to her and gazed down the hill. The waters of the Danube glimmered through gaps in the trees. 'It's beautiful here,' he said. 'So quiet.'

'You're going soft, Márkus. Since when did you start appreciating nature?'

He smiled then, and said, 'Kiss me.'

Krisztina squinted at him out of the corner of her eye. Laughing, she pushed him on to his back and slung a leg over him, her skirts trailing out around his waist. '"Kiss me," he says.' Her eyes sparkled as she mocked him. She was breathing hard, hands resting on his chest. 'Well, seeing as you asked so nicely.'

Krisztina bent down and opened her mouth to him. He kissed her, passionately, aggressively, the excitement fizzing in his blood. She grabbed his hair and thrust her tongue deeper into his mouth and when he felt himself stiffen, she moved her hips against him. The pressure was exquisite, unbearable.

Márkus reached up and took her breast, feeling for the first time its contours, its weight. He explored with his fingers and when, through the fabric of her dress, he dragged his thumb across her nipple he felt her hiss against his mouth.

The smell of her – so potent, so all-consuming – intoxicated him. He slid his hand up to the warm damp skin at the slope of her breast, and then snaked it inside the front of her dress. Krisztina kissed him with a relentless urgency, but as he quested further under her clothes she reared up, out of his reach.

Laughing, she wiped her mouth with the back of her hand. 'Now, now, Márkus. You're getting a little hot. Maybe you should cool down.'

He frowned. Pulled her to him once more. Again they kissed. When he moved to touch her again she pulled back.

'What's wrong?' he asked. He could feel the heat on his cheeks, the pulsing of his blood.

Krisztina rearranged the front of her dress, bent and bestowed upon him a final chaste kiss. 'You said we would wait. Said you wanted to.'

'I did?'

Smiling, she nodded.

He stared up at her, her scent filling his head. This girl, so earthy, so rich, so visceral, tantalised him and excited him and frustrated him. He memorised the image of her as she straddled him, the leafy canopy of the forest fanning out above her head. Márkus snorted. 'I lied.'

Grabbing her by the arms, he flipped her on to her back and reversed their positions. He seized the front of her dress and tore it open. Her breasts spilled free. Soft white flesh. Dark and puckered nipples.

Krisztina screamed. He pinned her to the earth by her throat. She scrabbled in the dirt with her free hand, and before he managed to secure it, her fingers found a rock. She clubbed him with it. Sparks exploded in his head and he nearly lost his grip on her. But he caught her wrist and bashed it against the ground until the rock flew from her fingers.

'Filthy *kurvá*,' he told her. 'You've teased me enough.'

When it was over, Márkus rolled off her and climbed to his feet. He buttoned his trousers.

On the mossy forest floor, Krisztina hugged her knees and stared up at him. Tears had washed clean lines through the grime on her face. A smear of blood clung to her mouth. Her voice trembled. 'What will you do?'

'About what?'

'Are you going to kill me?'

He drew a surprised breath, chuckled, and shook his head. 'Why on earth would I do that? We both knew this was coming, Krisztina. It just happened a little earlier than you expected, that's all. Nothing to get emotional about. I'll see you tomorrow.' Márkus turned his back and strolled away from her, whistling as he made his way down the hill. Above, the skies had darkened to full night.

He didn't go straight to the hotel, feeling the need to walk for a while. He loved his new ability to wander freely, do what he wanted, go where he chose. On an impulse, he visited the tavern where he'd first met his friends. He took a drink, and when he found that it did not quench his thirst, took several more. So high on adrenalin was he that he did not notice the effect the alcohol was having upon him until he was quite drunk. By that time, an opium pipe seemed a good idea, so he tried that too.

Some hours later, he returned to the Albrecht. The porter glared as he approached, but this was the third time they had fenced with each other, and the man opened the door without a word.

Up on the third floor, the entrance to his suite looked undisturbed. He put his ear to it. No sound issued from within. Satisfied, he unlocked the door and went inside.

On the floor, his friend was still bound tight to the legs of the bed. His eyes were open now, and when they saw him they bulged in shock. The young man struggled against his ropes, making muted grunts and moans through the gag in his mouth.

Lukács-Márkus shut the door, walked over to his friend and kicked him in the kidneys. 'Ungrateful shit,' he said. 'That's for calling me a *hülye*.' He went to the bed and stripped off his clothes. Naked, he performed a few stretches before lying down on the floor. He closed his eyes, relaxed his hands and feet, and concentrated on his breathing.

Opening his eyes, distracted, he turned to the young man, who was goggling at him in horror. 'For pity's sake, Márkus. This is difficult enough already, without you staring at me like that.'

Strangely, though, he discovered it was not that difficult at all. There was pain, yes, but the transformation in reverse was not nearly as strenuous. It felt as if his body poured into a memory of itself, a recognised groove. When he was complete, he opened his eyes and looked at Márkus. Colour had drained from the man's face.

'*Surprise!*' Lukács said, laughing as the absurdity struck him. Going to the mirror, he examined his face before pulling on his clothes. He swept up the hair he had left on the floor and threw it out of the window. Then he took a knife from his pocket.

Márkus flinched when he stood over him. Lukács bent down and sliced through the bonds. He cut off the gag and retreated to the bed.

'Get dressed,' he said.

His friend had been bound tightly for hours. He could not move quickly. Shivering, stumbling, he gathered his clothes, never once taking his eyes from Lukács's face.

Finally he found his voice. '*Hosszú élet*,' he whispered. 'You're *hosszú élet*.'

'An outstanding observation, Márkus.'

'Lukács . . . please. Don't kill me.'

He rolled his eyes towards the ceiling. 'Why does everyone think I want to kill them today?' He shook his head. 'I don't want to kill you, Márkus. I just want you to get dressed.'

Once Márkus had put on the rest of his clothes, Lukács led him out of the room and down through the hotel. Outside, he reached forward and plucked a piece of bracken from his friend's shirt. The young man seemed too terrified to do anything except stand and wait for instructions.

'I won't be seeing you again. Good luck with everything. Try not to speak ill of people in future. You never know when they might be listening. Here.' He delved into his pocket and removed the purse of money. When Márkus still made no move, he took his hand and pressed the purse into it. 'As recompense for this evening's inconvenience. Spend it well. And don't lose it.'

Winking, Lukács turned and walked away down the street.

CHAPTER 10

Gödöllö, Hungary

1873

Balázs József waited in the marble-floored hallway of the *tanács* townhouse and stared at the clock that hung on the wall in front of him. The timepiece was not one of his own, although the craftsmanship was passable. Its ponderous metal pendulum marked the passage of long seconds as he sat on a high-backed chair in the cool of the hallway, waiting to be called.

Two members of the *tanács* had interrupted his meeting with a customer in Pest and conveyed him here with hardly a word. When the destination of their coach became apparent, József fell silent. One did not question the motivations of the *Örökös Fönök*. He had been called before, but this time seemed different. A disquiet gnawed at him, growing with every tick of the clock.

A door opened at the end of the hallway and a hawkish old man with white hair and a black suit came across the marble floor. 'The *Fönök* will see you now,' he said.

József stood up. 'Of course.'

'He is in the rose garden. You may follow me.'

József accompanied the man to an intricately stuccoed antechamber that contained three doors, and through one of the doors to a quadrangle. The formal garden was surrounded

on all sides by a covered walkway, stone pillars supporting a
balcony level above. A water fountain stood at the centre of
the garden, approachable by four gravel paths. Roses, red and
white, lined each route. Near the trickling fountain, gazing
into a low wide pool, waited the *Örökös Főnök*. A white-suited
servant held a parasol above his head, shading him from the
sun.

As József approached, the *Főnök* turned to face him. The
skin of his ancient face had sagged into multiple wrinkled folds,
and his flesh had withered on his bones. But his eyes, when
they regarded József, were bright and glossy and alert: two chips
of cold jade.

József sank to one knee and bowed his head. 'Lord, I came
the moment I was called.'

The *Főnök* sighed, his breath rattling like wind through the
branches of a dead tree. 'Please, József, get up, get up. How
long have you and I known each other?'

József rose to his feet. He found the *Főnök* studying him
intently, and his disquiet matured into dread.

'How is Jani?'

Was that what this was about? József opened his hands
outwards. 'Jani's a headstrong boy. He's in love with the Zsinka
girl, and finds it difficult to be patient.'

'The *tanács* will make its decision soon. Patience is a valuable
skill. It will do him no harm to wait a little longer.'

'I agree, Lord.'

The *Főnök* nodded thoughtfully. He took another rattling
breath and turned to the servant holding the shade. 'Leave us,
please. József, lend me your arm. Walk with me to the bench.'

As the white-suited youth collapsed the parasol and retreated
to the house, József offered the old man his arm. He felt the
Főnök's fingers latch on to his flesh like the talons of an old
hunting bird. They walked together to a wooden bench on the
covered walkway and sat, looking out into the garden.

When József had entered the quad, two guards had been

flanking the nearest entrance. Now, from a doorway at the opposite end, a second pair emerged and took up positions either side of it. He felt a shrinking of his scalp.

'My old friend, this is painful. I wish you to know that. I'm afraid there's no gentle way to break this. Your boy, Lukács, did not attend the last two *végzets*.'

József stared at one of the stone pillars that supported the balcony above, not quite comprehending what he heard. 'That cannot be the case.'

'You think I am mistaken?'

He took a sharp breath, realising his error. 'No. Of course not. I would never suggest such a thing. But . . .' he floundered. 'I accompanied him to the second *végzet* myself. I saw him go inside.'

'I am told that your son slipped out of the courtyard moments after your carriage left the premises. Neither did he attend the third *végzet*.'

József felt his chest tightening, his stomach plummeting as if dropped into a well. He raised a hand to his face, and noticed that it was trembling. 'I . . . trusted him. I was proud, immeasurably so. I thought that despite his difficulties, he intended to fulfil his duty. He has made a mockery of that trust. Of me.'

The *Fönök* bowed his head. 'I am sorry.'

József looked away from the pillar, at the profile of the old man beside him. He straightened. 'Lukács is still my son. What will happen to him?'

'You understand the importance of maintaining our traditions.'

'I also know, Lord, you have the authority to dispense as you see fit.'

The old man nodded, then turned and looked at him. The chips of jade were flecked now with azure. 'I do, József. And I would hesitate to cast out any son of yours for a transgression even as serious as this. But other things have come to light.'

József closed his eyes.

'Last night in Buda a young woman was raped. Pretty thing, by all accounts. The girl has accused her betrothed of the crime.' The *Főnök* shook his head. 'It's not often an incident like that gets reported, or even taken seriously when it is, but this girl is a bit of a fighter, by all accounts.'

'And what does this have to do with my son?' József felt as if he balanced at the edge of a precipice, the *Főnök's* finger resting against his spine.

'Hopefully nothing, my friend. But they picked up the boy shortly afterwards and threw him in the cells. His defence is a strange one. He maintains he was kidnapped by a *hosszú élet* sharing your son's name, who supplanted him before going out to meet the girl. At this stage we know little more than that. We have not had a chance to speak to the boy ourselves.' The azure flecks in the *Főnök's* eyes had faded. 'The *palace* has asked us to investigate. That's unprecedented. Regardless of what has or has not taken place, the fact that the palace has even requested that we cooperate, demonstrates the lack of trust we now enjoy in some quarters. The king notices the tide turning, József, and seeks to distance himself. You must bring your son before the *tanács*, and give him an opportunity to clear his name.'

'Yes, Lord.' József hesitated. 'If I may ask: what will happen to the boy in the cells?'

'Guilty or innocent, he will hang. The stakes are too high for any alternative. Your task is simple, József. Go back to Gödöllő. Return here with your son.'

Lukács was looking down at the courtyard through the leaded windows of the music room when he saw his father ride in under the arch. He watched József dismount and hand the reins to a servant.

If you knew what I'm about to tell you, Father, perhaps you'd walk a little less upright.

Lukács headed down the stairs to his father's library. His stomach fluttered in anticipation. Not fear exactly; he had grown too confident for that. But even the most basic of interactions with his father brought nerves. Considering the magnitude of what he was about to reveal, it was testament to the changes he'd wrought in himself over recent weeks that he only needed to admit a slight anxiety. Overriding everything was his thirst to see the expression in his father's eyes when the man realised that, ultimately, he had failed to impose his will on his son. Lukács's situation was now a *fait accompli*. With his rejection of the *végzet* process, he had made his transition to *kirekesztett* inevitable. Nothing József could do now would change that. Perhaps if his father had listened, perhaps if he had consented to Lukács's requests, this might have ended differently. Instead, he had lost both his son and the respectability he valued above the feelings of his offspring. József had not listened; had never listened. Lukács would ensure that his father heard him – *properly* heard him – before he left Gödöllö for the last time.

Smirking as the door to the library swung open, unable to mask his smugness even as his stomach flipped and his heart raced, Lukács watched his father enter the room and come to an abrupt halt.

József stared. Lukács met his eyes and stared back.

His father took a breath and it seemed to catch in his throat. He shuddered. Bizarrely, his eyes filled with tears. Then he crossed the room, raised his fist and swung it at his son's head.

Lukács was so surprised that he failed to react. The blow caught him on the cheek with a force so brutal that he heard something *crack* in his face. He staggered, fell to his knees. When he looked up, József punched him again. Blood burst from his nose. He spluttered through it, pain blinding him. The fist slammed into his skull a third time and when he sprawled on the floor, József kicked him so hard in the stomach that the air exploded from his lungs.

Hands grabbed him, lifting him to his feet. He blinked away

tears to see his father's face, inches from his own, eyes a mad burst of colour. József snarled and hurled him backwards into a bookcase. Lukács's head struck a wooden shelf. He fell to the floor a second time, accompanied by a rain of books. His father strode to a bureau Mazarin, yanked out a drawer and began to rifle through its contents.

Lukács tried to focus on healing, on repairing the damage his father had done. But he was too shocked to concentrate. 'Wha . . . you doing?' he slurred.

'I *know*, Lukács, you hear me? *I KNOW!*' Shaking, his father dragged the entire drawer out of the desk and dumped it on top. 'The *Fönök* knows too. They all know, but they wish to offer me this. You knew what you did when you raped that girl, Lukács. You knew what the penalty would be. The *tanács* will not allow bad blood to thrive.'

'Wait, Father. *Rape?*' He tried to work out how anyone could know, and once he worked that out, wondered why anyone would give the story credence, especially so quickly. Especially his father.

Did they all think so little of him?

'Don't *lie* to me, Lukács. And don't make this harder than it already is.' József found what he was looking for. From the drawer, he picked up a dagger and unsheathed the weapon, turning it over in the light. Tears washed his cheeks. 'You've thrust a knife in me just as real as this.'

Lukács gasped through the pain. If he were found guilty by the *tanács*, the sentence would be capital. With sudden clarity, he understood that his father did not intend things to go that far. József would not suffer the humiliation of seeing his son on trial.

Coughing, spitting blood from his mouth, he used the bookcase to pull himself upright, gagging from the agony in his face and torso.

József sprang across the room, shoved him against the shelving and put the blade to his throat.

Lukács tried to move his head but he was pinned. Could he repair the damage quickly enough if his father cut his throat? Possibly. But what if József didn't stop there? What if he kept cutting? The thought panicked him and as Lukács struggled, the blade of the knife bit, its steel drawing a line of fire across his throat.

He was so close to his father's face he could see the individual pores of his skin, smell the tobacco on his breath, the mint oil, feel the wetness of his tears.

József moaned. He pressed his cheek against Lukács's forehead. 'I *loved* you, you stupid boy. Despite everything I loved you, always loved you, *always*. And then you did this. You did this to me. To your family. To yourself. To that stupid girl. Why, Lukács? *Why?* I don't want to do this, I really don't, but I must.'

'You don't have to do anything, Father.'

József bellowed. With his free hand he hauled Lukács away from the bookcase and slammed him back against it.

The shelf cracked his head and the knife sliced deeper. Lukács felt the blood beginning to course down his throat, hot and thick.

And then, with eyes now as black as the heart of a solar eclipse, with spittle hanging from his chin and with monstrous strength, József ripped the blade through his son's neck. Lukács's eyes bulged. He felt blood *erupt* from him. Saw it gush over József's forearms. Heard it spatter across the floor.

His father held him, face contorted.

Lukács tried to speak, tried to twist out of József's grip, tried to focus on his throat. But the pain was too great. He felt his legs buckle, and when they surrendered completely, his father braced him against the bookcase.

He coughed, choked. Spasmed.

Shadows rolled over him. His felt his head lighten. His thoughts began to spin away from him, unravelling in terror. His lungs emptied and this time when he took a breath, he found that he could not, found that his lips were numb, that his arms were numb, that his world was darkening, that his, that . . .

Balázs József relaxed his grip on his son's body and allowed it to thump to the floor. He turned, staggered to the bureau Mazarin and plunged the knife deep into its wood. Panting, sobbing, he roared again and upended the heavy wooden desk. Papers, candles and writing implements flew everywhere. József collapsed among the ruins. Weeping, he pressed his palms against his skull.

How could this have happened? *How?*

Was it his fault? Had he failed the boy somehow? He thought of his dead wife and moaned. He knew that the grief of her passing had made him retreat from the world, from the responsibility he bore to his sons. What would she think if she could see this? What would she say? Her middle son a rapist. Her husband soaked in his blood.

Raising his head, József forced himself to look at Lukács's body, at the gashed throat from which blood still pulsed in an ever-weakening tide. A dark image. A nightmare image. But it was for the best, he thought.

No.

Yes. It was. Kinder this way. Better for the boy.

You must not do this.

Better for everyone.

NO!

Shaking, mumbling, he crawled back across the floor. Reaching his son's side, he turned Lukács onto his back. The boy's eyes were closed. His chest was still.

József placed his hands over Lukács's ravaged throat, closed his eyes.

Pushed.

He felt a stinging in the flesh of his fingers, a resistance, as if he were pressing his hands into mounds of broken glass. The pain intensified and then, suddenly, he was through. Heat rushed through his wrists. Clenching his teeth, joined now to the boy's skin and muscle and flesh, he felt his blood surge out through his fingers.

'Come back,' he whispered. 'Please, son. Come back.'

As the warmth drained from him, József began to shiver. Thirst raged in him. He felt himself grow weaker, felt his stomach tighten and growl.

Beneath him, Lukács twitched. His hands flopped against the floor and his legs kicked. Then he sucked in a huge lungful of air, sat up and screamed.

József tore away his fingers, sending up a shower of scarlet rain. Lukács's throat was raw, dark handprints marking two patches stripped of skin. But even though the flesh beneath was livid, the gash had closed.

The boy opened his eyes, blinked. He stared at his father and József could not begin to imagine the thoughts that gathered behind them.

When Lukács spoke, his voice crackled like splintered wood. 'Was it not enough to kill me once?'

'Get out.'

His eyes were dreadful. They shone with terrible intensity. 'You loved me, you say. Am I to be appeased by that? You tell me you love me and then you—'

'Get out, *GET OUT!*' József shrieked. 'Curse me for being this weak but I cannot destroy my own flesh! They will hunt you for what you have done and rightly so. Leave now. Take what you must. I renounce you as my son. You are no longer *hosszú élet*. You've made your choice.' He hissed the last word like a curse: '*Kirekesztett.*'

Lukács stared. He clambered to his feet. One hand to his throat, he stumbled from the room.

'Balázs Jani is waiting outside, Lord.'

The *Főnök* took a breath and sighed it out, feeling his chest sink beneath his clothes. A week had passed since his first conversation with József. When the horologist returned to the *tanács* townhouse three days later, he came without his son and with an explanation of what had happened.

Quite how József could have been so convinced of his son's guilt, without even any further investigation, had confused them all at first. But it was, in its way, particularly damning. That he had let the boy escape brought its own consequence, one that pained the *Főnök* almost more than he could bear. The events of recent days had been the most difficult he had faced, but the security of the *hosszú életek* rested with him. He *must* remain dispassionate.

Sitting at the great table in the *tanács* chamber, the *Főnök* turned first to his right and then his left, meeting the eyes of the two elders beside him. Both wore the official horsehair head-pieces of office. He felt the weight of the periwig atop his own head. It was not a pressure that comforted him. 'Are we in complete agreement, then?'

Pakov, to his right, cleared his throat. 'We must do this, Lord. I feel for the boy, naturally, but it is not just tradition that demands our intervention. Dangerous forces are lining up against us. Public opinion is shifting. We act not to punish the crimes of a single son, but to protect the lives of all.'

'The greater good,' the *Főnök* muttered. He held out his hands before him, eyes tracing the network of veins, the liver spots, the age. How he hated this. How long had he served? And all of it meaningless if he failed now to navigate safe passage through the carnage Balázs Lukács had strewn in his wake.

He took a long breath, feeling the air filling his chest, listening to it rasp into his lungs, as if through dusty corridors and into forgotten catacombs.

To a chamber guard, he said, 'Send him in.'

The door opened and Balázs Jani, first son of Balázs József, stepped into the room. He was dressed sombrely. Black suit, dark shirt. Still not quite a man, his eyes betrayed his feelings:

silver flashes, green flecks. Fear, perhaps, tinged with anger; shame.

Jani approached the table, hands by his sides. He bowed his head. 'Lord. My lords.'

The *Főnök* strained to his feet and held out his hand.

Jani's eyebrows raised. He stared at the proffered hand for several seconds. Then he moved forward, bent and kissed it.

The *Főnök* took his seat. 'Jani, I am glad you have come.'

'You called me, Lord. What else would I do?'

'Of course, of course.'

'This is about my—' he caught himself. 'About the *kirekesztett*.'

The *Főnök* nodded. 'Yes, Jani. That is correct.'

'You asked my father to bring the *kirekesztett* to judgement. He failed to comply with your wishes. Lu— the *kirekesztett* . . . has fled.'

'We know that. Your father has told us what happened.'

'And now my father is to be judged.' A tear appeared on Jani's cheek. It seemed to anger the young man. His jaw clenched.

'Your father is a good man. Do not forget that. He has made a grave error, one that cannot easily be excused. But there is a graver matter here. More at stake. I wish to talk to you about that.'

Jani raised a hand and wiped away the tear. His face was set, determined. He gave a brisk nod.

The *Főnök* continued. 'When I first spoke to your father, we had only first reports of what happened in Buda. Since then, we have gathered more information. The accused boy has been interviewed. The additional details he provided lend credence to his story. The girl, after questioning, has corroborated it. I'm sorry to tell you this, Jani, but the *ördög* who raped Krisztina Dorfmeister was your brother.'

The young man bowed his head. 'I know. Like my father, I knew it the moment I heard.'

'So you also know what must be done.'

'His blood must be removed from the line.'

The *Fõnök* stared at Jani, studying him closely. 'And someone, as a consequence, must be sent to complete that task.'

Jani frowned. 'You're not suggesting that I—'

Pakov, to the right of the *Fõnök*, lurched forwards and banged the table with his fist. 'You *presume* to instruct the *Örökös Fõnök*?' he shouted.

'No. Of course not! I did not mean—'

'Enough!' The *Fõnök* held up his hand. 'I will not have this degenerate into a brawl. Jani, you will listen and you will obey. If you do not, we will have no choice but to rule against the entire Balázs family.

'The evidence before us is enough to rule *in absentia*. The *kirekesztett* formerly known as Balázs Lukács is cast out. His blood will be laid to rest. Your father has failed at his task. As the eldest son, that task now passes to you. You will hunt down the *kirekesztett* and bring him our justice. Do so, and the honour of your family will be restored. Until then, Jani, we have no choice. Your *végzet* judgement is suspended. You are refused rights to continue your courtship of the Zsinka girl. You will not see her, speak to her, communicate with her or her family in any way. Your brother Izsák is too young to aid you. Nevertheless, his future rights of *végzet* are equally revoked until this deed is done.'

The *Fõnök* leaned forward in his seat. Jani's face had blanched, eyes flickering in disbelief from face to face. 'Balázs Jani, do you understand the obligation you have been served by your *Fõnök*?'

Jani closed his eyes, opened them. The green flecks had chased the silver away. He pulled himself erect. 'I understand, Lord. And I obey. The *kirekesztett* will receive your justice. I will stand before you again and you will return to my family the honour this *ördög* has stolen.'

'I pray that is so, Jani. Know that we do this not out of spite, nor out of punishment, but out of duty.' He turned to the men who flanked him. 'Gentlemen, we have ruled. The *hosszú élet* known as Balázs Lukács is no more. From this day, until our justice is served, the disgraced *kirekesztett* son will be known as Jakab.'

CHAPTER 11

Snowdonia

Now

After her encounter with Gabriel at the lake, Hannah hurried back to the farmhouse. She sent her daughter to feed Moses, checked on Nate, and quickly returned outside. Slate clouds still tumbled towards the valley from the mountains. The air was heavy with the electric scent of ozone.

Unlocking the Discovery, Hannah slid behind the steering wheel and pulled the door shut. The 4x4's familiar battered cosiness was comforting, its muted strength reassuring. Until she remembered the blood.

The passenger seat was soaked with it, the grey upholstery stained brown where it had dried, and a sticky black where it had pooled so thickly it had still not fully congealed. It made her ill to look at it and she averted her eyes. Nate should have died in this car. How her husband still lived, she could not explain. How *anyone* could lose that much blood and cling to life was beyond her understanding. All she could do was thank God that Nate *had* clung on.

Hannah leaned over the ruined passenger seat and hooked the binoculars out of the door cavity. Crawling on to the back seats, she pointed them out of the rear window and raised the rubberised rims to her eyes.

The lake emerged out of a blur. She panned the binoculars

across its surface. No boat rocked on its waters now. No uninvited visitors fished its depths. Sweeping around, she spotted the rowing boat on the far shore, pulled up on to the stony beach and slewed over on its side. Its oars had gone. She could see no sign of Gabriel. Hannah scouted the rest of the valley, angling the binoculars at the slopes. No one lurked in the trees that she could see.

Hearing the sound of an engine, she shifted her position and lowered the glasses as a battered Defender drove around the corner of the farmhouse. A steel trailer trundled behind it. Sebastien. As his vehicle approached, Hannah opened the back door of the Discovery and jumped down on to gravel.

The old man parked and climbed out. 'Going to rain again,' he said, looking up at the clouds. 'Least it might keep the cold off us for a while. How's our patient?'

'Just like you said he'd be. Stiff, in pain, unable to move. But alive.'

Sebastien grunted. 'That's the main thing. I've brought you groceries. As much diesel as I could. Wood for the fire.'

'You're an angel from heaven, Seb.'

His emerald eyes appraised her for a moment, then a grin lit his face. 'An angel of death, maybe. I brought ammunition too.'

Hannah helped him carry the boxes of groceries into the house: vegetables, milk, bread, crumpets, cheese, fruit. She eyed a huge slab of Cadbury's chocolate. Lastly, Sebastien handed her two freshly shot ducks, which she hung on a hook outside.

In the kitchen, she put a kettle on the stove and busied herself putting away the groceries while Sebastien introduced himself to Leah. The girl was hesitant at first, until he got down on all fours and taught her how to make Moses roll over and bare his stomach for a rub.

On the sofa, Nate watched them play, eyes heavy with fatigue. Hannah handed him a mug of tea, smoothing his hair as he drank it. 'We met someone on our walk,' she said. When both men looked up sharply, she indicated with a flick of her head that they should talk carefully in front of Leah. 'Just now, on the lake.'

Sebastien moved to the window.

'He's gone,' she said. 'He was in a rowing boat. Had a couple of fishing rods with him.'

'What did he look like?' the old man asked.

'Tall, curly black hair. Irish accent.'

'Gabriel.'

Hannah sagged with relief. 'You know him. He said he lived across the valley. Comes down here sometimes to fish, and isn't very good at it.'

'I've bumped into him a few times. He keeps horses on his smallholding. Sociable fellow, always cracking jokes. Irritating as hell.'

'I wouldn't say that. But we don't want him around here all the same.'

'What did you talk about?'

'Not much. I gave him pretty short shrift. Told him he'd better find another lake to fish.'

'Good. Gabriel's harmless enough. Give him half a chance, though, and he'll be over here poking his head into things that don't concern him. Now, let's get to work.'

While Leah took the dog into the living room, they checked Nate's dressings. His stitches had held, and the wounds looked free of infection. They cleaned them again with swabbing alcohol and applied fresh bandages.

Outside, as raindrops began a slow beat on the car roofs, they unloaded logs and brought them inside, stacking them by the fireplaces in the kitchen, living room and master bedroom. They unhooked the trailer and wheeled it to one of the outbuildings. Lifting out a full drum of diesel, they rolled it inside and filled the generator's reservoir.

Noticing that Sebastien was becoming breathless, she forced him to sit on an empty crate, knocking away his protests. They watched the raindrops fall with gathering pace as wind began to stir the trees across the valley.

'I brought you something,' Sebastien said. He dug into the pocket of his Barbour. When he removed his hand he was holding a dragon-shaped brooch. Its scales were red enamel set into gold.

Hannah gasped when she saw it. She took it from him and turned it over in her hands. 'This is my mother's,' she said, wonderingly. 'I thought it was lost.'

'Your father left it with me once. Said he didn't want to carry it around any more. That perhaps one day, if you ever needed my help, it might persuade you to trust me.'

Hannah slid her fingers over the bumps of the dragon's enamelled scales. She looked up to see the old man watching her. 'I do trust you, Seb. I don't know what would have happened if you hadn't been here.'

The lines of his face creased. 'You would have coped. You've been doing it all your life. You'll go on doing it.'

'I don't feel like I'm coping.'

'I can see that. But you got Nate and Leah here safely. They're alive thanks to you, so don't forget it. This might seem an impossible situation, but you're surviving, Hannah. You all are. There'll be an end to this. We need to get your husband back on his feet. But then you'll move on.'

'I've been thinking about that. There's another place. I need to make a few arrangements first but it's safe, really safe. I set it up years ago. There's no link back. Not even my father knows about it. But it's a long trip. And until Nate's ready to travel, we'll have to sit things out here.'

Sebastien smiled. 'See? Just what I said.'

Hannah dropped the brooch into her pocket. She ran her fingers through her hair, stared at the concrete floor. 'My father—'

'Don't torture yourself, Hannah. You don't know. I don't know. Maybe we'll find out, maybe we never will. Charles prepared himself years ago. He loved you – loves you, I mean.'

'Don't write him off,' she said.

'I won't. But you need to accept—'

Hannah stood up and stuffed her hands into the pockets of her jeans. 'Let's go inside.'

That afternoon, she taught Leah how to prepare the waterfowl Sebastien had brought them, immersing the birds in boiling water before plucking feathers, cutting off heads and feet and removing organs, entrails and crop.

As the clouds purpled and the day surrendered its light, Hannah cooked a dinner of roasted duck, dauphinoise potatoes, green beans and thick buttered slabs of granary bread.

Because Nate could not move from the sofa, Sebastien cleared the circular table in the kitchen and laid it with an odd assortment of cutlery, dinner mats and glassware. He built up the fire from the restocked log pile, lit two candles, opened a dusty bottle of Cabernet Sauvignon and helped Hannah dish up four plates of food. While Nate, head propped behind cushions, fed himself from a tray balanced on his chest, Hannah sat with the others at the table.

Over dinner, Sebastien entertained Leah with folk tales. Hannah was thankful to him. She felt sapped of energy after a day caring for her husband, talking and playing with her daughter, and making plans. She had made a few calls that afternoon, in preparation for their move to the hideaway in southern France. She wanted to put as much distance, and as many obstacles, between Jakab and her family as possible. Not for the first time that day, Hannah caught herself thinking about her father and wondering where he was, whether he was alive, whether she would ever see him again. It was agonising – the not-knowing – but she forced herself to bury those thoughts. She could not allow herself to lose focus, to lose sight of her ultimate responsibility: keeping her daughter and her husband safe.

After dinner, Sebastien allowed Leah to fill a bowl with leftovers so that Moses could feed. Shortly after that, Hannah took the girl upstairs, filled the bath with hot water and scrubbed her until her skin glowed. In the master bedroom, she tucked Leah under the covers.

'Sebastien's funny, isn't he, Mummy?'

'Yes, darling. He's a very sweet man.'

'When I first saw him, I thought he was the Bad Man.'

Hannah stroked her hair. The quiet fear in her daughter's voice filled her with sorrow. What kind of childhood was she giving the girl, that the simple act of meeting a stranger created so much anxiety? If a parent's success was measured in the confidence they instilled in their children, she had failed utterly. Yet what was her alternative? Bring up Leah ignorant of the threat she faced? Grant her the happy childhood that she herself had craved, but leave the girl completely vulnerable if something did happen? Which was the greater betrayal?

'He's not the Bad Man, Leah,' she said. 'He's got a dog called Moses.'

'Daddy looks better.'

'Yes, he does. I think he's going to be all right.'

'Are *you* all right?'

The question ambushed her, blurred her vision. Clenching her jaw, Hannah forced a smile and pulled her daughter into an embrace. She buried her face into Leah's hair, wanting to lose herself in its clean youthful smell, yearning to be free of the decisions and the responsibilities she had to bear. After gripping Leah fiercely for some moments, she recovered herself and pulled away.

'It'll be OK, Mummy.'

Shame stole over her then, that she should sit here and accept assurances from a nine-year-old girl – that she would risk contributing to Leah's anxiety even as she sought to deflect it. 'Oh, will it now?' she replied loftily, gathering herself. 'Not for you, scamp, unless you get off to sleep. Come on, I heard Seb say he'd teach you a few tricks tomorrow if you got a good night's rest. Now give me a kiss and lie down. I'll be back in a bit.'

Downstairs, she found Sebastien had washed up the dinner plates and had settled in an armchair opposite her husband. He held a glass of wine.

Nate looked up. 'Did she settle?'

'Eventually. She's scared stiff but she won't admit it. And I hate myself for what I've put her through. For all of this.'

'It's not your fault.'

Hannah sat on the floor by his sofa. 'It's not her fault either. This . . . we have to stop this, Nate.'

'We will.' He reached out a hand and she took it. When he squeezed her fingers she was relieved to feel his renewed strength.

Hannah leaned forwards and touched her brow to his. 'Oh, Nate, will we? Really?'

'You couldn't do more than you're doing, Han. I know you feel like this is too much, that you're powerless, but I've never seen anyone stronger. You saved me. Christ, you saved us all. I'm meant to be your Tarzan here, and you pretty much slung me over your shoulder and walked out of the jungle.' He grinned. 'If I hadn't lost a couple of pints of blood, I'd probably be blushing.'

Suddenly she was laughing. Laughing and kissing him, feeling energised by both his conversation and the rush of love she felt for him. No matter how difficult their situation, Nate knew with uncanny precision the exact words needed to steer her out of her dejection, pick her up, dust her down and set her back on her feet. She loved him for so many things. Right now, his innate understanding of her, his ability always to know what to do or say to lift her, was the lifebuoy holding her above the water.

And then, breaking the spell between them, she remembered they were not alone, and that Sebastien was sitting at the table watching them. Laughing this time with embarrassment, Hannah found that she was the one blushing. 'Sweet talker,' she said, getting to her feet and slapping him on the arm. 'Sorry Seb, we're like a couple of teenagers over here.'

The old man grinned. 'Want me to separate you?'

'How about you pour me a glass of wine instead.'

'Gladly.'

On the table, her phone started ringing.

Sebastien hesitated, one hand on the wine bottle, looking down at the black rubber-sheathed phone vibrating across the table. The old man scanned the read-out, and then turned to Hannah.

When she caught his expression, she felt her stomach twist with dismay. He wore a haunted look that she could not decipher. She snatched up the phone. The screen displayed a single word: *Dad*.

Hannah was unprepared for the explosion of emotion that detonated inside her. She could not think properly, could not for a moment even remember how the phone worked. Desperate, she fumbled with it, nearly dropped it, finally activated it, and, gasping, aching, felt her voice crack as she asked, 'Dad?'

Silence on the other end of the line. Then, 'Hannah. Oh thank God.'

Her father's voice.

Hannah's sobs came in shuddering, heaving breaths. Tears streamed down her face. She sagged to the floor, bending over, pressing the phone to her ear, her forehead to the flagstones as she repeated her father's name over and over. It was a long time before she calmed enough to hear his soothing sounds, hushing her.

'Where are you?' she asked. 'What happened? I thought you were dead.'

'There's a lot to tell. But I'm fine, Hannah. I'm OK. That's the main thing for now. I had to stay out of touch for a while. I won't tell you where I am. It's best you don't know. There was . . . it was a mess, Hannah.' She heard strain in her father's voice, a note she had never heard before. 'Such a mess.'

'Where's Jakab?'

'Gone. Dead. He's finally dead. That part of it is finished. But the police are crawling all over the place. They're looking for me. But you escaped. That's the main thing. You escaped and it's all over. Are you hurt?'

'No, I'm fine. Really. I'm good.'

'Where are you now? Is Nate OK?'

'Where are we?'

Sebastien's fingers found her shoulder and squeezed so painfully that she jerked backwards. Hannah stared up into the old man's face, into eyes blazing with emerald fire. She glanced over at Nate, who wore a matching expression of horror. And then her stupidity suddenly dawned on her, her relief at hearing her father's voice blinding her to the darker possibilities.

After all these years, had she learned nothing?

'Hannah?'

'I'm still here, Dad. What . . .' She forced herself to think. 'What was the name of your friend at the university, the twitchy one who was always talking folklore and clapping his hands and getting on everyone's nerves?'

'Hannah, what's that got to do with anything?'

'Dad, please. Answer the question.'

'You mean Beckett? Why?'

She closed her eyes at his answer, but when she opened them she saw Sebastien shaking his head and gesturing at her to continue. It had been a weak question. A soft validation. 'I met one of your old friends yesterday. He gave me something. Something you bought Mum a long time ago. Do you remember?'

A crackle of static on the line. 'Hannah, I gave away so many things. I know you need to know it's me. What can I tell you?'

She could feel pain beginning to constrict her throat, her

hope turning to grief. 'You must remember this, Dad. You bought it for her on the holiday we had in Berne. Please, Dad. *Please.*'

'Hannah, love. It's been such a difficult twenty-four hours. I'm exhausted. Tell me where you are. Let me come to you. It's over, Hannah. You don't need to be frightened any more. Jakab is dead.'

With an awful wrenching sorrow that originated at her core, radiated out through her limbs and flooded her head, she realised that the voice on the other end of the phone was not the father she loved, not that man at all, but a despicable impostor who had wreaked destruction on her family, who had tried to murder her husband, had tried to supplant him and slide into her life like an invisible cancer, poisoning everything he touched.

'What have you done with my father, you *sick bastard*?'

Silence now.

On the phone. In the room.

Sebastien relaxed his grip on her shoulder, his face long with distress. Nate slid off the sofa to his knees. He reached out to her.

When the voice returned, it had lost all resemblance to her father's. 'You know, that's what I call some unbelievably bad luck. Years waiting to talk to you, and we get off on the wrong foot straight away.' Jakab paused. 'I hold my hands up. That was a crass approach and I apologise. It's probably nerves on my part. Stage fright, if you like. Easier to hide behind a persona than to bare one's soul. I'm really not the monster you think I am. I just wanted to talk to you unencumbered by all these complications, all this . . . *history.*'

She realised she was still kneeling on the floor, and jumped to her feet. Her grief boiled into rage. She needed to stand, to fight. 'Where is he?'

Jakab laughed. 'Hannah, please. Give me some credit. Your father is fine. It would be a rather unusual strategy, would it not, to attempt to ingratiate myself by causing your father harm before we even met.'

'It hasn't stopped you before.'

A sigh. 'Myths, Hannah. Untruths. You weren't there and you can't know. I've been taking good care of Charles. He's sitting in front of me even as I talk to you now.'

'Put him on.'

'With pleasure.'

A pause, and then her father's voice on the line. 'Hannah?'

'Dad?' If this really was her father, he sounded broken.

'I love you,' he said. 'Always. OK? Be brave. We know this is the end. Don't do it. Don't ask me. You won't know who talks next. I'll always be with you. Now, go.'

He was saying goodbye. He had decided this was the last time he would talk to her, and he was trying to remain dignified.

She clutched a hand to her mouth, pressing it over her lips, wondering why she did it. Such a pointless gesture.

Jakab's voice now. 'Hannah, please. Listen to me. I was serious in what I said. I'm not the monster you think. I'm not going to hurt him. I give you my word on that. This has gone on too long. I'm tired. I want to see you, yes. I want to talk to you. But I don't want to take anyone's place. It's too late for that, and it never would have worked for long anyway. I'll keep your father safe. All I ask is this: meet me. Just you, and just me. Anywhere you want. Out in the open. You name the place. Just let me see you once. Talk. Explain. There have been so many untruths, I don't blame you for being confused.'

'You attacked Nate. Where's the untruth in that?'

'He *shot* me. What did you want me to do? Stand there and let him put another bullet in me? Come on, Hannah. I was protecting myself. I never intended to kill him. Is he OK? Did he survive?'

'Put my father back on.'

'Can we talk? Meet?'

'Put my father back on. Let me talk to him, talk freely to him. Grant me that, and then we'll see. Prove to me that I can trust you.'

'I can't ask for more than that. Here's your father.'

Charles's voice again. 'Hannah, I told you. Please don't do this.'

'Dad, I know what I'm doing.' Her voice trembled. She fought to contain her emotions. 'Do you remember the Christmas you built me the doll's house?'

'I'll never forget.'

'Do you remember what happened?'

'The paint hadn't dried and we ruined your dress, the carpet, my trousers, and your mother's vase in the hall.'

'Do you remember how much we laughed?' She heard his soft sigh. He already sounded so far away. So unattainable now.

She strove to remain lucid through her grief. 'Dad, do you remember what I told you?'

'Yes.'

'That you were the best dad in the world, and how much I loved you for spending all that time making something especially for me.'

'I remember.'

Now she had accepted that this was the last time they would ever talk, Hannah wanted to share a final memory with him. It was the only gift she could give – the snapshot of a perfect moment together.

'I meant it then and I mean it now,' she told him. 'Dad, I love you so much.'

'I love you too, darling. I'm so sorry.'

'Don't be sorry. Never sorry. Don't you dare apologise. What you did, what you've done. You've saved us. All of us. It's down to you. We're here because of you. I love you. For that, for everything.'

'Time to say goodbye, love.'

'I know.' She cried out. 'Oh, Dad.'

'Say it, Hannah.'

'I love you. Goodbye.'

Hannah hurled the phone across the room and collapsed into Nate's waiting arms.

CHAPTER 12

Keszthely, Hungary

1874

The sun was dissolving into liquid fire over the hills behind Keszthely as Jakab left his hotel room and walked down to the shore of Lake Balaton to meet Erna Novák. It was nine o'clock, a midsummer evening, and the day had been hot and humid. Now, at its end, a breeze began to stir, tickling at Jakab's sweat-damped clothes and drying the perspiration on his forehead.

Coming to the edge of the lake after a short walk through Keszthely's streets, he stared out across Balaton's water. Its vastness still awed him, even eight weeks after first seeing it. To the south-east he could faintly see the far shore; to the north-east the lake stretched virtually to the horizon.

He had spent much of the day in his hotel room, seeking refuge from the heat, grateful for the breeze that blew in off the water and chased the curtains around his sill. From his balcony view, with the sun overhead, the lake had reflected a shade of turquoise so vivid it lifted Jakab's soul. Now, as that same sun drew blood from the clouds and sank towards the horizon, the water shed its colour and became instead a fathomless bowl of mercury.

He could feel his senses fizzing in anticipation of the girl's arrival. The light mottled and faded, and the singing of the crickets intensified, filling the air with their chitter. He fancied he could smell the sap of the pine trees growing on the hills to the west. Their scent mingled with the mineral smell of the lake, the citrus tang of his cologne, and the underlying sourness of his sweat.

Could it have really been two months since he had arrived in Keszthely? Much of his fondness for the place was doubtless due to the girl. But even discounting her influence he was sure he had never experienced such peace in his surroundings, such comfortable anonymity.

After leaving Gödöllö, he had taken a steamer south, following the Danube through Serbia and between Romania and Bulgaria, before realising that by trailing the river he made pursuit needlessly easy for anyone who wished to do so. Abandoning *a Duna* altogether, he travelled north to Bucharest and crossed the mountains back into Hungary, arriving at the natural spectacle of Lake Balaton in time for summer, and Erna Novák.

As the last red sliver of sun disappeared behind the hills, the waters of the lake darkened and a colder breeze seemed to break around him.

'Jakab?'

He turned, and there she was behind him. So powerful was her effect that his breath came in a rush, a flower blossoming in his chest. Here she stood, in rough linen shift dress and leather sandals, face and arms tanned from the sun, confident of the feelings she stirred in him but lacking any plurality, any motive. Her hair fell unbound about her face, the naturally dark tresses bleached to honey by the sun. Chocolate brown eyes, striated with olive and caramel, flashed over him and set his heart pounding.

Jakab pulled her towards him, pressing his lips against her mouth. He entwined his fingers into hers. 'The sun is only just setting. Let's walk along the shore a while. I want to—'

'Jakab, wait. There's something I must tell you.'

He smiled. 'Tell me later. We have the whole evening ahead

of us. I have a surprise for you.' He let go of her hand and took her arm. Her skin was warm and deliciously moist against his fingers. 'Come on, it's this way. I promise it'll be worth it.'

For a moment she allowed him to pull her along the shore. Then she slowed, her face creased with lines of worry. 'Jakab, no. Please. I think this is important.'

'What is it?'

Erna searched his face with her eyes. 'Strangers. This afternoon in my father's tavern. Asking questions about you.'

Jakab felt as if someone had poured iced water down his spine. 'What strangers? How many?'

'Two of them. One tall and broad. A few years older than you, perhaps. Dark hair. The other man was fifty or so. Scarred face, dangerous eyes.'

Trying to keep his expression empty of emotion, not wanting her to see his alarm, he guided her along the trail through the long grasses. 'What questions?'

'Jakab, are you in trouble?'

'No, of course not. Tell me, what questions were they asking?'

'They were talking to my father when I came back from the *piac*. Asking him questions about you. About how long he had known you, how long you had known me. Where they could find you.'

'Did they see you?'

'I don't think so.'

'Did they say who they were?'

'I wasn't there when they arrived. From what I heard, they made out they were old friends of yours. But there was something about them. Especially the older one. Who are they, Jakab?'

Jakab. When he had heard about the *kirekesztett* name the *tanács* had given him he had adopted it as readily as his new status. It had been a prideful and indulgent act, a childish thumbing of the nose. Far better to have taken a name with no connection to his past life. He knew the *hosszú életek* hunted him, intent on forcing him to answer for his actions in Budapest. Why had he made it any easier for them?

When he thought back to the events leading to his departure from Gödöllö, he did not recognise the person he had been. That time held dreadful memories, of deeds for which he now felt shame. Whatever pressures he had faced, whatever conflict had raged within him, nothing could excuse his treatment of Krisztina. In Bucharest he had read in a newspaper that Márkus Thúry had hanged. Jakab regretted that too, although not nearly as much as his treatment of the girl. He had supplanted Márkus in the belief that it was a short cut to her seduction. Still scarred by his experience at the *végzet*, he'd been unable to see that Krisztina's refusal had not been a rejection of him, but of Márkus. At the time, that refusal had blinded him with rage, and Jakab cringed at his recollection of its consequences.

He had been running ever since. Initially, because he was shamed by the memories of what he had done; later, out of necessity. In Belgrade, he had chanced upon a *hosszú élet* merchant who told him of the scandal in Budapest and how the *tanács* hunted their own. When the merchant deduced his identity, Jakab killed him. He regretted that too, briefly, until he was almost caught by his pursuers; the trauma of that experience quickly erased any remorse.

He had known for weeks that he had lingered too long in Keszthely. But what could he do? By then he had met Erna Novák. For the first time, he had found someone he loved, someone who reciprocated that feeling, and he could not abandon her here. *Would* not. Even though he had known her only two short months, the prospect of life without her was already too bleak to contemplate.

'Jakab? Please, tell me. They're your people, aren't they.'

Sharing with her the truth of his lineage had been the biggest risk he had taken so far. The revelation had frightened her at first; *hosszú életek* were a near myth to most. She had asked him to show her, and he had complied. Incredibly, her fear had surrendered to wonder and she accepted it, accepted him – just one of the many reasons he would not give her up. 'Yes,' he said. 'They're probably *hosszú életek*.'

'And they're not your friends.'

He laughed, a hard bitter sound. 'Unlikely.'

'What do they want with you?'

'Erna, I can't tell you that. I've told you so much, shared all I can with you, but you must trust me on this. Do you love me?'

'You know I do.'

'Then believe me when I say it is far better that you do not know.'

They had arrived at a secluded part of the shore, where a rise hid the town at their backs. On the sloping grass below them lay a blanket. Upon it was a wicker basket covered with a cloth. Inside, he knew, was bread, cheese, cold meat, slabs of chocolate. A bottle of wine and two glasses stood next to the basket.

Erna's eyebrows rose. 'Did you do this?'

Jakab shrugged. He had planned a romantic evening, and her news had soured all of that.

'Oh, Jakab. What are you going to do?'

He forced a smile. 'Well, for a start, I'm going to open that bottle. Will you have a glass?'

Curled together on the blanket, they ate the food and sipped at the wine. As the skies darkened and the crickets sang, they held each other and stared out across Balaton's waters.

'I'm going to have to go away for a while,' he said.

Erna's body tensed. 'I knew you would say that. Is there no other way?'

'Not right now.'

'But you're *hosszú élet*. Can't you just . . . disguise yourself? Change?'

'It's not as simple as that. There's no change I could make that would stop them recognising who I am eventually. It's difficult to explain, but they'd know.' He put down his wine glass, took her hands and turned to face her. 'You should go home. I need to find out more about these strangers. Now. Tonight.'

'Promise me you'll be careful.'

'Of course. Can you meet me later?'

'Where?'

'The woods behind your father's tavern. When you hear me whistle, come down.'

She kissed him. 'I'll see you again, won't I?'

He felt his stomach twist at the uncertainty in her voice, and wrapped his arms around her.

Nightfall brought cooler air and a breeze that danced through Keszthely's streets. Jakab followed Erna as she crossed the square alongside Kossuth Lajos Utca, weaving his way through throngs of people seeking respite from the heat.

Her father's tavern stood on a street in a cluster of commercial premises, flanked by a general store and an apothecary. As Erna approached the entrance, Jakab hung back, watching from an alley behind a row of houses.

Outside the tavern, groups of men sat at rickety tables, drinking and smoking. He heard laughter, the clink of glasses, the buzz of conversation. He felt a flash of anger at the leers Erna drew as she walked to the tavern door and went inside, but he stilled his body. Now was not a time to allow emotion to distract him.

They were here. He could feel them.

Whether it was a previously dormant *élet* sense that alerted him, he did not know. No disguise, he knew, could ensure invisibility from his compatriots for ever, but they would still need to meet him face to face to confirm he was the one they sought. *This* feeling was something different, an indescribable pull towards the building, a vague itch behind his eyes. He shook his head against its effects, disturbed and confused.

The front door of the tavern opened and a man came out, his tall frame silhouetted by the candlelight that shone from the windows. Jakab felt a shiver of awareness. The man placed a cigar between his lips and when he struck a match, his face was illuminated in its flare: square jaw, eyebrows like tangled hedgerows, dark locks shiny with grease, a crooked scar that ran from the left corner of his mouth across his cheek. Jakab had never seen him before, but that strange sense was screaming at him now, insisting that he had found one of his pursuers. The man lit his cigar, puffed out smoke. He slouched by the entrance of the tavern, staring into the night.

In the alley, Jakab remained wreathed in shadows, but he felt the prickle of the stranger's eyes nonetheless.

Fear rolled through him. Relations between the *hosszú életek* and Budapest's ruling classes had always been fractious, and he knew his actions the previous year had soured those relations further. The *tanács* needed to appease their critics by making an example of him. If he were caught, his life would be forfeit.

From a gap between two tenements, another figure appeared. It approached the first man and conferred with him. The two talked for a few minutes. Jakab edged closer. All of a sudden, the newcomer stiffened and turned towards the alley. For the briefest instant, light spilling from the tavern windows shone on his face.

Jani.

Jakab felt his heart quicken. His blood surged through his arteries. His stomach cramped. His head began to pound.

Of course.

They had sent his brother after him. The discovery outraged him, but it was an obvious move, now he thought about it. While his fellow *hosszú életek* could identify him up close, tracking him at a distance presented far more of a challenge.

But a relative, a *brother* – that was different. Jani had the *vérérzet*, the blood tie that allowed him to intuit his brother's whereabouts in the same way a diviner found water.

Until now, Jakab had thought he lacked that particular gift: just one more example of his stunted growth. But this explained the nagging *watched* feeling he had experienced earlier. His own ability was clearly meagre compared to Jani's, who had managed to follow him here from however many hundreds of miles away.

He watched, mouth dry of moisture, as his brother led the scar-faced stranger back into the tavern. What had he done to deserve betrayal like this? What had they promised Jani in return for bringing him back to Budapest?

Jakab had been planning to kill his pursuers tonight. How, though, could he take Jani's life? And, just as distressing – how could he ever hope to be free, ever hope to make a life with Erna, if he did not? He had no idea how long they would look for him. A year had passed since the *végzet*. Would they still be looking for him another year from now? Another ten?

With Jani out of sight, comforted by the knowledge that the *vérérzet* manifested as a vague directional pull rather than a bright beacon, Jakab emerged from the alley and followed a route between the buildings to the woods behind the tavern.

Erna arrived minutes after his low whistle from the cover of the trees. He watched her move through the long grass, the moon dusting her shoulders with milky light. The realisation that this might be the last he saw of her for some time distressed him more than he could bear. She spotted him lurking at the edge of the wood and when she reached him, flinging her arms around his neck, he felt hot tears sting his eyes as he embraced her.

They stayed that way for a while, motionless except for the slow rise of their chests, listening as a thousand crickets mourned them.

'I saw them,' he said.

'You did?'

'You were right to tell me. You probably saved my life.'

'What will you do?'

'I have to go. I have to end this. Otherwise we will never have any peace.'

'Is it safe? Will you be all right?'

'I'll be all right if you say that you'll wait for me.'

'What are you going to do? How long will you be gone?'

'I don't know exactly. But I won't be long, I promise you that. I don't think I *could* stay away from you for long.' He hesitated. 'These are hardly the circumstances I'd imagined, but I brought you down to the lake tonight so I could ask you to be my wife.'

Tears brimmed in her eyes now too. 'Whoever those people at the tavern are, whatever they want with you, you know my answer, Jakab.'

'You'll wait for me, then?'

She kissed him, and he felt her desperation in the press of her lips. 'Why must I? Let me come with you.'

'Erna, no.'

'Why not?'

'There are things I must do, things I would protect you from. Your place is here until I can finish this. I'll come back. Soon. When I do, I'll speak to your father. And we'll do this the right way.'

'Promise me.'

Jakab kissed her again, her tears wet against his cheek. He could feel his anger rising, a cold fury that made him clench his fists at the injustice of what they faced. The *hosszú életek* had cast him out and he had gone willingly, yet they were not content to leave him alone. Along these shores he had found happiness, and now they interfered with that too, jeopardising everything he held precious.

For now, he would run. He was unprepared for a confrontation. He needed time to plan. But he would return to Erna, and he would kill anyone that got in his way.

In his pocket, he felt the weight of the gold ring he had bought her, pressing against his leg. It seemed to mock him.

Jakab was sitting in a restaurant near the Festetics Palace when he next saw Erna Novák. It was spring, and he had been back in Keszthely two days. This was a different town to the one he had left baking under the hot eye of a summer sun. Now, cool air rolling down from the mountains slid across the warmer waters of Lake Balaton, rising into a mist that draped the entire area like a shroud.

The mist brought a strange serenity to Keszthely. Sounds were muted, so that when a dog barked or a church bell rang – coming as if from the bottom of a well – Jakab found it impossible to pinpoint its direction.

He had known that returning would feel like a homecoming, and the mist unfurled its own welcome, a protective anonymity that gathered him in its arms and cradled him with its peace.

How he needed that peace. He could not be sure exactly how long he had been away, but his experiences in between leaving Keszthely and returning already seemed a troubled memory. How long had he run, moving from one town to the next, leaving in the depths of night, taking random train journeys, crossing rivers and mountains, doubling back?

When he had fled the Lake Balaton region, he had not forged much of a plan. He told himself to get as far ahead of Jani as possible, and find somewhere he could prepare for his arrival. At the outset, the thought of harming his brother sickened him, but the further he travelled from Keszthely and Erna Novák, the less the prospect troubled him.

Even so, on those occasions when he did get far enough ahead, finding himself in some insipid town or village, he was unable to decide what to do when Jani caught up. Summer arrived, and still Jakab was no closer to returning to Keszthely. As that season slipped away, and then as autumn leaves surrendered to winter snow, he began to acknowledge that the challenge of killing two *hosszú életek*, one of whom could track him however many miles he put between them, was tormenting him so much that he was inventing excuses for his inaction. Rather than fighting back, he was finding more and more reasons to flee. Disgusted by his lack of resolve, he vowed to take the next opportunity that came along.

In Pozsony, he seized his chance. He reached the city knowing he had gained a few weeks on his pursuers. Renting an extravagantly large house in the Rusovce borough, Jakab played the role of an eccentric and introverted aristocrat. He paid for the services of a lawyer, who in turn paid for the services of a dubious yet reliable character called Alexej who spent all his time inside the house, watching each night for the approach of Jani and his accomplice.

It must have been February, or possibly March, when they finally appeared. Alexej woke him in the early hours. Two men, he whispered, had scaled the gates at the front of the house.

The first intruder approached the building's main entrance. The second crept round to the rear, climbing a wisteria vine to the first-floor balcony that overlooked the garden. Waiting in the master bedroom, enveloped in shadow, Jakab watched him swing over the balustrade and pad to one of the tall sash windows. Finding it unlocked, the intruder, still a faceless silhouette, lifted it open. Jakab stepped out of the darkness, pressed a Colt revolver to the man's forehead and pulled the trigger.

It was only in the flash from the gun's muzzle that he recognised Jani's startled eyes. His brother's head broke apart in the same instant. The thunder of that shot echoed around the house and ricocheted through Jakab's soul. He watched Jani's lifeless body pitch backwards over the balcony, landing in the shrubbery below.

Hours later, he would marvel at how easy – and how quick – that murderous act had been. But at the time, with the sharp stench of gunpowder in his nostrils, he found himself fascinated at the way the chips of Jani's skull glittered on the moonlit leaves of the rhododendrons below.

Staring down at his brother's corpse, thinking of all the history they had shared, he tried to summon grief. It seemed appropriate somehow. Yet all he could feel as he stood at the balustrade was emptiness. No guilt, no remorse. Not even any satisfaction. He was an empty vessel, a vacuum, devoid of emotion.

While Jakab knew there had never been any path back to his old life, he still understood that this was a watershed moment. The *tanács* would exhaust every means possible to find him now. What option, though, had they given him? Jakab had been content to walk away from the *hosszú életek* but they had insisted on following, had even resorted to the spectacular cruelty of setting one brother against another. He had felt no great love for Jani, had spent most of his life hating him, but the number of people in the world with whom he shared a history had just contracted and for that, if nothing else, he supposed he should feel sadness.

Alexej walked out of the darkened bedroom and joined Jakab on the balcony. 'The other one bolted when he heard the shot,' he said, peering over the rail at Jani's corpse. 'Want me to get rid of that?'

Jakab examined Alexej for a moment, considering whether to put a bullet in his head too. Instead, he placed a hand on the man's shoulder and nodded. Alexej had served him well, and he did not know when he might need his services again. Far better to keep acquaintances like that.

Jakab packed his bags quickly, jumped the wall at the end of the garden and left Pozsony the same night. It was one hundred miles to Keszthely by train and carriage, a journey that took him two days to travel. He booked a room near the lake and spent the first day walking its shores, thinking about the best way to alert Erna of his return. He ached for her as much now as he had outside her father's tavern when they had said their goodbyes. He still had the ring. Its weight in his pocket was a constant, insistent reminder.

Strange, but he discovered he was nervous at the prospect of seeing her again. He could not work out why. Almost, it seemed as if his time away from Erna – and his confrontation with Jani – had been the price fate demanded for his redemption. Jakab had lifted his chin and accepted the challenge, and now his mistakes in Buda could be forgotten. With Jani dead, the *tanács* would find it impossible to locate him. He would not be able to stay in Keszthely, but he still had money, certainly enough to buy a house far from here and raise a family with Erna in peace.

That evening he lay down on the rug in his hotel room and resurrected Márkus Thúry with a familiar flesh-searing agony that nearly split his teeth and set his heels drumming on the floor.

Afterwards he gorged himself on food and wine, crawling on to the bed to recover. A few hours later, settled in his borrowed face, he walked into her father's tavern. He sat at the bar all evening but Erna did not appear. Her father served him several times, sharing jokes and local news, but Jakab resisted the urge to enquire of her.

Now, a day later, sitting in a restaurant overlooking the palace, gazing out at the mist that hung over the town and beaded the windows, he studied a woman walking along the street and felt a jolt of recognition.

Jakab held his breath as she approached, placing his hands on the white tablecloth. The cutlery began to vibrate.

Erna.

There could be no doubt.

She looked different. Older, somehow. Thicker around the hips, heavier breasts. Her expression was distant and he was ashamed to find himself hunting for signs of pain in her features, some evidence of heartache. As she passed the windows she glanced inside and for a moment their eyes met. Erna smiled as she walked by, a simple courtesy for a briefly glimpsed stranger. And then Jakab noticed she was carrying an infant on her hip.

The sight confused him, stalling his thoughts. He glanced about the room, at the clock on the wall, at the silver teapot in front of him, trying to make sense of it. A startling thought occurred to him, but one he knew was impossible even as he considered it. They had been too careful, and the child too old, for it to be plausible.

Realising he was in danger of losing her to the mist, Jakab jumped up, overturning a vase and sending water cascading across the white linen. Cursing, he threw down some coins and ran outside to the street.

Erna had crossed the road towards the palace and was walking along an avenue of trees, their branches studded with green buds. He ran after her, shouting her name, laughing with jubilation.

Erna turned, and when she saw him approaching she hesitated and looked around her, as if hoping to see passers-by.

Panting, Jakab closed the last few yards.

'Do I know you?' she asked.

In his haste, he had forgotten the obvious. Instead of her betrothed standing before her, she saw a tanned and sweating Márkus Thúry. Not, he supposed, an attractive proposition. 'Erna, I'm sorry.' He grinned. 'It's me.'

'I'm afraid you have the advantage. Are you a friend of Hans's?'

'It's Jakab, Erna. *Your* Jakab. I promised you I'd be back. Here I am.'

Her eyes widened, and he was disconcerted to see a shadow of fear cross her face. She began to take a step backwards, noticed what she was doing, and stopped herself. Her chest rose and fell as she stared at him. 'Jakab?'

He opened his arms.

'What do you want?'

The question jolted him, the same way the look in her eyes

jolted him. 'What do I want? Erna, I'm back. It's done. I know this must be a shock for you, but—'

'A shock? How . . . Jakab. For a start, how do I know it's you? How do I know you're not one of those two *hosszú életek* that questioned my father that time?'

'It's *me*. Can't you hear it in my voice? I can prove it if you need me to. Not here. But you shouldn't need to see that. How many other men have taken you down to the shore to ask you to marry them?' He reached for her arms and when he touched her flesh she stiffened.

Erna gaped at him as if he had lifted away the top of a crypt and clambered out. 'What are you doing here, Jakab?'

Her reaction had transformed his elation into bemusement. 'I'm here for you. For us.'

On her hip, the young boy pointed a finger at him. 'Mama, who—'

Erna reached for his hand and hushed him.

Jakab stared at the infant. *What* had he just called her? 'Who's the boy?'

'Jakab, do you know how long you've been away?'

'Who's the *boy*, Erna?'

'I thought you were dead!'

He was shouting now. '*Erna*, WHO *IS* HE?'

The boy started crying. She pressed his face to her breast, soothing him. 'This is my son. This is Carl. I don't know what you think you're doing here, and I don't know why you suddenly decided to come back. What we had . . . it was a long time ago.'

'How can you say—'

She shook her head. 'I don't know what happened, where you went, what you've done, but you're not thinking clearly. It's been *years*. You can't just come back like this, out of the blue. It's cruel. I have a husband now, a family.'

He did not understand what she was saying, did not know how her words could be true. A slow horror was descending on him. The child was at least two years old. He had left Keszthely when? A year ago at most? Surely? He tried to count the months, even the seasons, and found himself staring at her, open-mouthed. He could not work out how long it had been.

Jakab felt something inside him threatening to rupture, and he braced himself against it. It felt like a dream was shattering, while he clutched at the broken shards.

No.

Furious, he turned his back on that thought.

She was in shock, that was all.

But she has a son!

He thought about her lying with another man and wanted to scream. 'Erna, I should have thought more about this before I came to you. I know that. This was a clumsy way to return. Let's start again. At the beginning, I mean. I—'

'Jakab, I have to go.'

'Wait, no. Don't say that. Don't just dismiss me like that. You said to me you'd wait.'

'I thought you were dead.'

'You said to me you'd wait!' He was shouting again, and she was backing away. He wanted nothing more than to reach for her and kiss her face. He resisted, clasping his hands together. This was the most precarious conversation of his life. 'Please. You have to talk to me. I . . . I've been away a long time. I hadn't realised how long, and I don't know why. Erna, I love you. You know that. I've been carrying that with me, undiminished, the entire time I've been gone. I know you love me too. Things may have happened since, life may have happened in between, but—'

'Jakab, I'm sorry, I can't listen to this now. I really do have to go. I have to feed Carl. I have to cook dinner for my husband.'

That word – *husband* – wounded him more than anything she had said so far – a pair of forge-heated tongs clamping on to his heart. 'Then meet me later. Tonight.'

'I can't do that.'

'Erna, I insist—'

Her face darkened. 'Careful with your tongue, Jakab. You lost the right to insist on anything a long time ago.'

He stumbled backwards, holding out his hands, feeling tears welling in his eyes. He looked up at the sky, shaking his head, then back at her. 'Please, I didn't come here to make you angry. I'm making a mess of this. I know it. But I'm half mad from seeing you again. Please, Erna, I beg you, meet me later. Let me explain.'

'Jakab, I can't, don't you see? I can't just walk out of the house at night to go and meet someone. I told you, I have a family, responsibilities, a man I love.'

'You loved me.'

She paused, and he sensed that his tears had softened her. She looked on him more gently, although her expression was so close to pity it wrenched him. 'Give me a few days,' she said. 'To arrange something. Then we'll talk.'

'That's all I want.'

She nodded. 'And Jakab – that's all you'll get. I've made a promise to someone. I've made vows, and neither you nor I can break them. Our time passed. I'm sorry it did. I waited for you for two years. Two *years*, Jakab. No clue that you were still alive, not a letter nor a message. Do you know how deeply I mourned you? No. You never will. To the northeast, a mile along the shore, there's an old boat shed with a wooden jetty; you can't miss it. I'll meet you there in three days. At dawn.'

'I understand.'

It was a lie. He did not understand at all.

Erna rearranged her son on her hip and walked away. He watched her until she was consumed by the mist.

Back in the town, he bought a newspaper and studied the date on it: 24th April, 1879.

He sat down on a wall and started working back.

Five years.

He had been away *five years*.

Jakab dropped the newspaper and moaned, holding his head in his hands. How had he let this happen? How could he have let *five whole years* go by without even realising, without even considering the consequences for his life back in Keszthely? She had said she waited two years for him. If she had met someone shortly after, and wed within the year, it explained the age of her boy.

Erna had a son. A husband. A life without him.

Despite all of that, despite everything she had said, he refused to believe it was too late. A love as intense as theirs came along only once. He would stake everything upon it. He had killed his own brother so that they could be together. When she discovered that, when she understood the extent of the commitment he had made to her, she would see sense.

It had been a shock, that was all. He could forgive her the harsh words she had spoken. He had handled their reunion badly. Once she accepted his reappearance into her life, she would see how hastily she had rejected him. She would regret her words. It would work itself out.

Jakab arrived, just as she requested, shortly before sunrise. So thick was the mist at this time of day he found it impossible to judge from which direction the sun would appear. He sat on a tree stump next to the wreckage of a rowing boat and waited, stomach tossing in anticipation.

The boat shed loomed, a single-storey wooden shell with a sagging roof and two wide doors at its front, one of which had collapsed into the weeds that surrounded it. Paint had peeled from the shed walls, and the suns of countless summers had warped and baked the silvered timbers beneath. Moss and lichen spotted the building's shaded side like a spreading cancer. The side facing the lake stood open to the elements. Long ago someone had removed the single door that had once slid forth

on oiled metal runners. Its opening led to a concrete launch
ramp. Next to it, a jetty thrust out into the water.

Erna emerged from the mist, hurrying down the grassy track
from the main road. He jumped up as she approached, opening
his mouth to greet her, but she shook her head vigorously and
held up her hands. 'No, Jakab, there is no time. You have to
go. Now. They're coming for you.'

He frowned. 'What are you talking about?'

'There's no time to explain. You have to get out of here *right
now*. Please, Jakab. I'm so sorry, I never meant for this to happen.
Your people. They know you are here. They're coming.'

He was finding it difficult to keep up with her. 'Is this a
trick?'

'A trick? Jakab, do you think I would trick you about
something like this?'

He stared, watching her eyes carefully. 'You seemed keen
enough to get rid of me three days ago.'

'For heaven's sake, what kind of woman do you think I am?'
She grabbed him by his coat sleeve. 'Come *on*. Don't go back
to the main road. Follow the shoreline northeast to Gyenesdiás.
You'll find passage from there. Don't come back to Keszthely.
Promise me, Jakab. Do you have money? Look, I brought you
this. It's not much, but it might help.'

Erna delved into her skirts and withdrew a handful of coins.
As she tried to press them on him, he flung her arm away,
suddenly furious. Coins tumbled from her fingers. Crying out,
she knelt in the dirt to gather them up.

'Do you think I need your peasant charity?' he snarled. 'How
do they know? How do you know they're coming for me?'

She snatched up the scattered coins. 'Jakab, please. *Please* just
trust me. Take the money. It's not a trick, I swear to you. After
everything we had, do you think I could betray you? Do you
think that badly of me?' She sobbed. 'You have no time. They'll
be here any minute.'

'Balázs Lukács! Balázs Jakab!'

At the sound of his given name, Jakab leaped away from her. The condensation in the air was even thicker now, a shifting veil that roiled around them, obscuring their surroundings and making it impossible to tell from which direction the voice came. Moisture clung to Jakab's coat, licked at his face and cheeks and hair.

'Balázs *Lukács*! Balázs *Jakab*!'

A male voice, jarringly effeminate. Jakab sensed the scorn in its challenge. He heard the accompanying bray of a horse. Twisting on the balls of his feet, he faced the track leading from the boat shed to the main road.

A shadow moved inside the mist. It darkened, coalescing into a horse and rider. The horseman wore a black wide-brimmed hat and a leather overcoat spattered with mud. His mount, an enormous grey stallion, blew steam from its nostrils and clattered great iron-shod hooves on the pebbles.

Raising his head, the rider examined Jakab with eyes that were cold yellow pools. Flecks of ivory and malachite sailed upon them. His skin had the pallor of a forest fungus and his albino hair was oiled and scraped into a ponytail. When he smiled, his face folded into cracks like the bark of a tree. Little humanity resided in his expression.

Fear erupted in Jakab, emptying his lungs and wicking the moisture from his throat. His feet anchored themselves to the ground. He knew who this man was, what he was, even though he had never met him.

The *Fönök*'s *Merénylő*.

Every seat of power had a creature like this: a beast sent to complete the distasteful assignments, the unpleasant tasks that were nonetheless vital to the maintenance of that power. The workload of this particular specimen seemed to have corrupted its very flesh.

'And here, then, Balázs,' the *Merénylő* began, in a high-pitched, sing-song voice, 'we arrive at the end of your road. You led us a merry dance.'

Jakab searched his surroundings, muscles twitching, mouth as dry as sawdust. Scrubland lay to his left, the boat shed and its wooden jetty to his right. More scrub on the far side of the ruined building, leading north along the shore towards Gyenesdiás. At his back, the rippling waters of the lake, quickly surrendering to mist.

Erna still knelt before him. She stared up at the rider, her mouth hanging open in dismay.

Jakab motioned to her. 'Get up.' Then, when she didn't respond, more urgently: 'Erna, get *up*. Now.'

Perhaps she detected the anxiety in his voice, his concern for her, because she scrabbled to her feet, backing away from the rider.

'Touching.' The *Merénylő* chuckled. He pulled a silk hand-kerchief from the pocket of his coat and dabbed at his upper lip. 'I take it you haven't raped this one yet then, Balázs.'

The scrub to his left provided the most promising escape route. The undergrowth was thick, tangled, and while he could pick his way through, a horse and rider would have more difficulty. He only needed twenty yards of distance before the mist swallowed him up. If he could just let Erna know his intention; he would not abandon her here with the *Főnök*'s assassin.

A crack sounded from the scrub, a dead branch snapping, just beyond the patch of ground he had been contemplating. As the bank of mist drifted and thinned, Jakab caught sight of a second rider navigating through the bracken towards him.

The newcomer looked up and grinned. His teeth were brown and rotten, his eyes flat. No *hosszú élet*, this one. Although from the look of him, almost as dangerous.

The *Merénylő* eased his heels into the grey's flanks and the animal took a step towards Jakab, its hooves clacking and scraping on the wet stones. 'You want to run. I understand that. I do believe you almost found the courage just then, until cowardice unmanned you.' The flecks of ivory in the assassin's eyes had faded, but his smile remained. 'I'm not going to stop you, Jakab. Not right away. This has been a long race. Far too long, and far too dull, most of the time. Let's make a little sport of it, shall we, now we're at its conclusion? We both know how this ends. I drag you kicking and screaming and bucking and biting all the way back to Buda, and whatever's left of you once we arrive we'll string up, eviscerate, boil, shred and feed to the wolves. How do you like the sound of that?'

'Erna. *Erna!*' A new voice, frantic and disembodied, broke through the mist.

Erna moaned, dropping her head. 'Hans, no. Why did you come?'

Out of the pillowy white crashed a young man. He was taller and slimmer than Jakab. Handsome, had his face not been pale and his eyes wide with panic. He skidded to a halt a few yards from the *Merénylő*, glanced at the riders, at Erna, and finally at Jakab. In his hands he clutched an axe, and now he beckoned with it. 'Erna, come here. Come away.'

Jakab put a hand on her shoulder. 'Don't move.'

Hans turned to the *Merénylő*, his expression accusatory. 'What is this? You said we would be safe. You said we could trust you.'

The *hosszú élet* assassin never took his mocking eyes from Jakab's face. 'What I *said*, woodsman, was that if you both stayed out of the way, you would not see any of us again. Yet here we are and I find first your wife and now you. I must say I hardly describe that as staying out of the way. Do you? Besides, I don't believe I've done anything to risk the safety of either your wife or your good self. I'm simply sitting here, on my horse, passing the time of day with a rapist and murderer who doesn't know he's dead yet. Why don't you go into town and spend some of that coin with which we so graciously rewarded you?' The *Merénylő*'s grin widened, but it never reached his eyes. They burned like twin suns, penetrating Jakab's mind, anticipating him, deriding him.

Jakab felt as if someone had battered him with an iron bar. Blood drained from his stomach. Tightening his grip on Erna's shoulder, he whispered, 'You *sold* me to them?'

She shook her head, trying to shrug off his hand. 'Jakab, no. That's not how it happened. Don't listen to him. He—'

'You thought you'd exchange me for a few pitiful handfuls of *coin*?'

The rush of emotion unbalanced him, his initial outrage eclipsed by an all-consuming grief. How could she have done this? Out of all the people he had ever known, to be betrayed by her . . . it was too shocking, too devastating, to contain in a single thought. He had thought she loved him, truly loved him, yet all this time she had been capable of betrayal as callous as this.

And what next? After all this was done, with him no doubt bound hand and foot and dragged through the mud behind the *Merénylő*'s horse, what was her plan? To return to her life shared with the simpleton standing beside the *hosszú élet* assassin? To return to her baby and her blood money and her snug little life?

Moving almost without conscious thought, as if his body acted of its own volition, his free hand dropped to his belt. His fingers slid along it, ducked inside and pulled the knife from its sheath inside his trousers. As he lifted the weapon in an arc around the front of Erna's body, he caught a reflection of her lips in the polished steel of its blade: lips he had waited five years to kiss; lips that had laughed with him, that had talked of future plans with him, that had once caressed his skin.

When Jakab placed the knife against her throat she screamed and thrashed, until the point pricked her flesh and she stilled.

Hans yelled, terror in his eyes. He lifted a foot, placed it back down. 'Please! Whatever you're thinking, don't. I'm begging you.'

Looking to his right, the only direction he could go, Jakab checked the wooden jetty. Its planks were stained black from the damp air. He sidestepped towards it, pulling Erna along with him. A single bead of blood appeared at her throat. It rolled down her neck.

'Well, this *is* interesting,' the *Merénylő* announced. 'Bizarre, yet interesting nonetheless. I have to admit I hadn't expected you to do that.'

The jetty was right behind him now. Jakab backed on to it, dragging Erna after him.

To his left, the second rider emerged from the scrub, guiding his mount over brambles. The man unsheathed a rapier and brought his horse to a halt, waiting for instructions.

Jakab continued to back down the slippery planks of the jetty.

The *Merénylő* reached down. When he straightened he was holding a crossbow, a bolt sitting in the channel before the cocked and latched bow. 'You know, Jakab, I think that's far enough. I mean, what can you possibly do next? My grubby associate here is hungry, and he becomes tiresome on an empty stomach. There's a place in town that serves the most delectable spiced sausage, and I've promised him his fill once we've finished here. And we *are* finished here, Jakab. There's nowhere left to go.'

Erna's husband dropped his axe. He regarded each of them in turn, eyes pleading.

Erna took a breath, and Jakab felt her press herself against him. She leaned back, her voice low and calm. 'Jakab, listen to me. If you do nothing else for the rest of your life, just listen now. You've got this wrong. All of it. When you found me a few days ago, I went home and told Hans what had happened. I'll admit that. But that's *all* I did. Hans already knew about you, had known about you for years. My God, you were the reason he found it so difficult to court me in the first place. I thought for so long you were coming back that I—'

'I *did* come back,' he hissed.

'Five years later, Jakab. Five *years*. Maybe a blink of an eye for you but not for me. I thought you were dead. I swear it. A few years ago your people came back, asking questions. I told them nothing – there was nothing to tell – but they explained how we could contact them if you returned.'

'And when I showed up, the money was just too much of a temptation.'

'No! That's just it. I told Hans I had to see you one last time, to talk to you. To say goodbye. At first he agreed. But then he contacted them, Jakab. I didn't know. He was scared and he contacted them. He was scared of you, of the *hosszú életek*. Scared he might lose me.

'Jakab, please listen. Hans is a good man. A wonderful man. He loves me and he loves our son, provides for us well. He was just doing what he thought he had to do to protect his family. I'm telling you the truth, Jakab. Five years ago I was in love with you so utterly I thought I might go mad from it. Our time may have passed but I still love you. I always will. I could never betray you. Not for money, not for anything.'

She looked over her shoulder and when Jakab met her eyes he felt himself floundering in the honesty of her gaze. She was telling the truth. Everything had happened exactly as she had described it; he suddenly had no doubt. At the realisation that she had not sold his freedom, had even risked her safety to give him a chance to escape, his emotions churned anew.

He had never had a chance of winning her back. She was too faithful for that. Even though she had moved on, had married and started to raise a family, her love for him had never deteriorated into bitterness. Even now, she was trying to protect him.

His vision blurred – tears of despair, that he would never have the opportunity to share her life. After everything, after all he had done to be here, the cruelty of it was too much to face. 'I'm sorry,' he choked, voice cracking with the strain. 'I mean it. I want you to know that. But if I can't have you like this—'

'Oh, how long do we have to wait, Balázs?' The *Merénylő* shook his head. 'There are two of us on horse. You're on foot.

Cut the girl's throat if you must. So what? It's the same unhappy ending for you whether you kill this fellow's wife or not. Did I tell you I'm hungry? I don't think I've eaten since last night.'

Even in his agony, Jakab noticed the way Erna's husband reacted to the *Merénylő*'s words. The man's eyes widened in outrage. Bending to the earth, he retrieved his axe.

Even though Hans stood just outside the *Merénylő*'s field of vision, Jakab did not doubt that the assassin knew exactly where he was positioned. What the *Merénylő* might not have anticipated was how his casual dismissal of Erna's life had affected her husband. Hans lifted the axe, rested the haft on his shoulder, and took a silent step closer to the assassin's horse. Then he switched his attention to Jakab.

Jakab returned the stare with loathing. How could this man, this lowly *woodsman*, have won Erna's heart? He might have laughed had it not been so tragic. He had sacrificed five years, had taken his own brother's life, and had returned to Keszthely, prepared to take Erna away with him and lead a far more basic existence than he would have otherwise accepted. In the meantime, this low-bred peasant had happened along and stolen everything Jakab had worked for; worse, he had *polluted* her with his seed so that she had spawned his child.

Jakab inched his fingers around the handle of the knife, switching his grip. The weapon was Austrian-made, fashioned from a single piece of forged steel, and was balanced so that it could be thrown from either end. He had spent so many hours sharpening its blade he preferred to throw it from the handle. Far less chance of cutting himself that way.

While he could not change the fact that Erna was in love with Hans, he was damned if he was going to stand by and let that peasant imbecile steal his rightful place with her. He studied Hans's face, his long nose, angular jaw and large, frightened eyes. Such an easy face to remember; such an easy face to become. If Jakab had not been caught by the *Főnök*'s man, things could still have worked out. He watched the woodsman take another step nearer the assassin, fingers flexing on the axe.

The *Merénylő* shifted in his saddle and turned his attention to Hans. 'My boy, please don't even think of involving yourself in—'

Jakab pulled Erna to his left, drew back his hand and threw the knife. Even as the blade left his fingers he realised he had misread the assassin's focus. The *Merénylő* was moving before his eyes found the blade's trajectory. He threw himself back in his saddle as the weapon whickered towards him.

The assassin rolled in a fluid arc, the blade spinning through the space he had just vacated. Rising back up in the saddle, he raised the crossbow as Hans lunged for the reins of the horse.

Jakab watched, paralysed, as the *Merénylő* pulled the crossbow trigger. He heard a *thwick* as the sinew bowstring contracted, picked up the bolt and accelerated it down the stock. He felt the impact of the projectile before the pain, the force of it knocking him back a step.

Hans was screaming. The *Merénylő* dropped the crossbow to the ground and drew the sword sheathed at his waist. The second rider shouted, kicking his heels into the flanks of his mount.

Concentrate on the pain, Jakab urged himself. *Grit your teeth and explore its edges. Force the wound to pucker and kiss. Knit the flesh back together.*

He hoped the bolt had not lodged in his body. It would make this far more difficult.

Hans loosed a second wrenching scream, swung his axe and buried the bit deep in the *Merénylő*'s spine. The assassin's eyes bulged.

Erna issued an alien keening.

There's no pain. None at all.

Jakab turned. The crossbow bolt had buried itself inside Erna's head, entering her skull just below her right eye. Her cheekbone had imploded from the impact, giving the side of her face an obscene concave look. Her eye was a blood-filled mess, leaking fluid down her cheek.

Only the end of the bolt remained visible. Jakab saw wooden flights attached to its shaft. Erna's jaw dropped open and a mindless *clacking* sound escaped her lips. She bucked and spasmed, her teeth snapping at the air, and as he released her she pitched forward on to the slimy planks of the jetty. When he saw the bolt's iron head protruding from the curve of her skull, and the remains of her beautiful mind and her memories dripping from its spike, Jakab felt his diaphragm contract and then he was loosing his own wretched scream that ricocheted inside his head, a tortured sound that would never stop, *could* never stop.

Hans yanked the axehead out of the *Merénylő*'s spine and the *Főnök*'s man slid from the saddle, his face hitting the ground with a slap. The woodsman stepped over the body, hefted the axe above his head and brought it down a second time. This time the blade sliced through the soft flesh of the assassin's neck and sheared through his vertebrae. Hans let go of the handle, staggered, collapsed to his knees. He raised both hands over his head.

Jakab forced himself to look at Erna, forced himself to retain every awful detail. He had walked away from the *hosszú életek* willingly, yet they had followed, sending his brother after him. After forcing him to kill Jani, they had sent this vile creature slumped before him.

And now the *Merénylő* was dead too. But not before he had succeeded in ending Jakab's life. Perhaps not by stealing his last breath, but he had taken something just as valuable.

It was over. He could not think of what to do.

It was over.

Everything.

Jakab let out the breath in his lungs, hearing its hiss as it passed his lips. An expunging, an outpouring. He lifted his arms until they pointed away from his body, outstretched. A ruinous calm settled upon him.

Nothing left at all now.

He gave the remaining rider a defeated, sickened smile. And then he allowed his body to fall backwards. Momentum took him. He felt an icy shock as he hit the water. The surface of the lake parted, and then it accepted him, coldness flooding him as he sank beneath, drifting, a funeral roaring in his ears.

The mist closed around the diminishing ripples of his wake.

CHAPTER 13

Paris

1979

Sitting opposite Charles at the small cafe table, Nicole Dubois stirred a sugar lump into her espresso. They were sitting beneath the beige awning of the Café de Flore, on the corner of the Boulevard Saint-Germain and the Rue Saint-Benoit.

Traffic flowed along the boulevard. Charles watched as a battered Citroën swerved, but did not brake, to avoid a group of tourists negotiating the junction. The car veered around the corner in a black cough of exhaust fumes, its driver holding the wheel with one hand and gesticulating out of the window with the other.

Nicole looked up at him, her expression grim. 'Later that morning,' she said, 'half mad with grief, Hans Fischer buries his wife in a makeshift grave by the side of Lake Balaton.'

'Erna Novák,' Charles replied.

Before Nicole had left England, she had given him a translation of the earliest diaries, written by Hans. It had taken him two evenings to read them. He had seen enough of the originals to know that the copies were accurate reproductions. They had left him feeling far more disturbed than he had expected.

Nicole nodded. 'My great-great-grandmother. It was 1879. She was twenty-seven years old. She'd been married to Hans for just three years. She died because she tried to protect Jakab from the people who were hunting him. After burying Erna, Hans walks back into Keszthely, packs a bag of belongings, says goodbye to his parents and leaves with his son Carl the same morning. That boy, my great-grandfather, is less than two years old. They never go back.'

Whether it was pure fabrication or the result of a single shocking incident twisted by superstition, Charles did not know, but hearing the tale from Nicole's lips lifted it straight out of the past and into the present. While neither of them could know the complete truth of what had happened in Keszthely in 1879, something terrible had happened to Erna Novák. It had taken Charles some effort to research it, but Gerold Novák, Erna's father, had reported his daughter missing to the authorities in the spring of 1879. Two months later her corpse was discovered when a local farmer's pigs uprooted it. She had been shot in the head.

Had Hans Fischer murdered her? Or had she been killed much as the diaries described? Perhaps the trauma of seeing his wife's murder, coupled with an upbringing couched in superstition, had driven Hans to believe that *hosszú életek* were responsible. But even if that were true, it didn't explain the continuation of the family's beliefs long after he was dead.

Nicole paused as a waiter skirted their table and unloaded a tray of coffee and croissants on to two Frenchwomen sitting nearby. When he retreated, she continued. 'Hans and Carl eventually settle in the city of Sopron, near the Austrian border. He changes their surname from Fischer to Richter.'

'When the diaries begin.'

'Hans writes the first. He starts it partly to come to terms with everything that has happened, and partly to capture all his memories of Erna, so he can pass them on to Carl when the boy is old enough.'

'He never saw any evidence of the *hosszú életek*'s abilities. Any proof whatsoever.'

'Charles, this is nineteenth-century provincial Hungary. Hans doesn't need evidence to accept what he hears about the *életek*. He's just seen his wife murdered by their *Merénylő*.'

'I understand that. I just wanted to be entirely clear.'

Nicole stared at him, her eyes narrowing. 'No, Charles, he never sees any evidence.'

'Sorry.' He held up his hands, placed them on the table. 'They settle in Sopron. Then, for years, no more contact.'

'Carl grows up, gets a job as a bookkeeper for the Sárközy family, one of the wine-producing dynasties in the region. He does well for himself, very well. In 1906 he marries Helene, Sárközy's eldest daughter.'

'Hans must have been pleased.'

'Immensely. It wasn't a time of great social mobility. Two years later Helene gives birth to Carl's daughter and my grandmother, Anna Richter. Life is good. Hans is now in his fifties, watching his son and granddaughter grow up. He continues to keep a diary, although not quite as regularly. Even so, the memory of Jakab and what happened to Erna never leaves his mind. Throughout his life, he collects stories of the *hosszú életek* and records them in the diary's pages. Despite all my years of research, some of the most useful information I have comes from the tales written down by my great–great-grandfather.'

'He was certainly meticulous in his record-keeping.'

'As Hans's granddaughter Anna grows up, her resemblance to Erna Novák is startling. You've read the copies I gave you. In his journal he references the similarity several times, and the poignancy seems as fresh now as it must have been then. In 1926, Anna turns eighteen. It's not long before she meets a young German chemist named Albert Bauer and falls in love. And it's not long after that things start to go wrong.'

Charles lifted the lid of the teapot and used a teaspoon to stir its contents. He poured himself a cup. Adding a splash of milk, he glanced back up at Nicole. He could see the strain in her face and it worried him. Two months had passed since she had left England with her mother. He had not heard from her for nearly three weeks before she telephoned him to say she was back in Paris, and safe. He had wanted to come out immediately, but it had taken a while to arrange leave with the college.

He still found it difficult to reconcile the serious, headstrong character she presented with the story she clearly believed. He had spent the weeks in England researching what he could of the *hosszú életek*. Beckett had been helpful, lending him a number of texts and pointing him in the direction of those he did not own. The information was sparse: he had found a few mentions in some of the oldest Hungarian texts, but the majority of the material was little more than badly worded ravings. Whereas Beckett made little distinction, Charles was conditioned to remain sceptical of every source. Nothing he had found gave him a reason to believe even a part of Nicole's story. There was simply nothing, anywhere, to support the fantasy she was wrapped up in.

And yet he loved her. He did not think he was capable of falling in love with someone who was insane, or paranoid, or confused. So where did that leave him?

Nicole seemed to have realised his mind had wandered, because she tilted her head and smiled, lips pressed together. 'You think I'm crazy.'

He shook his head. 'That's just it. I don't. I don't know how to explain all this, and I can't accept what I've read as fact. But I wouldn't be here if I thought you were crazy. You said things started to go wrong not long after your grandmother met Albert Bauer. How old would Jakab have been at this point?'

She shrugged. 'Who knows? How old was he when he first met Erna? Hans believed she met him when Jakab was still a young man, but there's no way of knowing. Erna died in 1879. Anna Richter met Albert in 1926. Forty-seven years later.'

'So if Jakab was in his twenties when he met your great-great-grandmother, he would have been in his sixties or even seventies by the time Anna had grown up and met Albert.'

Nicole looked at him, studying his eyes. 'Yes.'

'This is where Hans's diary ends. What happened next?'

'Anna had been worried for some time before she finally confided in her grandfather. Albert Bauer was an academic, a fiercely intelligent man. But six months after they started courting she began to notice changes. Subtle things. He would forget the experiences they had shared, the things they had done together. He would question her, ask her to reminisce about how they had met. Anna kept a diary too. She recorded how Albert began to visit her at unusual times of the day, when he should have been at work. They'd have sex. Passionate, rough sex. Finally Anna confided in Hans, who became convinced that Jakab had found them. The only thing he wasn't sure of was whether Jakab had already supplanted Albert entirely, and the man's corpse was lying in a ditch somewhere.

'He wanted Anna to run, but he knew how much she loved Albert, and he promised to find out if her fiancé was still alive. Between them, they worked out a plan. When Anna next received a visit from the Albert they suspected was an impostor, Hans set off for the young chemist's laboratory.

'It worked. While Anna engaged the false Albert in conversation at the family home, Hans was talking to the real Albert five miles away in the centre of the city.'

Charles frowned as he listened. For the first time, he could not think of an obvious explanation. 'What did they do?'

'That night, just like her grandfather had done forty-eight years earlier, Anna packed a bag, packed the diaries her grandfather had given her, and left Sopron. Albert went with her. It's not clear from the records they left, but it seems the young man had seen something too, something that scared him enough not to persuade her to stay.'

'Did they ever return?'

Nicole shook her head. 'Anna wanted to. She was terribly homesick. Then, a month later, they read in the newspaper that her grandfather, mother and father had been found dead. Hans, Carl and Helene. All three had been tortured.'

Charles felt a twist of unease. Whether it was from Nicole's story, or the hunted look in her eyes as she told it, he did not know.

She took another sip from her espresso and grimaced. 'Jakab tied them to chairs in the living room. He savaged them without mercy. We think he was trying to get information, the where-abouts of Anna. He'd been almost ready to supplant Albert, had felt secure enough in his knowledge of the man's history and day-to-day habits to take on his persona. He was foiled at the last minute.'

'Of course, you don't *know* any of that,' Charles said, then winced at his insensitivity.

Nicole's eyes flashed with anger. 'Of course I don't. But it's not exactly a wild speculation, is it? The family had no enemies. Even the way they were tortured told its own tale: *see no evil, hear no evil, speak no evil.* I'll spare you the details.' She shook her head. 'Jakab couldn't find out where Anna had gone because Hans insisted she did not tell them. But Jakab would have found that difficult to believe. It had taken him forty-eight years to trace the family. When he did, he found a beautiful young girl who was the image of the Erna he'd lost all those years earlier. And then he lost her too. It drove him over the edge. And like the sick lunatic he is, he took out his fury on the family that tried to protect her.'

Charles blew out a breath. 'And then?'

'You know the rest. I told you before I left England. Anna and Albert ended up in Germany, where they married. Anna gave birth to my mother shortly afterwards. Then the Second World War broke out. Albert was conscripted into the army and lost his life to a sniper's bullet in Stalingrad. After the war, Anna fled Germany with my mother. They settled in France.'

Charles nodded, remembering the next part of the story and

trying to calculate how old Jakab would have been by the time he caught up with Eric Dubois.

'I was born in '52,' she said. 'Seventy-three years after Erna Novák died. And I remember what happened to my father, Eric.' Nicole shivered. 'Come on, Charles. Let's get out of here.'

He stood, leaving a handful of coins on the table. As they left the Café de Flore he found himself studying the waiters, watching to see if any were taking an interest in him.

They walked the busy afternoon streets of Paris, crossing the Seine at the Pont du Carrousel, turning west at the Louvre and arriving at the Jardin des Tuileries. When they passed the sculpture of Theseus and the Minotaur, Nicole slipped her hand around his arm. Charles was surprised enough by the gesture that he glanced across at her, but she didn't meet his eyes.

Above them the sky was a polished blue. Autumn sunlight lit the statues from a low angle, painting the milk-white stone with dark shadows. Parisians and tourists filled the gardens. Office workers strode past huddles of young mothers on park benches with prams lined up before them. A party of screaming and laughing schoolchildren followed a trio of sharp-eyed school mistresses. A tramp shuffled by, pushing an enormous wheeled contraption stuffed with clothes and topped by a fluttering tricolour.

Despite feeling foolish, Charles couldn't stop himself studying the strangers they passed, lingering on faces far longer than etiquette allowed. Some smiled; most ignored him, or frowned as they walked by.

'How do you do it?' he asked her eventually, as they passed *La Misère*.

'Do what, Charles?'

He took a breath of air, exhaled. 'Live your life like this. Constantly searching faces in the crowd, wondering which of them you can trust, which of them you can't.'

'What choice do I have?'

The choice to let go of this insanity, he wanted to say. The choice to refuse to believe in this nonsense any longer, to take back control of your life and leave the superstition and tragedy in the past where it belongs. But he couldn't tell her that. Not yet. Every conversation was a tightrope walk between her quick-tempered convictions and his disbelief. 'I don't know,' he admitted.

'Don't forget,' she said, 'it's not me that's in danger here. It's those closest to me. At this point, that's you.'

He glanced across at her, hoping to see the trace of a smile, and was depressed to find that her face was serious, distant. 'Have there been others?' he asked.

'I'm not a virgin, Charles, if that's what you're asking.'

'I wasn't. I just wondered whether you've confided in others before.'

'Once. Yes.' She laughed, a brittle sound. 'I said I wasn't going to make that mistake again.'

'It didn't work out.'

'To say the least.'

'But there was no intervention. What I mean . . . you've not encountered this Jakab as a result.'

'No. I don't believe so.'

'So the last time he made an appearance, as far as you're aware, was when you were living in Carcassonne as a little girl.'

'Yes.'

'Some twenty or so years ago.'

She nodded.

'So what is it you think he wants?' Charles asked.

'He wants Erna.'

'But she's dead.'

'He wants to recreate the life he lost with her. And he doesn't care who he has to kill to achieve it. Anna Bauer was the image of her grandmother. My mother tells me I look the same. Jakab knew that Anna would never submit to him

willingly. He intended to kill her husband, supplant him and
slide into her life unawares. Years later, after that attempt had
failed, he tried again, this time with my mother. He failed then
too, but I think he's learning, getting better at it.'

She slipped her hand down his arm and interlaced her fingers
with his. Charles would have sighed with pleasure had she not
looked so thoroughly miserable.

'What are we going to do?' she asked.

He knew she addressed the question to herself, but he
decided to answer it anyway. 'We're going to get some dinner,'
he told her. 'And then we're going to get roaringly drunk.'

Nicole laughed, and for the first time that afternoon it
sounded genuine. She squeezed his hand. 'The great Charles
Meredith, always thinking of his stomach.'

'I've only eaten a crêpe since getting off the ferry.'

'Then we must find you some proper sustenance.' She
tugged his hand. 'Come on. I know a place.'

They ate in a crowded and noisy bistro huddled on a street
just off the Champs-Elysées. Charles ordered a smoked mackerel
mousse, followed by calves' liver with bacon and rösti potatoes.
The food, when it arrived, was excellent. While he tucked his
head down and sated his appetite, Nicole picked at a cod fillet,
yielding the plate to Charles when she could not finish it.

'Something's distracting you,' he said, noting again how she
scrutinised the diners at other tables.

'I'm sorry. It's been a strange day. Seeing you again, here in
Paris, after the time we had in England.'

He studied her face. 'You don't make it sound a particularly
enjoyable experience.'

She smiled, and the weariness in that look made him yearn
to hold her, to discover the best way of knocking this senseless
superstition out of her head, to stop her ruining her life with it.
'I've loved seeing you again. How could I deny myself the
pleasure of your fabulous English pomp?'

'So what is it?'

'I can't be responsible for you. I don't know why we ended up together like this. It seems like fate and that always worries me. You're a wonderful man, and I'm attracted to you, but if you don't believe a word I've told you, not only do I lack your respect, I know you won't protect yourself by taking this seriously. If you lure him, Charles, he'll kill you. Simple as that.'

'Nicole, you have my respect, of course you do.'

'But you don't believe a word of this *hosszú életek* craziness.'

'I'm prepared to accept that something decidedly odd happened to Erna Novák and Eric Dubois. And –' he took a breath, wincing as he heard the lie escape his lips but knowing it was the only way to keep her – 'I'm prepared to keep an open mind about the rest of the diaries.'

Nicole blinked, tears glittering in the corners of her eyes. 'You are?'

'Scout's honour. I'd still like to read the rest of the extracts you've translated.'

'Of course.'

'And I'd like to continue my own research.'

'You'll be discreet?'

'I will. And, in return, if we discover anything else that might explain these events, I want you to at least consider it.'

'Charles, I'd like nothing more than there to be a simple explanation for all of this. I doubt you'll find one.'

He shrugged. 'So we're agreed?'

'On what?'

'I'll keep an open mind. So will you. We'll both do our research, and we'll be careful with what we unearth. In the meantime, considering I appear to be risking my very existence in my efforts to continue to see you, we'll take our pleasures wherever and whenever we can.'

He stopped, aghast at the way the sentence had spilled from his lips. He saw the flush rising on Nicole's cheeks.

'Is your hotel within walking distance?' she asked, raising an eyebrow.

'Not really.'

She laid her hand on his. 'Let's get a taxi then.'

After making love that first night, they lay on the king-size bed listening to the murmur of Parisian traffic through the open window. The moon cast its cold eye on the glass, painting stripes of shadow on to the wall.

They spent the following day immersed in each other's company, hardly leaving his hotel room except to take a walk along the Seine as the sun flung crimson streaks across the sky.

Charles remained in Paris for another four days before he returned to England. Shortly afterwards he managed to arrange passage for Nicole. This time she stayed for a month.

In the spring of 1980, he proposed. Nicole cried and refused, telling him that she could not take responsibility for him, that she loved him and that was why she could no longer see him. Charles reacted furiously, his anger a mask for his hurt. Over twenty years had passed, he reasoned, since something had happened to Eric Dubois – something that could or could not have been due to Jakab Balázs. Surely the fact that she would be married to him, with a new surname, made the chance of Jakab finding her even more remote. Nicole disagreed and he returned to England, disconsolate.

Three months later, she followed. In the spring of 1981, when he asked her to marry him a second time, she accepted. There were conditions. The ceremony would be discreet, with no official announcement. Charles would continue to lecture at Balliol and record his documentaries, but he would court no publicity, and would say nothing – in public or otherwise – of his wife, except to his most trusted friends.

Nicole moved into his Oxfordshire cottage, bringing a warmth and vitality to the place that had never before existed. She converted the small dining room into an artist's studio and taught herself how to paint. She picked out new furnishings and renovated the old. Just before the Christmas of '82, she gave birth to a daughter, whom they named Hannah. Charles grew thicker around the waist, happy in his work and his family. He sold another plot of land to a private developer for a fortune, and invested the money shrewdly. As they reached the end of that decade, it became clear they would not be blessed with more children, but the joy Hannah brought them was more than enough to compensate; the girl's tenacity and fire, clearly inherited from both parents, was moderated by a selflessness that neither recognised as a quality of their own.

In '97, Hannah celebrated her fifteenth birthday, Nicole commemorated thirty-nine years since her mother had set fire to the family home where a *hosszú élet* had taken up residence, and Charles celebrated two publishing achievements he would regret for the rest of his life.

The first was his first full-length hardback, *Legacy of the Germanic Peoples*. The book was reviewed favourably by a number of national newspapers, meaning that sales were higher than he might otherwise have hoped. His growing reputation as a broadcaster also helped.

When Nicole opened the book, she was stunned to discover that the inside back cover of the dust jacket featured a monochrome image of herself and Charles posing in his study. The photograph had been taken by Hannah a year earlier. A caption read: *Professor Charles Meredith relaxes with his wife at their Oxfordshire home.*

Charles had not been prepared for her fury. He had thought that the years of *hosszú életek* paranoia had ended. So disturbed was he by her reaction that he neglected to tell her of the second piece he had published, an article in a little-known quarterly called *The Mottram-Gardner Journal of European Folklore and Mythology*.

The piece, just over five thousand words, was buried towards the back. Its title, *Hosszú életek: the birth and death of a Hungarian legend*.

Charles was credited as its author.

CHAPTER 14

Snowdonia

Now

The thunderstorm that had threatened for the last three days had not descended; for now, the heavens had brokered an uneasy truce. Clouds tumbled across the skies, flashing purple underbellies at the valley floor. At their tattered edges, shafts of sunlight winked in and out, transforming patches of landscape into blazing greens and mauves before the thunderheads closed in and the colours bled away.

In the farmhouse, Hannah lit large fires in each of the rooms, determined to chase away the damp before the storm broke. While the house warmed up, she donned gloves and scrubbed the tiny bathroom until the porcelain shone and the steel glinted. She mopped the kitchen floor and bleached the sink, scoured the cooker and stacked the remaining wood Sebastien had brought them into piles by each mantelpiece. In one of the outbuildings she found planks, nails and a hammer, and used them to board up the smashed window in the living room. She burned Nate's bloodied garments, found spare clothing for him in one of the cupboards, washed and aired it. She ran Leah a bath and washed her hair, then settled the girl in Llyn Gwyr's dining room with an Enid Blyton novel.

With her daughter occupied, Hannah counted again the shotgun cartridge boxes and double-checked the contents of each box. She found three new hiding places for the ammunition, fearing each time that it was either not sufficiently close or that it was too convenient for Leah's curious fingers. She loaded and unloaded the shotgun, decided to clean it with a can of gun oil she found under the stairs, and reloaded it when she had finished. She tried not to think about her father.

Nate watched her, his face unreadable. Three days had passed since their arrival at Llyn Gwyr. She still found it difficult to believe that he could have lost as much blood as he had and survived.

But survived he had. The kitchen sofa by the fire had become his convalescence bed, from which he made steadily increasing requests for food, drink, and empty bottles with which to relieve himself. That morning he had insisted she help him shuffle to the toilet so that he could attend to himself in private. Despite her fear that the movement would tear open either of his two wounds, he managed it. A habitual optimist, that small success spurred him on, and when he playfully swatted her rear three times within an hour as she passed his couch, she knew he was recovering.

Twice she caught herself dwelling on what would have happened, what life would have been like, had he died. Both times her vision swam and her hands shook as she considered how lost she would have been. The prospect of trying to establish a new life for Leah without Nate's presence was so shattering she found it impossible even to feel around the edges of the thought. Without him, how could she protect Leah against what was coming – a storm far greater than the one that threatened overhead?

She knew that Jakab would find them, felt it at her core. Yet despite her belief that she could not face that confrontation alone, with Nate virtually immobile and her father most likely dead, the burden fell upon her to protect all three of them.

Meet me. Just you, and just me. Anywhere you want. Out in the open.

The recollection of Jakab's voice filled her with revulsion. She knew better than to believe a single word of his poison. Bizarrely, even though she knew that Jakab was a monster, a broken mind consumed by its own dark obsessions, she had felt unaccountably pulled by that voice.

You name the place. Just let me see you once. Talk. Explain. There have been so many untruths, I don't blame you for being confused.

It disturbed her to admit it, but perhaps after all these years, a tiny part of her was attracted to the thought of relinquishing control, of surrendering herself to fate. She had watched predators hunting in the wild, had been fascinated at the way their prey kept running until exhausted, expending every last trace of energy to avoid capture. Yet when hunter at last brought down hunted, its victim often seemed to relax, accepting its end. Those final moments, while horrific in one sense, were intimate in another. Perhaps when you finally realised you were beaten – that there really was no hope – something was triggered in the mind, allowing you to expunge, accept.

In the farmhouse kitchen, Hannah opened the cupboards and sorted through their supplies. It was only mid-morning, but she would need to feed everyone soon. As she passed Nate's couch, he stretched out an arm and took hold of her wrist.

'If you count those shotgun rounds a fourth time, Han, I'm going to have to find new lodgings. Twenty-five in a box. Two full boxes and one box with six spares. That's fifty-six cartridges plus the two in the breach. Fifty-eight in total. Fifty-eight last time you checked. And fifty-eight the time before that.'

She looked down at his twinkling eyes. 'I'm going mad, aren't I?'

'As a hatter. Drag up that chair,' he said, indicating the armchair on the far side of the fire. He let go of her wrist and she pulled it over. 'Sit.'

She complied.

'Give me your foot.'

Hannah lifted one booted foot and rested it on the edge of

the couch. Nate untied the laces, eased off the boot and pulled off her sock. He began to work his fingers into her toes.

She groaned and closed her eyes, arching her back. 'You don't know how good that feels.'

'It's why you married me.'

'I can think of a few other reasons.'

'So can I. But I don't think these stitches could handle it.'

Hannah opened her eyes and when she saw him grinning at her, she was filled with desire for him. They had always shared a close physical relationship: far closer, she suspected, than that of couples who lived their lives free of the constant threat of loss. Her hunger for him was fuelled by more than simple physical attraction; it took flame also from her trust in him, and the complete understanding they had of each other. Hannah was a product, she supposed, of her environment. Honesty, faith, security: they were the fundamentals of her world. The foundations of her relationship with Nate stood on rock. It was why the prospect of losing him was so utterly inconceivable. 'You still haven't told me the details,' she said, studying his face, pleased at the way its colour had begun to return.

'There's hardly been a moment.'

'When Dad took us into his study, he said he thought we'd been compromised. Someone new at his solicitor's office not knowing the protocols and handing out information over the phone. That's all I heard before I went out to look for Leah.'

Nate slid his hands up to the arch of her foot, pressing the tension out of her. 'Charles said the solicitor thing had happened weeks earlier, which meant it was likely Jakab was already on the farm.'

Her father employed four people to help him run the estate on the outskirts of Chipping Ditton. Nora Trencher, in her late sixties, worked as Charles's part-time housekeeper. Nora's husband, Bill, was a regular visitor too, even though he was now too old to do any meaningful work; Leah had grown up around the couple and Charles liked having them there. The final two workers were brothers, and local lads: Tom and Alex Tavistock.

Nate's eyes wandered from her face, settling on the flames in the hearth. 'We were trying to figure out who it could be. Who had been acting strangely. I went into the wet room to grab our panic packs. I'd already unlocked the gun cabinet and taken out that old Luger Charles keeps in there. It was in my coat pocket, loaded.

'Nora came into the room, asking if I needed any help. When she saw our packs and the open gun cabinet, she . . .' Nate blew out his cheeks, and when he looked at her his face was gaunt. 'She smiled at me, but I knew it wasn't her. Those eyes. I've never seen anything like that. Never. It was old Nora right down to the mole on her cheek. Except for the expression in those eyes.'

Hannah dropped her head.

Nora Trencher. The woman had shared their lives for six years, had acted like a grandmother to Leah. The odds that she was still alive were almost nil. Her husband Bill, who had built Leah a beautiful doll's house two summers ago, had started to lose his sight over the last six months. He'd begun to depend on his wife even more. Hannah wondered what would happen to the man, sickened at the thought of him marooned in his rural cottage, blind and alone.

'I thought I'd prepared for this,' Nate said. 'I never expected the reality of it to shock me like that. Seeing her standing there, knowing what she was . . . it only paralysed me for a second but that's all it took. She was so damned *fast,* Han. I never even saw the knife until after she stabbed me.' He indicated the higher of his two wounds. 'Here first. Then here. You know the worst? When she realised I wasn't going to shout out, she stepped back and just watched me, head tilted to one side like she was trying to memorise my face, my mannerisms. Storing them up.' Nate shook his head. 'I keep saying *her.* I should say *him. It.*'

He lifted a hand from her foot and passed it through his hair.

Sweat had beaded on his forehead and he wiped it away. 'I managed to pull the Luger from my pocket. And that's when I shot her. Right in the chest. Should have killed her. The momentum took her back through the doorway. I fired again. Missed with that one. When I finally dragged myself into the hall, she'd gone.'

Hannah watched him in silence.

There have been so many untruths, I don't blame you for being confused.

This was the reality of what they faced. This was the truth of it. Jakab had killed Nora Trencher. She could not know that for certain, but that he had tried to kill her husband was clear. 'He said you shot him first,' she said.

'Of course he did.'

'He said he was protecting himself.'

Nate grunted, his disgust evident.

Hannah slid off the armchair, kneeling by the couch. She leaned over and kissed him, closing her eyes as he lifted an arm and held her.

Resting her forehead against Nate's shoulder, she asked, 'Did he say anything?'

'Nothing. Not a word, during the entire exchange. You know, I've been thinking about it non-stop. Jakab could have killed me there and then. There were far better ways to do it. I think when he knew his cover was blown and we were escaping, he just lost control and lashed out. I should be dead.'

'Don't say that.'

'I'm not being morbid. I think I was lucky.'

'I'm the one who's lucky.'

'Charles employed me to keep you safe.'

'You married me, didn't you?'

Nate laughed. 'Not exactly what he had in mind.'

'This isn't a normal situation.'

'I was trained to handle abnormal situations.'

'Not like this one, you weren't.'

'No. Not like this one.' Nate rubbed her back, and then lifted her chin so that he could look at her. 'Hannah, we have to end this.'

'I know,' she whispered.

'He's like a wounded animal, mad with pain, lashing out at everything that comes near.'

'Worse than that. A wounded animal isn't vindictive like this. He's driven by far darker motives.'

'We can't let this spread to Leah. It has to end with us. We need to do whatever it takes.' He hesitated. 'I love you. Both of you. I think you know how much. And if it takes my life to end this, I'll trade it.'

She nodded, her throat constricting. 'I've been thinking exactly the same thing.'

It was too painful to look into his eyes just then and see the commitment he was making. She climbed to her feet, conscious again that she was on the edge of tears, not wanting him to see how much his words affected her.

From the dining room, Leah screamed.

Hannah whirled at the sound, her first thought the where-abouts of the shotgun. On the pantry shelf.

Loaded.

Four spare cartridges tucked into the pockets of her jeans.

Before she moved from Nate's couch, Leah screamed again and ran into the kitchen. It dawned on Hannah that her daughter was screaming with delight.

'Horses, Mummy! Horses!'

Hannah went to the girl and crouched at her feet. 'Leah, slow down. Horses? What have you seen?'

'Out of the window. Three of them!'

'OK, scamp. Hush a moment.'

The crackle of burning logs in the fireplace was the kitchen's only sound. Then something new overlaid it, growing more distinct: the clatter and crunch of hooves on gravel. The flank of an enormous chestnut gelding passed the kitchen windows.

Astride it, wearing jeans, boots and a scruffy jacket, sat Gabriel. He wore a battered felt stetson on his head.

'It's the fisherman!' Leah shouted.

Gabriel's expression was relaxed and calm. The glint of humour crinkled his eyes and tugged at the side of his mouth, as if he contemplated a private joke. A solemn brown mare with a reddish mane followed his horse, roped behind it. The mare, wearing full saddle and bridle, led in turn a smaller grey colt, this one's head high and jerking at its rope.

'Don't move,' Hannah hissed, her eyes flaring at the girl. She yanked open the pantry door and grabbed the gun from the shelf. Two rounds already in the breech, she thought.

Poking her head around the door, checking that Gabriel could not see into the kitchen, Hannah crossed the tiles to Nate's couch and laid the weapon alongside him. She dug into her pockets and touched the cold brass caps of her two spare rounds.

What was Gabriel doing here? Why the horses? Her head buzzed as she tried to consider the potential threats, the best way of handling this intrusion. She looked down at Nate. The back of his couch shielded him from the windows. 'What do you think?'

'I thought you warned him off.'

'Doesn't seem to have worked, does it? I'll find out what he wants. Then I'll get rid of him.'

'Han, wait. Don't be too short with him. We don't want to raise suspicions here. He's persistent, this guy.'

'Too persistent.'

'Agreed. But let's slow down a bit. Can you think of any way that Jakab could have found us yet?'

She couldn't. And surely he wouldn't have contacted her, attempting to trick her into revealing their location, if he already knew. Still, something about the Irishman's presence frightened her. 'I don't like it.'

'Nor do I. But we're fighting a war now. We need to think

strategically. On the slightest chance that Jakab makes it here, he's likely to use someone like Gabriel against us. It might be useful to know something about the man. Something we can use; something we can validate.'

The way Nate so matter-of-factly raised the possibility of Gabriel's supplanting, and how they could armour themselves against its consequences, chilled her deeply. Yet he had only voiced the same thought that had entered her head.

Were they beginning to lose a vital part of their humanity? She didn't want anyone else to be pulled into their nightmare; too many people had died already. But she only had Nate and Leah left. Right or wrong, she would trade the lives of any number of strangers for theirs. If Gabriel insisted on interfering, she would not add his safety to those she already sought to protect. As Nate said, a little knowledge could be indispensable.

Outside, she saw the Irishman pull off a leather glove and flex his freed fingers. He swung himself down from the gelding and strode to the back door. 'Leah, remember what we discussed.'

As Gabriel caught sight of Hannah through the glass, he grinned, and she found herself surprised once more at the contrast of his cobalt blue eyes against the whiteness of his teeth.

Heart thumping hard in her chest, Hannah walked to the door. She replayed what Sebastien had told her of Gabriel.

Sociable fellow. Always making jokes. Irritating as hell. Give him half a chance and he'll be over here poking his head into things that don't concern him.

The old man had certainly been right about that last part. Hannah put her hand to the door handle and opened it.

'Well, there's a sight,' Gabriel greeted her, putting his hands on his hips. 'The vision of Llyn Gwyr stands before me. Mistress of the lake, admonisher of poachers. Protector of fish!'

'What are you doing here, Gabriel?'

He filled his lungs with Welsh mountain air and exhaled, his face joyous. Raising his arms, he performed a slow pirouette and shouted, 'Living! Breathing! Exulting under God's sky! Did you ever witness a day with as much promise as this?'

'There's a storm on its way.'

'Oh, no. Not today. The storm's coming, all right. And we should prepare, because when it arrives it'll be savage, no doubt. But it won't come today. Today is a day for celebrating life, commemorating its passing, and witnessing nature's swansong. Autumn, in all its pageantry.' He raised an eyebrow. 'Your daughter said you ride?'

'I do.' Hannah found the man's words beginning to weave their spell on her, much as they had before. The more he talked, the more at ease she felt, and the more dangerous she felt the situation become.

Don't lower your guard. Something is wrong here. I don't know what, but something is wrong.

'Will you join me for a ride?' Gabriel said. 'I'd ask you by name, but you haven't given me that honour.'

'I can't leave my daughter on her own.'

At this, he turned and with a flourish gestured at the mounts. 'Behold three horses. One for the feckless Gabe. One for the little miss, and one for the tall miss.'

Leah jumped into the gap between Hannah and the doorway. She peered at the horses and squealed in excitement. 'Mummy, can we go? Please? Just for a while? You know you'll love it! *Please*, Mummy!'

Gabriel laughed. 'Well, that sounds like an endorsement to me.'

Hannah folded her arms. 'We don't have riding hats.'

'Brought you a couple.'

'It's close to noon. Leah needs to eat.' She flinched, shocked that she had so carelessly revealed her daughter's name.

Gabriel's eyes glinted. Was that triumph she saw reflected there? He indicated the pack attached to his saddle. 'I come bearing bread, cold meats, cheese. Flasks of soup and chocolate biscuits. Ambrosia. Food of the gods, no less.'

His manner was so absurd, so excessively theatrical, that she found it difficult to remain cautious of him.

Idiot! That's exactly why you have to be so careful.

'Come on,' he said. 'Give me the pleasure of your company for two hours and I'll show you and the little miss a few of the secrets these grand old mountains like to keep to themselves.' Gabriel tilted his head to one side. 'I ask you: will you receive a better offer than that today?'

They took the trail that followed the near shore of the lake, before curving north towards the first slopes of Cadair Idris. Gabriel led, followed by Leah on the grey colt. Hannah had been worried by the young horse's temperament at first, but it had behaved impeccably so far. She followed on the mare, eyes moving from her daughter every minute or so to linger on Gabriel's back, wondering at the man's motivations.

Torn clouds continued to jostle across the sky, filtering the sunlight. In the distance, she saw a falcon hanging in the air, gliding on a current. It watched their progress for a while before banking and diving to the earth.

Despite the unusual situation, it felt fantastic to be riding again. The union between horse and rider had always brought her peace. She leaned forward in the saddle and rubbed her mare's flank. The animal's ears twitched and it blew through its nostrils.

Ahead, the path widened and began to climb. Their horses' hooves scraped on the rocky moraine. As the slope grew more challenging, Hannah watched her daughter closely, but even though the colt she rode was young, it appeared to need only a light touch.

Moss-slicked boulders – ancient detritus from long-extinct glaciers – lay strewn across the landscape. Gabriel slowed his pace until his horse fell in step alongside her. They both watched Leah guide the grey up the incline.

Hannah felt Gabriel's eyes appraising her.

'How's she handling?' he asked.

'I'll give you one thing, you know how to train a horse. What's her name?'

'Landra.'

'And yours?'

'This is Salomon. Your daughter's riding Valantin.'

'Good names.'

He grinned. 'Yours is the only one I don't know.'

She studied him, eyes narrowing. Then, impulsively, she made a decision. 'Hannah,' she said. 'Hannah Wilde.' She saw no flash of recognition in his eyes as she told him.

Gabriel's grin widened and he touched his finger to the brim of his hat. 'Hannah Wilde. Lady of Llyn Gwyr, hidden gem of Snowdonia. I'm honoured to be formally introduced.'

'You're an unusual man, Gabriel.'

He laughed. 'Surely you mean charismatic?'

'I said unusual.'

'It's what living in these mountains with nothing but horses for company will do to you.'

'It's beautiful country.'

'Aye, it is that.'

'There's no Mrs Gabriel?'

A flicker of sorrow crossed his face, disappearing as quickly as it had arrived. 'Not yet, there isn't. A heinous crime, that, is it not?'

'Shocking.'

For a while they rode in silence. Then he said, 'After how angry you were the other day, I thought it unlikely you'd join me.'

'I wasn't angry. I just wasn't expecting company.'

'You were a wee bit angry.'

'You shouldn't have been on the lake. We came here for some peace.'

'Ah, well you couldn't pick a finer place for that. Am I forgiven, then? Truly, I didn't mean to intrude.'

'Turning up with three horses in tow isn't intruding?'

'Perhaps a little intrusive. I just had a feeling you'd enjoy this.'

She laughed drily. 'Because you know me so well.'

'Conversation with you is like playing poker with a great white.'

'Charming comparison.'

'You've got a much nicer mouth than a great white, if you don't mind me saying.'

'See? Unusual.'

Their eyes met.

'What about you, Hannah Wilde? You're wearing a wedding ring.'

'Very observant.'

'It's not just a device to ward off charismatic Irishmen?'

'I said unusual, not charismatic. And the answer's no, it's not.'

'You're married, then. Shall we turn back?' He grinned again to show he was joking. 'So where is the lucky man?'

'You ask a lot of questions.'

'I'm an unusual man.'

Hannah shook her head, exasperated, and squeezed Landra's flanks with her calves. The horse responded. She overtook Gabriel's gelding and caught up with Leah.

Just after midday they arrived at a series of huge boilerplate slabs, the overflowing stone ridges damp with condensation. Dismounting, they led the horses across. On the other side, they climbed back into the saddle and followed the trail further up the mountain. They rode through a wood, its steep floor veined with the mossy roots of trees seeking anchorage among the rocks. Pale grey fungi bloomed on their trunks.

The air was noticeably colder at this altitude. As they emerged from the trees the wind bit at them with sharper teeth. When they crested a ridge tufted with coarse grass, Hannah drew an awed breath. A huge glacial lake lay before them. Towering peaks of rock surrounded the basin on three sides, their shadowed cliff faces pocked and slashed with fissures. Below, the dark blue water of the lake shimmered as eddies of wind dimpled its surface. 'This is amazing. Where are we?'

Gabriel jumped from his mount and led the horse to the water's edge. 'Llyn Cau,' he told her. 'Beautiful, isn't it? Legend has it that the lake is bottomless.'

'Yeah, right,' Leah said, laughing.

'They also say the dragon Afanc lives at the bottom of it.' he told her. 'So you'd better be careful what you say, little miss.'

'Thought you said it didn't have a bottom,' Leah retorted, jumping down from Valantin and leading him towards the water – copying Gabriel, Hannah thought, with a prickle of unease.

Gabriel held up his hands in mock resignation. 'Ouch. Scuppered by a twelve year old.'

'You know, I'm actually only nine,' Leah told him, her face solemn.

'Thanks, little miss, but that makes it even worse. Here, let Valantin have a drink for a while. Once he's had his fill, we'll give him some grain. It's in one of the packs. I'll show you what to do. In the meantime,' he said, unfastening a pannier from Salomon, 'it's lunchtime, and unless I give you a decent feed, I've a feeling your ma's going to tan my hide.'

Gabriel spread two large blankets beside Llyn Cau's shore and weighed down their corners with rocks. From the pannier he produced baguettes, a side of ham wrapped in foil, roasted chicken, a block of cheddar. He set out plates and cups, and took out a knife. Its blade looked cold and sharp.

Unscrewing the cap from a large thermos, he asked, 'Who's for tomato soup?'

'Me!' Leah sat down on the blanket as Gabriel poured out three steaming servings. Hannah joined them, cradling a cup between her chilled fingers.

'Up there's the summit,' he said, nodding at the highest of the peaks before them. 'Penygadair. We won't tackle it today. It's a steep ascent. But on a good day the views are spectacular.'

'They're spectacular here.'

'Aye, they are. You should see this place on a clear night, with the moon on the water and the stars filling the sky.'

'You've come up here at night?' Leah asked, her eyes wide.

'Many times.'

'Why?'

Gabriel looked sideways at her. 'Searching for the *Cŵn Annwn*, of course.'

'What's that?'

'The *Cŵn Annwn*? The spectral hounds of Welsh folklore. Huge black dogs with burning red eyes. Fangs as long as my forearm, dripping with saliva. They only hunt on certain nights of the year, between Christmas Day and Twelfth Night, on the slopes of Cadair Idris. Right where we sit. And they bring death to anyone who hears their howl.'

Leah frowned. 'Why would you want to hear them, then?'

Gabriel scrunched up his face into a leer. 'Why, to find out if it's true, of course.'

The girl laughed.

Hannah shook her head, unable to prevent herself from smiling. 'Stop it, you'll frighten her.'

'No he won't. It's silly. There are no such things.'

Gabriel shrugged in defeat. 'Foiled again. By a nine year old.'

After their lunch, with the temperature dropping and the summit obscured by cloud, they packed up their picnic and folded the blankets. Gabriel took a sack of crushed barley from a pannier and showed Leah how to feed the horses.

Hannah watched them working together, noticing how happy and relaxed her daughter seemed. She was grateful for it.

The coming days would be a strain on the girl. Soon they would be moving on from Llyn Gwyr, relocating to another new environment where everything would be unfamiliar.

They mounted up, and Gabriel led the way back down the slope. When they passed through a ravine and saw a waterfall spilling down the rocks, its roaring waters white with foam, Hannah realised he was taking a different route. Emerging from the ravine, they descended further, down grassy slopes spotted with heather. The land dipped beneath them in a series of diminishing stacks. They skirted a rocky hillock to their right; beyond this, the lip of the next ridge plunged over a vertical cliff face. As they drew closer, and the land beneath came into view, she saw that the drop before them was at least a few hundred feet. Gabriel approached the precipice and turned to follow its line south.

As Hannah's horse neared the edge, she spotted a cottage nestled in the valley below. It was small, stone-built, with woodsmoke curling from its chimney. Two cars were parked out front. The first was a white Audi Q7, mud streaking its sides. The second was a battered blue Land Rover Defender.

With a jolt, she realised that the Defender was Sebastien's. As she watched, three men came into view around the side of the building. Sebastien's tall frame and fuzz of white hair were unmistakable. Hannah did not recognise the other two men. One wore a red mountaineering jacket and was powerfully built, his face covered by a dark thatch of beard. The second man, shorter and considerably older than the first, and dressed in a grey suit, seemed to be talking while the other two listened.

A feeling of dread began to creep over her. She sensed Gabriel ride up beside her, and she glanced across at him.

He peered down into the valley. 'Your closest neighbour,' he said, nodding towards the cottage.

Hannah watched as the three men walked towards the Audi.

Had Gabriel purposely brought her along this route to show her this? She dismissed the thought as ridiculous.

Who the hell is Sebastien talking to down there?

In front of the cottage, the two strangers shook hands with Sebastien and climbed into the Audi. The car turned in a wide circle, kicking up mud, and headed along the track to the main road. Behind it, Sebastien raised his arm in farewell.

'Do you know him?' Gabriel asked.

She shook her head.

'Really?'

'Nope.'

'That might be for the best,' Gabriel said. When she turned back to him, all trace of his usual humour had vanished.

Ice crawled up her spine. 'Why do you say that?'

CHAPTER 15

Oxford

1997

Charles walked along the gravel path of the university botanic garden, searching its benches for Beckett.

The physic garden had always been one of his favourite places. He enjoyed its scents and its spectacle, its tranquillity and its history, its unique expression of the seasons. Usually a walk through its grounds was a tonic for his worries. But not today.

He had been feeling unsettled for weeks. Since the publication of his *Legacy of the Germanic Peoples,* with its jacket photograph of himself and Nicole, guilt had washed over him and the tide would not recede.

He recalled Nicole opening the book for the first time, the smile sliding off her face as she saw her image staring back at her. At first it had shocked her into paralysis. And then the anger exploded out of her. She ripped the book in two, flung away the torn halves, and launched herself at him with a scream.

How had he ever justified such a spectacularly selfish decision? The terrible irony was that he loved Nicole even more now than on the day of their wedding, yet with that one act he had blithely broken every promise he had made to her, had reduced the beliefs that framed her into a child's fantasy, a stale bogeyman ripe for euthanasia.

I know best, the photograph announced. *I've indulged your paranoia for eighteen years and now it's time we buried it.*

He knew *why* he had done it: pride. Even eighteen years after meeting her, he still thought Nicole was the most fascinating, most desirable, woman he had ever met. After all their years of secrecy, he had wanted to broadcast their relationship to the world, to announce that he, Charles Meredith, had had the good fortune to have snared a woman as incredible as Nicole Dubois. The thought that something as worthless as his own vanity could become the knife that severed them was so appalling it left him wretched.

At first Nicole talked, in a detached and emotionless voice, of leaving him, of packing a bag and disappearing. Later, after hours of tears from both of them, she suggested that they leave together: leave Oxford, leave the notoriety of his name, her new and unwanted publicity.

Yet after all the talk, they had not, finally, done anything. They loved each other too much to be apart, and the foundations of their lives had been sunk in Oxford soil for too many years to consider a relocation.

Although they remained together, their relationship had irrevocably changed. There was a carefulness now between them that had not existed before, a hesitancy before speaking, before acting. He mourned their old comfortable ways even as he castigated himself for their loss. They had not shared a physical closeness since that first fight. Nicole had not refused him. The truth was, he simply felt unworthy of her. It was what unsettled him most of all. That, and the fact he had not gathered the courage to admit his second act of betrayal – the piece he had written for the *Mottram-Gardner Journal of European Folklore and Mythology*.

It was that article, published a month ago, that drew him to the botanic garden, walking its paths and searching for the bird-like creature that was Patrick Beckett.

Charles found him on one of the benches that circled the water fountain. Beckett was wrapped in a woollen overcoat and hat. The man stared at the water lilies floating on the fountain's surface, tapping out a complicated rhythm on his knees. A briefcase rested beside him.

Beckett looked up as Charles approached. Age had not softened the academic's mannerisms. He twitched with recognition and jumped to his feet. 'Here he is! Professor Meredith, slayer of the almighty *hosszú életek*!'

Charles shook his head. 'Patrick.' He was in no mood for Beckett's theatrics.

The man jerked back in surprise, then clapped a hand on Charles's shoulder. 'Why so glum, my friend? I expected triumph, jubilation, perhaps a hint of false modesty – although only the merest crumb. Certainly not this troubled visage that presents itself. Come, sit! The bench is damp but you may share my blanket.' He gestured at a strip of tartan fabric lying on the wooden struts.

Charles sat down. 'You said you had something to discuss?'

'Straight to the point as always. No taste for small talk.' Beckett delved into a pocket and removed a silver hip flask. 'Before that, though, I must insist on a toast.' He unscrewed the cap of the flask, took a sip, clenched his teeth and swallowed. 'To the success of your *Germanic Peoples*. And, even more exciting, your quite startling emergence as a folklorist. *Birth and Death* was a revelation, Charles.' He proffered the flask.

'You read it, then?'

Beckett's eyes glittered. 'I devoured it.'

Charles took the flask and swigged from the neck. The syrupy liquid lit a fire in his throat. He coughed, blinking tears. 'Gods alive, Patrick, what have you got in here?'

Beckett grinned. 'You've not tasted Pálinka? A plum brandy, from Szatmar. It seemed a fitting tipple for our salute.'

Charles handed back the flask and wiped his mouth. 'I thought you didn't like spirits.'

'Tastes evolve, Charles, as one grows old. I had no idea you were so interested in the *hosszú életek*.'

'It must be nearly twenty years since I first approached you about them. I suppose you got me hooked.'

Beckett inclined his head. 'How extraordinary. And here you are after all that time, an authority.'

'I'd hardly say that.'

'Now you're being obtuse.'

'It was hardly a shattering thesis, Patrick.'

'Some of the material you referenced . . . I don't know how you could have discovered it.'

'The sources are all quoted.'

Beckett raised his eyebrows. 'Yet in most cases I haven't been able to follow your trail.'

'You've checked?'

'Dear Charles, please don't think I doubted their authenticity. You know I'm an addict for this stuff. I just like to read the texts first-hand where possible.'

'Well, I'm flattered by your interest.' He paused, uncomfortable. 'You said on the telephone—'

'Aha! I did, didn't I? I said I had something to show you, something I thought would tickle you, and I do. I've been sitting on it for years. Your paper mentioned something that drew me back to it. The great cull of the *hosszú életek* – a genocide of sorts – at some point in the late nineteenth century. Abysmal episode.'

Charles frowned. He disliked the way Beckett talked about folklore as if it were historical fact. 'They're stories, Patrick. Many individual renditions of the same basic premise. Those references to a cull appear in versions that originate around the turn of the century. You know my view on it. As society grew less superstitious – as supposed *életek* sightings dwindled as a result – it was a way perhaps of keeping the myth relevant. An explanation for the *életek*'s absence.' Charles shrugged. 'Who knows? It's just a theory.'

Beckett leaned forwards. 'You didn't discover any motive behind the cull?'

'No.'

'Interesting.'

'So what did you want to show me?'

Beckett twitched again, rubbing his hands. He bent to his briefcase, snapped open the clasps and took out a cardboard tube. It was stoppered with a plastic cap, which he removed. From inside, he withdrew a scroll, its thick paper brittle and stained with age.

Charles watched as Beckett unrolled the parchment. The handwritten text was Hungarian, and lavishly calligraphed. He spotted several mentions of *hosszú életek*. Three signatures lay at the bottom of the page, above a maroon wax seal faded to brown. The document was dated *3rd March 1880*.

'What is it?'

'See those signatures? That one is Emperor Franz Joseph's, the reigning monarch. The second belongs to Kálmán Tisza de Borosjenö. He was Hungarian Prime Minister from 1875 to 1890. The third I haven't been able to trace.'

'What does the text say?'

Beckett looked up from the paper, his eyes studying Charles hungrily. 'It's a Royal Decree. Quite a nasty one.'

'Yes?'

'It grants authorisation for the immediate extermination of the Budapest *hosszú életek*. Not just the ruling classes. Every last poor sod of them. "*Their stain to be forever cleansed from our society.*"'

'Where did you get this?'

Beckett smirked. 'Want to trade sources?'

'Have you authenticated it?'

'Oh, it's real, Charles. I can promise you that. What do you make of it?'

'I don't know. What do *you* make of it?'

'Buried in all these tales, perhaps there's a thread of truth.'

'Like what?'

'Imagine something happened back then. Something that

upset the balance. We know from the usual sources that there was an uneasy alliance between the *hosszú életek* and Budapest's nobility. They weren't exactly cosy bedfellows. Perhaps a particular incident sparked the unrest that led to this Decree.'

'And this is just your speculation?'

'Of course.'

'You sound as if you believe all this.'

'Don't you?'

Charles glanced up at the academic, his unease growing. Beckett's grin seemed to mock him. His eyes stared with intensity.

'And here's something else interesting,' Beckett continued. 'In all your research, did you ever come across mention of the Eleni?'

'I don't believe so.'

'The Eleni was the organisation tasked with carrying out the cull.'

'Eleni.' Charles paused. Now he thought about it, perhaps he had seen the name in some of Anna Bauer's diaries. He shook his head. 'No. Can't say it rings a bell.'

'Ah, what a shame. Never mind. They're mentioned here. See? In the second paragraph. You know what I find interesting? There's an Eleni Council in existence in Budapest to this day.'

'So?'

'You're right, of course. Just a coincidence.' Beckett laughed. 'There's a Round Table club in Oxford but I suspect its members aren't all chivalric knights.' He looked back at the document in his hands, rolled it up and inserted it back into its tube, replacing the cap. 'How's Nicole?'

His prickle of tension beginning to ease, Charles smiled. 'She's well.'

'Been a long time since I saw her. We should arrange something. Dinner.'

Charles stood. 'Yes. Let's set something up.'

They shook hands, and Charles walked back along the path

towards the Danby Gate. He glanced back at Beckett once on his way out. The older man was standing by the fountain, staring at the water lilies.

CHAPTER 16

Snowdonia

Now

Dusk had descended by the time Hannah, Gabriel and Leah arrived back at Llyn Gwyr. As the light leached from the sky, the temperature plunged. A numbing wind gusted around them.

They rode into the gravel courtyard at the back of the farmhouse, the breath of the horses pluming before them. The building stood in violet shadow. A solitary light in the kitchen window guarded against the approaching night.

Hannah brought the mare to a halt and dismounted. Her thighs ached, and she lifted each foot behind her, trying to ease the tension in her muscles. Gabriel watched her, sitting astride Salomon. 'Saddle-sore?' he asked.

She nodded. 'Thank you for today.'

'The pleasure was mine.' He turned to Leah. 'Did you enjoy yourself, little miss?'

Leah grinned, jumping down from the colt and rubbing its muzzle. 'I loved it. Valantin's a beautiful horse.'

'That he is.'

'Leah, it's time to say goodbye to Gabriel,' Hannah said. 'Go on into the house. I'll see you in a minute.'

Once the girl was inside, Hannah turned back to him.

Gabriel was staring at the windows of the farmhouse. 'Is he inside?'

'Who?'

'The master of Llyn Gwyr.'

'You keep asking about him.'

'Curiosity, nothing more. I want to measure myself against the man lucky enough to call Hannah Wilde his wife.' He laughed. 'See how I stack up.'

'You don't.'

Gabriel laughed harder. 'Ah, you're a cruel woman, Hannah.'

'And you're a terrible flirt.' Hannah unclipped the reins from Valantin and Landra, and used a rope to hitch the two together. She walked over to his horse, passed him the rope, then offered him her hand. 'We're leaving soon, so I probably won't see you. It was nice meeting you, Gabriel. Truly. I actually hope you don't end up meeting those hounds.'

Gabriel reached down and shook her hand. 'The *Cŵn Annwn* won't catch me.' He winked at her. 'Nice talking to someone with only two legs for once. Goodbye, Hannah Wilde.' Clicking his tongue at the horses, he rode out of the courtyard.

She watched him cross the river at the bridge and ride up the track to the main road.

In the kitchen, she found Nate in an armchair beside the fire, eating corned beef from a tin. Leah sat at his feet, warming herself before the embers and chattering excitedly.

Nate looked up as Hannah closed the kitchen door and locked it. 'How was our friend?'

'Strange,' she said. 'Stranger still, we went past Seb's place. Our hermit friend had company.'

'What? Who?'

'Two men I've never seen before. They drove off in a big Audi 4x4.' Hannah pulled down the blind above the glass in the door. She drew the curtains across the window. 'Anything happen here?'

'Not a thing.'

'I don't like this at all, Nate. Something's going on. I don't think we should hang around to find out what.'

'What did Gabriel have to say?'

'He asked a lot of questions about you.'

'He did?' Nate frowned, studied her. 'Do you think . . .'

'I don't know.' She blew out through her cheeks, trying to slow her heartbeat. 'I'm pretty damn freaked out right now. I think we should leave.'

'OK. Do you want to wait until first light?'

'Not really. I'd like us to go this minute. But it makes sense. We need to pack up.'

'We can secure this place for the night. Leave at sunrise.'

She nodded. 'We all sleep in the same room.'

'Agreed.'

'Mummy?'

She turned to her daughter, dismayed to see that Leah's face had paled. Hannah went to the girl, crouching at her feet. 'Oh, scamp. Come here.'

Leah clutched her. 'It's going to be OK, isn't it? We're not going to die?'

Nate reached out and stroked his daughter's head. 'Absolutely not. That's why Mummy and Daddy are here. To keep you safe. To keep us all safe.'

'He got you. The Bad Man. He hurt you.'

'And I'm getting better. We'll be out of here in the morning. Just wait till you see the place your Mummy found for us. You'll be safe there. The Bad Man won't find us. I promise you.'

Hannah cooked a stew, which they ate with the last of the bread. Afterwards, she put Leah to sleep in the master bedroom. She toured the ground floor of the house, checking locks, securing windows. She wanted to draw all the curtains, but with the lights off, she decided to keep them open. More chance of spotting intruders that way.

Once everything was locked up, she helped Nate upstairs to the bedroom. Leah was already asleep beneath the covers of the four-poster.

'I don't think I'm going to get much sleep,' Hannah said, her voice low.

'Want to take shifts?'

'I think that's wise. I'm sorry, Nate. I just have this really bad feeling.'

'Don't apologise, I trust your instincts. Shall I take the first stint?'

She shook her head, kissed him. 'I'm far too wired to doze off. Get some rest. You're still recovering.'

'You'll wake me?'

'If I'm flagging.' She knew she wouldn't. A long journey awaited them, and in his current condition it would be tough on him.

Nate was asleep in minutes. Hannah threw more logs on the fire. She moved to the side of the bedroom window, edging out her head for a look.

The darkness outside was almost absolute. Buried behind invisible cloud, the moon was a faint pearl smudge. She could just see the outline of the lake, the stone bridge over the river.

The land was still.

Jakab was out there. She had no idea how close. No way of telling. She wondered what was happening in the next valley where Sebastien's cottage stood. The sight of him talking to the two strangers had frightened her badly. He had told her he lived in isolation, had retired from the world.

And what of Gabriel? Several times during their ride he had led their conversation into dangerous territory. She had discovered little of him in return.

Perhaps it was all unconnected. Perhaps she was so exhausted that she was beginning to make connections where none existed. She looked over at the bed. Nate slept, his chest rising and falling under the blankets. Next to him, Leah had tucked her head into the crook of his arm. Hannah watched them, knowing that however exhausted she was, she would not give up. Could not.

Damn the odds, keep fighting until you have nothing left.

Her father's words. The thought of him made her chest heave with pain. That last phone call had been the most difficult conversation of her life. What had happened to him afterwards? The likelihood was that she would never find out.

Despite knowing she had locked all the doors, that no one could get into the room without crossing her first, she felt horribly exposed. The darkness outside was oppressive. It pushed at the windows.

She looked at the luminous dials of her watch. Twenty past three already. Four hours until sunrise. Three and a half hours until first light.

The longer she stayed in the room, the more her unease grew. If anything happened outside, or downstairs, she would only find out about it when it arrived at their door. Realising that her unease wasn't going to disappear, she stood up.

The shotgun was leaning in the far corner. She picked it up and, out of habit, broke the weapon. She checked that the chambers still held two rounds. They did. Spare cartridges were still tucked into the back pockets of her jeans. Into her front pocket she slid the long shaft of the Maglite. Going to the door of the bedroom, she opened it.

The hallway was a black void, from which faceless horrors could emerge. She wanted to use the torch, chase away the shadows. But she didn't want the light to be seen from outside.

Hannah stepped into the darkness, listening. Despite the fires she had kept stoked over the last few days, the air smelled musty, damp. The house creaked and settled. Wind rattled a window.

She knew there was a loose floorboard halfway along the landing, and edged around it. At the top of the stairs, she passed the display case. She felt the eyes of the dead falcon on her. Even though she knew they were only glass, she prickled at the sense of awareness. Why hadn't she taken the vile thing outside and burned it?

Hannah tiptoed past the case and down the stairs, until she was midway between floors. Silently, she lowered herself into a sitting position and rested the gun on one knee, pointing the barrels down into the gloom. She took the torch from her front pocket and placed it beside her.

Her eyes were gritty from lack of sleep. Her head throbbed. She just needed to get through the night. Tomorrow she would drive them away from here. Make sure they weren't followed. Find a hotel. Pay in cash. Sleep.

Hannah blinked at the darkness, stretched her neck from side to side, drifted.

When she opened her eyes, disorientated, she almost over-balanced. The metal of the shotgun was hot where her hands gripped it, slick with sweat. Her eyelids felt sticky. Had she dozed off?

Christ, Hannah!

She glanced at her watch, frowning at the dials, trying to make sense of the time. Fifteen minutes past five. Still dark outside. When had she left the bedroom? Three? She must have fallen asleep sitting upright, her head resting against the banisters.

With a loaded gun in your lap. Clever.

Biting off a yawn, she forced herself to focus. Had something woken her? The house was silent.

A chill waft of air caressed her. She shivered. Much colder now. The only fire still burning was in the bedroom.

Hannah tensed, raised the barrel of the gun.

Before going upstairs she had checked all the windows and doors. Earlier that day she had boarded over the smashed pane of glass in the living room. The cold draught could not be explained by the normal movement of air inside the house.

She clenched her teeth. Felt herself beginning to shake.

Focus on Nate. On Leah. Your husband, your beautiful daughter.

Don't you dare let them down. Don't you dare!

Someone was in the house with them. She knew it with a sudden dreadful certainty. Was it inconceivable that the intruder had already passed her while she slumbered? God, she didn't know.

Her left knee popped as she rose to her feet. She groped out a hand, searching for the torch.

If it's not there, I'll scream. I won't be able to help it.

Her fingers closed on it. She slipped it back into her pocket.

Eyes straining into the abyss at the bottom of the stairs, Hannah pressed her back to the wall and crept down to the hall.

At the base of the stairs, she leaned around the banister. Weak light from the porch window cast murky shapes across the floorboards. The door to the dining room was closed. Had it been like that when they'd gone up to bed? She thought it had.

Padding along the hall, she felt the wood under her feet flex with her weight. The next door on her right led to the living room. It was ajar. Beyond it, the hallway took a dogleg to the left, leading to the kitchen.

Don't leave an open door behind you.

Moving nearer to the living room allowed her to see past the corner to the kitchen. Its doorway was a black cavity. Keeping it in her peripheral vision, she ducked her head inside the living room, sweeping it with the gun.

Empty, as far as she could tell.

The large sofas might conceal someone. A tall bookcase in one corner bred impenetrable shadows. But the windows were closed and locked. The board over the smashed pane was nailed in place.

She exhaled a shallow breath and turned towards the kitchen just as Sebastien loomed out of the darkness.

Hannah gasped, choking off a scream. She staggered backwards, raising the gun. 'Jesus *Christ*! Get back!'

The old man hissed in surprise. 'Hannah? Thank God. You're—'

'What the hell, Seb? Stand back there where I can see you.'
She could see his eyes shining in the dark.

'Keep your voice down,' he whispered. 'He's here.'

'Jakab?'

'You have to get Nate and Leah. We're leaving. Now.'

'What's happened?'

'He surprised me at my place. I got away. He's *here*, Hannah.'

Her heart was thundering. She wedged the stock of the shotgun into her shoulder. 'How did you get in?'

'I have a key.'

She felt her lungs burning in her chest. Sucked down air. Strained to see him in the shadows. Strained to see his features. 'Where's Moses?'

'He's back at the house.'

'You left him?'

'Hannah, we've got to go.'

'What breed is he?'

'That's good. You're thinking. He's a Vizsla. Come on, wake them up. We don't have any time.'

Her skin felt as if lice were feeding on it. Her shaking was out of control. What if she dropped the gun? She fought the urge to wedge herself in the doorway.

Focus!

Her voice cracked. 'Sebastien, listen to me. When you last met Nate. Before all this. Where was it? And what did he eat?'

The shape in front of her hesitated. And then it *lunged*. Away from her. Towards the kitchen.

Hannah pulled the trigger. The shotgun roared, slamming into her shoulder. Its muzzle flash lit the passageway as the thunder of the blast rang in her ears.

She jumped forwards. Cold air rushed at her as the door to the kitchen slammed shut.

Points of light danced before her eyes. Blood pounded in her ears. Animal rage had overtaken her fear. The opportunity to end this, here, right now, was suddenly a reality. She charged at the door and rammed it with her shoulder. It bowed open a few inches. And then something hit it from the other side.

'You don't have to do this, Hannah. I want this to end as much as you do.'

His voice.

She heard a scrabbling. The pressure on the door ceased. Inside the kitchen, a table overturned with a crash.

Hannah stepped back and kicked the door open. 'Then let me help you,' she said, and fired into the darkness. She hadn't braced herself this time, and when the gun kicked, the stock cracked against her collarbone. The kitchen windows exploded.

A shout. Had she got him? A frantic shape danced by the back door. It wrestled with the handle. She ran towards it.

The shape yanked the door open and fled outside. Gravel chippings sprayed across the drive. Hannah skidded across the kitchen flagstones. The door slammed back against her head. Pain lashed her. She ignored it. Opened the door. Ran out into the night.

Jakab had reached the side of the house. He launched himself around it. Hannah followed, shrieking with fury. She turned the corner. Saw him running down the path towards the bridge. Saw a line of trees on his left. The river on his right.

She came to a stop. Put weight on her left leg. A shooter's stance. Lifted the gun. Tracked him.

Shotgun's empty, Hannah.

Swearing, she broke the weapon. Heard the spent cartridges jump out of the breech. Smelled the tang of gunpowder.

She fumbled in her back pocket for her spares. Slotted the first into the left-hand barrel. The second cartridge wouldn't fit. She was shaking too much. It popped from between her fingers. Fell to the ground.

Forget it. No time. Jakab was getting away. She snapped shut the gun and raised it to her shoulder. Braced properly this time. He was a vague shape in the darkness. She drew a line to him. Closed her left eye. Fired.

The gun kicked. The air *cracked*. Up ahead, she saw only darkness. Heard the fading crunch of feet on stones.

Hannah lowered the gun. She was hyperventilating. Sweat streamed from her. Stickiness in her left eye. She lifted a hand to her face, probed her forehead. Blood. A long gash, from the bridge of her nose to her hairline.

Then, to her left, the undergrowth exploded with movement. As she staggered backwards, a stag leaped from the trees.

It skittered to a stop on the gravel, hooves scrambling for purchase. Head swinging towards her, its liquid eyes met hers and it froze. Its flanks heaved as it snorted, condensation blasting from its snout. Steam rose from its hide. The animal was huge, its rack of antlers like the branches of a tree.

Hannah raised the gun. Knew that it wasn't loaded. Did it anyway.

The stag moved its head to one side, observing her. Then, incredibly, it bent its front legs and knelt. Hind legs tucking down behind it, the buck waited, prone.

Hannah stared at it, uncomprehending.

And then, slowly, she realised that the sounds coming from behind her, the sounds she had not even noticed until now, were the screams of her daughter.

CHAPTER 17

Oxford

1997

A thin mist of rain was beginning to fall as Charles parked his car two streets away from where Beckett lived.

A night had passed since their meeting in the Oxford botanic garden. Charles had not slept since, replaying their conversation as he lay in the darkness next to Nicole. At last, resigned to insomnia, he crept downstairs to his study. He pulled the drapes and sat at his desk. From a locked drawer he removed the diaries, their translations, and his indexed book of notes.

He cursed when he found three mentions of Eleni. Why had he never thought to check up on those references? Why also, he wondered, had he chosen to lie to Beckett about it? He thought back to the academic's words. *The Eleni was the organisation tasked with carrying out the cull.*

During his research, Charles had read several descriptions of the *hosszú életek* cull, including a memorable passage penned by Hans Fischer. In one rendition, the *életek* youth were barricaded inside their *végzet* venue and the building torched. In another, they were herded into the hold of a Danube river vessel, which was subsequently holed and sunk. The *életek* elders, when found, were hanged, decapitated, shot. Regardless of the individual methods, the result was the same: a massacre. Charles closed his notebook and went to his drinks cabinet. He poured himself a Glenlivet.

You're starting to have doubts, aren't you? Twenty years of having this tale drip-fed to you is beginning to have its effect. You've polluted your mind with it and now you can't sort myth from reality.

He returned to his chair, rolling the spirit around in his glass. Was he finally starting to lose his ability to reason? Taking a sip of whisky, letting the liquid trickle down his throat, he thought back to his meeting with Beckett. How could the academic have a signed Royal Decree in his possession? Why had he been so elusive about its origin? Throughout the conversation, Charles had felt Beckett's eyes measuring him, had felt that the man he had called a friend for more than two decades was mocking him.

Has Beckett been supplanted?

Charles coughed, nearly choked. He sat up in his chair and put the glass down on the desk. Whisky sloshed on to his notes. 'Get a hold on yourself, fool,' he muttered. 'You've been caught up in this too long. It's wrecked Nicole's mind. Now it's wrecking yours.'

'How's Nicole?'

'She's well.'

'Been a long time since I saw her. We should arrange something. Dinner.'

Charles felt the blood drain from his stomach as the realisation hit him. He was suddenly certain: in twenty years, Beckett had never met Nicole, had never even asked after her. The man was a fanatical bachelor, renowned for his view that women were a distraction and a nuisance. As for going out for dinner, a bag of pork scratchings at the Eagle and Child was about as close as Beckett had ever previously come to suggesting a shared meal.

Charles stared at the spine of his *Legacy of the Germanic Peoples* on the bookshelf opposite – the copy Nicole had not torn in half. Next to it was the much slimmer *Journal of European Folklore and Mythology*. Inside that, *Hosszú életek: the birth and death of a Hungarian legend*.

Had he, in an orgy of vanity, called down a monster upon them? Was there any chance that everything Hans Fischer and Anna Bauer had written about was true? Had Eric Dubois really been murdered by Jakab? Had Erna Novák really lost her life to a *Főnök*'s *Merénylő*?

His head throbbed. He drained the whisky and poured himself another.

That had been nine hours ago. Now, parked in the residential street a few hundred yards from Beckett's apartment, Charles switched off the ignition and unfastened his seat belt. He glanced at himself in the rear-view mirror. His eyes were blood-shot, a legacy from too much whisky and a night without sleep. His cheeks were grizzled with stubble. It was probably the first time he had not shaved in years.

A leather holdall sat on the seat next to him. Was he really going to do this?

Yes, he was. He had to know. He owed it to Nicole. Christ, he owed everything to Nicole.

Unzipping the holdall, he took out a metal box and placed it on his lap. He snapped open the two clasps and lifted the lid. His father's pistol lay inside, cushioned by strips of fabric. The weapon was a Luger 08, taken from a dead *Wehrmacht* officer in Berlin at the end of the war. Charles had no ammunition for it. Beckett, or the thing posing as Beckett, would not know that.

He cringed. How easy it was, suddenly, to believe. How frightening. Slipping the pistol into the pocket of his overcoat, Charles opened the car door and stepped out into the rain.

Beckett's home was one of two apartments converted from a sprawling Victorian townhouse. Cars lined the street outside. Charles walked along the pavement, head bowed against the drizzle. He climbed the steps to the front door, gathered himself, and pressed the buzzer to the academic's apartment. A minute later he heard footsteps descending a flight of stairs, and saw a shape appear on the other side of the glass.

The door opened and Beckett peered out. He broke into a grin. 'Charles! What a delight! As a matter of fact, I was just thinking about you. A fortuitous coincidence!'

'Hello Patrick.'

'Well, don't dally on the threshold. Come in, come in!' Beckett opened the door and Charles stepped over a pile of pizza fliers into the hallway. On the tiled floor, two elderly bicycles leaned against a cast-iron radiator. A black umbrella, on its side, dripped water.

Charles followed Beckett up the stairs and into the flat. The place smelled of dust and rancid cat litter. The hall was crammed with bookcases. When the shelving had run out, Beckett had resorted to stacking books in haphazard piles on the floor. A threadbare crimson rug covered an ancient carpet.

Beckett disappeared through a doorway into his snug, and Charles followed.

A standard lamp in one corner gave the room a warm glow. Beckett folded himself into an armchair and gestured at a throw-covered couch. Charles sat down on it, feeling the springs sag beneath his weight.

Books were piled everywhere here, too. An eighteenth-century map of Oxford hung above the fireplace. On the mantelpiece stood a framed sepia photograph of Beckett's mother. Beside it, on a wooden stand, a Gurkha knife. A unicycle was propped against a side table that held a black and white television. Three brightly coloured juggling skittles lay underneath it, thick with dust.

Beckett gasped, leaped to his feet. 'Forgive me, Charles! You come to my home and I fail to demonstrate the most basic of hospitality.' He rubbed his hands together. 'Drink? Pork pie?'

'Thank you, no.'

'Mind if I do?'

'Not at all.'

'Great. Right, then. I will. Back in a tick.' Beckett squeezed past a laden coffee table, upending a box of papers, and side-stepped out of the room.

Putting his hand into the pocket of his coat, Charles touched the cold metal of the Luger. Now he was here, the thought that Beckett could be an impostor was ludicrous. He watched as a cat padded into the room and jumped on to the arm of the couch. It regarded him indifferently, and yawned.

Beckett returned, holding a dimpled pint jug filled with ale. In his other hand he clutched a large pork pie, missing a bite. Noticing the cat, he cursed, spraying pastry crumbs. 'Ramses, get down! Seriously, these bloody cats. Can't stand the things half the time. Think I'm allergic, actually. Should have got dogs. Know where you are with dogs, don't you. Silly mistake.'

'How many cats do you have?'

'Five. Four. No, three. Lost one. Or two. Neighbour down-tairs hates them. Can't say I blame her. Wish I'd known you were coming. Would have tidied the place up a bit.' Beckett slurped from his glass. 'Cheers.'

'No Pálinka today, then.'

Beckett laughed. 'Good point. We probably should, given your recent achievements. I have a bottle somewhere. But to be honest, I hate the stuff.'

Charles stared. Beckett met his eyes for a moment, then looked across the room. Charles followed his gaze to the machete on the mantelpiece. Their eyes met again and Beckett smiled, displaying his enormous teeth. 'So, you're here. That's good. Nice to have a proper chat.'

'I wanted to follow up on our conversation.'

'You did?'

'To start, I wanted you to tell me more about the Eleni.'

'Ah.' Beckett took a large swallow of beer, then bit into his pie. He chewed for what seemed like an age. 'The good old Eleni. Should I say good? Or should I say downright bloody vile? The latter's more appropriate, isn't it? We thought Hitler was a sociopath. Well, he was. And so were the Eleni.'

'Tell me what you know about them.'

'You're the expert these days, Charles.'

'I'm interested nonetheless.'

Beckett settled back in his chair. 'Secret death squad, set up to wipe the *hosszú életek* from the face of the planet. From the evidence, they must have done a pretty good job.' He chuckled. 'Unless you know something I don't.'

'And they're still in existence today.'

'Ha. Battle re-enactors probably. You know how it goes with this kind of thing.'

'I'd like to see the scroll again.'

'Yes, of course.' Beckett blinked, looked over at Charles. 'Sorry?'

'The scroll. The one you showed me yesterday.'

The academic frowned. 'My dear boy, are you pulling Patrick's leg?'

'The Royal Decree.'

'Charles, frankly, I'm getting a bit old and a bit slow. I must confess I have no idea what you're talking about. I was here all day yesterday.'

'I met you in the physic garden.'

'With my hay fever? I can't even go there in the depths of winter. You think cats are bad. Try me with pollen. I sneeze out a lung even thinking about the place.'

Charles felt his chest tightening. 'Patrick, when did you last see Nicole?'

'Who?' The academic scratched his head. 'Is this some kind of initiation rite?'

Jumping to his feet, Charles sprinted through the flat, down the flight of stairs and out into the street.

Nicole was lying on the bed, a crocheted pillow in her arms, when the back door slammed and Charles called out her name.

'Up here.' Nicole heard his feet pounding up the stairs and when the door to the bedroom opened, she rolled over and smiled at him.

He looked terrible. For the first time since she'd known him, he hadn't shaved. And his eyes looked different. Haunted.

'Hi.' He stared down at her, and then he noticed the journal propped open on the bed: *European Folklore and Mythology.* 'You've read it, then.'

She shrugged. 'Curiosity got the better of me in the end.'

'It gets us all.'

'Are you OK?'

He shut the door and came over to the bed. 'I think we need to talk about some things.'

She patted the covers. 'I think we probably do.'

'Nicole—' His voice cracked. He sat down, his head bowed.

'Charles, are you crying?'

Wiping his eyes, he shook his head.

'What is it?' She propped herself up on one arm. 'What's wrong?'

'Nicole . . . My God, Nicole. However did I have the good grace to find you?'

'Overwhelming luck, probably.' Reaching for him, she tugged him on to the bed.

'If I ever lost you—'

'You came spectacularly close.'

'Do you really want to stay here?' he asked. 'In Oxford?'

'Don't you?'

He sighed, touched her face. 'I love you so much.'

'I know. You've a strange way of showing it sometimes, but I know you do. Come here.'

She pulled him to her. And then, for the first time in weeks, they made love. Afterwards, lying naked in his arms, Nicole reflected just how much she had missed their closeness. She had never seen him cry, had never seen him so vulnerable. It troubled her. She wondered what had caused it.

Stirring, Charles rolled on to his side and stared into her eyes. 'I'll do whatever you want.'

She reached out a hand, ruffling his hair. 'I'm a lucky girl indeed. The great Professor Meredith, prostrate before me, prepared to grant my every whim.'

'I'm serious. Whatever you want.' He looked over at the bedside table, where the diaries of her ancestors lay in a pile. 'What are those?'

Nicole smiled. She managed not to jerk away from him. Hoped that her face did not betray her. 'Just some old books.'

He nodded.

Wanting to gasp for air, forcing herself instead to take a measured breath, she studied his face – the line of his jaw, the sagging skin at his throat, his bushy eyebrows, matted hair.

And then, as calmly as she could, Nicole rose naked from the bed. She felt his eyes on her body as she pulled on her dressing gown. When she turned back to him, he was smirking, a predator's smile.

'I'm going to make some coffee,' she said.

'I'll join you.'

Nicole went out into the hall. She blotted two tears from her eyes.

Don't let him see. Don't let him suspect.

Was Charles dead? Was it already too late? Down the hall to the landing. Down a twisting flight of stairs to the lobby. Through to the kitchen, where she filled the kettle, plugged it in and turned to see that the man who looked like her husband but might not be had followed her into the room.

Trembling, she opened a cupboard and removed two cups. Took the pouch of coffee from the fridge. Spooned grains into the cafetière. Fumbled the container trying to put it back in the fridge. Dropped it.

Coffee grains slid across the floor in a brown tide. 'Jesus.'

The creature that might not be Charles shook its head. 'Never mind. Is there a brush?'

'I can do it.' Nicole fetched the brush and swept up the grains, teeth grinding. She emptied the dustpan into the bin as the kettle boiled, then poured water into the cafetière. 'I saw Sarah this morning.'

'Oh yes?'

There was no Sarah. Facing the counter, her back to him, Nicole suppressed a sob. 'She said you've agreed to teach her French class again.'

'I did?'

'Apparently.'

'I don't remember. But I'm happy to.'

Next to the cafetière stood the kettle. Next to the kettle, the toaster. Next to the toaster, a wooden block containing six incredibly sharp Sabatier knives Nicole had brought back from Thiers.

She glanced over her shoulder. In the breakfast nook, he had plucked a photo frame from the windowsill and was studying it intently. The picture was of Hannah, taken when she was thirteen. The girl sat in a canoe, life jacket over a summer vest, smiling up at the camera. They had been on a family holiday along the Dordogne. Two weeks of camping by the river, cooking over a stove, telling stories underneath the stars.

The man that might be Charles looked up at her and grinned, and Nicole finally admitted to herself that he was an impostor. She turned back to the kitchen counter, thinking that her legs might give way. Imagine that. Sprawled on the floor with that monster behind her. She swallowed, forced herself not to run.

In Carcassonne, how long had Petre impersonated her father before killing him? Days? Weeks? Was this the first time Jakab had visited her? The tenth? If it had not been for that simple error upstairs, she would never have even suspected.

You made love to him.

Charles's recent publishing success must have brought him here. The book, with its dust jacket photograph. The journal article. Both had been published within the last month. How long had it taken Jakab to discover them? How long to track Charles down? He couldn't have been here more than a few weeks, perhaps only a few days. Perhaps this was the first time he had visited. If that were the case, then her husband was probably still alive.

Maybe.

Possibly.

'The jeweller phoned,' she said.

'Oh yes?'

'Said your watch was ready.'

'I'll pick it up in the morning.'

Nicole heard him walk up behind her. There was no jeweller. No watch.

She turned around.

Jakab was standing in front of her, the picture of Hannah still in his hands. He was laughing.

She picked up the cafetière from the counter and flung its contents in his face. Boiling coffee engulfed him and he screamed, staggering backwards. The photo frame dropped from his hands. It smashed on the tiled floor.

'Do you have any idea how much that *hurts*?' he roared. When he straightened, she saw that the skin of his face was a bright, scalded red. Coffee grains and liquid dripped from his chin. Crazily, he *laughed* again. 'Damn, but it wakes you up, doesn't it? That's what they say about good coffee. Gives you a kick.'

Nicole yanked a carving knife out of the block. The wooden cube bounced off the counter. Knives clattered to the floor, steel shafts spinning. She jumped forwards and slashed at him. He was fast – too fast – shielding his face with an arm. The blade sliced through the fabric of his jacket. Blood flicked across the room.

Nicole lunged, intent this time on burying the knife in his face. He dodged. Before she managed to pull back the blade far enough to thrust at him a second time, her foot slipped in the boiling coffee. She toppled backwards, cracking her head against the counter as she fell.

Sprawled on the tiles, Nicole felt coffee burning her legs. The blow had stunned her, the shock too intense to let her move. Glancing down, she saw that her dressing gown gaped open, exposing her nakedness. She gasped at the horror of it.

Jakab tore a tea towel from the back of a chair and mopped his face. Already the red blotches were fading. He tossed away the cloth and examined the tear in his jacket. 'Oh, you absolute bitch. Look what you've done. Seriously, Nicole, look at this. Do you know how much I liked this jacket? I saw Charles wearing something similar last week and looked everywhere for one.'

On the floor to her left, a small filleting knife lay just within reach. She inched out her fingers towards it.

Jakab paced up and down in front of her, holding his hands against the sides of his head. 'Calm down, Jakab, calm down. It's not too late, it's not. Salvage it, that's what you do. Yes. That's what you're good at.'

Nicole touched the cold handle of the filleting knife. Her stomach flipped. She thought she might be sick.

Jakab snatched the smashed photo frame from the floor and brought it over to her. 'Who's this? Who is it?'

Her fingers crabbed over the handle of the knife. Closed around it.

'It's Erna, that's who it is. How? She's dead, Nicole. *Dead*. This is a *colour photograph*.' He thrust the picture at her.

She dragged the knife across the tiles.

'Oh, do you have to?' He lifted his foot and stamped down.

The bones in her wrist crunched. She screamed, pulling her shattered arm towards her.

Jakab kicked the filleting knife across the room. He noticed the other knives, and kicked them all away from her. 'All this time looking for you, Nicole. All these years. And look at you.

Old. Old and *spiteful*. Vicious.' He paused, sucked in a breath. 'Who is the girl?'

'It's me, Jakab.'

'Liar! Get up.'

She scissored her legs in front of her. 'Where's Charles?'

'Get up!'

'What have you done to him?'

'He's dead. Now answer my question.'

She cried out, her heart unravelling.

Jakab grabbed her arm and yanked her to her feet. He shoved her back against the counter. 'I'm going to ask you a final time. *Who* is she? *Where* is she?'

Tears coursing down her cheeks, Nicole stared at him, at the monster that looked like her husband but was not.

Jakab pulled back his fist and punched her in the face.

She woke, slumped on a chair in the corner of the breakfast nook. Her right eye was gummed shut. Her mouth tasted of blood. She raised her head drunkenly, looked about her.

Jakab sat across the table. He had removed the ruined jacket and was dressed in one of Charles's cashmere jumpers. Oxford Blue.

On the table, arranged in front of her, stood eight photo frames. He must have toured the house for them while she was unconscious. Each frame contained a different picture of Hannah.

Hannah dressed as an angel at a school play. Hannah posing on a sports field with hockey stick and ball. Hannah on a trampoline. Hannah and Charles splashing in the sea.

'Her name's Hannah,' Jakab said. 'And she's your daughter.'

Nicole said nothing. She looked up at him. Stared into his dead eyes.

'You know, I really didn't want this to happen,' he continued. 'I really wanted to make this work. Despite what I said – about you being old and spiteful – I enjoyed what we did earlier. There's definitely a positive element to your aggressive streak.'

She spat at him. A thick curdle of blood. It splattered across his cheek.

He sighed. 'But you are vicious. It's a shame. Where can I find her?'

'I'll kill you first.'

Jakab raised a hand to his face and wiped away the clot of blood and saliva. He stood up and walked across the kitchen, returning with a cloth. He used it to clean his fingers.

Moving around the table, he sat on the chair beside her. 'You're not going to tell me. I didn't think you would. Not really. You're stubborn, just like the rest of them. It's not an attractive trait, Nicole.'

He reached out to her. She flinched away from him, but her movement caused the room to tilt and spin.

Jakab began to talk, soothingly, as if to a wounded bird he was hoping to mend.

Perhaps that's what I am, she thought. A wounded bird. Too badly broken now.

'I'm going to gently – very gently – take your head in my hands,' he said, reaching out, sliding his fingers through the hair above her ears. 'And you're going to let me, *that's* it, just like that, exactly like that. You see, you might not know this, you probably don't, but there's this old *hosszú élet* parlour trick. It's quite a good one. I don't know how it works, I don't even know how I do it. But it does work, and that's all that really matters.'

She felt the palms of his hands against her temples, felt a sudden warmth from them. Nicole tried to turn her head away, but Jakab eased it back towards him, smiling, always smiling. The warmth in his hands became a heat, and suddenly she felt a lance of pain in her head.

'It won't hurt for long,' he told her. 'That's it, relax.'

She felt her heart begin to thump in her chest, its beat

accelerating. Dropping her mouth open, she panted, feeling the blood in her arteries beginning to race. A huge pressure was building in her throat, in her head. The walls of her skull felt like they were bulging. Her ears popped.

Then, quite suddenly, Nicole felt something rupture in her left eye, found herself blinking at him through a tide of crimson. She opened her mouth to shriek.

Jakab tilted his head as he watched her. 'I always find this part fascinating. Where *do* you go?'

Charles parked on the street outside his house, switched off the engine and unclipped his seat belt. He rubbed his face and stared at the sweat glistening on his fingers. One question repeated in his mind.

What have you done?

The man he had visited earlier was undoubtedly Beckett. The creature he had met in the physic garden yesterday undoubtedly was not. They had looked identical, sounded identical, acted identical. But the impostor who had shown him the Royal Decree had seemed pleased at Charles's discomfort. Had mocked him with his eyes.

Charles stared at his house, at the home he had shared with Nicole for the last twelve years. What did they do now? The experiences of those who had already travelled this path suggested only one option. Flee. Immediately. Pack up the necessary things, the few precious and irreplaceable things – letters, photographs. Find Nicole. Collect Hannah from her school. Leave.

What have you done?

He knew where their passports were, knew the whereabouts of his important documents. He had about a thousand pounds in cash inside the house. Enough for their immediate needs. He could quickly get more.

A shadow passed across the bevelled glass of the front door. Instinctively, Charles ducked down on to the passenger seat.

Raising his head, he watched the door open and saw an identical Charles Meredith step outside.

'Oh my God, no.'

The creature was wearing his favourite Oxford Blue sweater. It shut the door behind it and walked down the path to the street.

Charles rolled off the seat and wedged himself in the floor well. He realised he was shivering, convulsing. He did not know how long he lay there, but when he sat up, looking up and down the street, his nightmare double had gone. Charles clambered out of the car. He felt his jaw moving, his teeth clattering together in his mouth.

In the hall, he called out his wife's name. All the lights were on. He walked down the corridor to the kitchen, noticing that many of the photographs that lined the wall had disappeared. Discoloured oblongs of wallpaper announced their absence.

He opened the door to the kitchen and found a pool of what looked like coffee on the floor. Footprints had skidded and slipped through it, leaving trails. In one corner lay an empty knife block. In another, its collection of knives. A bloodied tea towel was bunched up on the work surface. On the kitchen table he saw a collection of photo frames, their backs towards him. On a chair, facing him, sat Nicole.

Charles closed the door behind him, shutting them both inside the room. The phone hung from a bracket on the wall beside the fridge. Pinned to a cork board above it was a list of important numbers. Nicole had put them there for him, as he was always misplacing things. Charles stared at the list for a while, looking for the number he needed. Then he picked up the phone and dialled.

A woman answered.

He cleared his throat and explained that he needed to speak to Hannah Meredith, that he was her father, and that it was urgent. The woman listened, and put him on hold while someone was sent to fetch his daughter from her class.

From the breakfast nook, his dead wife watched him. It looked as if, at the end, she had wept tears of blood. Her left eye was closed. Beads of blood oozed from beneath her eyelid. Her right eye stared at him, a bright red orb. He didn't like to look at it for long. Didn't want to remember her that way. Her bathrobe was open. Blood had gushed from her nose. It had splashed down her breasts on to the round curve of her stomach.

He didn't understand this. He had thought that Jakab wanted her. Had thought that had been the point.

'Dad?'

'Hannah.'

'What's happened? Everything all right?'

'No. Not really.' Charles paused, turned his back on his wife. It was difficult to concentrate with her staring at him like that. 'I'm afraid I need you to walk out of school. Right now. Once I finish talking, you need to hang up and just go. Do you understand?'

A pause on the other end of the line. '. . . Did he come?'

'Yes, Hannah, he did.'

'Is Mum with you?'

'Listen to me. Can you find your way to St Mary's Church?'

'Sure.'

'Good. Go there. Wait for me. I'll be there within the hour.' He paused. 'Is there anything you want me to bring? From the house?'

'No, Dad. Just you, and Mum.'

CHAPTER 18

Budapest

Now

With his eyes closed, the rising sound beneath him could have been the hum of some vast human machine. Whispers, coughs, smothered laughter. The creak of seat backs. The rustle of paper.

Then, stirring, the orchestra. A solitary oboe note at first, long and mournful. The vibration of horsehair on string announcing violins. Viola, cello and double bass adding their voice. A swell of trumpet, trombone and horn. Somewhere a breathy flute arpeggio, leaping among them.

Lorant Vince opened his eyes and breathed in the golden magnificence of the Budapest Opera House as its orchestra tuned its instruments. He sat alone in the royal box, on a straight-backed chair of maroon velvet. Above him, the auditorium's huge chandelier lit the ceiling frescos of Károly Lotz: startling images of Olympus and the Greek gods. Three golden storeys of private boxes curved away from him in a horseshoe around the stage. With the exception of the Royal Palace, the Opera House was Lorant's favourite building in Budapest.

As the orchestra continued to tune its instruments, the door behind him opened and Lorant heard someone enter. 'You're late,' he whispered.

The chair beside him scraped. Lorant turned in his seat. He

had been expecting Károly Gera, and while he could muster little love these days for the *signeur*, Lorant found the man beside him far more disquieting

Benjámin Vass looked down at the orchestra, at the audience in the stalls, the gilt and velvet splendour of the auditorium. Then he turned to Lorant. Vass's face was fleshy and placid, empty of expression, eyes hooded by drooping lids. His breath smelled of spiced meat, as if he had just eaten a plate of *gyulai kolbász*.

'Károly sends his apologies, *Presidente*. He asked me to attend you instead.'

'Károly requests a meeting with me and then sends his *second*?'

'His illness has worsened. I'm acting in his interest.'

Lorant felt his jaw tighten. No one acted in the interest of the Eleni's three *ülnökök*. No *ülnök* acted in his own interest, either; an *ülnök* acted in the sole interest of the Eleni Council. 'I'm sorry to hear that,' he said.

It was true. Károly was an old man, nearly as old as Lorant, dying from a disease he had spent the last six months battling. While Lorant would not grieve his death when it arrived, he would grieve for the man Károly had once been. What really concerned Lorant was that Károly's death increased the threat of Vass's elevation to *signeur*. As *Presidente,* Lorant could veto that appointment, but if the remaining *ülnökök* voted for Vass, his own position would become untenable.

Do I even want this burden any more? Probably not. I'm too old, too tired. And what, after all, have I achieved in all this time?

Regardless, he knew that if he did nothing else before stepping down, he had to do everything possible to prevent Vass from rising any higher. The man would twist the Council's manifesto, warp its objectives, tear it apart.

'Károly demands to know—'

'He *demands*?'

Vass hesitated. Then he smiled. 'Károly begs, he *grovels*, to discover why you've flown Dániel Meyer and others to London and have not deemed it pertinent to inform him.'

Lorant stared at Vass, forcing himself to maintain eye contact. Meyer was the only *ülnök* whose judgement Lorant could still trust. It was why he had sent him. 'You may tell Károly that I feel no pressing need to answer that.'

'He asks me to remind you that if the *ülnökök* majority raise a question, the *Presidente* is obliged to answer.'

'I see no *ülnökök* majority before me. I see no *ülnök* at all, nor the likelihood of one.'

If Vass was stung by that, he gave no sign. 'I will remind you, Lorant. I am acting for Károly. Which means I'm acting with the full authority of the *signeur* and—'

'You *have* no authority!'

'And I'm sure when I speak to Földessy he'll be equally keen to find out what is going on. There are your two *ülnökök*, Lorant. There is your majority.'

'You speak for Földessy now, too?'

'Of course not. But I think it's a safe assumption that he'll want to know what's happening as much as I do.' Vass smiled. 'As much as Károly does, I should say.'

Vass was correct. It was a safe assumption. Földessy had become impatient in recent years: impatient and hard-line. It was exactly the reason Lorant had confided in Dániel Meyer alone.

Below them, the notes of the orchestra faded. The audience settled, expectant.

'Well?' Vass asked.

Forcing his voice to remain calm even as his fingers clutched the arms of his chair, Lorant said, 'If the *signeur* wishes to force my hand, he knows what he needs to do. I will not negotiate with a messenger.'

Vass held Lorant's stare. He blinked his hooded eyes twice. 'Enjoy the opera, *Presidente*.'

★ ★ ★

The cab took Benjámin Vass across the city, circling the Városliget and dropping him outside the entrance to the Széchenyi Baths. He paid the fare, walked up the steps of the building's neo-baroque frontage and passed its enormous stone pillars. Against the night sky, its spotlit walls glowed a rich egg-yolk yellow. Vass showed his card to a guard in the marble-floored entrance lobby and walked through an archway to the three huge outdoor baths.

Illuminated by lamps on wrought-iron posts, two semi-circular pools book-ended a central oblong bath. Surrounding them rose the colossal towers, domes, balconies and fountains that dominated the building's architecture. Doorways led to a further fifteen indoor baths, all fed from two artesian wells tapping the thermal spring deep below the city park.

Steam coalesced on the surface of the water, obscuring the features of the hundred or so bathers. The smell of the minerals sharp in his nose, Vass walked across the stone paving to the furthest semi-circular pool. He found Károly Gera soaking near the steps, following a chess game two patrons had erected on a plinth jutting into the water.

Flesh hung off the man like melted candle wax. The skin of his face was a stained hessian, unable to soften the sharp ridges of his hairless skull. His eyes blinked from sunken sockets. Each rib of his liver-spotted torso strained against skin like the spines of a bat's wing.

Recognising Vass, Károly eased himself away from the chess players, moving through the water to a secluded spot at the edge of the pool. Vass squatted down opposite him.

'You saw him?' the *signeur* asked. He held a glass in his right hand. It contained a measure of spirit and a single cube of ice.

Vass nodded.

'Well? Out with it, then.'

Vass smirked. 'He's scared.'

'Nothing new there. Lorant's always been scared. What's he up to? Why has he sent Meyer to London?'

'He wouldn't say.'

Károly's face puckered into a scowl. 'That's outrageous. Have you spoken to Földessy?'

'Not yet.'

'I gave you very specific instructions.'

'I wanted you to see this first.' Vass unsnapped the clasps of a leather satchel and removed a clear plastic sleeve. It held an English newspaper clipping. 'I found this. It was published two days ago.'

Károly snatched up the document and squinted at it. He was silent for a minute and then he thrust the sleeve back at Vass. 'Suspected murder. Missing persons. So what?'

'The missing person is Anthony Pearson. Isn't that one of the identities Lorant arranged for Charles Meredith? After his wife's death?'

Károly lurched forwards. '*Te jó ég!*' he said, eyes glittering. 'Balázs Jakab. He's found them.'

Vass moved the *signeur's* wheelchair to the edge of the pool and helped the old man out of the water. In the moonlight, Károly's body was a milk-white membrane, sloughing off steam. Vass slung a robe around his shoulders and eased him into the chair.

Leukaemia was survivable in many of its forms. But once the cancer passed from the blood to the central nervous system, as it had with Károly, the prognosis was dismal; the median survival rate was one hundred and eight days.

The *signeur's* fingers twitched at the air. He swung towards Vass. 'We need to intercept. You have to arrange flights immediately.'

'We need to find out exactly where Meyer's gone first. We don't even have a contact over there.'

'Don't argue with me,' Károly snapped. 'Remember our deal.'

Vass stopped himself from smiling. 'Yes, *signeur*. Can I ask this, then? *Do* we have a contact?'

'We did. A long time ago.'

'Who?'

'His name is Sebastien Lang.'

'Sounds familiar.'

'It should, Benjámin. Lang was *signeur* before me.'

'And you know his whereabouts?'

'I have a suspicion.'

'Can we trust him?'

Károly grinned, his teeth luminous in the moonlight. 'You don't need to worry about that.'

CHAPTER 19

Snowdonia

Now

Hannah slammed through the back door of the farmhouse and ran through the kitchen into the hallway, flicking on lights as she went. Leah was screaming. Nate was shouting her name.

Upstairs. Both of them.

Sprinting along the hall, she grabbed the banister and swung herself around.

Nate was standing at the top of the stairs. In one hand he clutched a metal poker. His other arm clasped their daughter.

When Leah spotted Hannah her screams turned to sobs. 'Mummy!' She tried to extricate herself from Nate but he held her firmly, staring down the stairs with distrust in his eyes.

'The meal you cooked that night in the Cairngorms,' he said. 'What was it?'

'Chicken mole. Never again.'

He nodded. 'My first car?'

'Volkswagen Scirocco. White, with a leaky passenger door.'

Nate released his grip on Leah. The girl thundered down the stairs and leaped at her mother. Hannah cradled her with one arm, unwilling to let go of the shotgun, worried that she had not yet reloaded it.

'It's OK, scamp. It's OK,' she murmured into the girl's hair.

'He came, didn't he? The Bad Man came.'

'Yes, he came. But he's gone now. Mummy frightened him away. You're safe. I'm here. Your dad's here.'

'What happened?' Nate asked.

'He broke in through the back door. Pretending to be Seb.'

'Your head—'

'Just a cut.'

'It looks bad.'

'I'm OK. Really.'

He nodded. 'You didn't wake me.'

'I'm stupid, that's why. I couldn't sleep so I came downstairs, surprised him. Reckless. I could have ruined everything.'

'You didn't. We're all still here. You might even have—' He cursed, put a hand to his abdomen.

Hannah dropped her gaze to the bottom of his shirt. A dark stain was spreading across the fabric. 'Oh Nate, you're bleeding.'

He frowned down at his clothing. 'I jumped out of bed when I heard the gun shots. Must have torn the stitches.'

Blood was beginning to drip from the hem of his shirt.

For the first time, Hannah felt truly helpless.

Jakab was somewhere outside. And now this.

'What are we going to do?' she asked, hating the desperation in her voice.

Nate winced. 'One thing at a time, as always. Come on. Help me downstairs.'

Between them, they managed to get him down to the hall. Leah opened the door to the dining room and switched on the lights. Hannah helped her husband inside. She felt light-headed. Not enough sleep. Too much adrenalin. Too much fear, panic.

Beyond a mahogany dining table, two armchairs flanked the window. She guided Nate towards one and eased him into it. Breaking open the shotgun, ejecting the single spent round, she pulled two cartridges from her back pocket and slotted them into the breech. Hannah snapped the gun back together, closed the dining-room door, crouched down beside her daughter. She put one hand to the girl's face. Stroked her cheek. 'Leah, remember all those times when we talked about this moment? About a time when you'd have to be strong?'

The girl nodded. Her pupils were huge.

'Well, honey, that time is now. You know we love you, your daddy and I. More than anything else in the world. It's vital you remember that.'

'You think one of you is going to die.'

Hannah felt a tear roll down her cheek, cursed herself. 'No, darling. No one thinks that. But even if there's a tiny chance, we have to prepare for it. Just so we know what to do if it happens. You're a strong girl. Brave. Intelligent. All you need to do is keep thinking, keep questioning, keep a close watch. Trust your instincts, react fast, just as we've always taught you. Now, do you remember we showed you how to use one of these?' Hannah asked, indicating the shotgun.

'Yes.'

'What's this slider?'

'The safety.'

'How do you disengage it?'

'Push it forwards.'

'Good.'

'How will I know who he is?'

'You remember how we validate each other?'

'Yes.'

'If you're unsure, that's how. Now, come here.' Hannah pulled her daughter into an embrace.

Then Nate said, 'Car.'

Hannah moved to the side of the window. Dawn had bleached away the darkness, sketching the landscape in shades of grey. A battered blue Defender was rattling down the track from the main road.

The 4x4 bounced over the bridge and accelerated towards the farmhouse, headlights cutting a white beam through the shadows. It skidded to a stop twenty yards from the house. The engine idled for a few moments and then it died. Its lights went out.

Nate twisted his head. 'What do you see?'

'Sebastien's Land Rover.'

'Can you see him?'

The windscreen was a dark slab of glass. She could feel the gaze of the vehicle's occupant upon her. 'No. Leah, watch the car. If it moves, if anyone gets out, shout.'

The girl was gripping one of the dining-room chairs. Her knuckles were white. 'Where are you going?'

'To get the spare ammunition. I won't be long. Count to ten. I'll be back.' Hannah threw open the door and ran into the hallway. She skidded around the corner to the kitchen. The back door was hanging open, slamming in the wind. Two of the windows were broken, where she had tried to shoot Jakab. A smattering of shot was lodged in the frame.

Flinging open the pantry door, she grabbed two boxes of cartridges and ran back to the dining room.

'It didn't move.'

'Good girl. Now take these boxes. Open them up. I want you to lay the cartridges in a nice long row, so I can reach them easily if I need to. OK?'

Leah nodded. She put the first box on a chair. Opening the second, she began to arrange the rounds in a neat line, brass casings upwards.

Hannah moved back to the wall beside the window. Outside, the Defender's door banged open. She saw a blur of movement in the gap between the driver's compartment and the frame. Moses jumped down on to the gravel. He dropped his head to the chippings, turning in a slow circle. He looked up at Llyn Gwyr, then back at the 4x4. Nose close to the ground, he ran towards the farmhouse as if following a scent. 'It's his dog,' she said.

'Moses?'

She nodded. The dog ran past the window, raising his head and meeting her eyes. Then he was gone.

'Keep talking to me, Hannah.'

She glanced down. Nate's shirt was wet with blood now. The sight of it made her want to retch or scream or both.

You have to get him to a hospital! He's not strong enough for this!

'Nothing happening yet,' she replied. 'No movement.'

A bang somewhere in the house. A metal object falling over with a crash. Leah moaned with fear. She clamped a hand to her mouth.

A skittering in the hallway outside. A thump against the dining-room door. A low woof.

Hannah flicked off the safety on the shotgun. She took her left hand from the weapon and pried open the door a crack. Moses nosed into the room. She shut the door behind him.

The dog dropped his head and sniffed her feet, her legs, her crotch. He moved his nose up and down her free hand and licked her. Turning away, he approached Leah, enquiring, investigating. He moved his nose all over her body, licked her fingers and then he trotted over to Nate.

Moses stopped when he saw the blood.

'It's OK, boy,' Nate said, holding out his hand.

The dog turned his head away, first towards Hannah and then towards Leah. Whined.

'Go on, Moses,' Hannah said. She felt her stomach contracting, her scalp buzzing. She moved her free hand back to the barrel of the shotgun. The safety was already disengaged. Her daughter was far enough away from her husband's chair.

The dog took a step forwards, dropped his head and sniffed Nate's shoes. He looked up and whined a second time. Closer now, he sniffed her husband's legs, his crotch. Nate waggled his fingers. The dog nosed them. Then he licked them.

Hannah sagged against the door frame, breath exploding from her.

Nate raised his eyebrows at the animal. 'Thanks buddy. You nearly got me shot.'

Moses padded to the window and jumped up. He placed his front paws on the sill, and barked twice.

Outside, Sebastien climbed out of the Land Rover. He put his hands to his mouth and shouted Hannah's name.

She joined the dog at the window and opened it. 'Seb?'

'I heard shooting. Anyone hurt?'

Hannah glanced down at Nate, at the glistening pool of blood in his lap. 'No one was shot.'

'He was here?'

Hannah nodded.

'I'm coming in.'

'Front door.' Moving from the window, she handed the shotgun to Nate.

'Mummy, what are you doing?'

'It's Sebastien, sweetheart. I'm going to let him in.'

'What if it isn't? What if it's the Bad Man?'

'I don't think it is. Moses wouldn't ride in a car with the Bad Man, would he?'

'What if he trapped Moses in there with him?'

'OK, Leah, here's what you do. When I bring Sebastien in, I want you to watch Moses very carefully. If he starts acting strangely – hostile – I want you to nod at Daddy. He'll know what to do. OK?'

'Please be careful.'

Hannah went to the front door, seeing the distorted shape of Sebastien's head through the central bulb of glass. She hesitated, hand on the latch, and then she opened it.

Sebastien stared at her, his emerald eyes unreadable. 'Your father's favourite Bordeaux.'

'Château Latour. The name of your second dog.'

'Cyrus.' He blinked. 'Where are the others?'

'Follow me.' Hannah led him into the dining room. Moses jumped up to greet him.

Sebastien ruffled the dog's head. He turned to Nate, noticing first the pain in his eyes, and then the blood. 'Hellfire. They've torn loose.'

'Kind of bad timing,' Nate replied.

Sebastien turned back to Hannah. 'What happened?'

'I don't know yet. What's worse, Seb, I don't even know how you fit into all this.'

The old man frowned. 'Meaning?'

'We were out riding yesterday, near your cottage. Quite a party you were having. Not exactly the hermit lifestyle you'd led me to believe. What's going on?'

'Riding? Riding what?'

'Answer the question, Seb. Who were those men you were with?'

'It's good that you're suspicious. But there's a time for that. You need to tell me what happened here. So I can help. Your husband is injured. We need to—'

Nate lifted the barrels of the shotgun. 'Answer my wife.'

Sebastien hesitated. He looked from Nate to Hannah, and then back to Nate. 'Bloody-minded, the pair of you,' he snapped. 'Fine. I didn't realise you were spying on me. The two men you saw were Eleni.'

'I thought you'd severed your ties,' she said.

'I had.'

'So what? That was just a social visit?'

'Of course not. I contacted them. Just one of them. In confidence. I thought they might be able to help.'

'Just one of them?'

'That's what I said.'

'And yet two showed up. Some confidence, Seb. How many others know about us now, I wonder?' She paused, expecting a reply, but he remained silent. 'You didn't think we might want to be consulted about that? It didn't occur to you to ask us about involving another one, two, three or however the hell many more of those people now know about us?'

'I was trying to help,' he said quietly. His tone was so incongruous it made her pause, and with sudden clarity she realised how deeply she had wounded him.

And yet he'd had no right to do what he had done. She was absolutely right to be furious with him. 'Where are they now?' she demanded.

'They've gone back to town. They've rented a place there.'

'You tell them to stay the hell away from us.'

His jaw tightened. 'Can I examine your husband now?'

Then, upstairs, Hannah's phone began to ring. She had left it on the dressing table. 'I need to get that,' she said. 'It could be him. Could be Dad.'

'Mummy, don't go.'

Sebastien moved to the door. 'I'll do it.'

Hannah locked eyes with him. Then she stood aside and let him pass. She listened to the tread of his boots as they moved up the stairs, on to the landing, across the first-floor hall. Above, the bedroom door creaked. A loose floorboard squealed.

Hannah moved to the window. She scanned the nearby hills, the river, the road. No one. No people. No animals. No movement. Sebastien's Defender stood on the track, silent and alone.

Upstairs, the phone stopped ringing. A thump. Another creak, followed by footsteps back down the stairs and across the hall. Hannah opened the door and Sebastien slipped into the room. He handed the phone to her.

She checked the missed call log. No number had been recorded. She was about to put the phone on the dining table when it rang in her hands.

Hannah stared down at it, watching it warble and vibrate. She wondered what chance there was that her father was calling. Silly to torture herself. Thumbing the call button, Hannah raised the phone to her ear. She heard empty static. And then a voice.

'This isn't really working out, is it?' Jakab said.

'If I'd had another half a second to aim, it would have worked out a lot better.'

'Ouch.' He laughed. 'Come on, this isn't like you.'

'You don't know me.'

'I feel like I do.'

'Then you're deluded.'

'Ah, Hannah, it pains me to hear this anger in your voice.'

She stepped back to the window and looked outside. Was the purpose of his call a distraction? 'You tried to kill Nate. What did you expect?'

'We've talked about this. Your husband shot me. What did you want me to do? Lie down and die?'

'That's exactly what I want you to do.'

'I have no interest in harming your family.'

'You murdered my mother.'

'Another misunderstanding. I don't blame you for being confused. You've been fed so many lies over the years, so much vitriol. No one seems to recognise the truth any more.'

'And you do.'

'I know my truth.'

'What do you want?'

'The only thing I've ever wanted, Hannah. A small and simple thing: something so inconsequential it would cost you virtually nothing to grant it. I want to see you, just once. I want to sit down in a room with you and look at your face while I talk. I want to show you who I really am. And if at the end of all that, you still want to walk away, if you still insist that this has to end, then so be it. I'll honour your wishes.'

'As simple as that?'

'As simple as that.'

'What have you done with my father?'

'He's perfectly safe.'

'Put him on.'

'I can't do that right now, Hannah. But he's safe, I promise you. In fact, you'll have him back with you very soon.'

'You're lying.'

'Lying gives me indigestion. I prefer to tell the truth.'

She turned away from the window. Saw her daughter, balancing the last of the shotgun cartridges at the rear of a curving line. Saw the fear and the determination in her face. She looked across to the armchair where Nate sat, met his eyes, glanced down at his abdomen and the spreading stain of blood.

'OK. I'll meet you.'

An intake of breath. 'You will?'

'I just said so. Come on, then. Tell me where.'

'Tell you . . . now?'

'I can't think of a better time.'

'This is unexpected. I—'

'I'm sure it is. So you'd better hurry up. I might change my mind.'

Silence at the other end. Then: 'I'll call you back. Goodbye, Hannah. You've made the right decision.'

She hung up the phone and closed her eyes, leaning against the door.

'It's a trick,' Sebastien said. 'He doesn't want to meet you like this. It's against his nature. He won't simply let you show up and confront him. He prefers masks. Subterfuge.'

'I have no intention of meeting him. I have every intention of killing him. If he's distracted, if he's busy thinking about that instead, maybe it gives us an edge.'

Nate shrugged. 'It's the only tactic we have.'

'Now we need to think about how we get out of here.'

'We have to assume he's watching the house,' he replied. 'We've got two cars. Only one obvious way out. Over the bridge and up to the main road.'

Hannah turned to Sebastien. 'Any other routes out?'

The old man grimaced. 'Plenty. But all across open ground. The river flows in and out of the lake. There's no crossing to the east. To the west, about two miles upstream, there's a ford.

The other option is behind us. The long way round. But the terrain is pretty unforgiving. I don't think we can risk it.'

'We've got 4x4's.'

'It's not that.' He inclined his head, ever so slightly, in Nate's direction.

She knew he was right. Now that her husband's wounds had reopened, they couldn't afford a lengthy traverse across broken ground. They needed to get off the mountain. Shake Jakab loose. Find a hospital. Fast.

'So we take the main road,' she said. 'Assume he'll follow. Try to lose him in the mountains. Some kind of diversion.'

Sebastien nodded. He looked about as pleased at the prospect as she felt. 'Two cars or one?'

'We go together.'

'Two cars gives us more options.'

'I'm not splitting the three of us.'

'Then don't. You go in one car. I'll take the other.'

Her phone rang. They all stared at it. It rang a second time. She activated it and held it to her ear.

'Me again.'

'That was quick.'

'I'm a quick worker.'

'And?'

'I've been thinking about something. You don't trust me.'

'Perceptive.'

'If it wasn't for the sarcasm I'd thank you. It's clear I need to do something to build a little trust with you, before we see each other. A gesture of goodwill. Otherwise I fear we'll both walk away from our conversation unfulfilled. First, a confession: I haven't always made the right choices. There, I've said it. Some of the choices I've made have been bad, a few of them have been terrible. A lot of mistakes, but all of them in the past. Some made with worthy intentions, some without. When you live a long time, you get to collect a lot of mistakes. I won't make excuses for all of mine, but I will tell you my story, when

I see you. Some of it is distasteful. I'm objective enough to see that. But I'm hoping that after we talk you'll at least understand a fraction of what I've lost, what I've suffered, what I've sacrificed.' He hesitated, and she heard his breathing quicken. 'Look out of the window, Hannah. I'm giving you your father back.'

The line crackled and died.

Nate raised his eyebrows. 'What did he say?'

Hannah took the phone away from her ear. She frowned, staring at it.

'Hon?'

Moving to the window, she looked outside. Dawn had coloured the sky with a wash of pink that seeped around dish-water clouds. In the distance, a black Ford pickup rolled over the stone bridge. It reached the side nearest Llyn Gwyr and slowed to a halt. As she watched, the driver's side door opened.

Her father climbed out.

'Oh, my God.'

'What is it?' Sebastien joined her at the window, and hissed out a breath.

Nate put out a hand to Hannah. She helped him to his feet.

Charles Meredith shut the door of the truck and raised both hands above his head. He looked towards the farmhouse. Then he walked to the front of the vehicle, knelt down and laced his fingers behind his head.

Hannah stared, unable to move, unable to think. It couldn't be possible. Could it?

It's clear I need to do something to build a little trust with you, before we see each other. A gesture of goodwill.

Could she even begin to believe that her father was out there, that he was really still alive?

'I don't like this,' Sebastien muttered.

Her father looked tired, ill, but he seemed uninjured. She wished she could talk to him, validate him. But Jakab hadn't offered that, had sprung this surprise on her. Why?

She couldn't afford to take him at his word.

Could she?

When you've lived for a long time, you get to collect a lot of mistakes.

'Mummy, look at Moses.'

I'm giving you your father back.

'Mummy, *look*.'

Leah's words finally reached Hannah and she switched her attention to the dog. Moses had trotted to the dining-room door, and now he sat an inch away from it, ears raised, deathly still.

She glanced back at the road. The truck was still parked by the bridge. Her father still knelt in front of it.

Moses began to keen softly.

She looked at Sebastien. 'What is it?'

He put his hand into his coat pocket and when he removed it he was holding his knife. 'Trouble.'

The dog rose up on all fours. Lifted his nose to the door jamb. Growled.

From the kitchen, a soft thump.

'Mummy?'

'Go stand behind Daddy, scamp,' Hannah whispered. She took the shotgun from Nate. Took a step towards Moses. Towards the door.

A click, somewhere in the hallway. Footsteps? Then, the squeal of a door hinge. Living room. Had to be. The door from the kitchen stood permanently open. Someone had come through the back door of the farmhouse. They'd walked into the hall and then the living room.

The dog growled again. Sebastien clicked his tongue and the animal fell silent. If Hannah were to surprise their intruder, the best time was now – get into the hallway before he came back out of the living room. Be there waiting for him.

She reached out a hand to the door handle, touched its metal with sweat-slicked fingers, gripped it in her palm, turned it anticlockwise, prayed that its moving metal parts wouldn't betray her, and pulled the door open, towards her, ready to let go of the handle and hold the shotgun in both hands the moment she saw movement.

The hallway was empty.

Hannah planted a foot on to a floorboard she knew was solid. She swung the gun to the right, advanced fully into the hall, blinking, itching, wanting to rub the graininess out of her eyes, wanting to rub her face and loosen the tension there, knowing that she should do nothing but brace the stock of the weapon into the meat of her shoulder. Gabriel walked out of the living room.

He turned towards her and raised his eyebrows when he saw her aiming both barrels at his head. 'Have I come at a bad time?' he asked. When he grinned, the expression didn't reach his eyes. His cobalt stare measured her with frightening detachment.

'Shut up.' She backed away from him, keeping the sight hovering between his eyes. When she had given herself enough space between him and the dining-room door, she indicated where she wanted him to go with a flick of the gun. 'In there. Now.'

Gabriel shrugged. 'You really don't need to point that thing at me, Hannah. But I'm guessing you're going to ignore whatever I say.'

'Get inside.'

Hands raised, he obeyed.

Hannah followed, keeping the sight of the gun inches from the back of his head. 'Take the chair furthest from the window. I'm sure you'll figure out just how still you need to sit to avoid me unloading this into your face.'

As Gabriel slid around the dining table, Moses backed away from him until he was crouching in front of Sebastien, lips pulled back from his teeth, muscles twitching.

Gabriel sat down on the chair Hannah had indicated. He

gazed about the room. Finally he returned his attention to Hannah. 'Quite the welcoming party,' he said.

She checked the bridge. Her father still knelt in front of the pickup. He wore a woollen winter jacket, but only a light pair of trousers. It was cold outside. Damp.

'Little miss,' Gabriel said. 'That's a pretty pattern you've made right there with those shotgun rounds.' He looked back up at Hannah. 'Nothing sinister about that at all.'

'Don't talk to her.'

'You, by the window,' Gabriel continued. 'You must be Nate. I've been wanting to meet you, shake your hand and tell you what a lucky man you are. You've a fine wife.'

Nate's expression hardened. 'We've met before.'

'Oh, I don't think so. Not like this. A man of your calibre – I think I'd remember. But I'd say that luck of yours has taken a bit of a knock, judging from all that blood. I'm no expert, but I'd say you need something a bit more comprehensive than a sticking plaster to fix you up. And you,' he added, turning to Sebastien. 'Sebastien, isn't it? The old hermit guy. That's what you'd like people to think. Always popping up, though, aren't you? Like some persistently bad-tempered old leprechaun. OK, I place myself at your mercies. Perhaps one of you would like to tell me where we all go from here.'

'Why is my father out there?' Hannah demanded, edging towards him. 'What do you hope to gain from this?'

Gabriel's eyes never left her face. 'I don't intend to gain anything from this.'

'What were you doing in the house? What was your plan?'

'There was no plan.'

'*Liar.* Why were you in the house?'

'I heard gunshots. I came over. The back windows were blown out.'

She shook her head. She would not kill him here, not in front of her daughter, not without getting the truth from him.

Hannah looked out of the window at the gravel track where

her father knelt. She grappled with her emotions: love, hate, fear, indecision. Something was wrong here. So many things were wrong. She thought there were likely very few safe paths through this situation. Perhaps none. Even with the barrel of the gun trained on Gabriel – or Jakab, or whatever he was really called – she felt unsafe. He had planned a trap. That's why he was sitting there so comfortably. She was staring into the face of that trap, but she could not see its trigger. Yet what, she thought, was stopping her from taking him outside, out of Leah's sight, and putting a round of shot through the back of his head?

An admission, that's what. Despite everything, until he looks into my eyes and admits the truth, until I know without doubt that I'm not killing an innocent man, I won't be able to do it. And somehow, he knows.

She needed her father. With his help, with his recounting of events, perhaps she would be able to piece this together sufficiently to bring it to an end.

Keeping the shotgun aimed at Gabriel, she moved around until she stood next to Nate. 'I'm going out there.'

'What?'

'I'm going to get my father.'

'You can't, Han.'

'I can. I have to. He's the key to this.'

'I agree. But you're not going anywhere. It's too risky.'

'I'm not worried about myself.'

'I know that,' he said softly, putting a hand on her back. 'It's not what I meant. Your role is here. In this room. This entire situation revolves around you. It always has. You need to be here at the heart of it. For Leah, for us. I'll get Charles.'

'You? Nate, you're injured. You can barely walk.'

'You need to stay here, Hannah. And I need to do this.' He locked his eyes on her and she saw that he would not be turned away.

She felt herself beginning to shake. Felt herself wanting to be sick. Instead she kissed him. Then she walked towards Gabriel. 'Leah, close your eyes,' she said. Hannah slammed the butt of the shotgun into the Irishman's head.

The blow knocked him off the chair. He crashed into the wall, pitched backwards and sprawled on the floor, eyes rolled back in his head. She turned to her husband. 'Don't take any risks. Promise me, Nate. Something's not right here.'

He nodded. Opening the door to the dining room, he slipped into the hall. A minute later she heard their Discovery's engine turn over. A few moments after that, the vehicle passed the front of the farmhouse, heading along the track towards the bridge.

Overhead, the pink stain behind the clouds had become a crimson blush. A flock of geese flew honking across the sky. Down on the ground her father waited, hands laced behind his head.

The Discovery kicked up stones and mud as it bounced down the track. She thought of the blood flowing from Nate's wounds.

How did you agree to this? You need to get him to a hospital, have his injuries treated.

As soon as he got back, she would. As soon as they had finished this.

She felt Sebastien move closer to the window, move closer to her. She glanced at him, at his close-cropped white-haired scalp, his emerald eyes, the fuzz of stubble on his cheeks.

Nate brought the Discovery to a stop three yards from where her father knelt. He opened the door. Slowly, gingerly, he climbed out. Even from here, she could see the effort it caused him. He had left the engine running. She could see the exhaust pipe shaking, the blue diesel fumes chugging into the air.

Nate appeared from the far side of the Discovery, and her father stood up. She saw Nate say something. Her father responded. Nate started towards him and then her father pulled a pistol from his pocket and shot him.

The gun, Charles's favourite old German Luger, bucked in his hand, and two circles of colour bloomed on the back of Nate's shirt. The air cracked twice, the sharp retorts echoing across the valley floor. Nate rocked on his feet. He fell backwards to the ground.

Hannah rubbed her eyes, trying to make sense of what she saw. The air seemed to be ringing, screaming. In the corner of the room, she saw Gabriel begin to stir, and wondered if she should shoot him now before this became any more complicated.

She looked back out of the window. Her father – not her father, definitely not her father – was gazing towards the farmhouse. He had lowered the gun. He held a telephone to his ear.

Still the air screamed and rang. The screaming, she realised, was coming from Leah. Sebastien had grabbed the girl, was holding her tight. The ringing was coming from the phone on the table. Hannah lifted it to her ear.

'Before you get angry, you have to admit that he shot me first,' Jakab said. 'With this same gun, ironically. I meant everything I said to you earlier, Hannah. But I couldn't let him get away with that.'

Hannah dropped the phone, vaguely aware of the shriek that tore out of her, that clove her. She turned around and around. Her mind wouldn't work. Somehow she was in the hall, scrabbling at the lock on the front door. Then she was sprinting down the track towards her husband, towards the creature wearing her father's face.

The moment he saw she was armed, Jakab scrambled back towards the pickup. Hannah stopped, raised the shotgun and fired. An instinctive reaction. Wasteful. She was too far away for an effective shot. She ran on.

Jakab swung open the truck's door and climbed into the driver's seat. Still Hannah ran. Closer now. The vehicle shuddered as the engine coughed, revved. The wheels spun in reverse, bit into gravel. It hurtled backwards over the bridge.

She raised the weapon and fired again. This time a plate-sized section of windscreen exploded. Leaning on squealing wheels, the pickup swung around until it pointed up the hill towards the main road. Then it accelerated.

She heard thunder behind her.

No. Not thunder. Something else. Hooves, pounding on gravel. Growing louder.

In a blur of movement, Gabriel charged past, crouched low upon his mount. The horse leaped the hump of the bridge, landing in a shower of stones. It raced after Jakab's truck, its stride lengthening.

Within a few seconds, vehicle, horse and rider disappeared over the top of the ridge.

Silence returned to the valley.

Hannah dropped the shotgun. She walked over to her husband. Knelt down beside him.

Nate's eyes were open. She picked up his hand.

The first bullet had smashed through his sternum. The second had drilled through the right side of his chest. Beyond the ragged entry points she could see splintered bone, torn flesh. A lake of blood was emerging underneath him. 'Oh, Nate, my darling, my love. What has he done, what has he done? This can't be. This can't be.'

Nate gripped her hand. He opened his mouth, tried to speak.

Behind her, she was aware of footsteps, of people drawing close, but that didn't matter, none of it mattered. Not now.

She stared into Nate's eyes and told him that she loved him and held his hand and smoothed his hair away from his face. It took him a further minute to die, and then it was all over.

CHAPTER 20

Sopron, Hungary

1927

Sitting on the steps of the baroque Trinity Column in Sopron's main square, Jakab watched the city's residents hurry past on morning business, swaddled in gloves and hats and overcoats. Breath steamed from their mouths. The previous night had been cloudless and pure, and the heavens had sucked away what warmth remained on the city's streets. Now the sky was a brittle blue, as if dipped with a ceramic glaze.

Opening the paper bag on his lap, Jakab tore off another fat strip of strudel and shovelled it into his mouth. The pastry was gloriously warm, the flavours fizzling on his tongue: sugary apple, cinnamon, nutmeg, cloves. Days earlier he had discovered an Austrian bakery on the Várkerület that made the finest strudels he had ever tasted. This morning, he had purchased three, and not just for the taste alone: his body would require plenty of energy from him today.

Crumpling the top of the bag closed and dusting flakes of pastry from his clothes, Jakab reached inside his coat and withdrew his watch. He snapped open its gold hunter case and checked the time: quarter to eight. If his luck held, he should spot Albert Bauer crossing the square some time in the next five minutes. The chemist, he had learned, was reassuringly punctual.

Out of habit, Jakab turned the watch over and slid his thumb across the inscription on the back plate.

Balázs Lukács
Végzet 1873

Fifty-four years after his father had presented it to him in their carriage outside Buda Palace, the watch still faithfully recorded the beats of his life. How many times had he traced with a finger the looping lines of those eighteen letters? Even now, over a half-century later, the engraved words stirred emotions in him he would rather not confront. He recalled his father's blade at his throat, the line of fire it drew across his flesh. The blood.

Jakab snapped shut the case and slipped the watch back into his pocket.

He looked up, searching the cold-flushed faces of the people crossing the square for the one he hunted, and then, with a surge of excitement, he spotted Albert walking towards him from the direction of the Firewatch Tower. Jakab clambered to his feet, shaking the numbness from his legs where they had pressed against the frozen steps.

Albert, hatless, was wrapped in a heavy woollen overcoat that hung awkwardly on his tall frame. His skull was all sharp angles. Combined with a hook-like nose, it gave him the appearance of a hawk. Jakab had studied those features relentlessly over the last few months. He knew every cleft and dimple, the precise contours of the man's protruding ears, the line of his thin lips. As usual, Albert had slicked his hair with tonic and parted it to one side. Jakab's hair matched exactly.

He waited until the chemist had walked by, and then fell in step behind him. He only intended to follow Albert as far as his workplace; he needed to confirm that the man would follow his usual routine.

Are you enjoying the crisp winter air, Albert? Are you thinking about your young sweetheart? I wonder if she ever mentioned that she was already betrothed. I wonder if she shared that secret with you. Fear not; I'll be sharing that knowledge sooner than you'd probably hope.

In front, Albert peeled off along Kolostor utca. Jakab followed him down two more streets and watched him bound up the steps of a tall cream-coloured building that served as an apothecary and private laboratory.

Satisfied, Jakab strode back to the main square and to the street where he'd parked his motorcar: a maroon Mercedes-Benz 630K. It was hardly a vehicle suitable for this kind of work, but he had seen it in a showroom in Munich and had been smitten by its muscular lines and chromed brilliance. The super-charged six cylinders could deliver a speed of nearly ninety miles an hour – not that he'd come anything close to that on the streets of Sopron.

Jakab started the vehicle and followed the road southeast out of the city, towards the mansion where Erna Novák's grand-daughter lived with her parents, Carl and Helene Richter, and her grandfather, Hans.

The decades following Erna's death had slid past in a fugue of bitterness and sorrow, fury and grief. Jakab hated the world, raged at the injustice of it. Those were the black years; the lost years. He had allowed himself to become the victim of events, rather than their master.

He recalled little of his lifestyle during that period, and what he did disgusted him. He had sampled every vice, savoured every depravity. By the time he had emerged, clear-headed and healed, nearly fifty years had passed. He wondered how it was possible for such a huge tranche of time to be eaten away. Still, however long it had taken him, he *had* emerged, with renewed strength, renewed purpose. He had attained an awareness of the power he possessed to shape his reality, and the possibilities thrilled him.

It had been clever of Hans to change the family's name from Fischer to Richter. But with a typical lack of imagination, the woodsman had neglected to change their first names too. Once

Jakab decided to find the family again, it took him less than twelve months. And what he discovered startled him.

Anna Richter.

The girl was a few years younger than her grandmother had been during Jakab's first visit to Lake Balaton. Younger, fresher, yet somehow wiser. Her eyes were the same deep chocolate, shot through with olive and caramel, and her hair was the same glossy brown. Jakab had feared that he would find the beauty and grace Erna gifted to her descendants corrupted, diluted, by Hans's seed. Those fears were extinguished the first afternoon he caught sight of Anna. Far from corrupting Erna's legacy, the woodsman's influence had helped to produce a creature even more exquisite than the woman Jakab had known during his time in Keszthely. He fell in love that same afternoon.

In Anna, he had been given a second chance of happiness. He would not squander it.

A mile from the Richter residence, on a forested road that was frozen mud and stones and little else, Jakab slowed the Mercedes and steered it into a depression amongst the trees. He cringed at the sound of brambles and holly snapping against the vehicle's coachwork.

Switching off the engine, he lay back in his seat, concentrated on the memory of Albert Bauer's face and clenched his fists against the familiar flaring of pain as he moulded himself into the young man's countenance. Tearing open the paper bag, he stuffed the remaining strudels into his mouth, barely chewing the pastry before swallowing. He took a silver compact mirror from the seat beside him, flicked it open and studied his face. Angular cheekbones, thin lips, ears that stood proud of his head.

The nose wasn't quite right. He strained, *pushed*. Checked the mirror again. Better. No, perfect.

Flexing his shoulders, Jakab climbed out of the car, careful not to snag his trousers on the undergrowth.

The Richter residence was a wide-fronted mansion in the classical style, with ornate pilasters across the width of its facade and a porch supported by four stone columns. The walls were a lemon yellow. Imitating Albert Bauer's graceless walk, filling out the mask he had created with mannerisms that were a perfect replica of the German chemist's, Jakab climbed the steps and pressed the bell. He was expecting a maid to answer, so when the door swung open and revealed Anna, he took a surprised step backwards and nearly tripped.

Her eyebrows rose when she saw him standing there. 'Albert? What a surprise! I thought you'd be at the laboratory today.'

He gazed at her face, chest swelling, thinking about all the ways it reminded him of Erna. And all the ways it didn't.

'Albert?'

'I . . . yes. I was there. But I thought I'd pay you a visit. Silly, but I wanted to see you again.'

She pulled a face. 'Won't you get into trouble?'

'Not a chance. I've been working hard. I deserve a little time of my own.'

Anna opened the door wider. 'Well, come in, come in. You must be half frozen. It's not much warmer inside, to tell you the truth, but there's a good fire going in the drawing room. I'll bring us some coffee if you like.'

'Are your parents home?'

'Father's working in his study. But he won't mind.'

'And Hans?'

'He went into the city.'

'Right.' Jakab walked into the hallway. Anna shut the door behind him. She led him into the drawing room.

This was not the first time he had dared to visit her at home. The first three occasions had been fleeting. He had waited outside the house until he saw Albert Bauer leave and then, on the pretext of forgetting some trinket or other, had rung the bell and had been admitted to hunt for the lost item, snatching a few lines of conversation with Anna, flexing his new skin. On his fourth visit, he arrived in the middle of the day, when he knew Albert would be at the laboratory. He discovered her alone in the house, and an hour later discovered himself in bed with her. He had repeated that experience several times since. Although he didn't feel confident enough yet to supplant Albert completely, he found himself unable to stay away from her. He was, he knew, taking a huge risk.

While Anna perched on the arm of one of the two sofas beside the log fire, Jakab settled himself into a wingback chair and folded his hands in his lap. He drank her in. Over a grey dress of some diaphanous fabric, she had pulled a man's woollen cardigan. Unlaced leather work boots adorned her feet. The skin of her calves was creamy and smooth. He tried not to stare.

Again, Anna smiled brightly at him. 'Coffee, then.'

'Please.'

Once she had left, Jakab looked around the room. A rug with a geometric pattern lay on the parquet floor. Marble-topped side tables supported a ceramic bust of a philosopher he didn't recognise, a glass vase of ostrich feathers, a tortoiseshell cigar box, a Victrola gramophone and stack of 78s. Over the fireplace hung an enormous gilt mirror. In one corner, a lacquered Chinese screen was alive with the twisting bodies of dragons. Her father's writing desk stood in another.

Jakab rose to his feet and went to one of the windows. Outside, frost bearded the leaves of rhododendron bushes yet to be touched by sun.

He moved to the writing desk. A leather-bound diary lay on its surface beside a Waterman fountain pen. On the desk's single shelf stood a row of older journals. Some of their spines displayed a year etched in gold foil; most of them were blank. Opening the volume before him, Jakab saw a bookplate attached to the inside front cover. Illustrated with twisting vines, wolves and deer, the handwritten message read:

Diary of Fischer Hans
1923–

He flicked through the pages of pale-blue handwriting, seeing the names of Carl, Helene, Anna and Albert. He selected an entry at random, and had just started to read the text when he heard a noise from the hallway outside. Something about the sound had been furtive, not quite right. Quickly, he dropped the book and moved to the door. In the hall, he saw Anna standing beside a walnut occasional table. In one hand she held the shaft of a telephone mouthpiece. To her ear, she held the receiver.

'. . . I won't, I promise you,' she said quietly. Noticing him by the door, she grinned, replaced the phone on the table, and sauntered up to him. 'Coffee,' she said, playfully prodding his chest with her finger. 'Coming right up.'

He nodded towards the telephone. 'Problem?'

'No, no.' She swerved past him, heading deeper into the house, and Jakab returned to the living room where he checked his appearance in the mirror.

Albert Bauer stared back at him.

He shouldn't be here. It had been foolish – desperately so – to visit her again. Especially so soon. How easy for his presence to be revealed; how easy for her to mention today's encounter to the real Albert and ruin everything. Intoxicated by the intimacy they had shared, he had abandoned all caution in his haste to repeat the experience.

Jakab took a breath, exhaled. He would have liked longer to study the chemist, longer to learn about the man's background, his work, the history of his relationship with Anna. But it was too late. If Anna was suspicious, he could deal with that, could mend it, given time. As long as the real Albert Bauer was rotting under six feet of frozen loam.

You can't afford to mess this up.

He wouldn't. He loved her. Had loved her all his life.

Knowing that to leave the house without saying goodbye would strike her as odd, but suddenly convinced it was the right thing to do, Jakab tiptoed into the hall, slipped out of the front door and ran back down the road to his car.

★ ★ ★

In Sopron, he took lunch at the Pannonia Hotel and retired to his suite on the second floor, where he spent the rest of the afternoon thinking about Albert Bauer. Already, he had discovered plenty of information about the young chemist. The man was an orphan, sponsored by a wealthy uncle who lived in Vienna. He had lived in Sopron for two years, moving to the area from Leipzig, where he had studied at the university. He was a keen philatelist, disliked jazz, and was awkward in social situations. He stammered when nervous, spoke with an accent, suffered from mild bouts of psoriasis.

While Jakab would not be able to convincingly continue the man's career as a chemist, a quickly arranged Viennese inheritance would solve that problem. His only concern was that he still knew relatively little about Albert's relationship with Anna. This morning, however, he had discovered Hans's diaries. He was sure that many of the answers he needed lay within those pages.

At the dressing room table, Jakab studied Albert's reflection. 'We'll visit you first, my boy. And then we're going to arrange a burglary.' He shook his head. 'Who'd want to live in Sopron, eh?'

After nightfall, he parked his car in the narrow street outside Albert's apartment. The cold weather had swept the majority of Sopron's residents indoors. Stars glimmered in a cloudless sky, with only the merest chip of a moon. The windows of the chemist's first-floor apartment were dark.

Unusual for Albert to be out on a Wednesday evening. The man usually ate supper at a bistro in the adjacent street before returning to his apartment, where he worked for a few hours before retiring.

Jakab pulled out his watch and squinted at it. Nine o'clock. His feet were already growing numb. Deciding that he might as well wait inside the apartment where it was warm, he got out of the car.

Crossing the street, he felt in his pocket for his set of keys and used one of them to open the outer door. The hallway within was unlit. Jakab climbed the stairs to the first floor, paused and listened outside Albert's rooms.

Silence.

He used a second key to unlock the front door, and opened it. Again he paused, listening for sounds in the darkness. Muffled laughter drifted to him from further along the passage. But the darkness inside Albert's apartment was still. Replacing the keys in his pocket, Jakab took out his knife. He went inside.

Easing the door shut behind him, he reached out a hand to the wall, feeling for the bakelite switch that activated the light. As the ceiling bulb winked on, he spun around in the small space. No one cried out, no one lunged at him. He saw Albert's writing table. The sofa and chair by the fireplace. The bookcase.

The table, usually a jumble of scientific papers, scribbled notes and writing instruments, was clear. The shelves of the bookcase were bare. Above the fireplace, where previously a mediocre watercolour had hung, only a brass nail remained.

An image replayed in his mind: Anna, standing in the hall, telephone mouthpiece held to her lips.

'. . . I won't, I promise you . . .'

She had grinned at him. And for the briefest instant, as she had replaced the telephone on the table, he'd seen a furtive look cross her face.

Striding into the bedroom, Jakab switched on the light. The doors to the room's two cupboards hung open. Empty drawers gaped. The bed had been stripped. Albert's radio had vanished.

Crying out, he tore two of the drawers from their runners and hurled them across the room. They broke apart in a splintering crash. He kicked one of the cupboard doors off its hinges. 'No! No, no, no!'

Jakab charged out of the apartment, thundered down the stairs and out into the street. It took him a couple of attempts to start the car, partly due to the cold, and partly because his hands were shaking, his vision blurred by tears.

Even this afternoon, he thought, when she had deceived him in the hallway of her parents' home, she had done it gracefully. How perfect she was. He ached for her.

The Mercedes lurched forwards and Jakab navigated it along the narrow street, keeping his speed down until he reached the wider roads where he could push the car harder.

Would she still be at home? Unlikely. But where else could he begin his search? Would *any* of the family be there? He was so distracted at the thought of losing her that he nearly missed the turning on to the forested road that led to the Richter house, and when he hauled the wheel over he almost hit a vehicle travelling without lights, barrelling along in the opposite direction.

You have to calm down. You have to think. You can't afford to handle this badly.

A few hundred yards from the property, he ran the Mercedes off the road. The car ploughed a muddy channel as it slid to a halt. He killed the engine.

Ahead, lights were burning inside the house. From a leather case on the passenger seat beside him Jakab pulled out a Gasser revolver. He jumped out of the car, wiped his eyes clear of tears and sprinted along the drive. He leaped up the front steps. Rang the bell. Heard it trilling, somewhere deep inside the house.

His lungs were burning. His head was buzzing. Wrong. All wrong. He wasn't thinking clearly. He hadn't thought this through. He had no plan, no idea of what to do next. Overwhelmed, he collapsed to his knees, steadied himself with one hand on the stones. Concentrated on his breathing.

Was he too late? Had he lost her? Hans had been careless enough to change only his family's surname. He didn't think a man of Albert's intellect would make the same mistake.

He heard a latch rattling. Looked up. The door swung open, revealing the face of an old enemy.

'Albert?' Hans Richter squinted down at him. 'What did you forget? What is it?'

Jakab stood, bared his teeth.

'You're not—'

Lunging, he grabbed the old man's arm and yanked him out of the house. As Hans tumbled down the steps, Jakab clubbed him on the back of the head with the revolver. The woodsman crumpled to the paving stones. He groaned, half turned. Jakab sprang at him. He raised the revolver and drove the butt down on to the top of Hans's skull. Moments later he caught sight of further movement in the doorway.

Helene Richter stood framed in light, wrapped in a shawl, a hammer clasped in her hands.

Eyes still wet with tears, Jakab stared up at her. 'Help us,' he croaked.

He had built up the fire in the drawing room to a crackling blaze, and finally he was beginning to feel warm. Reflected flames danced in each of the three tall windows that looked out on to the night.

Jakab walked around the room, recovering his breath. He let his fingers trail through the display of ostrich feathers, ran them over the smooth tortoiseshell cigar box, brushed the heavy drapes beside the windows.

Hans's writing desk stood exactly where it had this morning. The Waterman fountain pen still lay on its surface, but the old man's leather-bound diary had gone. The shelf above, which had contained more volumes of the Richters' history, was empty.

Taking his time, Jakab returned to the windows and closed each set of curtains. He walked to the centre of the room and sat down on a wingback chair. Closing his eyes, he breathed deeply and allowed the anger and the worry and the pain to drain out of him.

He opened his eyes.

Helene Richter sat on the sofa to his left. Her arms were tied behind her. Her ankles were bound together. Her silk blouse was ripped. She stared at the rug on the parquet floor, eyes wide and disbelieving. Beside Helene sat her husband. Carl wore an open-necked shirt, dark trousers. Unlike his wife's, Carl's eyes scanned the room, although they were careful never to rest on Jakab's face.

Only Hans, roped to a chair opposite his son and daughter-in-law, dared to look at him. A flap of the old man's scalp hung over his ear. Blood had soaked his jacket and his shirt. He would not take his eyes off Jakab. 'Whatever you decide to do to me,' Hans said, 'I'd ask you to remember one thing. Carl is Erna's son. Her blood, Jakab. Think about that. He's as much a part of her as Anna is.'

Jakab was silent for a while. Finally, he said, 'You'd ask me to remember. I remember a lot, woodsman. I remember how you stole my wife.'

Hans stared. Finally he shook his head. 'She was never your wife.'

The truth of those words – their stark and cold reality – cut Jakab more deeply than anything in the forty-eight years since Erna's death. In an instant he was transported back to the night she had met him on Balaton's shore and told him of the strangers at her father's tavern. He remembered how his joy at her closeness had transformed to terror at the knowledge that the *hosszú életek* had found him. He remembered the feel of her tears against his cheek as he kissed her and promised that he would return. He remembered the way she had looked at him five years later as she tried to give him money and make him leave, remembered the way the coins had sparkled and tumbled in the air as he shoved her away from him. He saw the *Merénylő*, all sickly skin and poisonous eyes, rising up in his saddle and pulling the crossbow's trigger. He remembered how he thought he'd been shot, remembered the awful, terrible pain of what happened next: the dreadful *clacking* sound emerging from

Erna's lips; the sight of her teeth snapping at the air; the feel of her slipping from his arms; the gleam of the blood-slicked bolt protruding from her skull; the discovery that in the time it took for a shaft of wood and metal to cross a few yards of empty space he had lost everything, everything.

Jakab found that he was crying. His chest heaved and great shuddering breaths escaped him. He pressed his hands between his knees, rocking back and forth as the tears spilled down his cheeks.

Slowly, he recovered himself.

He wiped his nose, his face. When he looked up, he saw tears glistening in the eyes of the old man too.

'Where is Anna?' he asked.

'Jakab, I loved her just as dearly as you did.'

'Where has Albert taken her?'

'If I'd known what those men would do, if I'd known how it would end, I never would have called them. I was scared, Jakab: scared of you, scared of losing her to you.'

'I have to find her.'

'You won't, though. I'm sorry for you. But she has her own life. The right to lead it with whomever she chooses. You must allow her that. Your involvement with her ends here. In this room.'

From his pocket, Jakab pulled out the knife, turned it over in his hands, ran his thumb along the blade and drew a line of scarlet. On the sofa, Helene Richter moaned. She sagged back in her seat.

'I don't want any more bloodshed,' he said.

'Then don't do this—'

'But I must find her. Please. All of you. It's a simple enough question.'

'Jakab, don't you see? We don't know where she's gone. None of us do. We helped them leave, yes. But they won't come back. Not now. We've said our goodbyes.'

He stood, walked into the midst of them. Studied the way

the flames in the hearth reflected off the knife's blade. 'Of course you know. You must know.'

'Please don't do this, Jakab.'

He went to Helene, reached out a hand to her face. She strained away from him, but she could only move so far, and he took her chin and lifted her head. She would still not meet his eyes. Softly, he asked, 'Where can I find her?'

The woman sobbed.

Behind him, Hans said, 'Jakab, you know this is wrong. You must know that. Think about Erna. What she would have wanted.'

'What do you know of what Erna wanted?'

'Jakab, I was married to her.'

'And the next time you insist on telling me that, I'm going to cut the lips off your son's bride.' He turned to Carl, using the tip of his knife to tilt the man's face towards him. 'Look at me, Carl. Just look at me. There, see? That wasn't so bad. I'm no monster, am I? I don't wish your daughter any harm. I don't wish *you* any harm. But you must tell me where Anna's gone. I know that, deep down, you understand that. I love her, Carl. I must find her.'

The man's face had lost all its colour. His Adam's apple bobbed. 'We don't know where they've gone. Why on earth would they tell us that? *They* don't even know where they're going.'

'A father would know.'

'I promise you, I—'

'*A FATHER WOULD KNOW!*'

Jakab dropped the blade from Carl's chin, hauled himself away, forced himself to retreat from the man. Pacing, circling the room, his mind filled with thoughts of Anna, of Erna, of Anna. And immediately those thoughts turned darker, began to mock him, gloating, insistent.

He imagined Anna and Albert driving through the night, the German chemist at the wheel, Anna's hand resting on his thigh.

He imagined them stopping at a hotel, terrified at what they had just escaped but also energised, alive, thrilled. That energy would find its release in passion, drawing them together, giving them the confidence to believe they could prevail.

He felt as if a tumour had burst inside his skull.

Striding around the sofa, snapping Helene's head back and brandishing the knife high above him, he said, 'Last chance, Hans, I swear it. You tell me where they've gone right now or I'll make her so damned ugly you won't suffer yourself to look at her again.'

On the wingback chair, Hans bowed his head. He began to pray.

Beside Helene, Carl opened his mouth and joined him.

Jakab remained frozen, one hand pressed against Helene's forehead, the other clutching the knife.

'. . . *and forgive us our trespasses, as we forgive those who trespass against us . . .*'

He slashed downwards.

Helene Richter gagged, bucked.

'. . . *deliver us from evil . . .*'

Lips pulled back against his teeth, determined to drown out their words, determined to demonstrate the futility of their prayer, Jakab carved into her face.

Later, much later, after the screaming had abated and the life had left them and the only sound in the room was the steady *drip-drip-drip* of blood falling on the rug, Jakab acknowledged that the old man had been telling the truth. He had not known; none of them had known.

It was too late by then, of course. And it would hardly have mattered. Because once Jakab had started cutting, he became too upset to stop.

CHAPTER 21

Aquitaine region, France

Now

Days passed, but they could have been hours or weeks. Hannah curled around the horror and the pain of her loss, drawing its spike ever deeper, letting its poison travel her veins and its barb twist inside her, eviscerating her of all her hope, her memories, her meaning.

Sebastien dug a grave on the shore of the lake, working as fast as he could in the chill autumn air. The ground was frozen and rocky, and he was unable to dig deep. A mist of rain harried him, and he looked up often and scanned the hills, as if feeling the eyes of her husband's killer upon him as he worked.

With the shallow site prepared, the old man dragged Nate's body over the lip and laid it inside as gently as he could. Earlier, Hannah had washed the blood from Nate's face and hands. She wanted Leah to remember her father without the stains of violence upon his body.

The girl, white-faced and silent, lips pressed together as if she concentrated on a reel of horrors spooling before her eyes, bent and tucked a letter into the pocket of Nate's shirt. Hannah saw the hard, urgent scratches of her daughter's handwriting and had not the courage to ponder what questions they asked.

In the shadow of the mountain, Sebastien read words from the Book of Common Prayer as Hannah gripped Leah's hand.

We brought nothing into this world and it is certain we can carry nothing out. The Lord gave, and The Lord hath taken away; blessed be the Name of the Lord.

Nate might have brought nothing into this world, but with his departure he had carried off every opportunity for Hannah's happiness, her peace. She screamed when Sebastien threw the first shovel of dirt over him and the grains of soil skittered across his face. She collapsed to her knees, the cold mud soaking through her jeans. She would have thrown herself on Nate's body, pressing her lips to his cheek, if Sebastien had not tossed away his shovel and grabbed her, gathering up Leah and holding her too.

Hannah screamed again, guttural and forlorn, when Sebastien pushed her away, picked up his spade and continued to shovel. She watched, gulping down air in disbelief, as the level of earth grew up over Nate's chest, around the tops of his boots.

The soil buried his right hand first, the hand that had held her as she panted and heaved and brought Leah into the world. She wept a goodbye to the fingers that had caressed her face, massaged her feet. His left hand disappeared next, absent of the wedding ring she had hung from the chain around her neck.

It took three shovels of earth to cover his face. Lips that had kissed her – had laughed with her, had spoken vows to her – surrendered to wet mud and worms and stones. Eyes that had watched their daughter grow, ears that had heard her profess her love for him, all succumbed to the cold press of earth. A lock of hair and a pale strip of forehead was the last she saw of him.

As Sebastien hammered a simple wooden cross into the soil, Hannah felt her vision flickering, her scalp prickling, and she slumped to the ground, useless and spent. Hollow and lost.

Of their journey from Llyn Gwyr, she remembered little. Sebastien carried her to the car while she mumbled and shuddered and told him of her plans, the whereabouts of their documents, their passports, their money. As he drove them over the stone bridge, her grief overcame her. She flung open the door of the Land Rover and tried to launch herself out of the seat, the tangle of her seat belt the only thing stopping her from plummeting into the river below.

He sedated her then. Something powerful from his canvas military kit that wrapped pillows around her pain and dropped it into a well, leaving her pliable, awake, yet virtually idiotic from its effects. Had she seen her father's corpse, propped beneath the painted sign for Llyn Gwyr, his frozen hands clutching a copy of his last work? Or had that been a macabre hallucination gifted to her by Sebastien's drugs?

She recollected a cottage, somewhere in Snowdonia, the faces of men she did not know, their features molten in the soup of her thoughts. An aeroplane interior, its fuselage shorter and narrower than of any aircraft she had travelled in before. Another car journey, this one by night. Whispered conversations, the agony of her daughter's quiet sobbing, the guilt as she lay senseless and anaesthetised, too selfish to lift her head from the mercy of the sedative's embrace.

Someone opened the car door and carried her across a crunching gravel path. The night air was warmer here. A different country now, a different life. A key turned in a lock. Footsteps echoed on flagstones. Scents of ginger, cinnamon and cloves. Upwards to a dark room, starched sheets, shuttered windows. Silence. Sleep.

She woke in the night, eyelids gummed shut and mouth like chalk dust, and stumbled down a bare staircase to a kitchen with simple wooden furniture and whitewashed walls. Sebastien sat in one of two armchairs clustered around an unlit wood stove, reading a newspaper in the light thrown from a table lamp. Hannah searched through cupboards until she found what she needed – a bottle of brandy and a single glass. She poured herself a shot, swallowed it and poured another. Sebastien put down his newspaper, folded his hands in his lap and opened his mouth to speak. She shook her head at him, threw back another shot and carried the brandy bottle back to her bed. When she woke next, light was filtering through the gap in the shutters, and a congealed breakfast of eggs and toast sat on a tray beside her bed. She gulped brandy from the neck of the bottle and embraced unconsciousness once more.

When she next opened her eyes, night had returned. Head thumping and stomach clenching, she didn't manage to reach the bedroom door before she vomited a bitter and stinging stream of bile on to the floorboards.

Staggering back down the stairs, she found the kitchen empty. The smell of roasted chicken hung in the air. Dishes stood drying on the rack. Someone – probably Leah – had been drawing pictures at the table. A man lying down. Flowers on his chest. A woman and a girl holding hands. A sun. A bird. A mountain.

The french windows were ajar, and Sebastien walked into the kitchen while Hannah was searching for another bottle. There was no more brandy, and by the time she found wine and a corkscrew, her hands were shaking so badly that she slipped and cut a gash in her thumb and dropped the corkscrew and started crying.

Silent, Sebastien took her hand and led her to the sink. He ran her thumb under the cold tap, wrapped a kitchen towel around it and lowered her into a chair. He boiled a kettle and made her a mug of tea, and when she took a sip of it, scraping her hair away from her face, he said, 'She needs you.'

'I can't.'

'There's no one else.'

'I know.'

'She's an incredible girl, Hannah. But she can't cope with this without you. She needs your strength.'

'And what do *I* need?'

She cringed, shamed by the brutality of her words. Lifting her head, she was shocked at the strain she saw in Sebastien's features. His skin was waxy and shadowed, his eyes dull and laced with red.

'You lost a husband,' he replied. 'She lost her father. Will you let her lose her mother too?'

'There's no hope.'

'That's letting him win.'

'He *has* won. Look at us. Look at what's left.'

'You've still got a daughter.'

'For how long?'

Swearing, Sebastien strode to the kitchen counter. He snatched a glass from the draining board, found a half-litre bottle of gin in a cupboard she hadn't checked, and filled the glass to brimming. He thrust it in front of her. Spirits slopped on to her legs. 'Go on, then, if you must! Take the easy way out. It's not what I expected of you, but everyone disappoints if you give them long enough, don't they? I thought—'

'He's *dead*, Seb! He's *DEAD*!' she shrieked, batting the glass out of his hands. It shattered on the floor.

'I know! It's horrific, and nothing you or I can do will change that! But you have a little girl that needs you, so pull yourself together and think about that instead! How did you feel when your mother died? What did you need? Did Charles abandon you to a bottle of brandy? My God.'

Hannah placed her hands over her ears as the tears coursed down her cheeks. 'Stop, please stop,' she whispered. 'I'm sorry, Seb, I'm sorry, just please . . . stop.' Rocking back and forth in the chair, she hugged herself. Shivered. 'What am I going to do?'

Sebastien turned his back and walked out of the room. When he returned, he was carrying a blanket. He draped it across her shoulders. 'You're going to survive, that's what. Bury this grief for now. Turn it into anger. You have to.'

'When you sedated me, back at the farmhouse. I thought I saw . . .' She raised her eyes to him. 'Did I see my father?'

Sebastien bowed his head. 'I'd hoped you wouldn't remember that.'

'I hoped I'd dreamt it. I've lost him too, and I can't even summon any more grief. I'm empty.'

'I know.'

'Jakab placed him there to taunt me, didn't he? To punish me. He propped him up with that damned journal in his hands. Do you think it was quick?' She shook her head, dismissing the question. She really didn't want an answer. 'That creature killed my grandfather, my mother. Now he's taken my father and my husband.'

'I've said it once before, but it's an evil thing, this. It has to end. I'll do everything I can to make sure it does.'

'We're at the endgame now, aren't we?'

'It feels that way.'

'If it comes to it, and I don't survive, will you make sure that Leah is looked after?'

'You don't need to ask me that.'

'But I do need to hear it from you. I've a feeling we're close too, the last throw of the dice. If I have a chance to kill him, and if that chance means my life, I'll take it if I know she'll be all right. I'm sorry. There's no one else to ask.'

Sebastien crouched in front of her and enfolded her hands in his. 'If it comes to it, Hannah, I'll ensure Leah is provided for. And not just by me. You won't be abandoning her to a solitary life in the mountains. She'll be safe. Loved.'

'Thank you, Seb. Thank you for everything.' She raised one hand to her mouth. 'We didn't even bury him. Is he still under that sign?'

'I have people dealing with it.'

'Your old contacts.'

'Some of the good ones.'

'Did we go to see them?'

'Briefly.'

She nodded. And then something else occurred to her. 'Gabriel.'

'What about him?'

'I don't know. Do you think it was odd, him riding off like that?'

'After you threatened to kill him, and then knocked him unconscious?'

'Another mistake. I've made so many of them, haven't I?'

'I didn't mean it like that.'

'It just doesn't make sense to me. If he was trying to escape, surely he would have taken a different route?'

'Rather than one that took him right past you, right into the path of your shotgun.'

'It seemed more as if he were chasing Jakab, rather than trying to get away from us.'

Sebastien grunted. 'I'm a bloody idiot. I hadn't even considered that. Now you mention it, I can't disagree with you.'

'I always felt he was laughing at me. That he knew something. At the time I put it down to paranoia. I should have trusted my instincts. I wonder where he is now.'

'I'm right here.'

Gabriel walked into the kitchen and closed the french windows behind him. He paused at the far end of the room, watching their reactions with eyes like blue azurite. In his right hand he held a duffel bag, which he dropped to the floor. Stubble grazed his cheeks. His face was grave, absent of all humour.

Hannah surprised herself with her lack of movement. Perhaps it was the lingering effect of Sebastien's sedative, or the alcohol, or both, but she felt anchored to the chair. She glanced around the room, searching for weapons. She could see none. The kitchen worktop held only a kettle, a coffee maker and the dishes stacked on the drainer. A basket stood next to the wood stove, but it contained no logs.

Hannah looked up at him. 'What do you want?'

'I want to help you.'

'Why?'

'Because of the tragedy that's found you. Because I began to like the woman I met in the mountains. Because it's the right thing to do. Because there's no one else who can.'

Aware that Sebastien's hand was creeping towards the pocket of his trousers, aware that she needed to hold Gabriel's attention, Hannah asked, 'How did you find us?'

'It wasn't that difficult.'

'Who are you?'

Gabriel moved further into the room. Hannah climbed to her feet. Next to her, she felt Sebastien rising.

'I'm guessing that's a blade you're reaching for, old man,' the Irishman said. 'Please, don't. I'm very tired. I'm not here to hurt anyone.'

'Who are you?' Hannah repeated.

Gabriel studied her face. Finally he said, 'I'm *hosszú élet*.'

His words were like a fist in her stomach, driving the air from her lungs. She sucked in a breath. 'What happened to Gabriel? What did you do with him?'

The man before her frowned, and then his face softened. 'Hannah, I *am* Gabriel. That same guy. I can understand, based on your experience, why you'd think we're all as monstrous as Jakab, using and discarding people as if they were little more than a fresh set of clothes. But I assure you we're not.' He glanced away from her. 'I think even Sebastien would agree with me on that.'

'Don't tell me what I think,' the old man snapped. 'You have no idea who I am, no idea at all. And if you were really *hosszú élet*—'

'You're Sebastien Lang,' Gabriel interrupted calmly. 'You were born and raised in Vienna and you studied medicine at Semmelweis University in Budapest. While you were still an undergraduate you met a *hosszú élet* woman named Éva Maria-Magdalena Szöllösi. Éva mistook you for one of us. The Eleni cull was still fresh in her memory and secrecy remained the watchword. By the time she revealed herself to you and discovered her mistake, you'd both fallen in love. She admitted the truth, and then she fled.'

Sebastien stumbled to the armchair and fell into it. He raised shaking hands to his face, covered his eyes.

'Éva pleaded with you to forget her but you were heart-broken, devastated. You began researching the *hosszú életek*. Everything you could read, everything you could hear. Finally you stumbled across the Eleni. The organisation tasked with wiping out the *hosszú életek* was searching for its few survivors. Not to kill, this time: to exploit. But you didn't care about any of that. You just wanted to find Éva.'

'I did care,' Sebastien croaked.

'You rose up through the ranks and finally became *signeur*, right hand to the *Presidente* and responsible for finding the *hosszú életek* using whatever means possible. During one of your botched attempts, a young *hosszú élet* girl was killed. She was one year away from her first *végzet*. She might have met some-one and fallen in love. She might have had children. She might have delayed the inevitable for another generation or more.' Gabriel's eyes narrowed. 'So tell me again, Sebastien Lang. Tell me that I have no idea who you are.'

'That girl was never meant to die,' he whispered, raising his head to reveal eyes wet with tears. 'It should never have happened. The whole thing was a disaster from the start.'

'A disaster for us.'

'You think I don't know that? Why do you think I walked away?'

'I'm not here to answer that,' Gabriel replied. 'I'm here to help Hannah.'

Hannah laid a hand on Sebastien's shoulder. She didn't like the animosity that was building between the two of them. To Gabriel, she asked, 'How do you know so much about Seb?'

'When your family – your society – is obliterated in a genocide that history charmingly labels a *cull*, you tend to keep a close eye on those who choose to do you harm.'

'I never wished to do you any harm,' Sebastien said. 'God's sakes, I was in love with her. I just wanted to find her again.'

As if he had never spoken, Gabriel said, 'We don't know the identity of all the Eleni Council members. But the ones we do are watched. When he relocated to Snowdonia, I agreed to keep an eye on him. I moved into a place across the valley from his cottage.'

'How long ago?' Hannah asked.

'About eight years.'

'Eight years? That's a hell of a long time to live alone in a place like that, just to monitor the comings and goings of one old man.'

Gabriel shrugged. 'Eight years isn't so bad. It was an important thing to do.'

Hannah recalled how desperately lonely Gabriel had seemed during their ride up Cadair Idris. She wasn't sure she agreed. 'How do I know that any of this is true? How do I know that you're not Jakab?'

'Can we sit at the table?'

'Why?'

'If you'll grant me just two minutes grace, I'll show you.'

Hannah looked from Gabriel to Sebastien, and then back to the Irishman. 'Why should I trust you?'

'You shouldn't. But what have you got to lose?'

After staring at him a moment longer, Hannah pulled up a high-backed wooden chair and sat down at the table.

Gabriel sat opposite her. 'There's one thing you might not know about Balázs Jakab. A birth defect. Rare, and unfortunate.'

'His eyes,' she replied. 'He couldn't control their colour.'

'Full marks. You've done your homework. But the *lélekfeltárás* – our term for it – is more than just a colour change, a means of disguise. It's how we reveal ourselves to each other. You could say it's our most intimate form of expression. There are different levels, of course. A full *lélekfeltárás* is shared only between lovers. Or potential lovers.'

'Show me.'

He raised his eyebrows.

'Don't flatter yourself. Show me.'

Gabriel reached out and took her hands. She flinched at his first touch, forced herself to relax. She had to know. Had to see this.

His grip on her was soft, the tips of his fingers warm. 'Look at me,' he said. 'Don't think, don't tense. Just open your eyes, and look into mine.'

Hannah gazed into pupils encircled by startling blue irises. She had read about the *lélekfeltárás*, having discovered a rambling passage on the subject in one of Hans Fischer's diaries. As she concentrated, she noticed that the cobalt hue of Gabriel's eyes was actually the dominant colouring of three distinct shades of blue. Deeper notes, of ultramarine and navy, were confined to the outer edges.

His eyes seemed to flare, to pulse, and as she watched, a wheel of golden points began to emerge around the borders of his pupils. The dots of fire grew brighter, detached themselves and floated like Chinese lanterns across an ocean towards the white of his sclera. She felt her heart quicken, her skin begin to tingle. Another ring of golden lights surfaced, broke loose and floated across Gabriel's eyes. The cobalt hue began to darken, blushed with mauve.

Hannah's hands tightened on his. The top of her head prickled. Her cheeks burned. Her breath came in quick shallow gasps. She was suddenly aware of every nerve ending in her body. She could feel the caress of the night air on her lips, the rub of her clothing against her breasts, the cold press of the chair upon her legs.

The golden points continued to emerge, detach and sail, and the colours at the edges of his irises began to rotate from deep blue to violet to indigo. Around her, the kitchen had ceased to exist. All she could see was the light, the dark, the colours and the gold. All she could hear was the thunder of her blood pounding in her ears.

And now, as if the swirling colours were a whirlpool

tumbling her inexorably towards a vacuum at the heart of him, she felt pulled, drawn, *dragged*, into the darkness of those pupils, leaving the wonder of the shifting hues behind, reducing her world to a terrifying void that rushed at her, called to her, clamoured for her.

Hannah shuddered, squirmed, felt her fingers twitch and stutter in Gabriel's grip. She felt her throat constricting, a scream building. She tried to look away. Couldn't.

It seemed like an age, a lifetime, and perhaps it was no more than the merest of moments, but finally Gabriel flung away her fingers and lurched up from the table.

Their link broken, Hannah jerked back in her chair. Gasping for breath, raising her hands to her face, she felt the tracks of tears on her cheeks. 'My God,' she breathed. 'I felt . . .'

Gabriel studied her from the far side of the kitchen, shaken. 'Are you all right?'

'I thought I was losing myself.'

'I'm sorry. It's the first time I've ever done that. I forgot that you – that you're not . . .'

'*Hosszú élet.*'

He stared at her, his expression hollow.

Hannah wiped perspiration from her forehead. She stood up. Dizziness assailed her and she gripped the table for support. Breathing heavily, she turned to Sebastien. 'It's not him. It's not Jakab.'

With a last look at Gabriel, she fled to the hall and climbed the stairs to the first-floor landing. A window there was open to the night. She was grateful for the movement of air against her flushed cheeks. As the tingling faded from her skin, as her fear receded, she felt a warmth flooding her, as if someone had opened the top of her head and filled her with heated syrup.

Leah's bedroom was a boxroom, containing a single bed that stretched the length of the far wall. The shutters above it were closed. The girl lay beneath them, cocooned in an embroidered quilt.

On a side table, in a pile, lay the diaries started by Hans Fischer. The string that usually bound them was balled on the floor.

So Leah had finally read them. Perhaps, she thought, it was time.

Hannah walked into the room, sank down on to the bed and curled around her daughter's body.

'I thought you were dying,' Leah whispered into the darkness. 'I kept coming to see you but you never wanted to wake up.'

'I'm here now. And I'm going nowhere. I'm here and you're safe.'

She turned over. 'I cooked you some eggs but you didn't eat them,' the girl said. 'I didn't know what else to do.'

Hannah pulled her close, bowing her head so that she could fill her nose with the scent of Leah's hair. The warmth that had immersed her still radiated. Now, with her daughter in her arms, she felt a moment of calm for the first time since Nate's death.

For three days and nights, she had replayed the moment when her father had risen to his feet and shot her husband dead. The image played every time she closed her eyes. For three days and nights, she had asked herself what she could have done to stop Jakab, how she could have prevented him from killing Nate.

Here, in the sanctuary of her daughter's bedroom, that scene had temporarily lost its power to torment her. The questions faded from her mind. She breathed the fragrance of Leah's hair, felt the heat of her body, reached out for sleep.

Jakab was coming. She knew that. The only remaining uncertainty was how many people would die when he arrived, and whether Hannah could ensure that he was one of them.

CHAPTER 22

Snowdonia

Now

Dániel Meyer watched as his *second*, Nikola Pálinkás, shovelled the last spade of earth over the grave and tamped it down. Pálinkás was in his late thirties, six foot five, with a weightlifter's chest. It seemed the only areas of his body not covered with wild black hair were the two triangles of skin beneath his eyes, currently hidden behind gold–framed Aviators. His beard reminded Dániel of the bristles of a boar's fur.

This place was so cold.

The first flakes of snow were beginning to fall from a tombstone sky, and the temperature had plunged below freezing. But it was the wind and the damp that wrapped around Dániel's limbs and squeezed his bones until they ached. Beneath his feet, the ground was as hard as steel.

Despite the conditions, sweat had beaded on Pálinkás's brow. Dániel clapped the man on the back. He blew air into his cupped hands and turned. Behind them, in the lap of the mountain, stood the farmhouse of Llyn Gwyr, a sad and silent monolith. Whether it was the building's empty windows or something else, he did not know, but ever since they had arrived, Dániel had felt *watched*. It was not a pleasant feeling.

They had discovered Professor Charles Meredith moments after turning on to the track that served the farm. His corpse, frozen and white, reclined against the sign exactly where Sebastien had directed them.

Lifting the cadaver into the back of their rented 4x4 had caused them some difficulty – manoeuvring it into the farmhouse had been even harder. Once inside Llyn Gwyr's kitchen, they'd had to prop his body on a chair in front of a crackling fire for two hours before he thawed enough to enable them to prise the booklet from his fingers and unbend his limbs until they lay flat.

A series of burns decorated the professor's chest. Two of his fingers had been snipped off. But however agonising those injuries, they had not been life-threatening. Dániel had not been able to pinpoint the cause of death.

They decided to bury him next to the grave of Nathaniel Wilde, the husband of the girl Sebastien had brought to them. Hannah Wilde. Poor thing, to be caught up in something as awful as this.

'I'll be inside.' Dániel walked towards the building, studying its blank windows. So much loss, he thought. Such a melancholy place.

In the kitchen, he gazed again at the shattered windows, the broken glass on the flagstones. He went down the hall and into the dining room, where he saw the broken line of shotgun cartridges that snaked across the table.

It was going to be a last stand. Yet they managed to escape. Although not without a price.

Dániel shivered, his thermal layers inadequate inside this draughty mausoleum. He heard footsteps in the hall. Pálinkás came into the room.

The big man nodded towards the windows. 'Chopper approaching.'

Dániel moved to the sill and looked out. He could already hear the distant beat of rotor blades. 'Is it finished?'

'It's not pretty, but it'll keep the scavengers off him.'

'We've done what we can.'

'Did you ever meet him?' Pálinkás asked.

'Once. A long time ago now. Just after his wife died. He was half mad with grief, suddenly responsible for the safety of a fifteen-year-old girl who half loved him, half hated him for what had happened. I didn't think they had a chance. It's a miracle he stayed alive as long as he did.'

The helicopter, a Bell 206 JetRanger, appeared over the trees and arced around the front of the building, a growling beast of black and silver. The bass thrum of its engine and the *whup-whup-whup* of its blades seemed wrong in the funereal stillness of the valley: obscene. Llyn Gwyr was a cemetery now. Its dead begged for silence.

The helicopter circled the house, hovered and began to descend, stirring the snowflakes into a maelstrom. Seconds after landing, its doors opened and three men jumped out. All of them wore insulated winter clothing. Dániel recognised one of them. He stiffened.

Benjámin Vass, chubby-faced *second* to the *signeur*, leaned back inside the craft and removed a wheelchair. His two associates helped a fourth man out of the aircraft and into it. This time Dániel blew air from his cheeks.

Károly Gera.

The Eleni *signeur* looked about as alive as the corpse they had buried earlier. The thick padding of his jacket did little to disguise the frailty of his body. His eyes held a dangerously fanatical shine.

Pálinkás appeared at Dániel's side. 'This isn't good.'

'No.'

'You want me to call Lorant?'

'There's nothing the *Presidente* can do from Budapest.'

Pálinkás nodded. They both watched the four men approach the farmhouse.

Benjámin Vass pushed the *signeur*'s chair into the dining room and parked him in front of the fire. When he turned to face

Dániel he was smiling, face shiny with perspiration. He clapped his hands, two hard punctuations, and rubbed them together. 'Nice place. Remote, admittedly. Basic. But I could grow to appreciate it. Perhaps. What do you think, Dániel?'

'About what?'

'About your farmhouse, of course. Let me guess. Holiday home? Investment property? Just somewhere you can come to get away from it all? I'm presuming that's why you're here.'

'I'm sure you know that's not why I'm here.'

Vass went to the sideboard, picked up a china figurine, studied it. 'Ah. Of course. There's been some trouble, I understand. Two fresh graves by the lake. Perhaps not such a nice place after all. Oh, well. I'm not intending to stay long. Just long enough, in fact, for you to tell me where I can find Hannah Wilde and that cantankerous old goat, Sebastien.'

Dániel felt his temper rising. 'You forget yourself, and you forget your position, Benjámin. People have died here. I've no wish to listen to your insolence.'

'Insolence? Oh, Dániel, I can't express how much that hurts. Every morning I wake up and tell myself how I need to win the respect of my *acadeim*, win the trust of the loyal, unimpeachable Dániel Meyer. And now you cut me like that.'

Károly gripped the armrests of his wheelchair with clawed fingers. His voice was a rasping whip. 'God damn you both, *stop it!*' The words seemed to exhaust him. He collapsed back in his chair. 'Dániel, come here. Sit down. Listen to me. We know what happened. The important part, at least. We need to know where they went.'

'*Signeur*, I can't tell you that.'

'The woman and the girl are in danger.'

'I know.' He glanced across at Vass, who was staring out of the window. 'I'm trying to ensure we don't add to it.'

'Your motives are good, Dániel, but you're not making the right decisions. We can protect them.'

'Sebastien is already protecting them.'

Vass turned from the window. 'I know that one of those graves contains the woman's husband. I'm guessing the other contains her father. Dropping like flies, aren't they? If that's the kind of protection Sebastien's providing, it makes me feel a little sorry for her.'

'Benjámin, that's enough!' the *signeur* barked. 'Dániel, you're not a fool. I admit we have a chance to turn this to our advantage. But the positive side effect is that we can save the lives of this woman and her daughter. I know I speak as only one *ülnök*. I can dial Földessy right now and give you a majority decision if you wish. But I believe we're beyond Eleni politics at this point. It's become a very simple choice. Whose side do you want to be on?'

The *signeur* studied Dániel's face. He seemed disappointed with what he saw. Sighing, he inclined his head at his *second*.

Dániel felt Vass approach him from behind. The man's breath, spicy and meaty, filled his nostrils.

'It's unpleasant being on the other side, Dániel,' he said. 'If you're interested in seeing *how* unpleasant, I'd be more than happy to demonstrate.'

CHAPTER 23

Aquitaine region, France

Now

Hannah discovered the note while she was preparing Leah's breakfast.

She had woken when the first pale light of morning slipped between the slats of the shutters in her daughter's room. The girl was asleep beside her, warm and at peace, and it took all Hannah's will to force herself up from the bed and down the stairs to the kitchen.

She had, for too long, allowed her grief to consume her. It had been an unforgivable dereliction of the girl. The knowledge of her failure was like a steady drip of poison in her veins, and while she would force herself to bury the agony of Nate's death for now – stifle it, smother it, drown it – she would not forgive herself for the three days she had abandoned Leah to her loss.

He makes monsters of us all.

No.

Too easy, Hannah. That failure had nothing to do with Jakab. That was your weakness alone.

Nate's passing, she knew, had destroyed something in her that could never be healed. That life was over, its echoes already faint, and now that she had emerged from her paralysis into this cold new existence, she found she had only one goal. Last night she had extracted a promise from Sebastien to find Leah a loving home should she not survive a final encounter with Jakab. She had asked him because she felt the conclusion of their struggle lay near, and because she planned to kill him at whatever cost to herself.

The prospect of death did not raise in her the slightest fear. Perhaps, she thought, it was the one advantage she had over the creature that stalked them. She no longer placed any value on her life.

On the kitchen worktop she found two baguettes from the day before, still soft beneath their crusts. The fridge yielded a box of soft cheese, a paper bag of sausages, a ham, six eggs, apples, a jar of plum jam, orange juice and milk. In one of the cupboards, she found tea bags and coffee. She discovered the note, written on a single sheet of watermarked paper, propped on the windowsill between pots of basil and tarragon. The handwriting was a graceful looping of ink.

Hannah, I'll be down at the river. My people are coming. Gabriel.

She turned the note over in her hands. The experience they had shared the previous evening had filled her with wonder at first, although it had quickly been overtaken by fear. Perhaps she shouldn't have been surprised by that: despite her inclination to trust Gabriel, he was still *hosszú élet*, inextricably linked to the nightmare that had claimed her for so much of her life. Oddly, though, the experience seemed to have shaken him too. For whatever reason, the sadness she had glimpsed in him during their ride up Cadair Idris had surfaced once more; she had caught an aching loneliness in his eyes.

My people are coming.

Hearing the creak of floorboards from Leah's room and the soft thump as her daughter descended the stairs, Hannah poured juice, filled a kettle and began to lay the table.

Leah slouched into the room, bare feet scuffing along the floor, and pulled up a chair. The girl's face was puffy and flushed. She yawned and squinted up at her mother.

'Want some breakfast, kiddo?' Hannah asked, forcing a brightness into her voice.

Leah blinked, nodded.

'That's my girl.'

After they had breakfasted on bread, cheese and ham, washing it down with tall glasses of orange juice, she rinsed the dishes, dressed them both and took Leah outside. Hannah had not left the house since they had arrived. She wanted to see how the place had changed since her last visit – wanted to assess its privacy, its security.

'Is this going to be our new home?' Leah asked.

'Yes, it is. Do you like it?'

'Does it have a name?'

'Le Moulin Bellerose.'

'French.'

'That's right.'

'Can you speak French?'

Hannah smiled, slinging her arm around her daughter. 'Yes, I can. And so will you.' She had owned Le Moulin Bellerose for nearly nine years. No one but Nate knew of her connection to it. After her mother's death, Charles had liquidated his investments. He used the funds to purchase a couple of inexpensive properties in remote locations – he liked to call them his safe-houses – which they could use as a temporary refuge should Jakab ever find them. When Leah was born, and Charles became even more fearful for their safety, he gifted Hannah a sum of money.

Buy a place, somewhere far from here. Somewhere you can all go, in anonymity, should the worst happen. Don't tell me where it is. I don't want to know. Less chance of me betraying you that way.

Hannah had found the farm during a family trip through France when Leah was six months old. She only needed half the money her father had given her to buy it, and with good reason. The roof of the honeyed-limestone farmhouse had collapsed. It had no heating, no electricity, no water. A tree grew in one of the rooms.

The following summer, Nate spent a fortnight sawing timber and hammering joists, re-laying all the old roof tiles that had survived, and replacing those that hadn't. The summer after that, he connected a water supply and added an oil tank and furnace. Between them they made Le Moulin Bellerose their secret retreat. Not just their bolt-hole, but their idyll.

At the front of the property stood two wheat fields, separated by a tree-lined track that stretched away to the main road. Their land was encircled by a forest of oak, sweet chestnut and walnut. Among the trees they saw roe deer, red squirrel, bright yellow Cleopatra butterflies. During the day they listened to the song of mistle thrush and goldfinch, and in the evening to the reedy call of tawny owls and the looping music of nightingales.

The farmhouse kitchen faced south. It opened on to a small plum orchard, neglected and overgrown when they bought the farm, but flourishing since. Below the orchard, a track led through woodland to the north bank of the Vézère River, one of the tributaries of the Dordogne to the southwest. The farm, and its land, was cupped in a horseshoe bend of the river. Early in the last century a mill race had been cut to syphon water from the river to a watermill that still stood on the property's western border.

Like the farmhouse, the mill had been in ruins when they first arrived, home to a colony of pipistrelle bats that hung from its rafters like a rippling fur coat. Nate had repaired the roof and reglazed all but one of its broken windows, allowing the bats to continue their tenure. He had talked of converting the mill to produce their own electricity. His sketched plans still lay in the drawer of the living-room bureau.

Le Moulin Bellerose was a place of beauty, the backdrop to a thousand precious memories, and as Hannah walked outside with Leah and smelled the familiar sweetness of the plums that had split open on the ground, the warmth of those memories – now so fragile, already so distant – made the ache of her loss flare into bright new pain.

She picked a plum from the nearest tree and handed it to Leah. 'Here, try one of these while you can. We're at the end of the season.'

The girl took a bite, smiled. 'It's sweet.'

'I watched your dad eat so many plums one summer he had stomach-ache for two whole days.'

At the mention of her father Leah's face tightened. 'Where are we going?'

Hannah saw the sparkle of tears welling in the girl's eyes. Knowing that Leah did not want her to see, she took her hand and pointed down the path. 'This takes us to the river. Do you want to have a look?'

Leah nodded, took another bite of the plum.

They followed the trail through a patch of woodland, crunching over dead leaves. The morning sun was low and the sky was pale and clear. In the deep shade of the trees off to their left, two carrion crows pecked at something red and wet in the undergrowth. One of the birds looked up and screamed at them as they passed.

The path meandered through the trees until it arrived at the Vézère's northern bank. The river was wide and slow at this stage of its journey, olive-coloured and speckled with the crisp carcasses of dead leaves. A swarm of midges hovered above the water, offering themselves as food to the birds that swooped from the trees.

Upstream, the river curved away from them. Downstream, it ran straight for a while before curving back behind them. The opposite bank was steep, thick with forest.

Gabriel stood at the edge of the water, hands stuffed into the pockets of his jacket. He turned at their approach, and Hannah thought he looked older this morning. Melancholy. 'Wish I had a fishing rod,' he said.

'There's one at the house. Nate used to come down here all the time and catch our dinner. Pike, trout, all sorts.'

He nodded, and then his eyes found Leah and his face

brightened. 'Little miss! Now, I bet I can guess what you've been eating.'

'Plums.'

Gabriel slapped his head. 'How am I supposed to guess if you tell me the answer, eh? What sort of game is that?'

Leah almost found a smile for him. 'A game I won.'

'Oh, you did, did you?' He laughed. 'Do you like the river, little miss? You see that log, half submerged, over by the far bank? I saw a kingfisher perched there a minute ago. If you watch, he might come back. Beautiful bird, the kingfisher. A real treat to see one.'

Leah's eyes moved between Gabriel and where he pointed, as if deciding whether he was teasing her. Appearing to rule in his favour, she approached the bank and crouched down. Chewing her lip, she stared intently at the log.

Hannah went to Gabriel's side. 'Your note said your people were coming.'

'They want to meet you.'

'Why?'

'A few reasons. Not least because of what you've suffered at the hands of one of our own.'

'I suppose their desire to find Jakab doesn't rank highly in that decision.'

'I hoped you'd consider us a more compassionate people than that, Hannah.'

'Would you? In my shoes?'

He bowed his head. 'I suppose not. No.'

If he had argued or rebuked her instead of accepting her words, she knew he would have provoked her to anger. Instead, his lack of defence unbalanced her and she felt a twinge of guilt.

'We may have our own reasons for wanting to find Jakab,' he continued, 'but that doesn't preclude us from agonising over the devastation he's wrought on you.'

'What *are* those reasons, Gabriel?'

'You'll find out very soon,' he said. 'From someone who

can explain far better than I.' Gabriel lifted his head and looked upstream to where the river curved into the forest.

'Who are you meeting here?'

He smiled distractedly, his eyes fixed on the far bank.

'I don't like surprises, Gabriel,' she murmured.

Hannah didn't have to wait long. She heard the quiet chugging of an outboard engine, and soon the bow of an open-topped wooden boat slid into view around the bend, cutting the water before it. As more of the vessel emerged, she was reminded of the sleek lines of a Venetian gondola. The boat motored towards them, its varnished woodwork glimmering in the sunlight,

Hannah counted four figures within. At the bow knelt a tall man with pale skin, and auburn hair scraped into a ponytail. Dark glasses hid his eyes, and he wore a black zippered gilet over a cream polo neck. His mouth was a tight line; Hannah felt his eyes behind their glasses measuring her as she stood on the bank.

Two other men sat at the stern. They wore the same guarded expressions, and studied her just as stonily. One rested his hand on the tiller while the other had his fingers steepled together. All three looked solemn, strong, alert. But it was the tall presence in the centre of the boat, dressed in a loose ivory suit, that captured and held Hannah's attention.

A silk cowl, the fabric flowing like liquid copper, covered its head and obscured its face in shadow. Hannah felt her heart begin to thump in her chest, and she wondered what prompted such a rush of expectation. She clenched her fists, fingernails cutting into her palms. Her leg muscles twitched.

The stranger sat motionless, hands folded beneath the trailing fabric of the cowl. Hannah felt a hand slide into hers, and she glanced down to see that Leah had moved to her side.

As the grim-faced skipper swung the craft towards them and killed the engine, the man in the bow tossed a coil of rope to Gabriel. He caught the end of it and reeled in the boat. When its gunwales bumped against the bank, he secured the line around a tree root. 'Welcome,' he said.

The figure in the middle of the boat raised its hands and lifted the cowl away from its face. Hannah felt as if the breath had been sucked from her lungs. Seated before her was the most coldly beautiful woman she had ever seen. Slender-limbed, with fair hair that fell to her shoulders and a face carved from the sharpest contours of bone, the woman's skin was as pale and smooth as a magnolia petal. Her years were impossible to guess. Lavender eyes, clear and sharp like a predator's, studied Hannah with such intensity that she retreated from the bank. A frightening power radiated from the woman. Hannah felt Leah's hand tighten around her own.

'Greetings, Hannah Wilde,' the woman said. When her lips lifted into a smile, that cold countenance melted into an expression of empathy so pure and so genuine that it closed Hannah's throat. Not knowing what to do or say, she bowed her head, pulling Leah even closer to her side.

Assisted by the sombre man with the ponytail, the stranger stepped on to the bank. She went first to Gabriel. After kissing him on both cheeks, she embraced him. 'How do you fare?'

'Better for seeing you.'

'You still have that brogue.'

'You're the one who sent me to Ireland.'

'It's a beautiful accent.'

'I think it's here to stay.'

She smiled and turned to her companion. 'You can leave me now, Illes. Thank you for getting me here safely.'

The man frowned. 'I'd prefer to stay at your side.'

'You can see I am in safe hands.'

'But *Főnök*—'

'Illes, do you question me?'

He dropped his head, dismayed. 'No, of course not.'

'Oh, Illes, I did not intend that as a slight.' Her face softened. 'You bruise so easily. Go on. You know where I am. You know that I'm safe. I'll let you know when I'm ready to leave.'

Illes cast Hannah a distrustful look, then muttered his acquiescence. He climbed back into the boat and Gabriel cast them off. The craft turned in a lazy circle before heading back upstream.

Taking Hannah's arm, the *Főnök* steered her up the path that led to the house. 'I want you to know how sorry I was when Gabriel told me what happened. No woman your age should have to suffer the loss of her spouse. No woman of any age should suffer that loss because of another.'

Hannah feared her composure would dissolve if she acknowledged the woman's words. Conscious of Leah at her side, mindful of her vow to show strength in front of the girl, she forced the conversation into a new direction. 'You're the *Örökös Főnök?*'

The woman smiled. 'Such an ancient old title.'

'I thought the position was always taken by a man.'

'Sometimes I wish that were true.'

'You didn't want to be *Főnök?*'

'I didn't want to be the last,' the woman replied, as they emerged from the woodland that bordered the plum orchard. Arriving at a bench, its slats silvered and warped by the suns of past summers, she slowed and glanced up at the house. For the first time since her arrival, she looked uncertain. 'Is he inside?' she asked, turning to Gabriel.

'He went out for supplies. He'll be back soon.'

She appeared to consider this for a moment, and then said, 'You know, I think Hannah and I need to talk a while. Perhaps, Gabriel, you'd be good enough to bring us some tea.'

Hannah found that she enjoyed the airy way the *Főnök* commanded him. She met Gabriel's eyes and when he shrugged helplessly at her she grinned. As he returned her smile, Hannah noticed a troubled look cross the *Főnök*'s face.

'Perhaps you could find yourself a little helper, too,' the woman added.

'Yes, mother,' he replied, bowing low. Gabriel turned to Leah. 'Come on, little miss. I'll show you how the Irish make tea.'

Hannah watched them go, and turned back to the *Főnök*. 'Gabriel's your son?'

'That boy is a number of things, not all of them useful and several of them irksome,' the woman replied. 'But, yes, I'm proud to call him my son. Come, let's sit.'

Hannah settled on the bench beside her. Together, they listened to the laughing call of a woodpecker somewhere in the forest. For a while, neither of them spoke, yet the lack of words did not feel uncomfortable. Eventually, Hannah said, 'You mentioned something just now. About being *Főnök*.'

'About being the last?'

'What did you mean by that?'

A fine delta of lines appeared at the edges of the woman's eyes. 'It's a difficult thing to offer leadership to a people who have lost control over their future. But offer it I must. And when I look around me and see the dignity displayed by our last generation, see their elegance and their grace, it fills me with pride even as it tears at my heart.' The *Főnök*'s chest rose and fell, and she turned her lavender eyes upon Hannah. 'We're dying, you see. As a people.'

'Dying?' Hannah frowned. 'How can that be?'

'What do you know of our history?'

'More than you might think. Nowhere near as much as I'd like.'

'You've heard, I suppose, of the *hosszú életek* . . . cull.' She grimaced as she spoke the word.

'A little.'

The *Főnök*'s eyes unfocused and she began to talk. In the nineteenth century, although they had begun to spread out across the world, the largest population of *hosszú életek* remained concentrated in Hungary – the majority of those in Budapest. For centuries they had lived in virtual anonymity among the populace. But as the towns and cities filled, and as records of births and deaths became more stringent, it became harder for them to keep their secrets. The nobility had always been aware of them and, perhaps due to their dynastic nature, had forged many cross-generational trading relationships with *hosszú élet* families over the years.

Perhaps it was inevitable, but some of the Budapest nobility began to covet their longevity, and envied their ability to disguise themselves. To the peasantry and common folk, the *hosszú életek* were still little more than an entertaining yarn, but as envy among the nobility developed into jealousy, and jealousy bred mistrust, those entertaining fireside yarns developed a more sinister note.

It was, the *Főnök* explained, a mountain of powder kegs waiting for someone to light the fuse. 'And then,' she said, 'Balázs Jakab attended his first *végzet* at the palace of Buda, and was rejected in cruel and callous fashion by his peers.'

Hannah straightened. 'Jakab? *Jakab* had something to with the cull?'

'Jakab *was* that fuse, Hannah. The *végzet* did not go well for him. He stormed out of the palace, ending up in the company of a couple of young rascals down at the riverfront. The young man's name was Márkus Thúry. The girl was called Krisztina Dorfmeister. Jakab went drinking with them and they developed a relationship of sorts. It's unclear exactly what happened next, but it seems that Jakab became interested in the girl. Perhaps she spurned his advances. We'll probably never know. What we do know is that he kidnapped the young man, supplanted him, and took the girl up into the hills, where he raped her. The truth emerged eventually, but not before Thúry was hanged for the crime.

'By then, that mountain of powder kegs had been lit. It was a long fuse but, facing increasing pressure, the palace finally signed our death warrant. The following summer, after biding their time and planning their strategy, the newly formed Eleni murdered our entire *tanács* with their first strike. It happened the same night as the first *végzet*. That particular *végzet* wasn't held at the palace that year. Franz Joseph would not allow it. But he did allow it at a specially built timber-framed building two miles further down the river. With our children inside, and our elders already dead, the Eleni boarded up the doors and burned it to the ground.'

'My God.'

'*Végzet*s in other cities were attacked and destroyed in similar ways. They didn't find all of us. Many escaped. But the damage had been done. Too many of us had died.'

'I don't understand. If there were survivors . . .'

'Hannah, maybe it's something you've yet to learn about us, but we don't bear children easily. Much study has gone into why that's the case, but no one really knows the answer. We have few children, and we're fertile for only a very brief period in our lives. A few hundred years ago, an annual *végzet* was held in every major city more than two days' journey from Budapest: Debrecen, Vienna, Bucharest, Lviv. In the north too: Moscow, Minsk, Warsaw, Berlin. The year after the cull, no *végzet* was held anywhere in Eastern Europe, or, indeed, the world. Two years later, in the most paranoid secrecy, we managed to arrange a single event. In total, twenty youngsters attended, and some of those were siblings, limiting the possibilities even further. I can't remember the last time a *végzet* was convened.'

The *Főnök* laid her hands on her lap and studied her smooth skin. 'It's painful to bring a child into the world and watch him grow, knowing that he will never have the chance to enjoy children of his own.'

'Gabriel . . . you mean there's no one?'

'There are no more available *hosszú életek* his age, Hannah. None.'

She reeled at the woman's words. Losing Nate had brought her pain almost beyond endurance, but the thought of never even meeting him, of never meeting *anyone*, was too bleak to

imagine. She recalled the expression on Gabriel's face as he recounted the Eleni's involvement in a young *hosszú élet* woman's
death. 'But there are alternatives, surely? Why must he restrict
himself to a *hosszú élet* girl?'

'Can you imagine the special agony of watching someone
you love age and die, all within what seemed to you like a
matter of years? Would you want anyone to experience that
horror?'

'No. I wouldn't. But we're not just talking about a life
partner for Gabriel here, are we? We're talking about your
survival. If he has children . . .'

'It can't be.'

'But—'

The *Főnök's* eyes darkened in anger. 'Do you think if it were
that easy we wouldn't have considered it? Do you think I'd sit
back and watch us fade away if there were any chance of what
you've just described? It's been tried before and the results were
. . . you wouldn't have wished to see the results. The only
mercy was that they did not live long.' She sighed, and reached
out her hands to Hannah as the lavender hue returned to her
eyes. 'I'm sorry. This is difficult and you were right to ask. But
it's outlawed, Hannah. Our blood just doesn't mix.'

'You don't need to apologise. It's tragic. All of this is a
tragedy. I had no idea about Gabriel, about what he's lost. It's
hard to think that he'll never even share the *lélekfeltárás* with
someone who can reciprocate it.'

'He told you about that?'

'He showed me.'

'He *showed* you?' Alarm crossed the *Főnök's* face, and then it
dissipated into weary resignation. 'He should never have done
that. It wasn't right.'

'Maybe not. But I asked.' Hannah shrugged, and then she
laughed, a brittle sound. 'Let's face it, inside that house we're a
collection of broken people.'

The woman rose to her feet. 'Speaking of Gabriel, he never

brought us that tea. Another thing to have words with him about. Come on, it's time we went to see the others. It's been a long time since I enjoyed the company of a child.'

By the time Sebastien returned, the four of them were gathered around the table, drinking tea. Hannah heard the front door slam and the skittering of paws on wood as Moses scampered along the hall into the kitchen.

His hackles raised, the dog paused in the doorway, staring at the *Főnök*. He barked once.

Behind him, the old man backed through the door, a paper sack of groceries under each arm. 'Out of the way, Moses. Damned dog's confused as hell since Gabriel turned up. I found a gun shop. Filled out all the forms but it's going to be . . .' He turned towards the group and his voice drifted away to silence as he noticed the woman on Hannah's left.

Moving to the counter, he set down the bags. His arms fell to his sides. He took a step towards her, his breath rasping in his throat. 'Éva?'

The *Főnök*'s face was a tumult of conflicting emotions. 'Hello, Sebastien.'

The old man tilted his head away to the side, his eyes losing their focus. When they returned to her, his jaw began to tremble and his hands began to shake. He looked down at his fingers, as if surprised that they should betray him like that And then his eyes widened and he lifted his hands to his face.

'Sebastien, I—'

'No!'

'It's OK. You—'

'*Don't LOOK at me!*'

He was too old to run. Perhaps, if he had been younger, more agile, he would have tried. A terrible wail escaped him. Spying the french windows hanging ajar, he fled outside, covering his face with his hands. Staggering between the trees of the orchard, he clutched at his hair, his ears.

The *Főnök* stood, her face a grimace of pain. A flush had appeared on her cheeks. 'Leave this to me.'

Hannah watched her follow Sebastien. She turned to Gabriel. 'The woman he met as a young man. Éva. She's your mother?'

Gabriel nodded.

Hannah turned her eyes back to the orchard. The *Főnök* had caught up with Sebastien. She took him by the arm and led him to the bench.

Can you imagine the special agony of watching someone you love age and die, all within what seemed to you like a matter of years? Would you want anyone to experience that horror?

Witnessing the pain on Éva's face as she followed Sebastien had made Hannah see the hard truth of those words. What must it be like for Sebastien, too, to see the woman he loved, as young now as she had been when he had met her fifty or sixty years earlier? Éva's beauty was undiminished by time. The four-score years that Sebastien had walked the earth were etched into every furrow of his face, were evident in every liver spot, every gnarled vein, every swollen knuckle. His hair had receded, his skin had sagged. His muscles had contracted, his joints had stiffened. His eyes – eyes that had perhaps caused Éva to mistake him for *hosszú élet* all those years ago – had remained a startling emerald. But everything else had changed, aged, worn away. To Hannah, he was a beautiful old man, headstrong and brave, unsentimental yet compassionate. But for all of that, it would have been churlish not to recognise the physical diminishment time had dealt him.

Hannah wondered what Sebastien thought as he contemplated that diminishment. She wondered what he saw when he looked at Éva. And she wondered what Éva must see when she looked at the young man she had loved and saw him battered and made fragile with the passing of the years.

Outside, the couple had sat down on the bench. Sebastien slumped forwards, staring at the ground. Éva talked softly to him. When she reached out and laid one hand over his, he flinched, but accepted her touch.

'Your mother explained a lot,' Hannah said. 'It doesn't make Nate's death any easier to face, but she made me see that it's not just Leah and I affected by all this.'

'She told you everything?'

'She said you were likely to be one of the last *hosszú életek*.'

'What an honour, eh?'

Mirroring the *Főnök*'s actions, she reached across the table and placed her hand over his. 'Are you OK?'

Gabriel looked down at her hand, withdrew his own from beneath it and nodded. 'Yeah.'

On the kitchen floor, Moses raised his ears. Moments later, Gabriel looked towards the window.

'What is it?' Hannah asked, frowning.

'Vehicles,' he said, rising to his feet. 'Approaching the house.'

CHAPTER 24

Aquitaine region, France

Now

Hannah leaped up from her chair the instant she heard Gabriel's words. Her scalp prickled and her skin shivered, as if an army of beetles marched across her flesh. The conviction seized her that this was finally the moment; this was the beginning of her reckoning with Jakab. Leah's future would be won or lost today on the strength of her actions. The burden of that responsibility wicked the blood from her stomach and sent it crashing through her arteries. She put her hands out to the table, her vision doubling, dizzied and overwhelmed by her emotions, fearing that she might fall to the floor.

'What's wrong?'

She shook her head at Gabriel. No time to explain. No time to be weak.

They were in the wrong part of the house. The kitchen's french windows opened on to the orchard and the path down to the river. From here, they were blind to the approach of vehicles from the road.

But there's no way Jakab can have found us. Surely? I've been so careful. Nobody else knew about this place. Just Nate and I. And we kept it so secret.

But that's not entirely true, is it, Hannah? Who knows what happened during your three-day disappearing act into oblivion. You handed all responsibility to Seb. All the checks you would have made, all the precautions you would have taken, handed to an old man you barely know. Jakab could have followed you through any number of mistakes and you'd never know which of them led him here.

Gripping the worktop, Hannah blinked away the fog of her thoughts, forced herself to focus. She had no time. And a huge decision to make. Did she better protect Leah by finding her a hiding place, or by keeping her close? How would she have felt, at the same age, knowing that danger approached and being asked to face it alone? Hannah knew the answer to that should not influence her decision. But it had been less than a week since the girl had watched her father murdered by a monster masquerading as her grandfather. 'Leah, stay close to me.' Hannah crossed to the hall and ducked into the dining room.

Two white Audi Q7s were bouncing up the track that bisected the wheat fields, kicking up tails of dust from their huge tyres. A third Q7 had parked where the track met the main road. Already, men were spilling from its doors. None of them wore uniform, but they organised themselves like a military unit, quickly sealing off the farm's entrance.

Hearing Leah's rush of breath, Hannah glanced across at her. A single teardrop trembled on the girl's right eyelash as she watched the approaching vehicles. 'He's coming, isn't he? The man that killed Daddy.'

Hannah opened her mouth to reply, and struggled to find any response. What response was there to a question like that?

Leah turned to face her, and when she smiled the tear hovering on her eyelash spilled down her cheek. 'It's OK, I'm ready. I won't let you down.'

Hannah's throat tightened. She swept Leah into an embrace, pressing her nose into the girl's hair. It smelled of vanilla and green apples, of innocence and vitality, of trust and love and hope. Teeth clenched, she heard herself snarl out words in a voice feral in its savagery. 'We're going to beat him, Leah. I promise you. Today's the last time you'll have to hear the name

Jakab. I swear, I'm going to end this. For you. For Daddy. You're going to be safe. I promise you, Leah, you're going to be safe.' Noticing that she was clutching the girl far too hard, Hannah kissed the top of her daughter's head and released her grip.

Leah's lips were pressed together in a firm line. Her face was flushed. She lifted her chin and wiped the tear from her cheek. 'I'm a bit scared but not too much, really. I think the Bad Man should be more scared of you.'

Hannah laughed at that. She felt the small release of pressure fortify her. 'Come on, hold my hand. Do what I say, and remember everything I've taught you. A new life starts today.'

Her throat was dry, and her skin still felt as if insects crawled over it. But a fire was growing inside her, fuelled by outrage that her daughter should endure emotions like these and by a determination to destroy this scourge upon them, this curse. Too many lives had been lost. Too many dear people.

Behind her, Hannah heard the kitchen door slam. She whirled around. When Sebastien appeared in the doorway with Éva, she puffed her cheeks with relief that the intruders had not breached the house. The old man's eyes were rimmed red but alert. He joined her at the window, scowling when he saw the 4x4s accelerating towards them.

Hannah turned to the *Fönök*. 'Could they be *életek*? Your guards?'

Éva shook her head. 'Too many of them. Too crude.'

The lead Audi arrived at the crescent driveway in front of the house. Losing no speed, it swerved and bounced on to the rutted trail that led to the orchard at the rear. The second vehicle braked hard, sending up a shower of gravel and dust. It slid to a halt a few feet from the dining-room window. Its engine died.

A breathless stillness descended. The Audi's radiator grille was so close that Hannah could hear the tick and ping of its engine block as it began to cool. Sunlight sparkled off its windscreen, turning the glass into a mirror that shielded its occupants from view.

'They're not *életek*,' Sebastien said. 'They're Eleni.'

Hannah lifted her eyes to the ex-*signeur*, daring him to meet her gaze. 'You brought *Eleni* here?'

His jaw tightened. When he faced her, his eyes were bright with resentment. 'I didn't *bring* them, Hannah. I—'

'Then tell me how they managed to find us.'

'I had to confide in someone! I needed to get you and Leah out of the country. Do you think I could have flown you here safely, could have avoided your names appearing on passenger lists, without Eleni help? I couldn't reach you, Hannah. You'd shut me out.'

She cringed at his words, her anger at him receding as quickly as it had arrived. For a moment she fought to hold his gaze. Then she turned away from him, her cheeks hot with shame. He had done everything he could to protect them. And still she castigated him. 'Seb, I'm sorry. You're right.'

He batted away her apology, turning back to the window as the Audi's passenger door swung open.

The man who climbed out of the car was nearly as old as Sebastien. His grey hair was oiled and combed to one side, and his moustache was carefully trimmed. When he moved, it was with the exaggerated care of one whose joints pained him, and when he glanced towards the house, Hannah thought she caught a trace of apprehension in his eyes.

'Oh, god*damn* it,' Sebastien muttered in disgust.

'What is it?'

'That old fool is Dániel Meyer. Dániel is *acadeim*. One of the *ülnökök*.'

'One of your good guys?'

Sebastien glanced at her and she saw his pained expression. 'He's a good guy. Whether we can trust him or not is another matter.'

But you did, Seb. And now he's here.

And you keep blaming him. Even though it's not his fault.

Dániel Meyer ran a finger around the collar of his shirt and went to the front door. He knocked.

To Éva, Hannah said, 'That man you brought here with you. Illes. Can you reach him?'

'I've sent him a message.'

'How quickly will he get here?'

'I can't say.'

Sebastien snapped his fingers and gestured at the door. 'Back into the kitchen, all of you. Let me handle this. I know Dániel. I'll find out what he wants.' To Éva and Gabriel, he said, 'He doesn't know your identities. He won't know that you're *hosszú életek*. Let's keep it like that.'

Hannah searched Sebastien's eyes, willing herself to detect any trace of duplicity, any hint of betrayal, and found none. She held out her hand to Leah. 'Seb's right. He knows these people. Come on, let's go.'

When she returned to the kitchen, Hannah saw four men standing in the plum orchard. One of them held the chains of two adult Vizslas. The stranger met her gaze, his eyes flat.

She heard the latch on the front door disengage. A weary voice said, 'I'm sorry, Sebastien. I had no choice.'

Footsteps clattered down the hall and Dániel Meyer appeared in the kitchen. When his gaze found Hannah, she felt a twinge of recognition. Was his one of the faces she had seen during her hallucinatory journey from Llyn Gwyr to Le Moulin Bellerose?

Meyer came to her and took her hands. 'Hannah, my name is Dániel. You may not remember me; you probably don't. I didn't think I'd see you again, but now I find myself once more in your company I must tell you how incredibly sorry I am for your loss. Your husband's death was a tragedy for us all. As was your father's. I won't be crass enough to suggest I know how loss like that must feel. I'm just glad that Sebastien managed to find you, and glad that our organisation was able to help in some small way by getting you here safely.'

The quiet sincerity of his tone, and the compassion it conveyed, robbed her anger at his intrusion of much of its heat. Even so, she eyed him warily as he let go of her hands. 'What are you doing here, Dániel?'

Meyer pursed his lips at her question. He opened his mouth to reply but before he found any words Moses interrupted with a bark. The dog trotted to the windows, pacing up and down beside them. Gabriel tilted his head.

'What is it?'

Hannah didn't need to wait for an answer. The sound was already a rhythmic chopping at the very limits of her hearing. Quickly it grew more distinct, more violent, more urgent, until she realised she was listening to the approach of a helicopter.

My God, it's coming in fast. Reckless.

In the orchard, a whirlwind of autumn leaves began to dance. The whistling fury of the helicopter's rotor blades and the bass thrum of its engine vibrated in Hannah's chest and rattled the windows in their frames. She glimpsed the aircraft's landing skids first, and then saw it touch down on a patch of open ground beyond the plum trees. It was black with yellow trim, a fat and angry wasp, with a belly full of men visible through its curved glass. To Meyer, she asked, 'More of you?'

The *acadeim* nodded.

'Could you be any less subtle?'

'I'm afraid that's not a word our *signeur* would understand.'

Sebastien thumped the window with his fist. He turned, face mottled red with anger. 'You brought the *signeur* here, Dániel? Of everyone, you brought *him*?'

'I told you. I didn't have any choice.' Meyer turned back to Hannah, tugging at the wedding band on his finger. 'Sebastien told me where you'd gone. And they knew it. I don't know how, but they did. They're desperate now. They'll do anything to find the *hosszú életek*. They know time is running out, that Jakab is their best chance, that you are their greatest lead. It makes them even more determined. Ruthless. I don't wish you any harm, Hannah. I don't wish anyone any harm. Please just cooperate with them. For all our sakes. And soon this will be over.'

'You betrayed me,' Sebastien whispered, taking a step towards the *acadeim*.

Meyer's laugh was hollow. 'I know you think I had a choice. You confided in me and when the pressure was on, I broke that confidence. So yes, maybe I did betray you.'

Outside, one of the helicopter's doors opened. A man jumped from the seat beside the pilot. The flesh of his face was soft and puffy and his eyes, hooded by low lids, made him look lazy and bored. He wore chinos too short for his legs. Their seams strained against his thighs. He pulled a wheelchair from the helicopter and unfolded it.

'Sebastien, I've lost track of the years I've counted you as a friend,' Meyer said. 'There's little I wouldn't do for you if I could. But when I promised to keep this secret, it was never on the understanding that I'd risk my life for it. I'm sorry if that means you think I've played Judas. But I never agreed to play this game for these stakes. Look at me. I'm an old man now. I have a wife, grandchildren. Putting my life at risk was never part of the agreement.'

'Your *life*?' Sebastien scoffed. 'You've always been soft, Dániel, but never as pathetic as this. Károly might spit and scratch, but I'm sure whatever the *signeur*'s done to frighten you this badly is just posturing. Since when did the Council become so fragmented that it threatened its own?'

'Since you left,' Meyer replied. 'I doubt you'd recognise the organisation we've become.'

'Even if you're right, Károly is hardly in a position to threaten your life.'

'No,' Meyer agreed. He nodded towards the man who had emerged from the helicopter. 'But he is.'

Sebastien turned back to the window. He swore when he saw the chino-wearing stranger the *acadeim* had indicated.

Hannah frowned. 'Who's that?'

'Benjámin Vass,' Sebastien told her. For the first time, she detected unease in the old man's voice. It chilled her. 'He's the *signeur's* second.'

The nearside rear door of the helicopter swung open and another man jumped out. Vass snapped a command at him. Reaching into the aircraft, the man lifted out a third figure and lowered him into the wheelchair.

Hannah stared at the chair's elderly occupant. The skin of his face was as dry and crisp as dead leaves. Listless eyes stared out of shadowed sockets. She thought he could not have weighed more than seven stone.

'The one in the wheelchair is Károly Gera,' Sebastien said. 'He's the *signeur.*'

Gabriel, silent until now, moved closer to the window. 'The one you told me about last night?'

'The one who killed that *hosszú élet* girl. He's dying, if it's any consolation. By the look of it, he doesn't have much time left.'

Vass bent down and shouted something to the old man. Then he walked towards the farmhouse.

Hannah watched him approach. Her landscape had changed once again, and even though her thirst for closure raged just as fiercely, she felt her earlier confidence wavering. Vass was an unknown, a threat she had not conceived.

If you'd held it together, if you hadn't caved in to the grief of Nate's death, hadn't abandoned Leah so selfishly, you could have brought her here without divulging the existence of this house to anyone. And they never could have found you.

'It's probably best that I leave you now,' Meyer said. 'Sebastien—'

'Just get out. I've no more words for you.'

Hanging his head, murmuring his apologies, Dániel Meyer went back into the hall and out of the house.

Moments later, Vass appeared at the french windows. He

tested the doorknob. When it turned in his grip he opened it and entered the room. Behind him, one of his lieutenants manhandled Károly's wheelchair over the step and set it down on the kitchen floor.

Silent, Vass surveyed the room. A sheen of sweat greased his forehead. He opened his arms wide to them and beamed. 'Somebody told me you were having a party. I thought I'd be the first to arrive, but it seems I'm fashionably late. I'm afraid I didn't come bearing gifts. Remiss of me. Which one of you is Hannah?'

'This wasn't a party anyone invited you to, Benjámin,' Sebastien muttered.

Vass turned and studied the ex-*signeur* from beneath the soft folds of his eyelids. 'Ah, *Sebastien*. As delightfully crotchety as ever, I see. Please, don't consider me a guest. Perhaps you'd prefer to think of me as your complimentary security. I've reason to believe that your friend Jakab Balázs is on his way here. While I've no doubt that the care you've provided Hannah and her daughter has been exemplary, this development makes our presence a sensible precaution.'

Hannah's stomach clenched at the mention of Jakab's name. 'What makes you think he's coming here?'

'I'm guessing that you're Hannah. Wonderful.' He gestured at the cadaverous creature in the chair. 'Allow me to introduce our esteemed *signeur*, Károly Vega.'

'Answer my question.'

Vass smirked. 'The reason I think that your friend Jakab is coming here, Hannah Wilde, is because I invited him.'

The beetles resumed their march across her flesh. 'You did what?'

'A terrible thing happened at Llyn Gwyr. I don't think *atrocity* is too stark a word for it. I saw the aftermath – your husband's grave by the lake, not even a headstone to honour his memory. We buried your father next to him. Very sad.' He leaned forwards. 'Do you know something? The entire time I was there I had this crazy feeling I was being watched. Sixth sense, perhaps. I'd bet my grandmother's bones that Jakab descended out of those hills the moment we left. Which is why I left him an invitation to this cosy house-warming, with clear instructions how to find it. And which is why, Hannah Wilde, we have a wonderful opportunity to help each other. I want Jakab Balázs, and I imagine you want him to stop murdering members of your immediate family. I'd venture to suggest that places us in partnership.'

'You think he's going to walk in here and let you grab him?'

'I'm confident I'm capable of dealing with Jakab.'

'You're using us as bait.'

Vass considered this, and then his smile broadened. 'Yes, I suppose that's exactly what I'm doing. But please don't feel demeaned by it. You can consider yourself the very finest bait, used to catch the most elusive of fish. We hunt Moby Dick, no less, and I offer you my services as Captain Ahab.'

'Ahab died,' she spat, outraged by his casual mockery, unsettled by the lifelessness in his eyes when he smiled at her.

'Then I beseech you, Hannah. Help me craft a more satisfying conclusion for us both.' He walked back to the french windows. 'I think now would be a good time to bring in the dogs.'

Vass tapped on the glass and motioned for the stranger with the two Vizslas to come inside. While he waited he pulled a phone from his pocket. He dialled a number and held it to his ear, his gaze moving among the faces that watched him. 'Get everyone out of sight and into cover. Far away from the house. I want the cars off the drive and away from the entrance road. Get the helicopter out of here. This place needs to look like a morgue in exactly one minute.'

He terminated the call and looked at Hannah. '*Morgue*. Hardly the most sensitive of metaphors, considering recent events.' Feigning sheepishness, Vass turned his attention to Éva and Gabriel. 'Now that I've finally had the pleasure of meeting

Hannah Wilde, and I've reacquainted myself with the irascible Sebastien, I'm extraordinarily keen to find out who you good people are.'

'They're just friends of hers, Benjámin,' said Sebastien. 'No need to drag them into this.'

'I see. Just friends. Still, I'm curious nonetheless.'

'The devil take your curiosity.'

'I'm impressed by your protectiveness over them, but I'm only asking for an introduction. Are they so fragile they need an old man as chaperone? Do they have no tongues?'

The *signeur* lurched upright in his wheelchair, breath rattling in his throat. 'Benjámin, enough of the theatrics! We're here to do a job. That's all. There's no need to add to the growing list of people who find you offensive.'

Vass had turned to face the *signeur*, but now he returned his attention to Hannah. Rather than showing any resentment at his rebuke, he looked amused. He held up his hands and sighed. 'He's right, you know. Despite my best efforts, sometimes I just . . . *trample* on people. I really don't mean to. But even the best of us have our failings.'

Behind Vass, the stranger with the two Vizslas appeared by the french windows, the end of each chain wrapped around his fist. The first dog was the more powerfully built, with a ragged coat and a muzzle scarred from fighting. The second was younger, with clear eyes and a sleeker coat. It froze the instant it saw the two *hosszú életek*, one front paw suspended above the ground. When its companion noticed them it also paused mid-stride, back leg held aloft and absolutely still.

Hannah's chest grew tight. She found she was holding her breath. She remembered Sebastien warning Gabriel and Éva not to reveal themselves. Would Vass understand what he was seeing? She burned to see his expression, but wouldn't give in to the temptation of looking at him.

The larger Vizsla took a half-step into the room. Lips curled back from its teeth, ears flat against its head, it began to growl, low and menacing. Suddenly the younger dog lunged towards Éva, jaws snapping at the air. The animal almost pulled its handler off his feet. Swearing, the man hauled back on the chain.

Hannah risked a glance at Vass. He had been watching the Vizslas' display, and now he returned his attention to Gabriel and Éva. The hoods of his eyes retracted. He licked his lips.

He knows.

Vass smiled. 'Well . . . well . . . well. I really should have worn a dinner suit. Such esteemed company.' He put a hand into his pocket and drew out a revolver. It was an ugly thing – a gruesome black lump of metal. With the Vizslas growling behind him, loops of saliva dangling from their jaws, Vass took a careful step towards the *hosszú életek*. He examined their faces. 'Just like us,' he said. '*Just* like us. Please, sit down. All of you.'

Gripping Leah's hand, Hannah moved to the table and sat, tugging her daughter on to a chair beside her. Gabriel and Éva took the empty seats.

Drops of perspiration clung to Vass's forehead. A single bead dribbled down his temple. He glanced over at the *signeur*. 'How long have I promised to deliver you a single *hosszú élet*?' he asked. 'And now I find us two.'

The old man leaned forward, eyes glittering. 'Are you sure?'

Éva surprised Hannah then by rising to her feet. The woman's lavender eyes had darkened to crimson as she regarded Vass. When she spoke, her voice rang with power. 'My name is Éva Maria-Magdalena Szöllösi. I'm honoured to be named as *Örökös Főnök* to the *hosszú életek*. I'm likely to serve as the last. You're Eleni, which makes you responsible for the massacre of our children and the genocide of our race.'

Vass held her gaze. He shook his head. 'Oh, no, I'm not responsible for the massacre of anyone, Éva. The cull you speak of occurred nearly a hundred years before I was born. But I *am* very pleased to make your acquaintance.' To the *signeur*, he said, 'This changes everything. We don't even need to wait for Jakab.'

'Then let's do it,' spat the old man. 'And get out of here before he arrives.'

Vass raised his eyebrows at Gabriel, who had risen to stand alongside his mother. 'This is, I presume, where you introduce yourself?'

Gabriel's voice was flat, dangerous. 'I'm Gabriel Mounir Szöllösi. I'll give you this warning, Benjámin. You think you're prepared for what's coming. You're not. You think you understand the nature of your adversary. You don't. You think you'll prevail here today because you command greater manpower, greater firepower. You won't. I promise you this: the way you conduct yourself over the course of this day will have great bearing on how you complete it.'

Vass rolled his eyes. He pointed out Hannah and Gabriel to the Eleni lieutenant who had accompanied him from the helicopter. 'Rope these two to chairs. Take the girl and the woman upstairs. Secure them. Separate rooms.'

Hannah stared at the gun Vass dangled so casually from his fingers. How had it come to this? The monster that had destroyed her mother, her father and her husband was on his way here, to this place she had managed to keep secret for so long. And before she could even focus on that, she had to confront this far more immediate threat.

Your only concern is Leah. Vass is unpredictable, unhinged, and he's armed. Don't antagonise him. Don't fight, not yet. Choose your moment. You may have only one. Let Leah go. Let go of her hand and get her out of this room safely.

As Hannah tried to extricate herself from her daughter's grip the girl cried out, and the sound of it nearly broke her. Ruthlessly she peeled back Leah's fingers. 'Go with the man, Leah. I promise you, it'll be OK.'

'Mummy, *no!*'

'Scamp, listen to me. Remember all the things I ever taught

you. Think about everything I've said. Keep your eyes open, OK? Be brave. Trust your instincts. Everything will be all right if you do that, I promise. Now go.'

Eyes as wide and scared as Hannah had ever seen them, Leah rose to her feet. Vass's associate approached Gabriel with a length of rope and bound him to the chair.

When he advanced on Hannah, Sebastien shouted, 'Benjámin, this is barbaric! Károly, surely you can see there is absolutely no need—'

'Sebastien, *please*,' Hannah pleaded, terrified that the old man would risk his life for her. She could not bear to lose him too. 'Don't make this any harder. Don't do anything rash.' Sitting back in the chair, she allowed the stranger to bind her. His rope bit into the flesh of her wrists but she refused to let Leah see her pain.

After testing his handiwork, the man led Leah and Éva from the room.

Vass clapped his hands. 'Good. Excellent. We're getting somewhere. I hope we're all still friends?'

His voice low, Gabriel asked, 'What is it you want?'

Vass beamed at him. 'Oh, come *come*, Gabriel! Feigning ignorance at a time like this? You *hosszú életek*! You're like the spoilt children who get all the best toys but steadfastly refuse to share. Now, I can understand why you're suspicious of us. The actions of my antiquated predecessors were really rather crude, even if they *were* acting on the orders of the Crown. But they envied you, you see. All of them. They envied you your long lives, and they grew distrustful of your ability to conceal yourselves among them. To make matters worse, you just wouldn't share.'

'Share what?'

'Why, the secret, of course.'

'Secret?'

'Someone's going to tell me I'm being too theatrical again if I'm not careful. I'm talking about the thing you've been unwilling to share with us since before the Eleni came into existence. I'm talking about the secret of your longevity.'

Gabriel opened his mouth to respond but Vass raised his revolver and waved it left and right. 'Yes, yes. I've heard the argument. If we all lived as long as you, we'd be in crisis. Population explosion. The stability of our society would fracture. Chaos. Anarchy. And perhaps there's a shred of truth in that.' Vass shrugged. 'Luckily for all of us, I don't want you to share your secret with a wider audience. I just want you to share it with me.'

He paused, and a thought appeared to occur to him. He glanced at the old man in the wheelchair. 'Forgive me, *signeur*. And, of course, you.'

Hannah heard a scrape and a thud from the room above. Would Vass's man tie Éva first or Leah? Probably Éva. Which meant Leah would be next, in a different room.

Vass withdrew a slim velvet case from his pocket and took it to the kitchen counter. He placed his revolver beside it, looked sideways at Sebastien, then retrieved the weapon and thrust it into the waistband of his chinos. 'I hope you wouldn't be silly enough to try,' he said. He gestured at the Eleni lieutenant holding the leashes of the two Vizslas. The man withdrew a pistol from a holster beneath his jacket. He stared impassively at Sebastien.

Satisfied, Vass returned his attention to the velvet case. He lifted the lid and withdrew a stainless steel and glass syringe. 'Consider me, Gabriel, the teacher who persuades you to share your toys.'

Vass lunged. He grabbed Gabriel's arm at the bicep and plunged the needle into a vein. Teeth bared, eyes shining, he extracted a full vial of blood and yanked the syringe out of the Irishman's flesh. Gabriel roared in anger.

Ignoring him, Vass held the vial up to the sunlight. The maroon liquid projected fractured rubies on to the wall. He wiped sweat from his forehead and turned to the *signeur*. 'Roll up your sleeve.'

Károly scowled. 'I have no desire to be your guinea pig, Benjámin. Try it on the girl first.'

'As you wish.' Vass turned towards Hannah.

Gabriel strained against his ropes. 'You're a *fool*!'

'Please don't interrupt,' Vass replied.

'You're insane if you think it's going to be as simple as that! You can't just expect to—'

Tutting with exasperation, Vass pulled the revolver from his waistband, pointed it at Gabriel's right foot and pulled the trigger. The thunder of the shot rolled through the house. Gabriel spasmed, his back arching. Hannah heard his teeth scrape as he tried to control the pain. The arteries in his neck pulsed, angry red cords.

'Leave him alone!' she screamed.

Calmly, Vass aimed the gun at Gabriel's left foot and shot him again. The Irishman's boot burst open in a flash of blood and leather. This time he cried out. Hannah heard an answering scream from upstairs.

Oh, Leah. my poor baby. She doesn't know what's happening. Two shots; she'll assume the worst. One bullet for me, one for Gabriel.

'I know that won't kill you,' Vass said. 'But I do know it hurts. I asked you not to interrupt. Please don't do it again.'

Hannah heard another thump from the floor above. She raised her eyes to the ceiling, trying to visualise the room beyond, trying to imagine what would make such a sound. She felt herself beginning to shake. Found she was unable to take a full breath.

In the wheelchair, Károly frowned. 'I don't like this, Benjámin.'

'Then leave,' Vass whispered. Silently, he placed the syringe on the countertop. He lifted his head, hooded eyes moving over the ceiling.

Near the door to the hall, one of the Vizslas turned in a circle. Its ears twitched.

In the corner, the refrigerator hummed. Coolant trickled

through its pipes. Gabriel's chair squealed under his weight.

A creak from upstairs. Hannah recognised it as the floorboard on the first floor landing, a few feet from the top stair. Vass turned, a half-step. Hannah closed her mouth and forced herself to be still. Something large and heavy clattered down the stairs, ripping pictures from the wall in a cacophony of splintering wood and shattering glass. She heard Leah scream again as the object continued its destructive path, culminating in a hard slap as it met the hardwood floor of the hall.

Both the Vizslas now turned in circles, uttering soft howls.

'Perhaps you might want to investigate that,' Sebastien said.

Vass stared at the ex-*signeur*, eyes hard. He gestured at the old man to approach the door.

Sebastien met Hannah's eyes. She sensed he tried to tell her something important with that look. All her senses screamed at her that opening the door was a bad idea, that he would invite a monster into the room with them. He crossed the kitchen, placed his hand on the knob, opened the door a fraction.

As he peered through the crack, the breath rushed out of him. He turned back to Vass. Shook his head. 'You thought you were being so clever, didn't you? You thought you'd send out an invitation to Jakab, offer Hannah as bait, and then you'd come here and wait for him. Your arrogance is utterly breathtaking, Benjámin. It only remains to be seen how many lives you've destroyed because of it. You didn't invite Jakab here. You haven't set a trap. *You've brought him with you.*'

Sebastien threw open the door to the hall. The man Vass had sent to restrain Leah and Éva lay on the floorboards, legs tangled on the stairs. His face was turned towards them. Both of his eyes had haemorrhaged. Dark blood leaked from his skull where it had cracked against the floor.

The pressure building in Hannah's head was unbearable, a ribbon of pain that ran from ear to ear.

He's HERE.

Jakab is HERE.

And while she was trapped in the kitchen, Leah was alone in one of the upstairs rooms. 'Have some *humanity*,' she moaned at Vass's back, tears coursing down her cheeks. 'Don't let him take my daughter. Please. Don't let her think I abandoned her. Not again. Please not again.'

Vass took a step towards the hall, inspecting the human wreckage on the floor. Then he turned and met Hannah's eyes. He smirked.

'*Jakab!*' he shouted. 'Jakab, listen to me! It seems you got here safely. That's good. I'm glad about that.' He laughed in delight. 'And I like a man who shares my affection for a dramatic entrance. I have what you want. What I promised you. She's a live one, I'll admit, but that makes it all the more interesting, doesn't it? I can't fault your taste. You know what, Jakab?' he asked, glancing first at Gabriel and then at the syringe that lay on the counter. 'I don't even want anything in return. I'll set her free, turn her outside, and you can just take her and go.'

He paused, listening for a reply.

Around them, the house waited.

One of the Vizslas dropped its head, snuffled the floorboards, raised it again. The second dog turned, its nose lifted high.

Beside Hannah, Gabriel whispered through gritted teeth. '*Look.*'

She turned to him, shocked when she saw the paleness of his face. She recalled the moment at Llyn Gwyr when she had switched on the Discovery's interior light and discovered how much blood Nate had lost. The memory raked fresh claws at her. Gabriel indicated the windows and Hannah untangled herself from the memory, following his gaze.

Illes strode through the plum orchard towards the house, his auburn tresses flowing unbound behind him. His eyes had darkened to black, and Hannah thought she knew the significance of that. His face was a mask, an approaching death, devoid of colour or emotion. In each hand he carried a gleaming steel pistol. Beside Illes walked a second *Főnök* guard. He carried a pistol of his own, and his eyes were as black as coal.

'Sebastien, stand back,' Gabriel hissed.

Illes was already halfway across the orchard. He passed in and out of sight through the trees. Hearing Gabriel's instruction, Sebastien turned and saw the *Főnök*'s man. He threw himself against the wall as Illes raised his gun and fired off four quick shots. The glass in the french windows exploded across the kitchen floor, a tidal wash of diamonds. Two rounds slammed into the cupboard beside Vass's head. Splinters of wood spun across the room. Another round punched through the door of the oven. The fourth destroyed a rack of metal cooking implements.

Vass dropped to the floor. He twisted around, trying to locate his attacker. When he saw the advancing *hosszú életek*, he bellowed, 'Dogs!'

Frantic, his Eleni lieutenant unclipped the chains from the Vizslas' collars. The animals surged across the kitchen and leaped through the broken windows, a fluid streak.

Illes appeared at the edge of the orchard. He raised his other pistol and fired off five more shots. Kitchen utensils and wooden cupboards exploded into shrapnel. Vass pressed himself to the floor.

The younger Vizsla reached Illes first. Jaws snapping, it hurled itself at his face. The *Főnök*'s man swatted the animal's skull with the butt of his gun. The dog tumbled to the grass, convulsing. The second Vizsla changed direction, vaulted the orchard fence and scrambled through the trees.

'Benjámin!' The *signeur*, hunched in his wheelchair, sat stranded in the middle of the kitchen. His eyes were wild, chest jerking as it rose and fell. 'Get me away from the window!'

Vass ignored him, slithering on his stomach across the floor. Blood flowed from his hands where broken glass had sliced them. He overturned the heavy oak table beside Hannah. Ducking behind it, he lifted his revolver over the top and fired three times into the garden.

Thunder cracked in her ears. She strained against the ropes that bound her.

You've no more time! You have to free yourself! Come on, Hannah! ACT!

'Shoot them!' Vass roared.

'*Benjámin!*' The signeur was shrieking in fear. 'Benjámin, as your *signeur* I *command* you!'

On his knees, across the room, Vass's lieutenant finally found his nerve. He rose into a shooter's stance and squeezed off a volley of shots. A bullet took Illes's companion in the heart, punching him backwards in a red spray. Another drilled through Illes's right arm, tearing out a lump of flesh. The impact spun him around, but he recovered his balance with barely a missed step. Illes raised the pistol in his left hand and returned fire.

Crockery and cupboard doors and glass and ceramic tiles exploded, filling the air with dancing shards and splinters and dust. A bullet opened the Eleni lieutenant's throat in a dark rain. Two more shredded his torso, pitching him on to the floor. His back arched as blood fountained from him, and his heels scrabbled against the floorboards as if they gloried in the scarlet murals they painted on the wood.

In the garden, Illes ejected the spent clip from his pistol. He tried to reach inside his coat, but his wounded arm prevented him. Instead, he closed his eyes. The muscles of his face slackened.

Vass peered around the side of the table. He saw Illes standing motionless in the garden and flashed his teeth. Lifting his revolver, he aimed it with both hands. The gun bucked, and the sound of his shot tore through the kitchen. Illes staggered backwards. A dark stain appeared in the centre of his cream polo neck, just below his breastbone. He glanced down at it, eyebrows lifting in surprise as it blossomed. He dropped to one knee. His remaining pistol fell from his hand.

Hannah's eyes found Sebastien's. The old man stood with

his back against the wall, shielded from the french windows by the stove-pipe.

'Seb. Please, Seb, I can't get loose. Find Leah. Don't let Jakab take her. Please don't let him take her from me.' She sobbed. Hated herself for it. But she was losing this. How much time had elapsed? How long had Jakab roamed the upper floor of the house?

'Nobody leaves this room,' Vass snapped. He broke open the cylinder of his revolver, shook his head at the empty casings. 'Oh, this just gets better and better.'

Across the kitchen, Sebastien nodded at Hannah, and her heart ached at the compassion she saw in his face. Leaving the safety of his alcove, he strode across the room and into the hall. From his pocket he pulled his short-bladed knife. She cringed when she considered what little protection it offered him. He disappeared up the stairs.

On hands and knees, slipping and sliding in blood, Vass crawled to where his lieutenant had fallen. He snatched up the dead man's pistol. Wiped it clean. Crabbed back towards the overturned table.

Outside, Illes was still down on one knee. He opened his eyes, picked his pistol from the grass. Lifting his wounded arm, he pulled a spare clip of ammunition from his jacket. He rose to his full height.

Halfway across the kitchen floor, Vass paused beneath the counter that held the stainless steel syringe. Its glass reservoir was undamaged. He reached out a hand and snagged it. The liquid rolled ruby reflections across his face.

Vass grinned, and then he was snatching at the button on his shirt cuff. He rolled up his sleeve. Revealed a fleshy forearm.

'Benjámin, what are you doing?' the *signeur* rasped.

Vass found a blue vein in the crook of his arm. 'I know, I know. You're dying, and I promised you. I hate breaking promises. But this might be the only chance I get.'

He depressed the plunger on the syringe. Gabriel's blood

swelled up through the needle and flooded into his arm. Grimacing, he pulled it free and tossed the empty vessel across the room.

The *signeur* twisted in his chair, mouth working soundlessly.

Hannah heard a loose floorboard creak above them. She watched Vass crawl back into cover behind the table, holding his plundered pistol close to his chest. He raised his eyes to her, and she saw that his pupils had dilated.

'Shit, this stuff's good,' he said. He opened his mouth wide and bit at the air. His arm twitched and he dropped the pistol.

In the garden, Illes pushed the spare clip into his gun. He took a step towards the house. Then another, raising his weapon.

Vass lifted his hand, examined his fingers. 'I can feel it flowing through me,' he murmured. 'No pain. Just a . . .' He clenched his fist, opened his fingers and picked up the pistol.

'Benjámin!' the *signeur* hissed.

Vass raised the gun in a fluid movement and shot the old man twice. The *signeur's* head burst like a rotten squash and his wheelchair rocked backwards. Sharp pieces of Károly's skull slid down the wall behind him.

'Don't *interrupt* me like that when I'm *thinking*,' Vass said. He frowned, looking first at the weapon in his hand and then at the *signeur's* corpse. Then, noticing Gabriel, he aimed the gun at the Irishman's face.

Hannah closed her eyes. She couldn't help Gabriel. The rope that bound her was too tight. She wondered if she could stop herself from screaming if she was hit by the spray from the shot that killed him.

Nothing she could do to intervene. She wouldn't watch him die in front of her.

So you'll keep your eyes closed and abandon him too.

She raged at that internal voice even as it shamed her into opening her eyes.

Vass's pupils vibrated as if powered by tiny springs 'What's happening?' he asked.

'You're dying,' Gabriel replied. 'You're a psychotic bastard, you're dying and it's going to hurt. You're going to feel more pain than you ever imagined you could feel. And when it's over you're going to wake in hell where it'll start all over again.'

Vass shivered. His cheek began to twitch. 'Then I'll take you with me,' he said, and pulled the trigger.

Gabriel jerked back in his chair as the blast echoed around the room and Hannah opened her mouth wide and screamed and screamed.

CHAPTER 25

Aquitaine region, France

Now

It had only been her bedroom for a few days, and it contained barely any of her belongings, but it was clean and brightly painted and it had felt snug.

She tried to tug her wrist away from the headboard. The plastic cuff that bound her to its slats cut into her skin and she screwed up her eyes with the pain. She had thought about chewing through it, but she couldn't get her teeth into the loop.

If only she could reach something metal – a screwdriver would be perfect – then perhaps she could twist the plastic with it, tightening it until it snapped. The pain would be awful, but at least she would be free. At least she would be able to creep downstairs and help Mummy fight the Bad Man.

She didn't want to think about Him, didn't want to even consider that she might have to meet Him. But she didn't want Mummy to die. And she didn't want to die either, mainly because it scared her but also because she didn't want Mummy to be alone.

It was no good though. There was no screwdriver in sight. She could see a pair of pyjamas and a paperback book and a Bratz doll and that was it. None of those things offered her any means of freeing herself, unless there was a chapter on how to escape from handcuffs in the book, and she knew there wasn't because she had read it before and it was mainly about horses in love.

The man who had tied her to the bed had done so in silence, refusing to look at her. First he had bound Éva in the larger bedroom next door. After that, he had taken a syringe and injected the woman with something. Éva's eyelids had drooped and she'd fallen asleep. Then he had led Leah into her bedroom, where he used two of the plastic strips to truss her up.

She heard sounds from the next room: a creak as the door swung open, voices, a whispered conversation. Moments later the door of her bedroom opened and Sebastien peered inside. His face was paler than she had ever seen it and he carried a stubby blade. When he saw her, he sagged with relief and moved to the bed.

'Are you hurt?'

She shook her head. 'Where's Mummy?'

'Downstairs.'

'Is she—'

'At the moment, she's fine. She'll be even better once we get you out of these cuffs and away from the house.'

'I tried to bite them off. But I couldn't reach.'

Sebastien nodded, motioning her to lower her voice. He slipped his blade inside the loops of plastic and sliced them off. Leah sat up on the bed, rubbing away the soreness from her wrist. She heard a soft thump, somewhere upstairs.

'Let's go,' he whispered.

Leah nodded and when he offered her his hand, she was grateful. It felt good to be that close to someone. Sebastien moved to the bedroom door and opened it a crack. He squinted through the gap. Satisfied, he opened it fully and moved into the hall. Leah followed, but when Sebastien headed towards the main stairs she tugged his hand and shook her head. He frowned at her. In response, she pointed along the corridor past her own room. *Balcony*, she mouthed. *Steps*.

The master bedroom lay at the end of the hall. It contained a set of doors that opened on to the roof of a single-storey annexe. A balustrade ran around it, except for a gap where a set of metal steps descended down one side of the house. It was the better option. They had no chance of making a silent escape via the main stairs. Almost every tread screamed or groaned under pressure.

Leah led Sebastien into the master bedroom and drew back the curtains. Opening one of the balcony doors, she walked out on to the roof. The sun was a white coin in the sky above them. She filled her lungs with air, relieved to be outside where no one could creep up on her, plunge a knife into her, or press a hand to her mouth and suffocate her. She thought about her mother downstairs. About how scared she must be.

'Let's go,' Sebastien said.

'Where are all those men from earlier?'

'They're probably dead,' he replied. 'We have to hurry.'

Heart accelerating at his words, she tightened her grip on his hand and accompanied him down the steps.

At the bottom, feet crunching on the gravel, Sebastien crouched down beside her. 'Listen to me, Leah. You see that car?' He pointed at one of the big white off-roaders the men had parked in front of the house. It sat empty, a few feet away from the dining-room window.

She nodded.

'When I say the word, we're going to run over to it and jump inside. You take the passenger seat. You know which one that is?'

A silly question, but she nodded anyway.

'Good. Get in and do up your seat belt. We're going to leave here fast. The car will make a lot of noise. Some of those men from earlier might turn up.'

'I thought you said they were dead.'

'*Probably* dead, I said. And I only said they might turn up. I want you to lie low in your seat. Make yourself small. Understand?'

Leah nodded. She discovered she was crying. 'What about Mummy?'

'We get you to safety first. Then I come back for her. OK?'

'OK.'

'You're sure?'

'Yes.'

'Go.'

Leah sprinted across the gravel. She tugged open the Audi's door and scrambled up into the seat. She slammed the door behind her and struggled into the seat belt. When she glanced at the driver's seat on her left she saw that a dark liquid had drenched it. It was still wet, and she was pretty sure it was blood.

Hannah didn't want to look, didn't want to see the evidence of Gabriel's ruined face, wanted to remember him as the proud *hosszú élet* that had accompanied her up the slopes of Cadair Idris. But in the end she couldn't stop herself, as if her eyes demanded that she witness the continuing tragedy of Jakab's legacy.

When she turned in her chair she found Gabriel staring back at her. 'Missed,' he said, eyes wide. 'Can you credit it?'

Vass's hands spasmed and he dropped the gun. He grinned, the skin of his mouth stretching far wider than it should have done, exposing teeth as far back as his molars. When the flesh on one side of his mouth split open all the way to his ear, he screamed. The loose flap of cheek flopped down under its own weight, revealing the pink gum along his jaw. Blood, in a torrent, flowed down his neck.

'*Son'thing whurong,*' he slurred, hands scrabbling on the floor for the pistol. His fingers slipped on the boards, leaving bloody trails. Hannah realised that the dark and gummy discs that glued themselves to the wood were his fingernails.

He raised his eyes to her and she saw that one of them bulged as if forced from its socket by pressure within. '*Helk-he,*' he said, gargling through the blood welling in his throat.

Help me.

Fluid gushed from his ear. It spattered on to his shoulder

'You want me to help you?' Gabriel asked. 'You untie me and give me your pistol. That's the only way I can help you now.'

'Helk-heeee.'

'You untie me now while you still can!'

Vass bucked and twitched. He tore at his clothes, ripping open his shirt and exposing the soft white folds of his flesh. He began to paw savagely at himself. Gobs of fat, like molten wax, came away in his hands. He screamed again. Teeth rained from his mouth, clattering on to the floorboards like ivory dice. He raked his fingers across his abdomen, tearing open a deep furrow. Hannah saw his organs lurking beneath, a dark and shining mass. Just as he was about to plunge a hand into that snake of intestines, a gun barked and the top of Vass's skull detonated like a bloody firework.

Leah watched Sebastien yank open the driver's door and swing himself up into the cabin. She thought she might be sick if she watched him settle into the seat already glossy and sticky with someone else's blood. When the fabric squelched beneath his weight, she felt her stomach clench, and tasted the acid burn of bile in her throat.

Sebastien cursed. 'What the hell happened in here?'

'I think somebody got killed,' she whispered. 'In fact I'm pretty sure about it.'

The old man nodded, turning the keys in the ignition. 'I think you might be right. Poor blighter, whoever he was. Hold on to your hat. This could get bumpy.'

When Hannah opened her eyes, she saw Benjámin Vass slumped against the overturned kitchen table. The top of his head was missing. Pieces of him clung to her top, her jeans.

So much violence. So much death. All in the space of

minutes. Yet she felt no horror at what she had witnessed, no nausea. Their lives – and their deaths – had not mattered to her.

Hearing the splintering of wood, she turned in her seat. Gabriel's eyes were closed. Teeth bared, tendons straining in his neck, he grunted. Something below him cracked. An unnatural ring of muscle had appeared around both his forearms. The pressure of his reshaped flesh against the ropes had shattered both arm rests, leaving vivid welts on his skin. Even as she watched, the marks faded. Gabriel lifted his hands and shook himself free of the rope. 'My God, that stings,' he said.

'Untie me.'

He nodded, first bending down and unfastening the rope that bound his legs.

Illes limped into the kitchen through the shattered french windows, eyes like black holes. His polo neck was soaked with blood. He stepped around the dead *signeur*'s wheelchair and over the flaccid carcass of Benjámin Vass. 'Where?' he demanded. 'Where's the *Főnök*?'

'Upstairs. They took her to one of the rooms.'

Illes dragged himself to the hall.

'Please, Gabriel,' Hannah begged. 'Hurry.'

Pulling the last of the rope from his legs, he lifted himself out of his chair, cried out as his wounded feet took his weight, and fell to his knees. He shuffled towards her, sweat glistening on his face. Unpicking the knots that bound her, Gabriel hissed his words through the pain. 'Bastard shot me twice. I can't walk, can't run.' He winced. 'I'm sorry, Hannah. I'm not much good to you yet. You need to hurry. Do you know where Seb's gone? Where he will have taken her?'

Hannah yanked her right arm loose as he removed the rope. 'We agreed a fall-back.' She started work on the knots that bound her left arm while Gabriel untied her feet. Suddenly she was free.

'Then go. Quickly. I'll find you.'

Hannah jumped up from the chair, unprepared for the spikes of pain that shot through her legs as the blood began to return. She fell to the counter, gripped it. Breathed deep. Steeling herself, she lurched across the room. She made it to the doorway, held on to the jamb, swung herself into the hall.

The dead man lay at the bottom of the stairs. She was about to step over him when she heard movement on the landing. The floorboards above her squealed, and then Sebastien appeared on the stairs. He froze when he saw her. Then his face changed – an awful look of pity. He shook his head.

She screamed.

No. She wouldn't believe it.

He was mistaken. He hadn't looked properly. He didn't know the house as well as she did. He didn't know all the hiding places.

'*LEAH!*'

It just wasn't possible that Sebastien could have checked all the places a girl as clever and as brave and as beautiful as Leah could have found. He couldn't be telling her that her little girl had gone.

But you know the truth. You know what's happened. You always knew this was going to happen if you weren't strong enough.

He found her, Hannah.

Jakab found her, and he took her. You have no one else to blame for that. And if you don't act now, use every second, you don't have the slightest chance of seeing Leah again.

She launched herself past Sebastien. Up the stairs. Kicked open the first door on the left. Saw the *Főnök* slumped on the bed. Saw Illes leaning over her. Backed into the hall. Yanked open the next door. Laundry cupboard. Piled with blankets. Hauled them out. Checked for hiding places. Found no one. Opened the door on the right. Leah's bedroom. Saw a yellow plastic cuff on the bed, sliced open.

He's got her. If you ever doubted it, now you know.

Back in the hall, into the bathroom.

White tiles. Bath. Towels. Toilet. Sink.

Nowhere to hide. Nowhere to hide. One last room to try. The bedroom at the end of the corridor. She ran to it. Flung open the door.

A king-size bed. Plenty of room underneath it. A wardrobe in the corner, old and echoey. Floor-length curtains. So many places to hide. But none of them matter. None of them. Because one of the balcony doors is standing open, and a breeze that smells of lavender and late autumn sun and the terrible finality of endings is pouring through the gap, and now she can no longer deny what has happened, can no longer hope, can only think of a little girl's face and a mother's promise that everything would be all right, and what a lie that had been.

CHAPTER 26

Aquitaine region, France

Now

Hannah turned and turned in circles, although she felt as if she were stationary and the room spun around her. The bedroom was a cathedral of light. Nate had whitewashed the walls, and he'd cut a skylight into the ceiling that sloped between the huge oak beams. Shafts of autumn sunlight struck her from above, and white rays reached through the balcony windows, bleaching her, purifying her.

For a moment she lost herself in the light, spinning in its brilliance. If the sun's heat could vaporise her as she turned, would she choose that? If she could command it to flare with energy and, in a single moment, incinerate her memories, strip away her pain, transform to ash every particle of her, every damaged fibre, boil away her tears and her grief and her guilt, would she open her arms and embrace it?

So disorientated was she by Leah's disappearance, by the realisation that she had made the wrong choice by failing to keep the girl close, by the light that poured in through the windows and seared her with its intensity, that Hannah wondered for a moment if the shock had killed her.

Yet surely no afterlife could be cruel enough to accept not just her soul but all her agony, her fear, her shame. If Nate waited for her here, how could she explain that she had abandoned their beautiful child to the monster they had evaded for so long?

No, this was not a cathartic light; it was a light of clarity. She knew her chances of finding Leah were fading. But even the smallest chance was worth nurturing. It was all she had. And for the moment it was all she needed.

Hannah ended her rotations. She forced herself to breathe, focused her eyes. The first thing she saw, pinned to the frame of the balcony window, was a tiny red bead. In an instant, she recognised what she was looking at. It was one of the enamelled scales of the dragon brooch her father had given to her mother. The same brooch Sebastien had given to her at Llyn Gwyr. The same brooch she had given to Leah a few days earlier. No accident had caused it to be pinned here. Hannah plucked it from the wood.

It was a beacon. A sign. Leah had left this for her. She was sure of it. What it meant, she did not know. But she clutched on to it, to what it represented, and dived through the balcony doors and into the light.

He had asked her to lie low and make herself small, and even though Leah knew it was sensible advice, she could not resist inching herself up in the seat high enough to see over the dashboard. Sebastien twisted the keys in the ignition. The engine of the big white off-roader woke with a cough.

'Elvis has left the building,' the old man murmured. He stamped down on the accelerator and the wheels spat gravel chippings, launching the vehicle backwards across the drive. Sebastien hauled the wheel over and the 4x4 slewed around in a circle until its nose pointed down the track that led to the main road. A cloud of white dust drifted across the windscreen. He glanced in the rear-view mirror at the farmhouse. Selected first gear.

'Not the main road, they'll be waiting for us!' Leah shouted, terrified that the Eleni she had seen guarding the gate would intercept them.

Sebastien turned to face her. She hadn't expected him to be grinning. It confused her. 'Clever girl,' he said. 'What do you suggest?'

She knew she had to make smart decisions. She couldn't sit back and let him do all the hard work. They needed to work together if they were to survive this. Most importantly, they had to find a way of rescuing Mummy.

Unbidden, an image surfaced in her mind: the tall Eleni man tying Mummy to the chair. It made her want to cry and she knew she couldn't afford to do that, so she got angry instead. 'Take the side road,' she said, pointing to the overgrown track on their left. 'Through the woods.'

Sebastien licked his teeth. Then he nodded. The Audi lurched forwards and Leah was flung back in her seat. Within moments they passed out of the sunshine and into the trees. The off-roader bounced and rocked on the twisting track, tyres scrambling for grip on its cracked mud surface. They hit a large pothole, and when Sebastien banged his head on the roof he said a word Leah had never thought to hear from his lips.

'When are we going back for Mummy?'

'Soon.'

'We can't leave her there with the Bad Man.'

'Which one?'

'You know, the Bad Man.'

'From where I was standing, they all looked pretty bad.'

Leah frowned, wondering if he was serious, wondering if he was being sarcastic. 'So when are we going back?'

'When we've got you far enough away.'

'But then we'll have to go all the way back again.'

'Shut up a while, OK?'

Leah nodded, brushing tears from her cheeks.

They were travelling even faster now. The track through the trees was only wide enough for a single vehicle. Branches snapped against the windscreen. Their tyres ripped up ferns and brambles.

When the car skidded around a bend, Leah saw a man lying on his back in the middle of the track. He wore a khaki jacket, and black trousers with lots of pockets. His eyes were open and the handle of a knife rose from his chest like the candle on a birthday cake. Blood had soaked through his coat, darkening the soil around him. 'We've got to help.'

'He's dead.'

'You have to stop,' she moaned, placing one hand on the dashboard, twisting her head away.

'There's no way round.'

'You can't just—'

Their vehicle bounced over the corpse, rocking on its suspension but losing no speed. Leah stuffed the front of her fist into her mouth, squeezing her eyes shut. She wanted to scream.

You have to be grown-up. You can't be a girl any more. All those times Mummy talked to you, she was trying to prepare you for this. She said it would be horrible, that you might have to do horrible things. Well she was right, wasn't she? You're lucky that Sebastien is here to guide you, because you've been pretty useless so far.

But the problem was that Sebastien was being horrible, too. It wasn't that he failed to stop when they found the man in the road. The stranger was dead. Anyone could see that; she just hadn't wanted to admit it. It wasn't even that he had driven over the man's body. They were running for their lives, and when you ran for your life you had to do things, brutal things. She thought the memory of driving over that man would be with her for ever, that she would hear the sound of their tyres punching into his corpse every night before she slept. But she also thought it had been part of the price of their escape, one of those nasty things they had to do. Because of Jakab.

Even though he hadn't stopped, even though he'd driven over the man's body, and even though she knew he'd been forced to do both those things, he also hadn't tried to help her through it – hadn't told her to look away, hadn't tried to shield her eyes from the sight.

When her front teeth cracked against the knuckle she had pressed into her mouth, she noticed how badly she had started to shake. She looked around the car, at the leather seats, at the dials on the dashboard, at Sebastien.

He hunched over the steering wheel, wrenching it left and right. The corner of his lip curled upwards, halfway between a grin and a sneer.

Reaching out a hand, Leah began fiddling with the controls on the central console. She pressed the button for the cigarette lighter, twirled the dials on the air conditioning, switched on the radio, dialled up the volume.

Dance music thumped from the car's speakers. Sebastien yelled, slapped her hands away. He jabbed a finger at the radio, killing it. 'What the hell's wrong with you?'

'We need to go back for Mummy.'

'I told you. We'll go back. Now, please. Let me concentrate.' He shot her a quick smile. 'Look, I know you're scared. But it's going to be all right. You're safe now.'

She looked at him. Really looked at him. At the fuzz of white hair on top of his sun-browned head. At the deep fissures that lined his skin. At the liver spots on the backs of his hands. She remembered he had an eagle tattoo on his wrist, but couldn't remember which one. His nearest wrist was bare. The one furthest from her was concealed by his coat.

Up ahead, the trees thinned, and Leah saw snatches of grassland between their trunks. She knew that somewhere on their left the river flanked them.

'Where did you first meet my daddy?' she asked.

Sebastien's eyes found hers for a moment. 'What?'

'I asked where you first met my daddy.'

'Leah, please—'

'You said you'd tell me. You said you'd tell me anything if I asked.'

'And I will. But we need to get away, Leah. We need to get away from Jakab.'

She felt her tummy twist when she heard that name on his lips. She sobbed, and when she heard how pitiful it sounded she forced her fingernails into her palms, forced herself to remember her mother's words.

Scamp, listen to me. Remember all the things I ever taught you. Think about everything I've said. Keep your eyes open, OK? Be brave. Trust your instincts. Everything will be all right if you do that, I promise.

Sebastien slid the car around a bend, tyres thrashing at the undergrowth. Leah gripped the sides of her seat, bracing herself until the vehicle righted itself.

On the dashboard, the cigarette lighter button popped out.

Trust your instincts.

Leah snatched the lighter from its socket. Its end glowed red. Grimacing, she jammed it down on to Sebastien's leg. He yelled, flung his arm at her, tried to bat her hand away. His fist caught her in the side. Leah's breath exploded from her. The pain was terrific, but she fought it, twisting the cigarette lighter into his flesh like a screw.

Shrieking now, Sebastien lifted both hands from the wheel. He grabbed her wrist and tore it away from his leg. She felt something crack. A bolt of agony shot up her arm all the way to her teeth. The cigarette lighter spun away into the footwell.

Screwing up her eyes at the agony in her wrist, she lunged at the steering wheel and caught it in her other hand.

Sebastien slapped at the burning embers of cloth that stuck to his leg. Leah hauled the steering wheel towards her.

They were travelling too fast. As the car lurched to the right, she realised that they were going to hit a tree, and that even if she survived that, Jakab was probably going to kill her.

Clasping the enamelled red dragon scale as if it were a talisman, Hannah sprinted across the annexe roof and down the covered steps. She ran to the front driveway, skidding and sliding on the loose gravel.

Where would he go? How would he flee? Earlier, a white Audi had been parked in front of the dining-room windows. Dániel Meyer and his bodyguard had arrived in it. Now it had gone. But had the Eleni taken it? Or Jakab?

He won't have escaped on foot. He'll have stolen a car or brought one with him. He can't melt away with a nine-year-old girl without one.

She turned, scouring the fields. She checked the track to the main road, the trail that led through the woods. The tree line.

No Eleni in sight. None of their vehicles.

A slick of what looked like blood marked the patch where the Q7 had stood. Hannah stared at it.

It isn't Leah's. That's all that matters. It isn't Leah's. He didn't take her just so that he could kill her out here. He's got much worse than that planned. Which is why you have no time.

Before they landed in France, Sebastien had rented a Jeep Cherokee – it had been waiting for them at the airfield. He kept it in one of the work sheds on the far side of the building. Hannah jumped across the blood-slicked gravel and sprinted past the front of the house. She wondered what would happen if any remaining Eleni caught sight of her. To retain any chance of finding Leah, she could not afford a single delay. Yet for all the gunfire that had erupted minutes earlier, it was bizarrely quiet outside.

The tool shed was a single-storey brick structure with a timber roof. Its wooden doors were warped, speckled with the ancient remains of red paint. Hannah slammed against one of them, using it to bring herself to a stop. She wrenched back the locking bolt and swung the door open. Darkness reached for her. She smelled sawdust, old motor oil, the antiseptic aroma of new motor vehicle. The Jeep's front grille glinted in the shadows, a shark's mouth full of teeth.

Hannah looked over her shoulder. She checked the paths, the drive. No one. No Eleni moved in the orchard, the wood. The helicopter was nowhere in sight.

She ducked into the shed, sliding down the narrow space between the 4x4 and the wall. As she edged past its wing mirror, fingers snatched at her. Hannah screamed, thrashed backwards, cracking her elbow, losing the skin of her knuckles.

Cobwebs. Just cobwebs, tangling in her hair. Cursing her skittishness, clawing the strands away from her face, she slid another few steps along the car and lifted her fingers to the driver's door. Her heart was pounding now. She could feel it knocking in her chest.

Please be unlocked. Please.

She had talked with Sebastien only that morning about leaving the Jeep ready in case they needed to make a swift escape. But had he remembered? She gripped the handle and prayed.

When the door clunked and swung open, Hannah almost cried out with relief. She clambered up into the cabin and slammed the door. Silence. The aroma of pine air freshener. Something jangled against her hand, cold and metallic.

Keys.

Twisting them in the ignition, she threw the 4x4 into gear and stamped on the accelerator. The big three-litre engine cleared its throat. As the car punched out of the tool shed, tearing the doors from their hinges, Hannah rocked back in her seat. Pieces of wood rained down on the path outside. She hauled on the wheel and just avoided clipping the corner of the house, yanking the wheel in the other direction the moment she was clear. The car lurched over, engine hollering, and she jammed on the brakes outside the front of the farmhouse.

Revving the engine, she scanned left and right.

Where have you gone, you bastard? Where have you taken her?

He had only one sensible option. Just fifteen miles north, the main road met the E70 route that crossed southern France. From there, Jakab could access any number of airports. Or he could just stay on the road. Westwards, it would take him to Spain. East, he could pass through Italy, Slovenia, Croatia,

Serbia, Romania. It even crossed the Danube between Giurgiu and Ruse.

Hannah could measure the time she had left in minutes. A chasm of darkness was rushing up behind her. If she did not outrun it, if she flinched before it, Leah would be lost. Knowing that already it could be too late, that already she could have failed, she screamed with frustration and anger and sorrow and hatred.

Earlier, Vass's henchmen had been guarding the main road. None of them remained in sight. But she wouldn't take the risk. The track through the woods followed the river and passed the mill, joining the same road. It was a better route. If she were delayed even a minute, it could give Jakab the margin he needed.

Jamming the accelerator to the floor, she clutched the wheel as the Jeep lunged forwards. When its front wheels hit the uneven surface of the track, it bounced and nearly threw her out of her seat. Hannah changed gears, pushing the vehicle as hard as it would go. A pothole unseated her a second time. She tugged her arm through the seat belt. Tried to fasten it. Secured herself.

Wheels tearing up clods of earth, the Jeep powered up the gradient that led into the trees. Within seconds, she was plunged into shade. Bracken and ivy snapped and ripped. Her tyres shredded dead leaves.

A tight turn ahead. She dared not lose any speed. Dared not hesitate. Like a wild thing, the Jeep slid and spat, clawing at the earth as it took the turn. The steering wheel bucked and spun. She would not let go. The back end lost traction and slid. The Jeep's right side slammed against the trunk of a tree. Hannah cracked her head against the window. Hard enough to dazzle her.

Keep going. Just keep going.

As the car righted itself and accelerated out of of the turn, she saw a crow perched on something in the road ahead.

Sickened, she realised it was a man's body. He could not still be alive. A knife protruded from his chest. His right leg was thrown across his body. One side of his skull had been crushed.

The track was too narrow. On each side, the trunks of chestnut, oak, beech and birch crowded close. She could not afford to stop and pull the man's body out of the way. She had to get through. Ahead, the crow exploded into flight. Hannah downshifted and accelerated.

I'm sorry. I don't know who you are. I'm sorry.

The Jeep rocketed up the slope, pistons detonating like cannons. Hannah forced herself to keep her eyes open as her vehicle thumped over the corpse with a jolt that flung her around in her seat.

She smelled the smoke before she saw it – acrid in her nose, bitter in her throat.

When she turned into the next bend, she saw the first drifts of it hanging in the dappled light. Another bend and the drifting smoke became a grey cloud, its shade darkening.

She barrelled around the next turn. Ahead, a boiling black soup obscured the entire track. Hannah braked hard. She slowed the Jeep to a crawl. Beyond the windscreen, visibility dropped to a few feet. Oily smoke, as dark and as glossy as tar, billowed all about her. Inching her way now, peering through the roiling mass, she strained to find its source. A few feet. A few feet more. The stink of burning rubber, burning plastic. The smoke pressed at every window. Hannah switched the headlights on to full beam. In front, something gleamed.

Coughing from the fumes leaching into her lungs, she nursed the Jeep forwards. Whatever had been reflected in its lights vanished as another mushroom of smoke erupted.

It appeared again. Unmistakable now. The back of a white Audi Q7.

And suddenly she knew that this was the car that had brought Dániel Meyer to Le Moulin Bellerose, and that this was the car that Jakab had used to take her daughter away from her, and as she nosed the Jeep through a break in the smoke, and autumn sunlight flooded its interior, she pulled up alongside the horribly wrecked Audi and found that her hands were shaking on the wheel, trembling like the filaments of a spider's web during a kill, and she could hear in her ears the pounding of blood through her arteries, and all because Jakab had been here, and so had her daughter, and oh how could anyone still be alive inside that twisted and blackened metal cage?

Without realising, she had brought the Jeep to a halt. She switched off the engine, unbuckled her belt. Opening the door, she slipped out of the car. She took a breath. Another. Stared at the burning Audi. Looked away. Thought she might be sick. Wondered why she should care about that; about such a trivial thing.

The black smoke rolled away from her, blowing in the direction of the farmhouse – that false refuge she had built with Nate. Hannah looked up and down the path. She moved closer to the wreckage.

The vehicle had left the road at a sharp angle, as if the driver had swerved to avoid an obstacle. Another few feet and it would have been out of the trees and into grassland. Instead, the car had slammed head-on into an oak. The impact had been so violent that its engine bay had fused with the tree trunk. Smoke poured from it: burning cables and rubber and dripping oil. Dark flames licked metal.

The Audi's windscreen had disappeared. Inside, the driver's seat was stained black with blood. There was so much of it.

She hugged herself. Forced herself to approach the car. The passenger seat was empty. But she could see blood there too. Bright and red and fresh. And, she thought, wanting to close her eyes, wanting to die, it had to be Leah's.

She may be close. She may have crawled into the bushes. She may be dying there, wanting to find somewhere peaceful, somewhere away from the sharp metal and the stink of burning and the violence and the madness. Or she's died already, alone and frightened and wondering where you were, why you broke your promise, why you allowed this to happen.

Hannah turned away. Peered between the trees. Peered through soot-grained eyes and tears and lost hope. Leah wasn't there. Nobody was there. And so she looked back at the car again, and that was when she saw the enamelled dragon scale.

It glimmered, a red circle edged in gold, pressed deep into the plastic of the Audi's dashboard. She felt her chest swell, her throat tighten, until she doused with cold logic the hope that had wanted to surface.

That the dragon scale was Leah's, she had no doubt. But nothing here indicated that she had left this marker *after* the crash.

Believe.

Such a simple idea. So difficult. So monumentally difficult, after all that had happened, after all the dreams that had died.

Believe.

She would search for her daughter until she had no more breath. And she would not take that last breath until Jakab Balázs was destroyed, utterly, was little more than a dark memory for the world, a filthy stain that time would bleach away.

And if she confirmed that Leah was dead and managed to kill Jakab, what then? What would she do? What *could* she do if the last person on earth that she loved had been taken from her? What choice would she have?

You know what you'll do. Even now you're thinking it. Even now. Well, no one will begrudge you that, and likely no one will care. You will have failed everyone that mattered.

But whatever happens, you don't miss your appointment with Jakab. The arms of those scales need to be balanced.

Hannah stepped away from the burning Audi, turning from the smoke and the stink and the crackle. Up ahead, the track emerged from the trees into grassland. Sunlight caressed browned stalks. A breeze whispered amongst them. To the south ran the river, and closer still the mill race, a man-made channel of water diverted from the Vézère to power the mill's wheel.

And there, in the distance, half in light and half in shadow, a gnarled and age-warped three-storey construction of timber and brick and stone, stood the old watermill itself. Le Moulin Bellerose.

It had cloaked itself, at the river's edge, in a circle of thin trees. Hannah felt the blank stare of its upper windows. They spoke of age and decay. Of atrophy and ruin. Of the inevitability of loss and the futility of hope.

Nate had patched the roof to protect the structure from the worst of the weather, and he had reglazed all but one of the windows. That single black maw remained, its sill spattered with guano, the entry point for the colony of pipistrelle bats that roosted in the building's dusty rafters.

A sound echoed throughout the forgotten structure, bouncing around its shell and spilling out of the broken window. The sound of a young girl's screams.

CHAPTER 27

Aquitaine region, France

Now

The weight of conflicting emotions that assaulted Hannah as she heard her daughter's cries threatened to overwhelm her, unravel her. Her heart clenched. Her mind grappled. The almost unbearable relief that Leah was close brought with it terror that even now Hannah might be too far away, too weak, too late. The anguish in those screams sparked fury so blisteringly acute, so animalistic and all-encompassing, that her body shook, her teeth grated and her eyes felt like they would burst from their sockets. Her skin rippled with electricity. It rose into goosebumps. It lifted the hairs of her arms and her neck. Her ears rang and her mouth tasted blood. Her nose filled with the reek of burning rubber and plastic and oil.

She had no weapons. No gun, no knife. In her flight from the house she had not even paused long enough to grab something – anything – with which she could confront Jakab.

Hannah rubbed at her face with shaking hands. Her skin felt both raw and numb, a strange sensory mix. She found herself glancing back at the Audi, at the solitary red dragon scale pinned to the dash, at all it represented.

And suddenly, magically, as she stared at that single enamelled button, she felt as if a plug had been pulled somewhere deep within her, and all of her emotions – her terror and her rage and her guilt and her hate – were spiralling away, draining out of her like poison gushing from an abscess. What remained was the clarity of a single thought.

She had to kill Jakab Balázs, or she had to die in the attempt. And she had to do that today. Now.

Find a weapon. Something. Anything. You need to improvise. You'll be no good to Leah if you go in unprepared. You have one chance. One final opportunity. For Leah. For Nate. For all of them.

Catlike, she darted back to the Jeep, wrenched open its passenger door. In the glove compartment she found an owner's handbook, a sheaf of papers from the rental company, a map of southern France, an alloy locking nut key in a polythene bag. No good.

She slid her hand into the door recess. Empty. Jumping into the passenger seat, she leaned over the gearstick and checked the driver's door pocket. Her fingers brushed against cloth. Closed around something. Lifting it out, she saw it was Sebastien's canvas medical kit – the same one he had brought to Llyn Gwyr. Hannah dropped it on the seat and unrolled it. Antiseptic wipes, painkillers, scissors, burns dressings. Inside individual pockets she found a surgical scalpel, and spare blades in sterile pouches. Separate folds yielded a tracheal tube, suture thread, a selection of syringes, a penlight torch.

She snatched up the scalpel and torch, bundled up the kit and tossed it on to the back seat. With her finds tucked into a pocket, she climbed out of the Jeep, opened its boot, peered inside. A folded tarpaulin, two blankets, a five-litre jerrycan and two cardboard boxes. Rifling through the first box, she found fishing line, a sack of dry dog food and two thermos flasks. The second box contained a dual gas stove, spare gas canisters, a box of all-weather matches, a butane lighter, several freeze-dried food packs.

God love you, Sebastien. You thought of everything.

Hannah grabbed the jerrycan, knowing from its weight that it was full. She stuffed the butane lighter into her shirt pocket.

As an afterthought, she opened the matchbox and crammed a handful of pink-tipped matches into her jeans.

You have to go. NOW.

Hannah skirted the Jeep, hefting the jerrycan alongside her, feeling the cold shape of the scalpel handle pressing against her leg. Out of the trees she ran, through long grass heavy with seed. It tugged at her legs and snagged her boots. She wondered if she was too late. She wondered what horrors were unfolding inside the mill.

Beyond the tree line, the land sloped down to the banks of the Vézère. Sunlight twinkled on its surface, reflecting cold blues and leaf greens and the brown shades of river stone and mud.

The mill race cut a narrow channel from further upstream, diverting water into the reservoir that fed the wheel. The sluice gate was closed; she could hear the overflow pouring down a stepped weir, emptying back into the river. Hannah stumbled on a rock hidden in the grass. Nearly twisted an ankle. The jerrycan slammed against her leg. She lurched onwards, swinging the container behind her.

The watermill, three storeys of brooding stone and brick, perched on a rocky outcrop thrusting out into the river. Its steeply pitched roof drooped where the timber beneath the tiles had warped and cracked. Moss clung in patches to its northern face. Its windows were blank voids, denying any glimpse of what lurked within.

The waterwheel itself, like some dark and twisted amusement park nightmare, hung from the wall that faced the river. Thirty feet in diameter, immense cast-iron spokes held its wooden paddles in place. With the sluice closed, the wheel was still. Its upper paddles, dried by the sun, were spotted with the dusty clumps of dead algae. Those nearer the water were slick and green with river slime.

A railed wooden platform surrounded the base of the building, partly supported by stilts where it jutted over the rocky outcrop. The mill race terminated at a sluice gate directly below the platform. A metal wheel operated a worm drive that raised or lowered it, controlling the flow of water.

Halfway along the nearest wall stood the mill's only door, a thick oak slab studded with ironwork. It hung open. Since hearing Leah's scream, Hannah had seen no one enter or leave by it. All the windows she could see were closed except for the unglazed hatch at the very top, and that was too far above the ground to provide an escape route. Anyone attempting to leave via the windows overlooking the Vézère faced a plunge into the rock-strewn shallows below.

Lungs burning, muscles aching, Hannah stopped at the balcony rail of the structure's wooden platform.

He's stronger than you. Faster than you. Cleverer. You've got to surprise him. Unbalance him somehow. He won't be thinking about you yet. Not with Leah here.

Hannah stared at the doorway, at the darkness that seeped out of it. She could feel her heart clenching and unclenching in her chest like a fist. Behind her, water tumbled over the weir in a roar. Crouching, she unscrewed the lid of the jerrycan.

She still had no idea what she was going to do. Throughout her ownership of Le Moulin Bellerose, the watermill had been the one place where she felt unsettled. Its enforced solitude, out here on this lonely outcrop, gave it a sad and dismal air. Now, it exuded malevolence.

Throw him off balance. Do something unexpected. Give yourself any advantage you can.

Standing, she grasped the metal wheel that controlled the sluice, twisted. Nothing. Tensing, she strained against it, bracing her legs and spine, watching as the skin on her knuckles whitened.

The wheel slipped an inch. It gripped and held fast. Again she heaved against it, feeling rust grate on the teeth of the rack. Then, in an instant, the resistance broke, and the wheel turned in her hands.

Below her the steel sluice plate began to rise. Water, at first a trickle and then a gush and then a flood, foamed and churned.

The wheel groaned. For a moment she thought the water's force was going to tear it loose, rip out the huge axle and bring the entire building crashing over the lip of the outcrop into the river below. Instead, it began to turn. Slowly it gathered speed, flinging white spray into the air as the paddles rotated through the seething water. She heard gears engaging inside the mill, the old machinery roused from sleep.

Hannah picked up the jerrycan. She pulled the scalpel from the pocket of her jeans. Stared at its blade.

He'll kill you. You know he'll kill you.

The great wheel turned. Water foamed and boiled and hissed. The platform beneath her feet vibrated with the power she had unleashed.

Hannah moved to the mill's heavy oak door, took a last breath and slipped inside.

CHAPTER 28

Aquitaine region, France

Now

From rich autumn light she stepped into a cloying abyss. The sun's heat had roasted the air inside the mill; it was thick with the smell of dust and timber and disintegrating linen sacks. Underlying it was a fouler odour. Some animal had crawled in here recently to die.

The windows were caked in filth. They allowed scant sunlight to filter through. To Hannah's left, the waterwheel's main shaft entered the room through a hole in the wall. Upon it sat a huge metal pit wheel. As the pit wheel turned it rotated a cog on a separate axle, converting horizontal motion into vertical. A toothed spur wheel drove a second spinning shaft that disappeared through the ceiling to the milling room upstairs.

The machinery clacked and shook and knocked and creaked. Its vibrations lifted a fine haze of flour into the air around her.

Slowly Hannah's eyes adjusted to the gloom. A collection of rusted farm tools were heaped in one corner. In another, a stack of firewood. Under a window stood the workbench Nate had used to patch the mill's roof and reglaze its windows. On it rested a chipped blue coffee mug, a china plate, several offcuts of glass.

Leah sat cross-legged in the middle of the room. The girl's pupils had dilated so much that her eyes looked like black holes.

Her face was smudged with dirt and blood. A lump like a halved plum swelled on her forehead. Her skin was white. Her left cheek was lacerated.

But she was here. In this same room. Alive.

On the floor, opposite her, sat Jakab.

Utterly still, his back to Hannah, legs tucked beneath him, he perfectly mirrored Leah's stance. He wore corduroy trousers, boots, an old army coat. Hannah would need only two steps to bring him within reach: the abomination from Gödöllö; the horror that had ripped through generations of her family like a sharpened scythe.

Her husband. Her mother and father. The grandfather she had never met. Erna Novák, little more than a name in an old diary, but a woman who had loved and feared and grieved and died. All of them gone. All because of this creature before her, this stalking beast.

She stared at the back of Jakab's head – at the tanned skin of his neck, at his dark hair – and felt her stomach seizing, her mouth flooding with saliva. To be this close, within touching distance of the source of so much death and pain, made her nauseous. Waves of insanity and corruption seemed to flow from him. She felt buffeted by their swells.

Leah lifted her gaze to Hannah. The girl's eyes were wild, lost. Her mouth hung slack.

Oh please God, am I too late? Has he ruined her already? Stolen away her mind?

She tightened her grip on the scalpel. Against Jakab, it was a mere talisman, but it was all she had. 'Leah, get up. Come away from him.'

The girl remained still, as if transfixed by some spell he had woven.

'*Leah.*'

Finally, her daughter blinked. 'It's OK, Mummy. He explained everything.'

Never before had Hannah heard that tone in Leah's voice. It

was caught somewhere between wonder and horror, denial and acceptance. 'Darling, please. I don't know what he's said. But you know who he is. What he is. Anything he's told you is a lie. I promise you that. Now stand up. Come away.'

Leah's face tightened, as if she tried to communicate with more than mere words. 'We don't have to be afraid any more.'

'You're right. We don't have to be afraid. Not of him – not ever again. Please, honey. Get up.'

Around them, the mill wheels clanked and turned. Dust shivered in the air. Floorboards vibrated. Leah untucked her feet from beneath her.

When the girl began to rise, Jakab copied her. Moving with preternatural grace, he unfolded his legs and pushed himself up from the floor: a single sinuous movement, like steam curling from a pot.

He turned and Hannah felt the breath whoosh from her lungs as if she had been kicked. Felt her fingers lose their grip on the jerrycan. Heard it thump to the floor. Felt her throat constricting as impossibly – *impossibly* – she found herself staring not at Jakab, not Jakab at all, but Nate.

Nate. Solid, incarnate. Standing before her.

Nate. Resurrected from the lifeless vessel she had abandoned at Llyn Gwyr.

The skin around his eyes crinkled as he smiled, and when Hannah saw the animation in that soft expression she thought her heart would burst from her chest. Her knees buckled and she stumbled. Managed, just about, to stay on her feet. Felt the scalpel, slick with her sweat, begin to slip through her fingers.

It's not him! You know it's not him!

The jerrycan had tipped on to its side. Fuel glugged, gushing from the nozzle, spreading across the floor. It soaked into the wooden boards beneath her feet, staining them black.

'Han,' he said. And it was Nate's voice. Unmistakably Nate's. His timbre and his accent. His playfulness and his strength.

A wretched sound bled out of her as she stared at him and wanted it to be true. She forced her eyes shut, squeezing out tears. Opened them again. Saw his face, his beautiful face. 'You're dead,' she whispered.

Nate sighed. His face creased, and he shook his head. 'Oh, Han. Don't say that. How can you stand there and say that? Don't write me off. Don't write *us* off.'

'You killed him.'

'Killed him? He's right here. He's *me*. I'm everything he was and more. I can take care of you, protect you, love you. Look at me, Hannah. Look at this man before you. How long have I searched? How long have I committed my life to looking for you, only ever for you? And now suddenly you're here, and I'm here, and Leah is here. And we can be together, the three of us, sustaining something you thought you'd lost for ever. Do you know how many times I've dreamt of this moment, dreamt of the things I'd say to you, the promises I'd make?'

'You killed all of them.'

He shook his head. 'It was a different time. A different world. A lifetime ago. For you, several lifetimes. Whatever happened before, this is where we are now. This moment. A turning point. No one can change the past. But I'm your Nate. The Nate you want me to be, the Nate you're so desperate to have back. I'm here, Hannah. Just let me in. That's all you have to do. We can't change the past but together we can make the future. Just give me a chance and let me in.'

Behind him, Leah retreated to the far wall, her eyes huge.

Nate smiled, reached out a hand. 'Hannah?'

From the heap of old tools in the corner, Leah picked up a wooden fork handle and swung it at her father's head. When it connected with Nate's skull it made a sound like a cricket bat striking a ball.

Not Nate.

Jakab.

Hannah blinked away her confusion. The creature wearing

her dead husband's face crashed to its knees and pitched over on one side, eyes rolling in their sockets.

Leah dropped the fork handle. She raised her hand to her mouth. Chewed her fingers.

'Leah, that was so brave of you,' Hannah told her. 'So very brave. And this is all going to be over soon. I promise. But first, I need you to go outside.'

The girl looked up at her.

'Leah, go on. Go outside and wait there until I come out.'

'Will you come with me?'

Hannah nodded her head. 'I will. But first I have to finish this. You don't need to see this part. Go on.'

Tears rolled down her cheeks. 'Can't we just leave? Right now? Do you have to hurt him? He looks so much like Daddy.'

'Please, scamp.'

Leah stumbled across the floor of the mill. When she reached the door, she hesitated, turned back. Hannah discerned something in the girl's expression that was grim and dark and ultimately accepting. And then she was gone, leaving Hannah alone with Jakab.

Around her, wheels turned, axles rotated. Upstairs, the millstones rasped and scraped as they ground together. Dust motes hovered and sparkled in the thickening air.

Hannah gripped the scalpel. Crouched over Jakab.

This, then, was where it ended for him. She wondered, if he had known his last moments would find him lying in filth before the woman who rejected him, if he would have asked himself what he had achieved from all his killing, what he had gained.

As she raised the scalpel to his throat, tensing her arm, preparing to plunge the blade into his carotid artery, he opened his eyes.

Not Nate's loving eyes.

Not Gabriel's magical eyes.

Not even the eyes of a demon.

These were too ordinary. Lustreless. Dull.

In them she saw madness and she saw fear.

Blood skated down the side of Jakab's face where the fork handle had opened his skin. His smile was forced, tight with pain. 'For a moment there,' he said, 'you considered it.'

She shook her head.

'Yes. Just for a second or two. But you did.'

'Never.'

'If you do this, Hannah, it'll make you no better than me.'

'That's a joke.'

'You'll really watch me die all over again?'

Scowling, she raised the scalpel, scanned his neck, saw the flicker where his artery pulsed. She glanced upon his face a final time. Not Nate's features, she told herself firmly, but the features of a killer who had stalked her through time, and whose time had finally run out.

Not Nate's face but so like it. Jakab was right, though. In the end, she couldn't watch, couldn't witness that awful sundering a second time.

Hannah scrunched up her eyes and plunged down with the blade. And even as she did, she knew she had hesitated a fraction too long and her opportunity had been lost. She felt his fingers encircle her wrist, gripping her so hard that she gasped in pain. He leaped to his feet, dragging her with him, and when she tried to transfer the scalpel from her trapped hand to the other, he wrenched her arm so savagely that it tumbled from her fingers and clattered across the floor.

Jakab panted, blood dripping from his face, mouth twisted into a snarl. 'You actually would have done it, too, you crazy bitch. You really thought it would be that easy? You thought I'd *allow* you to *kill* me?' He shook his head. 'I'm not even *here* for you, Hannah. I'm not even *interested* in you. It's Leah who's important. You've confused her. Poisoned her against me. Filled her head with nonsense and lies just like Nicole did with you. But it's not too late this time. She's young enough to heal. Once she's out of your reach.'

Hannah swung her left fist at him, intending to batter his face. He caught that wrist too and when he yanked her arms apart it took everything she had not to scream.

If you scream, Leah will come. Whatever happens, whatever he does, you can't allow that.

She drove her knee up into his groin. Eyes flaring, he pivoted and tossed her across the room. Hannah flew towards the mill machinery. Fearing she was going to be sucked into the gears, she put out a hand to grab hold of something and slow her momentum. Her fingers snagged on the teeth of the huge spur wheel.

It took less than a second. The cog yanked her in a half-circle, and as it dragged her hand into the teeth of the pinion wheel, three of her fingers burst apart in a wet spray.

Pain like white fire in her brain.

Don't scream.

The shredded meat of her hand had fouled the pinion. Its axle groaned and flexed. The pinion's teeth stuttered as they ground against bone.

Don't scream.

Her hand was a pulped mess. Severed fingers; torn skin. In the gloom of the mill, the blood painting the machinery looked like oil. Hannah tried to pull what remained of her hand out of the gears. Pain shrieked in her head. She was caught.

Across the room, Jakab smirked. 'That's unfortunate.' He ambled over to her, peering down at her ruined hand.

Her ears buzzed. Her eyelids fluttered.

So this is where you die. In a stinking millhouse.

You failed, Hannah. And now he wins, and you lose. And you die, and he gets Leah. He gets to destroy Leah's life because you failed.

Except she wouldn't let that happen. She didn't care about dying. Even if it *was* in a stinking millhouse. She wouldn't let

Jakab have her daughter. No way. She wouldn't risk the prospect of an afterlife where she had to explain that.

'I'll say one thing for you, Hannah Wilde. You never gave up.' Jakab glanced around the room, and when he looked back at her he saw that she held a butane lighter in her fingers. Her thumb rested on the flint wheel.

The jerrycan had emptied a gallon of petrol across the floorboards. The stench of the fumes was thick in the air. One spark. That was all she needed.

Something cracked and splintered in her trapped hand, and the spinning pinion snapped away a shard of bone. A shockwave raced up her arm and exploded in her head.

As fast and as lithe as a wild animal, Jakab sprang at her and snatched the lighter from her fingers. Shaking his head, he tucked it into the pocket of his army coat. 'Insane,' he said. 'Totally insane.'

She moaned, then. Moaned with grief at the thought of what would happen after she had gone. 'Nate.' Her voice cracked. 'Oh, Nate. I'm so sorry. I'm so sorry, I failed. I let her down. Leah. *Leah* . . .'

Jakab approached her. Eyes hungry. Head cocked to one side.

Not Jakab. Nate.

Hannah shook her head.

No, not Nate. *Not* Nate.

The creature with her husband's face took another step closer to her and lifted its hand to her cheek. Fingers caressed her skin. 'Hush,' it said. 'It'll all be over soon. Hush.'

It leaned towards her face. Nate – *not* Nate – *Jakab*. The pinion rotating on her ruined hand, on her crushed bones, clattered and wobbled on its axle. It bumped and stuttered.

A ghoul filled her vision. And now it was kissing her, although somehow it was Nate's mouth, unmistakably Nate's lips upon hers, kissing her the way he had always kissed her, while his fingers traced a line down her cheek, along her throat.

Now his hand was at her breast, squeezing, caressing, and his kiss became more urgent, and Hannah felt her knees sag, and then she did what she never thought she would do, never thought she *could* do, and found herself opening her lips to him. Even as his tongue entered her mouth and she felt the heat of his body against hers, she was digging her free hand out of her jeans.

Jakab broke their kiss. He pulled back from her and looked down at her hand, at the fingers that held a single pink-tipped match, its phosphorus head hovering an inch above the spinning metal spur wheel.

His eyes met hers. His tongue flickered out, licked his lips.

'I win,' she whispered.

Jakab lunged at her as she struck the match against the wheel.

A tiny black coil of smoke.

Nothing.

A white pinprick of light. A sudden flare.

Hannah's fingers opened and the burning match twirled to the floor. Even as it fell, the air spawned a yellowing light. Jakab slammed into her, the force of his body ripping the remains of her hand free of the cog's teeth.

She wrapped her arms around him as they fell. The air rippled into a golden sheet, sucking the air from her lungs. A wave of heat rolled over her, and now she was burning, falling into flames and fire as the heat became a furnace blast and the shrieking agony in her hand became nothing, *nothing* compared to this. She opened her mouth to breathe and fire leaped into her lungs.

It won't last. You've won.

You've won.

Jakab flailed and thrashed. She held fast as his elbow caught her in the face, smashing her nose. Her hair sizzled. Her flesh roasted, crackling and spitting like pork fat. She opened her eyes and in the instant before the inferno shrivelled them to hissing spheres, she glimpsed hell. Hell made real and burning all around her.

But you did it.

You failed Nate, but you didn't fail Leah. She'll live. You won't see it. But she'll live. And she'll no longer have to be afraid.

Still clinging to the *hosszú élet* ghoul, Hannah pitched backwards, backwards into the flames, backwards into the all-consuming heat.

CHAPTER 29

Aquitaine region, France

Now

Leah was standing on the wooden platform, holding on to the rail, when fire bloomed inside the watermill. Even from where she stood a few yards from the door, she felt the intensity of the heat as it lashed her.

Glass shattered. Smoke, thick and poisonous and black, erupted from the broken windows. Inside, she heard a cry. Then nothing but the roar and crackle of flames.

Her mother was at the centre of that firestorm. Leah had seen the look in Hannah's eyes, had known it meant something bad.

But not this. This was too terrible to have imagined.

Crimson flame exploded out of the nearest window. Inside the mill something heavy fell over with a crash. The waterwheel shuddered on its axle, groaned. Beneath her, she heard a thunderclap of splitting wood.

Leah stumbled from the platform to the grass. Already, the fire was a living beast, a hundred thrashing tongues. Deep inside the building, she heard a raw splintering. The huge waterwheel juddered again, and this time something buckled and snapped. As water continued to rotate its paddles, Leah watched, hands at her mouth, as the entire wheel canted sideways and angled into the building. When the wooden paddles bit into stone, they exploded into shards. The iron framework dragged and screamed, and in a single awful rotation the wheel consumed itself, shearing into twisted metal and splinters and dust. Pieces of it fell away and crashed into the surging waters beneath.

Now the studded oak door of the mill swung open. A vortex of dirty yellow fire twisted within.

And there, hunched in the doorway, crouched a terrible shape, blackened and crisp, human and yet not. The creature's face had burned away, skull charred and smoking. Its clothes were on fire. Like a broken marionette, it took three jerking steps and collapsed on to the grass.

Leah ran towards it. She stripped off her cardigan, used it to smother the flames, burned her hands and burned them again, but somehow managed to put out the fire.

She did not know who the figure was, but she knew it was damaged too badly to live. Its fingers twitched. Curled.

Gabriel slammed on the Audi's brakes and the vehicle slithered to a halt behind Sebastien's abandoned 4x4. Both of the Jeep's doors were open. No one sat inside. To the right of it, a second Audi was on fire.

Barefoot, feet still throbbing from his injuries, he threw open his driver's door. Limping to the burning Audi, he peered inside, steeling himself for what he might find. But the cabin was empty. It looked like someone had bled away their life on the driver's seat, but they weren't there now.

'*Look!*'

Sebastien climbed out of the passenger seat. The old man's face was pinched with horror, his finger raised and pointing towards a pillar of smoke and flame rolling out of a stone structure on the bank of the river. Tiny black shapes flickered out of a top floor window and spiralled round the column of smoke.

In front of the building, Leah knelt over a blackened lump.

★ ★ ★

At the end, she had discovered she didn't want to die in darkness, in the stink of a burning building, with only Jakab – and whatever animal rotted in the corner – for company.

Even though the fire had taken her eyes and she would never again see the sun, even though her nerves had been seared away and she would never feel its warmth, it had seemed important to be outside.

She lay on her side, feeling her muscles spasming, feeling her heart beginning to labour, feeling the breath that rasped in and out of her ruined lungs beginning to slow.

'Mummy, please don't leave me here alone.'

If Hannah could have wept for those words, she would have done. So cruel for life to end this way. She knew she had made the right choice. Knew she had set Leah free. Knew she had finally rid her of the curse that stalked them.

Sebastien would look after the girl. And if not him, Gabriel. Or perhaps Éva. She had not known any of them long. But she trusted them.

'I love you,' whispered her daughter. 'I don't want you to go too.'

Hannah opened her mouth to speak, but her voice was gone. So dreadful for Leah to see her like this. If only she could say goodbye. If only she could offer some comfort.

She wondered if Nate would be pleased with her. Wondered what he might say. Wondered if even now he watched her as she lay here, watched his wife and his daughter together under an autumn sun.

And now her pain was ebbing. And light was again starting to flare behind her eyes. This time it was not a burning light, not a scorching light, but a cathartic warmth, a glow, a peace, and Hannah felt herself sigh, felt herself let go of all the pain and the fear and the loss, and felt herself step into that peace and open her arms to it.

★ ★ ★

Leah slumped over into a heap as she watched her mother pass away. She knew it was her mother now, recognised her from the smouldering boots she wore – the only things left that identified her.

She had said everything would be all right. But it wasn't all right. Wasn't all right at all. She shouldn't have to see her parents die like this. Not both of them.

Hearing a shout from the woods, Leah looked up to see figures running towards her. Through her tears, she didn't know them. And then she did.

Gabriel reached her first. He stared down at the blackened husk on the grass. When he raised his beautiful cobalt eyes to her, she noticed that they were wet with tears. 'Is it Hannah? Is it your mother?'

She nodded.

'Oh, Leah. Oh, darling, I'm so sorry.' His face crumpled, and when she saw that she tried to rise. He closed the distance between them and swept her up into his arms, and she nestled her face into his shoulder and breathed his scent and pretended that everything was all right. Even though it would never be.

'Jakab.' Gabriel nodded towards the mill, at the dark flames boiling out of the building's windows. At the black smoke curling across the water. 'Is he in there?'

Leah nodded.

'She was the bravest woman I ever met, your mother. She kept her promise.'

'She promised everything would be all right.'

'And it will. It may take you a while, but you'll see.'

Now she heard a new sound, a dreadful wrenching cry, a mix of anger and disbelief and pain. When she opened her eyes she saw Sebastien stagger up to Hannah's body. He fell to his knees.

The old man reached out and seemed about to touch her roasted flesh. Instead he laced his fingers above his head and turned to Gabriel. '*Do something!*'

The Irishman slumped. 'What can I do? What can any of us do? Open your eyes, man. She's gone.'

'There's *life* in her.'

'No. And even if there was . . . Look at her, Seb; just look.'

Sebastien's eyes were wild. 'Haven't you paid any attention? Don't you see? When are you going to figure this out for yourself? She's one of *you*, Gabriel, one of your own. Hannah's *hosszú élet*. I'm sure of it. She's one of you and she can *heal*.'

Leah felt Gabriel stiffen. Suddenly she was slipping from his embrace, sliding down his frame.

'She can't be,' he said. 'That's impossible.'

Sebastien lurched to his feet. He paced, turned, raked fingers through his hair. 'Stupid, *stupid*. It was the one thing Charles and I fought over. I knew his intentions were noble, but I never agreed it was the right thing to do.'

Now Gabriel was the one shouting, his face flushed. '*You're not making any sense!*'

'It was Charles's theory, not mine,' the old man said, the words tumbling out of him. 'He'd done his research, interrogated the dates, realised there was a good chance. He had his suspicions about her mother, Nicole, even more so with Hannah as he watched her grow. But do you want me to tell you the story now while she dies at your feet? Or do you want to save her life and let me finish it later?'

Gabriel fell to his knees. 'If what you say is true . . .'

'God*damn* it, Gabe!'

Gabriel bent over Hannah and placed his ear against her cracked lips. He turned his head and looked into her ruined face. Then he raised his eyes to Sebastien. 'You're absolutely sure?'

Sebastien clenched his fists and rolled his eyes heavenward.

Placing one hand on Hannah's chest above her heart, Gabriel touched her temple with the other. He closed his eyes and exhaled.

Leah watched, her own breath shallow in her throat. She went to Sebastien, fitted her hand into his. 'What's he doing?' she whispered, afraid that she had confused what she had heard, afraid that the tiny ember of hope that glowed inside her would wink out.

Sebastien enfolded her fingers into his leathery palm. 'There's a chance. Just a chance, mind you. *Hosszú életek* can heal one another. It's risky and it's painful and it doesn't always work. Your mother is partly *hosszú élet*, I'm sure of it. But I can't say how potent that part of her is.' Sebastien turned to her. 'Do you believe in miracles?'

How in the world did she answer that?

On the grass, Gabriel hissed and his hands twitched. Leah watched as, minutely, his fingers appeared to sink into her mother's flesh. As they did he tilted back his head and moaned in pain.

The body beneath his hands trembled, bucked. And then it stilled. Gabriel sucked in a breath. He gritted his teeth. His face drained of colour so completely that he looked to Leah like a wraith. Again he opened his mouth to cry out, but this time no sound emerged. Finally, he tore his hands free. Leah saw that his fingers were raw with blood, and that he was sobbing. 'It's no good. She's too badly hurt.'

He bellowed with frustration, panted for breath. 'I can put all of myself into her. And I would. But I don't have enough to bring her back. It'd kill me and she'd still be dead.'

Leah let go of Sebastien's hand. 'Then you have to try harder!' she screamed. '*She* didn't give up! She *never* gave up!'

Gabriel's eyes had lost their cobalt hue, had faded to a sickly grey. 'Leah, I'm sorry—'

'No. *No!* Don't say that. Don't say you're sorry.'

She felt a hand on her shoulder, and when she turned to shrug it free she saw that it was a woman's, slender and smooth.

Éva stood behind her, and her eyes ached with compassion. 'He's right, Leah. She's too badly burned.' The *Örökös Fönök* raised her eyes to Gabriel. 'You can't do it alone. But you might with my help.'

His eyes flared as he saw his mother's expression. Some private understanding seemed to pass between them. Éva, tall and strong and beautiful, sank to her knees in the grass beside her son. She reached out her hands and settled them on to Hannah's blackened body. Then she turned to Gabriel and the smile she gave him pricked tears from his eyes. 'Let me do this for you.'

Gabriel took a shuddering breath. He stared at his mother for what seemed like an age. And then he placed his hands over hers.

Silent, the two *hosszú életek* closed their eyes.

Smoke and ash billowed up from the watermill into the autumn sky. Flames boiled inside the building. Forced from their daytime home, bats circled the smoke, swooping and diving and cavorting.

Leah looked away from them, to the river, to the foaming water that poured out of the mill race and crashed on to the debris of the shattered wheel below. She looked at the far bank, at the trees that lined it, at the sunlight that dappled through the leaves and spun cobwebs of silver on the water.

In the long grass, Éva slumped against her son, but she did not remove her hands from Hannah's body, and Gabriel did not move to catch her, even though he grimaced and set his jaw. As Leah watched, a lick of wind lifted a crisp flake of her mother's skin and bore it away.

Underneath was a small patch of pink.

Healthy skin. Hairless, but unblemished.

Leah stared at it. She heard Sebastien cry out behind her. At first she thought he wept for her mother, for the miracle of what had just happened, and then she realised that his tears were for Éva.

The elegant *hosszú élet Főnök* was growing old. Her skin crinkled, the flesh beneath it withered. In a matter of minutes

Éva aged thirty years, and she continued to change. Her cheeks sank. Her eyes clouded. Their colour leached away.

More flakes of blackened skin drifted up into the sky.

Éva sighed through shrunken lips. And finally, as the quickening flesh beneath her fingers twitched, as Hannah's lungs filled with air, the old woman collapsed into the grass, her eyes closed and her breath wheezing out of her, and Sebastien fell to his knees and whispered her name.

Epilogue

Gabriel sat beside her on the bench as the autumn sun sank below the horizon. She couldn't watch the sunset, couldn't see the golden light as it spread out across the sky, but she could feel the warmth of its rays on her face, and it felt good.

He wouldn't let her go outside during the day, fearful that the midday sun might damage her new skin. He wouldn't let her spend much time alone, either. She didn't mind that. In fact, she was grateful for it. The memories of what had happened were still too immense to face alone. Her body might have healed, but her mind hadn't. Not yet.

'You're quiet,' she said.

'I was just thinking,' he replied. 'About her. About them.'

'How is she?'

'She's dying. But she's happy.'

'Is she in pain?'

'A little – just the usual pains of old age. But you know what? She's not going to die today. Nor next week, most likely.'

'She sacrificed so much.' Hannah fought to steady her emotions. As much as anything, the salt of her tears would sting.

'She's happy, Hannah. That's the funny thing. My mother and Sebastien. It's incredible. She may have a week, maybe a year. How old is he? Eighty? He has no time either. Yet it's as if they're twenty-somethings again.'

The wind blew, and it brought the scent of autumn fruit. Hannah knew that he watched her. Self-consciously she raised a hand to her face, to the bandages over her eyes. 'Don't.'

'What?'

'Look at me.'

'You're going to be all right, you know.'

She took a breath. 'I miss him so badly, Gabe. Every hour. Every second. Nate's dead. I know that. I know I'll never see him again. Not in this life, at least. But I'm still in love with him.' She heard her voice crack. 'I'll always be in love with him.'

'And that's just as it should be.'

She reached out to him and found his arm, his hand. 'You've been so good to us. So patient.'

'I've got plenty of time on my hands.'

She could hear the grin on his lips and suddenly she found herself laughing. 'If everything I've heard is true, we've both got plenty of that.'

'Do you remember the night, in the kitchen, when I showed you the *lélekfeltárás*?'

'What about it?'

'I saw something in your eyes. Or thought I did. Just a flicker. For the briefest moment. And then it was gone.'

'Well, you won't be seeing it again.'

While they had been able to restore her life, she would not regain her sight.

'There are other things I can teach you. Things I can teach Leah. When you're both ready.'

'I'm not sure, Gabriel. I'm not sure I want that.'

'You might. In time.'

And he was right. She might. 'What I don't understand,' Hannah said. 'When I talked to your mother, she said it was impossible. Someone like me, I mean. Said that no one could be conceived that way.'

'It's what we thought. No, it's what we knew. A hundred times over. I can't explain it; I can't explain *you*. None of us can. You shouldn't exist, Hannah, and yet you do.' He laughed sheepishly. 'We're calling you a miracle.'

'I'm no miracle,' she said. 'But it's given you hope, hasn't it? It's given you all a shred of hope. For a future, I mean.'

Gabriel was silent for a while. Quietly, he said, 'That depends on you.'

She didn't know what to say to that. So she squeezed his hand instead.

'You haven't told me what you learned from Seb,' he said.

Hannah shrugged. 'He says my father worked it out. From the diaries. Don't ask me how. Do you remember I told you about Albert and Anna? My great-grandfather and great-grandmother? They lived in Sopron, fled to Germany when Jakab tracked them down. For a time, while he was preparing to kill Albert, Jakab supplanted him. Just like he supplanted my father. And when Anna fell pregnant, it was Jakab's baby growing in her belly.'

'Which means Jakab was your ancestor. Your great-grandfather, in fact. Do you think he knew?'

'No. And I don't think it would have made much difference if he had. He was too corrupted by that point. Too insane.' She shuddered. 'Come on. I don't want to hear his name any more. He's dead. Gone. Out of our lives forever. Where's Leah? Have you seen her?'

From the trees, Hannah heard a rustle of movement.

'I'm here.'

'Have you been sitting there all along?'

'Mostly.'

'Come over here, scamp.'

The aroma of toffee and chocolate. Of salty skin.

'What have you been doing?'

'Starting a diary,' the girl replied. 'One of my own.'

**Read on for an exclusive peek
into where Stephen Lloyd Jones is going
to take the story next . . .**

CHAPTER 1

Interlaken, Switzerland

The face contemplating Leah Wilde from the petrol station's restroom mirror was her own, but it wouldn't be for long. With the door locked, and the scent of disinfectant sharp on the air, she pulled a passport from her bag and studied the image of the woman it contained.

Pouched skin hanging beneath tired eyes. Cheekbones robed in fat, framing a fleshy nose. A filigree of lines branching from the lips, like the contours of a landscape glimpsed from space. A mole to the left of the chin. Earlobes like pale tears of candlewax.

Leah closed her eyes, took a breath, and heard Gabriel's words inside her head.

Create a mould, and pour yourself in. See what you want to be, and be. Don't fear the pain. Pain is good. Pain is the price.

But pain wasn't good. And now here it came: an unwelcome prickling at first, like the rash caused by a nettle's sting. Quickly it intensified, needles sinking deep into her face. She gritted her teeth, felt the skin around her mouth loosen and pucker, felt her heart thump in her chest as the blood surged into her head, her flesh swelling, stretching, slackening.

Reaching out, Leah gripped the wash basin. She held on tight, stomach slopping around inside her, waiting until the pain, finally, began to recede.

When she opened her eyes she saw beads of sweat shining on a forehead mapped with age lines and blemishes. An older face. A stranger's.

At some point she must have dropped the passport into the sink. She fished it out, shaking off droplets of water, and opened it back to the photograph.

Again she studied the woman's image. Compared it to the face watching her from the mirror.

Good.

She was ravenous now, stomach cramping with urgency, but her hunger would have to wait. She'd pulled into the petrol station near the town of Jestetten, a few miles from the Swiss-German border; she needed to get out of here, and fast. Removing a baseball cap from her bag, Leah jammed it down on to her head, keeping her eyes on the ground as she returned to her car.

At the crossing she showed the passport to a border guard, submitting herself to a cursory inspection before being waved through. In Zurich, she abandoned the car in a side street and checked into an anonymous chain hotel.

The next morning, under a different passport and a different face, Leah rented a motorbike from a garage in the city. After following the kinks of Lake Lucerne's shore to Altdorf, she turned west and rode through the Susten Pass, a route that wound among mountain peaks so extraordinary they drew the breath from her throat.

Perhaps it was the drama and raw beauty of the Bernese Oberland's landscape, but as Leah guided the bike along she felt the weight of her indecision begin to lift. No one knew she was here. They had forbidden her outright from coming, had forbidden her even from investigating this. But she knew it was the right thing to do. The only thing left she *could* do, however dangerous it might be.

She reached Interlaken a few hours after midday. The town perched between Lake Brienz in the east and Lake Thun in the west, twin cobalt bowls that reflected the blade-like sharpness of the Alpine sky. Looming above the town to the south, the fortress peaks of the Jungfrau, the Mönch and the Eiger, jagged brushstrokes of rock and snow.

Leah found a small hotel along the Aar, the river that connected the two great lakes and formed the town's northern border. Her first floor room was basic but clean: table and chairs in one corner, cupboard in another. Opposite the bed, a cabinet on which sat a TV, coffee maker and kettle. Shuttered French windows opened onto a narrow balcony. Below, slid the turquoise waters of the Aar.

Throwing her rucksack down on the bed, Leah returned to the door to check it was locked. A spy-hole gave her a distorted view of the deserted corridor outside.

She filled the coffee maker with water and set it to brew. Pulling off her boots, she lay back on the mattress and waited for the room's heat to thaw her limbs. During the four-hour ride through the mountains, the chill October air had stolen through her leathers and frozen her skin.

For the first time in her life, she was truly alone, no one within shouting distance should this plan of hers lead to disaster. Few among the remaining *hosszú életek* even knew what secret the town clasped in its bosom.

She wondered how long it would take before her mother and Gabriel discovered her disappearance. She wished she could reassure them of her safety, but it was too early for that. Too early to tell whether she *was* safe.

In the corner of the room the coffee machine began to hiss. Rising from the bed, Leah reached through the net curtains and checked that the French windows, too, were locked. She unzipped her rucksack, rifling through her gear until she found the pistol she had hidden there.

Leah turned it over in her hands. The Ruger was small enough to conceal on her person, but – loaded with hollow-point rounds – lethal enough to stop most threats with a single shot. She took out two spare magazines and stacked them on the bedside table.

Stripping off her motorcycle leathers, she carried the gun into the suite's tiny bathroom and left it on the basin while she steamed herself in the shower until her skin flushed red with heat.

Afterwards, wrapped in a bath sheet and with the pistol within easy reach, Leah poured herself a mug of coffee. Pulling a hardback book from the rucksack, she found a pen and sat at the table.

The volume, bound in black leather, was her current diary. She had lost count of how many she had filled over the years. But she had written an entry every day since that afternoon, fifteen years earlier, when her mother and Jakab had burned together at Le Moulin Bellerose.

Opening it, she re-read her words from the previous day, a simple list of activities: evading the *hosszú életek* security at the forest retreat in Calw; driving across the border into Switzerland; signing for the package that waited for her at the hotel reception in Zurich; unpacking the Ruger and its ammunition in her suite before folding herself between the bed sheets and finding sleep.

Leah tapped her pen against an empty page. She wondered how tonight's entry would read. Wondered whether there would be one.

After writing a summary of her trip through the mountains, she used the phone beside the bed to call down for room service. But when the food arrived twenty minutes later she couldn't eat it. Trepidation had shrunk her stomach, and the smells wafting from the tray threaded her with a nausea too acute to overcome. Moving to the French windows, she unlocked the shutters and pushed them open.

Frigid air feathered into the room, contracting her bare skin into goosebumps. Across the Aar, the mountain peaks south of the town rose like claws from a bear's upturned paw. They really were castles of stone; monuments of colossal proportions, as if a race of giants had raised them there in supplication to an angry god. She'd read about the Alps – her backpack was stuffed with guides and maps – but little of her time spent researching this place had focused on its topography. She had not expected the mountains to affect her as deeply as they did.

On her return to the table, she noticed something on the room service tray she hadn't seen before, poking out from beneath the leatherette wallet containing her bill. Frowning, she nudged the wallet aside, revealing a square envelope. Her name was intricately calligraphed across the front.

Heart knocking against her ribs, Leah snatched up the Ruger from the bed. Seven rounds in the magazine. Nine millimetre hollow-point. They would open like a flower on impact, punching fist-sized holes into whatever stood in her way.

Head cocked, ears straining, fingers greasy where they curled around the gun, Leah forced herself to be still. She knew that her hearing was sharp, knew that if anyone lurked in the corridor outside she would sense them – unless they, like her, were *hosszú élet*.

After two minutes had passed, and she had heard nothing but the muttering of water in the hotel's pipes, she removed one hand from the gun and reached behind her. Locking the French windows, she pulled the net curtains back into place.

Barefoot, Leah padded across the room to the door. She paused again, listening. When only silence greeted her, she pressed her eye to the tiny spy-hole. The lens warped her view, but she could see that the corridor remained deserted.

Returning to the tray, she picked up the envelope. The paper was thick, luxurious. Breaking it open, she withdrew a square of cream card. At the top it bore an embossed logo in gold and black: a series of interlinking chains, like a Celtic knot.

I warned you not to come. I am delighted you chose to ignore that advice. Let's dine together, tonight. A car will collect you

*from outside your hotel at eight o'clock and bring you here,
should you wish. Rather more convenient than a motorcycle – it
grows cold in these mountains on autumn evenings.*

*I cannot guarantee your safety from here on in, but of course
you know that.*

'*Az Kutya Herceg*'

A shiver took hold of Leah as she read the last line, borne as
much from fear as from the frisson of anticipation the words
produced. She dropped the card on to the table beside her,
spine tingling from a cold lick of distaste.

Az Kutya Herceg. The Dog Prince. A theatrical affectation,
but from what she had heard of the man, he enjoyed how his
reputation had developed among the *hosszú életek* until it had
gained an almost mythic status. Az Kutya Herceg was, she
knew, one of the more forgiving of his titles. It did not allude to
his ruthlessness, his monstrousness when provoked.

How could he have learned of her arrival so quickly?
She'd entered Switzerland using one fake passport, had rented
the motorbike using another. From the Susten Pass she'd
ridden directly to the hotel, memorising the route and the
names of Interlaken's streets in advance. The only people to
have seen her face were the middle-aged woman at reception
who handed her the room key, and the youth who brought in
her lunch.

Outside, the snow on the mountain peaks had blushed to
pink as the sun dipped towards the waters of Lake Brienz. The
Alps looked like they were bleeding.

At a quarter to eight, fifteen minutes before the car was due,
Leah opened her rucksack and pulled out a tissue-paper parcel.
From it she unwrapped a long-sleeved embroidered lace dress
in midnight blue. She changed quickly, slipping her feet into
nude patent shoes with a heel far higher than she usually wore.

Twisting up her hair into a pile on top of her head, she secured it with two steel chopsticks whose points had been filed to a needle sharpness.

She stared at herself in the mirror, turned her head from left to right, wondered what he expected to see. From a small travel bag, she removed lipstick and eyeliner and quickly applied make-up to her face, then examined herself again.

Better.

Pulling out a glass bottle of perfume, Leah considered it for a moment before replacing it, unused. She picked up the Ruger, checked that the safety was engaged and slid it into a sequinned clutch purse, then tucked her diary back into her rucksack and packed up the rest of her belongings. If she needed to leave here quickly, she wanted everything to be ready.

Beyond the window, except where the mountain peaks blocked their light, a sprinkling of stars pricked silver holes in the sky. Shrugging on her biker leather over the dress, she left her room and walked down the stairs to the foyer. The hotel's glass doors slid apart and Leah, holding the clutch purse as nonchalantly as she could, stepped outside.

Now that the sun had set the Alpine air was brittle, teasing a mist from her breath. She tasted something on her tongue, a subtle sourness, and thought she sensed an imminent change in the weather: a premonition, perhaps, of snow. She shook her head at the thought.

Across the street, a graphite Rolls-Royce Phantom, like an armoured rhinoceros, idled against the kerb.

Leah stared at the vehicle's enormous flat-fronted grille, the headlights like narrowed eyes and the winged Spirit of Ecstasy, poised for flight, perched on the bonnet.

Its windows were black, reflecting the night.

Don't let them see your fear.

Blowing air from her cheeks, Leah crossed the street, threw open the Phantom's rear door and slid into a world of mahogany and cream leather. She pulled the door shut behind her, there was a heavy-sounding clunk. Immediately, as if a switch had been flicked, the noise of the street traffic ceased.

No one occupied the seat beside her. In front, a man sat behind the steering wheel. She could see curls of black hair, a strong and tanned neck.

He turned in his seat, and when he saw her sitting there he flashed white teeth. His irises were feathered with violet, a shade she had never seen before in the eyes of a *hosszú élet*. Leah thought she caught something else lurking in that expression too: something that froze her blood a little. She recalled the line from the note:

I cannot guarantee your safety from here on in

Again, that frisson of expectation, stirring the hairs on the nape of her neck.

'Leah Wilde,' the man said.

She nodded. 'Who are you?'

He ignored her question. 'Lean forward for me. Before we go any further, I need to take a look at those pretty eyes.'

She slid to the edge of her seat, bringing her face to within a foot of his own. His eyes really were extraordinary. Striations of passion fruit and lavender. Unworldly, cold; and this close, unsettlingly intense. She watched as the streaks of violet intensified and began to bleed towards the edges of his irises, like dye leaching into a vat of ink. Leah gripped the leather seat with her fingertips, feeling her own eyes respond in kind. There followed a curious unspooling of fear and longing.

She could not remember how long it had been since she had met another *hosszú élet* for the first time. Her heart quickened in her chest; she felt its pulse in her ears. The scent of his cologne washed over her.

Flinching away, the man stared through the windscreen at the cars passing on the street. Then he turned back to her. 'How old are you, Leah?'

She held his gaze. 'Twenty-four.'

The moment seemed to lengthen, stretch out between them. His nostrils flared.

'So it's true,' he said.

'It's true.'

'And we're to believe that you came here, all on your own: a single girl, into the lion's den without any protection whatsoever.'

'You can believe anything you want,' she replied. 'But I'm here alone. Just as I promised.'

He stared at her, his expression hardening. Abruptly he turned away. Putting the Phantom into gear, he flicked on an indicator and pulled into traffic.

They drove south out of Interlaken, following a twisting road that threaded its way through dark pine forest as it rose towards the peaks. Theirs were the only lights on the road.

'We're leaving town?'

He found her eyes in the rear-view mirror. 'You wanted to meet Az Kutya Herceg.'

'I thought he lived nearby.'

'He doesn't.'

Leah clutched the purse on her lap, feeling the hard angles of the Ruger through its sequinned fabric. 'Is it far?'

'A while yet.'

The Rolls-Royce accelerated, powering them up the road's gradient and around its curves towards the starlit peaks of the Jungfrau, Mönch and Eiger. As Leah settled into the seat's leather embrace, she tried to avoid glancing too frequently at her driver. Every so often she sensed him lifting his eyes from the road to study her.

Are you sure about this? Are you absolutely sure?

Yes. It was the right thing to do. The only thing. She knew she wouldn't be thanked, knew that her actions tonight would sow even more division among the few *hosszú életek* that remained. But if *someone* didn't do something soon – something radical – then all that her mother and Gabriel had worked for in the years since her father's death would be undone.

Even so, by coming here alone, with no one aware of her destination, she placed herself in exceptional danger. Her driver had taunted her about walking into the lion's den, but Leah knew that was exactly what this involved. She had heard the stories. Some of them sickened her.

They wound up through black ranks of fir and pine, moonlight glimmering on frost-rimed needles. The air at this altitude looked sharp enough to cut her skin. All around them, the Bernese Alps presented dizzying faces.

Finally the Phantom slowed, turning down a private single-lane road that took a sharp ascent through the trees. A minute later they left the forest behind and emerged on to a rising strip of tarmac. When it swept around to the right, Leah gasped.

An enormous chalet complex rose up ahead: four curving levels of wood and glass, topped with multiple gabled roofs. The building glowed with a golden light, an architectural bauble clinging to the face of the mountain. The windows of its middle floors reached from floor to ceiling, at least four metres in height, served by crescent-shaped balconies that curved their entire width. Somewhere inside she could see the flickering reflections cast from a swimming pool.

To the left of the building a five-car garage had been chiselled directly out of the rock. Strip lights blazed inside. Below the house, a wide lawn receded into darkness. Across the valley, in full view of the huge viewing windows, rose the rocky monolith of the Jungfrau. Snow sparkled on its summit. On its north eastern shoulder loomed the Mönch and the Eiger.

Her driver brought the Phantom to a halt on the tarmac. He glanced around at her embroidered lace dress, then up at her scuffed motorcycle jacket. 'It's minus ten outside. You're not exactly dressed for mountain weather.'

'No.'

'Wait here.' He got out and went to the boot. Moments

later he appeared at her window, holding a calf-length fur. It shimmered silver in the moonlight. He opened her door and held out the coat to her. The air that raced into the car made her eyes sting at its bite. 'Put this on.'

Leah swivelled her legs and stood, feeling her skin burn with cold. Slipping her arms into the fur, she wrapped it around her body and followed him across the tarmac to the ground-floor entrance. The front door was a rounded slab of oak hung within a curving transom decorated with stained-glass panels. Its fittings were brass, polished to a liquid shine. Scorched into the centre of the wood she saw the same woven motif from her dinner invite.

Her driver opened the door, stepped into the entrance hall and beckoned her to follow. With a flutter of nerves in her belly, knowing that whatever reservations she'd entertained about tonight's encounter, it was now too late to change her mind, Leah crossed the threshold.

When the door closed behind her, she heard the clunk of several mortices engaging simultaneously, sealing her inside.

A Discovery of Witches

Deborah Harkness

It begins with absence and desire.
It begins with blood and fear.
It begins with a discovery of witches.

A world of witches, daemons and vampires.

A manuscript which holds the secrets of their past and the key to their future.

Diana and Matthew – the forbidden love at the heart of it.

'Intelligent and off-the-wall, it will be irresistible to *Twilight* fans' *The Sunday Times*

'Write what you know, debut novelists are told, and Professor Deborah Harkness has accordingly set hers in the world of academia . . . A bubbling cauldron of illicit desire . . . all the ingredients for an assured saga that blends romance with fantasy' *Daily Mail*

'An inventive addition to the supernatural craze . . . Historian Harkness's racy paranormal romance has exciting amounts of spells, kisses and battles, and is recounted with enchanting, page-turning panache' *Marie Claire*

'A romp through magical academia' *Guardian*

978 0 7553 7404 5

headline

LYNDSAY FAYE

The Gods of Gotham

August 1845

After a fire decimates a swathe of lower Manhattan,
and following years of passionate political dispute,
New York City at long last forms an official Police
Department.

That same summer, the great potato famine hits
Ireland.

These events will change the city of New York for
ever.

'A wonderful book. Lyndsay Faye's command of
historical detail is remarkable, and her knowledge of
human character even more so' Michael Connelly

'Executed with brio and packed with pungent
historical detail . . . this is a cracking yarn' *Daily Mail*

'*The Gods of Gotham* succeeds on many levels: as a
colourful, crackling evocation of an underworld
packed with desperados; as an unflinching glance
into the history of some of New York's shadiest and
most shameful corners; and as a cleverly crafted
crime story with a central character who deserves a
new case, and another book' *Metro*

978 0 7553 8676 5

headline
review

Pure

Julianna Baggott

THE DEATHLY HOUSES ALL FELL DOWN. THE
SICK SOULS WANDER 'ROUND AND 'ROUND.

Pressia barely remembers the Detonations. But, living
amongst the devastation, every day a dangerous
struggle for the survivors who are marked by their
fused, burnt, damaged bodies, she is starkly aware of
what has been lost.

BURN A PURE AND BREATHE THE ASH . . .

Partridge is one of the lucky few sheltered inside the
Dome. They escaped the apocalypse unmarked, pure.
But he doesn't feel safe. Smothered by the rigid order
of the Dome's regime, he suspects all is not as it
seems.

WHEN PRESSIA MEETS PARTRIDGE, THEIR
WORLDS SHATTER ALL OVER AGAIN.

'Sizzles with invention' *The Sunday Times*

978 0 7553 9359 6

headline

Now you can buy any of these other bestselling
titles from your bookshop or
direct from the publisher.

FREE P&P AND UK DELIVERY
(Overseas and Ireland £3.50 per book)

The Ocean at the End of The Lane	Neil Gaiman	£7.99
A Discovery of Witches	Deborah Harkness	£8.99
Shadow of Night	Deborah Harkness	£8.99
The Gods of Gotham	Lyndsay Faye	£6.99
Seven for a Secret	Lyndsay Faye	£7.99
Moth and Spark	Anne Leonard	£8.99
The Devil's Ark	Stephen Bywater	£8.99
Herald of the Storm	Richard Ford	£8.99
The Troop	Nick Cutter	£7.99

TO ORDER SIMPLY CALL THIS NUMBER

01235 400 414

or visit our website: www.headline.co.uk

Prices and availability subject to change without notice